Jenni Keer is a history graduate who embarked on a career in contract flooring before settling in the middle of the Suffolk countryside with her antique furniture restorer husband. She has valiantly attempted to master the ancient art of house-work but with four teenage boys in the house it remains a mystery. Instead, she spends her time at the keyboard writing women's fiction to combat the testosterone-fuelled atmos-phere with her number one fan #Blindcat by her side. Much younger in her head than she is on paper, she adores any excuse for fancy-dress and is part of a disco formation dance team.

Visit her website: **jennikeer.co.uk** and find her on Facebook **/jennikeerwriter** and Twitter **@JenniKeer**.

Praise for *The Secrets of Hawthorn Place*

'An exquisitely detailed and enchanting love story'
Heidi Swain

'A beautifully intriguing love story, that twists and turns
and stays with you long after the last page'
Rosie Hendry

'An epic love story, mixed with gorgeous settings,
a great deal of mystery and intrigue, lots of laughs,
a few tears and fabulous characters, made this an
absolute delight to read. I really loved it'
h

By Jenni Keer

The Hopes and Dreams of Lucy Baker
The Unlikely Life of Maisie Meadows
The Secrets of Hawthorn Place

The
Secrets
of
Hawthorn
Place

JENNI KEER

ACCENT

Copyright © 2021 Jennifer Keer

The right of Jenni Keer to be identified as the Author of
the Work has been asserted by her in accordance with the
Copyright, Designs and Patents Act 1988.

First published in 2021 by
HEADLINE ACCENT
An imprint of HEADLINE PUBLISHING GROUP

1

Translation of Medieval love poem c.1500, author unknown,
by Eleanor Parker. Used with permission.

Cataloguing in Publication Data is available from the British Library

ISBN 978 1 4722 8673 4

Typeset in 10.5/14pt Sabon Std by Jouve (UK), Milton Keynes

Printed and bound in Great Britain by Clays Ltd, Elcograf S.p.A.

HEADLINE PUBLISHING GROUP
An Hachette UK Company
Carmelite House
50 Victoria Embankment
London EC4Y 0DZ

www.headline.co.uk
www.hachette.co.uk

Louise Buckley
For your enduring faith in this book

For weal or woe I will not flee
To love that heart that loveth me.

That heart my heart hath in such grace
That of two hearts one heart make we;
That heart hath brought my heart in case
    To love that heart that loveth me.

This knot thus knit, who shall untwine,
    Since we that knit it do agree
To loose not nor slip, but both incline
    To love that heart that loveth me?

Farewell, of hearts that heart most fine,
    Farewell, dear heart, heartly to thee,
And keep this heart of mine for thine
    As heart for heart, for loving me.

Medieval love poem c.1500, author unknown
Translated by Eleanor Parker

Chapter 1
Percy Gladwell
1896

My darling Violet,

I have tried, I truly have, but I cannot continue this charade any longer. Two months shut away at my mother's house, unable to work and unwilling to socialise, and I fear I'm going mad. Being without you is killing me anyway, so let it be a done thing.

You will find my actions hard to understand, and perhaps harder to forgive, but since the day we first met, I have loved only you. Facing a life where I am denied even your friendship, is no life at all. I would not be living, I would be existing.

Know that I am sorry. Mother will weep, and that I regret, but there are others I have hurt who might even wish to stand behind me and give the final push. Oh, how the heart makes fools of us all . . .

Only last summer, I stood on top of the cliffs at West Bay, and on top of the world. It was a joyful time for me – a time when I could hardly believe your feelings were as powerful as my own. But we both knew, and have always known, it could never be. It is hard for me to return here now, and this visit is all the more poignant when I think of those happier times.

1

Do not feel sorrow, my love, feel only joy. I am still with you – in every brick and piece of polished oak, through every stained-glass window and even in your beloved petunia bed. The house was always our love letter, and I am content to know you will see out your days surrounded by these little pieces of me. I will watch over you from above, and pray God you have a long and happy life.

> *That heart my heart hath in such grace*
> *That of two hearts one heart make we;*
> *That heart hath brought my heart in case*
> *To love that heart that loveth me.*

Percy Gladwell

The letter was posted in town at two forty-five. By four o'clock most of a bottle of Cockburn's port had been consumed to give him the courage he needed to do the thing he was most afraid of.

At five past the hour, on the beautiful Jurassic coast of Dorset, Percy Gladwell stepped off the high cliffs at West Bay and a mother, paddling with her tiny child in the waters further down the beach, looked up at the cliffs and screamed.

Chapter 2
Present Day

I struggled up the steep stone steps as the taxi pulled away, rested my wheelie case on the top step and rang the bell. The key was somewhere in the jumble of my rucksack but it was taking every ounce of strength to hold it together, and one more hiccup, even as tiny as not locating the keys quickly enough, would catapult me into the sky of total despair. I knew Brian would answer any moment and offer to take the case up to my old bedroom. Good old Brian. Reliable, if nothing else.

'Molly, darling,' Mum said, swinging back the glossy scarlet door, which happened to match her nail-varnish, and glancing at my case. 'We weren't expecting you. Is Rupert away with work again?'

'No. Why?'

'Because you usually only descend when he's left you to your own devices.' She ushered me inside and studied my face. 'So, if Rupert isn't away with work, your dejected expression unfortunately speaks a thousand unuttered words. I'm guessing you need a large rhubarb gin and a hug?'

Her arm guided me down the large airy hallway of our three-storey Georgian London house and, as the warmth of her touch and the familiarity of home enveloped me, I succumbed to the emotions I'd been holding in since my long-term boyfriend had uttered those stomach-churning words, 'We need to talk . . .'

'Rupert's dumped me,' I admitted, and burst into tears.

'Oh, sweetie.' She threw her arms about me and held me close, patiently waiting for my initial wailing to simmer down into more gentle sobs, and finally fade into occasional sniffs and hiccups.

'I'm afraid broken hearts are part of life, my darling. You'll become a stronger person and learn from the experience. Take off your coat and I'll see to that drink.'

Five minutes later, nestled in the safety of one of the large white leather armchairs, clutching a fishbowl-sized glass full of glorious, fizzy, pale pink gin and tonic, I filled Mum in on the details. Rupert had met someone else. I was surplus to requirements.

'She was in his Thursday evening cordon bleu cookery course and over the last few months the friendship developed into something more.' I shrugged to pretend I didn't care, but I did. No one likes feeling they're replaceable. 'He said we'd drifted apart and that I don't share his interests, which is untrue. I adore his passion for good food, for example. I might not get involved with the preparation, but then when you live with a cooking whizz, why would you try to compete?'

'To expand your knowledge? Learn a new skill? Enjoy the experience of sharing an activity together?' Mum suggested. I chose not to react.

'And then he said we'd been heading this way for a while and everyone but me could see it.'

It was easy to look back now and spot the signs. I'd been doing that for the entire taxi journey, questioning why his announcement had been such a shock. Rupert had been my one serious relationship, the first man I'd lived with, and the only boyfriend I'd ever said 'I love you' to. We'd hooked up at uni and made life plans together, but in recent weeks Rupert had talked of them less. Now I knew why. He had someone else to share his future with and, unfortunately for me, his home.

Mum remained silent so I ploughed on, hitting her with the obvious solution to my unexpected homelessness. 'It's his flat so I had to move out, and I know you and Brian are off on holiday soon, so I was thinking . . .'

'Yes?' Mum raised a guarded eyebrow.

'. . . That I could stay here for the month and look after the place whilst you're away? We'd be helping each other out, if you think about it.'

'I'm not sure how my darling daughter, who can barely identify the cooker, never mind operate it, and who leaves a trail of belongings wherever she goes, is going to be much of a help. I love you very much, but I fear that going from home, to uni – where I happen to know Izzy did all the housework and cooking – and then to Rupert's hasn't done you any favours.'

'Are you implying I can't look after myself?' I crossed my arms over my non-existent chest. 'I'm perfectly capable of running a household.' Maybe I hadn't technically had much practice at independent living, but I certainly knew the principles involved.

'This is all rather irrelevant, sweetheart,' she said. 'I'm afraid you can't stay here.'

'Why not? You said my room was always here for me if I needed it.'

'Yes, but we won't be here from Monday—'

'I know. You'll be in New York. But I can be here to protect it from burglars,' I said, warming to my theme. 'It's not ideal to have this big property standing empty for a month.'

'You're right.' She paused. 'And that's why we decided to do a house swap.'

'A what?' I sat up straight and let my arms drop.

'A house swap. Oh, Molly, I swear you never listen to me. We're staying in an apartment overlooking Central Park, and the family who own it will be coming here. It's all been arranged and I'm afraid an extra house guest was not part of the package.'

I sank back into the large chair, letting the wide sides shield me from this unwelcome news. Being small and slender, perhaps I could slip neatly down the gap between the cushions and the seat if I wriggled my bottom back far enough. Maybe I could hide in the chair for a month, nipping out when it was dark for food and supplies – as it appeared I was now officially homeless – at least until Mum and Brian returned from their holiday.

As I contemplated the utter disaster that was my current situation, I heard the front door close and a beaming Brian appeared, clutching a ridiculously ostentatious bunch of lilies. Their sickly scent wafted into the room, along with what I could only assume was a guilty man. Surely no one buys flowers unless they have something to hide? Because, now that I thought about it, Rupert had come back with flowers on a few occasions since starting the evening course.

'For you, dar— Oh. Molly, what a pleasant surprise!' His eyes lit up and his smile spread even further across his face.

That was the thing about Brian – he'd tried, he really had, particularly to begin with, but he'd butted in to our happy little life without being asked. Well, I certainly hadn't invited him in. Mum informed me when I was nine that she had a 'special friend'. Within a year, they were married and our contented twosome became a crowded threesome. Having been used to exclusive dibs on my mother, suddenly there was this stranger in my life, taking over the bedtime stories, buying me expensive gifts, and praising every little thing I did to a ridiculous degree. But surely it was all for my mother's benefit, because everyone knows that if you fall in love with someone and they already have a child, she's the nine-year-old fly in the otherwise perfect ointment.

'Rupert has finished with Molly,' Mum explained. 'But I've told her that she can't stay here as our American house-swap guests are coming.'

She gave him an intense stare. They did that a lot. It was a being in love thing, apparently, which, fair play, they still were after fifteen years. A slow dawning of comprehension replaced Brian's puzzled expression as he realised the true extent of my catastrophic circumstances.

'Can you bunk with a friend for a few weeks?' he asked, depositing the bouquet on the glass-topped coffee table and giving me a hopeful smile.

'I could try Izzy, I suppose, but she lives too far from work. I'd have over an hour commute.'

I hated my job; I'd been forced to take a part-time telemarketing post selling solar panels when a year of post-university job hunting had drawn a blank and Brian had called time on my allowance. The majority of my salary was bonus-related, but it turns out I'm not great at cold-calling. Still, it earned me enough to get by. Or rather, it had until Rupert had put me out with the carefully crushed and spotlessly clean recycling.

'Some people have much longer commutes than that, Molly. You'll simply have to get up earlier,' Mum unhelpfully pointed out. 'Perhaps you can rent a room somewhere? You *are* earning, and Rupert never asked you for rent. Perhaps you could pick up another job, or ask for more shifts at work? It's not like you have much else to fill your time.'

That's where she was wrong. I was extremely busy outside my working hours. I'd amassed a large following on Instagram and posted artistic shots of Rupert's restaurant-quality meals daily. Catching up on Snapchat took ages, and I was forever stumbling across must-see Netflix box sets. As for exercise, there was nothing of me already. If I took up a sport, I'd be a hologram within a fortnight.

'Any chance of reinstating my allowance, Bri?' I asked, giving him the biggest smile I could muster. That would be the easiest option all round, and Brian wasn't short of money.

'Um, no, sorry, Molly.' His round face went pink as he cast another look at Mum. 'We supported you without question through university, and for a year afterwards, but there has to come a time when you're responsible for yourself. You're a graduate now and the world is your undiscovered oyster.'

I wriggled in my seat, my knees tucked under me, and clutched a huge cream cushion to my chest like a shield. As I'd limped out of university with a third in history, my degree was hardly anything to shout about. Studying the past had seemed like an easy ride, but it became a dry and dusty chore when I had to choose between writing essays about nineteenth-century industrialisation or hanging around the student union bar. Yes, I'd chosen to focus on the social aspects of university life, but I was certain my people-skills were top notch as a result. Except when I was trying to sell solar panels.

'But I need a bit of support to bail me out of an horrific situation that isn't my fault. A short-term loan? An early birthday present? It's the last time. Honest. All my mates fell into good jobs and I was so unlucky. I applied for hundreds of high-salaried positions, but no one wanted me and I've had to settle for stupid telemarketing.' Perhaps hundreds was an exaggeration, but I didn't understand why I hadn't been snapped up. A degree was a degree, after all.

'Telesales is a perfectly good starting point. You don't just walk into the top jobs, Molly. You have to earn them. Kids today expect everything to fall into their ungrateful laps.'

I wanted to point out that every generation has it tough in different ways. We were going to inherit a world that his generation had screwed up – the political instability, global warming, and pollution of the oceans for starters. Plus, gone were the student grants that had cushioned Brian through university. Most of my friends had finished with astronomical debts – although Brian made sure I finished debt free, but that wasn't the point.

My mobile pinged to let me know there was a Snapchat notification, reminding me that my stepfather was the CEO of a telecommunications company and my adolescent years had been financed by the exponential growth of the mobile phone. I half-leaned forward to investigate but pulled back. Mum and Brian always joked that my world revolved around my phone and I was trying to present myself as a motivated and deserving case, not a social-media-obsessed dependant.

'I'll leave you to think about that loan then,' I finished hopefully, giving Brian another wide smile and standing up. Now was a good time to make my exit. Besides, I was itching to see the Snapchat notification, optimistically hoping that Rupert had realised the error of his ways and was begging me to come back.

I launched myself across my bed, pushed a stack of graphic novels and some folded black T-shirts to the floor, where the cleaner must have piled them after I'd moved out, and swiped open my mobile to see my Snapchat notification. Unfortunately, it was not a repentant Rupert, so I messaged Izzy for some sympathy. Surely she'd come through for me in my hour of need. I pinged her a sad face emoji – the one where the tears are practically rivers pouring from the eyes of the yellow-faced blob – and she responded immediately.

What's up, hon?

Homeless. Rupert's dumped me and Brian's house is temporarily out of the equation. Any chance of me bunking on the sofa for a couple of weeks?

It took her a worryingly long time to reply.

Not permitted in my tenancy agreement. Sorry.

As I'd never rented outside of uni, I knew nothing of acceptable terms and conditions, but it seemed a rotten old world if you were forbidden from helping a mate out in an emergency.

There was a knock at the bedroom door and Mum's head poked around the frame.

'Room for a little one?' she asked, as I continued to tap away on my phone and fill Izzy in on my troubles.

'Of course, as long as you're alone. I'm not Brian's number one fan right now.'

She picked up a pillow that I'd accidentally sent flying, and leaned it against the white metal bedstead. Settling herself next to me, she tried hard not to focus on all the things I'd just thrown to the floor and launched into Ninja Mum mode, deliberately not making eye contact, which I'm guessing she read somewhere in some How-to-Bring-Up-Awkward-Daughters manual. Small talk was the order of the day, but I knew her games.

'I love the vibrant wallpaper in here,' she said. 'And you have the best views in the house – across the park. You insisted on this room when we moved in and Brian moved his study into that poky north-facing room on the third floor, remember?'

Mum was reminding me Brian was a good guy and that I was being unreasonable. One point to her. As for the garish wallpaper, bright turquoise with tiny scarlet birds perched on snow white trees, I'd chosen it because everything else in the house was so excruciatingly white, or slight variations thereof. I thought they'd kick up a fuss, but instead Brian quietly wrestled with wallpaper-hanging for a fortnight several summers ago.

Perhaps I was being harsh on him, but he wasn't my biological father, and he sometimes stepped into shoes that weren't his. The problem was, I had no idea whose shoes they were – the mystery of my paternity the only thing I ever quarrelled with Mum about. I would ask and she would shut down. But after twenty years of 'Trust me, Molly, it's for the best,' her evasiveness was wearing see-through thin.

'I love how the changing seasons are reflected by our view of the park,' she continued. 'It's easy to forget we're so urban when you sit in this room and the treetops fill the skyline – although it's a shame you can't fully appreciate the view.'

Make that two points. Your room is so cluttered no one can get near the window.

'But I guess it's a good place to escape to when you feel the world has dealt you a crummy hand,' she added.

And there was the hat trick. How was it that I knew, even though she was ostensibly backing me up, that she was implying my messy life was my own doing? Ah, yes, the addition of the words 'you feel'.

She didn't speak for a moment and put out her arm for me to nestle into – which I did, of course. Hugs make everything better.

'I understand that the house swap stops me from living here next month, but surely Brian can help me out financially in the short-term?' I said, wafts of Chanel's Gabrielle floating like an invisible mist between us. 'Just to see me through until you return?'

'I'm afraid not, my darling, and I'm behind him one hundred per cent. We can't keep bailing you out. You have to stand on your own two feet and take some responsibility.'

'Can't you have a word and—'

'No, Molly. Sometimes it's only through adversity that we

find ourselves. I'm certain that you will meet the challenges of this situation and come out victorious.'

A low groan came from somewhere inside. 'Oh, Mum, what am I going to do?'

She lifted up her other arm and stroked my hair, brushing my short, feathery fringe away from my face and running her hand down my cheek. More of her ninja motherhood skills – a simple action to remind me how disappointed she'd been when I cut it all off. Although she never said so, unlike Brian who almost cried the day I walked in, all my glorious, thick, long, black hair now a wispy choppy frame around my pale face.

I looked up at her, finally meeting her eyes.

'You are twenty-four years old, Molly. Old enough to work this thing out all by yourself,' she said. 'And I have every faith that you will.'

Chapter 3
Percy Gladwell

1894

Until that day, my career had been my morning, noon and evening. Long hours and late nights. Pencil dust and T-squares. Backache from leaning over drafting tables, and eye strain from working unsociable hours under poor light.

I hadn't given much thought to the fairer sex. I assumed I'd acquire a wife in time. Mother relentlessly paraded a string of sensible women before me, worried that I would see out my days a bachelor. But my sole focus in recent years had been establishing a successful practice. To have my own offices before my thirtieth year was a considerable achievement, and partly through sheer luck, partly through hard work and my growing reputation, I had an impressive and expanding client list. A commission from an earl had increased my standing and I'd recently completed a summer retreat for one of Rosebery's cabinet ministers – although he had proved such a disagreeable fellow to work with that I doubted he would last long in office.

I was not, however, averse to the benefits of a sweet smile and gentle disposition. It led to many pleasant evenings at the theatre and musical recitals. But no one truly moved me. No one connected. There was no column to support my arch, no flowing lines, no combination of the beauty and practicality which was my very essence.

And then Violet Marston walked into my offices.

A pale complexion and a fragile quality, she was straight from a painting at the hand of Waterhouse or Burne-Jones. It was as if the Lady of Shalott had floated downstream and into my life. Wild, flaxen hair barely tamed into submission and an unworldly look that spoke of passion and fire. My mouth went dry and no words came readily to my lips.

'Mr Gladwell, thank you for agreeing to see me at such short notice. I've been looking forward to this meeting,' she said and proffered a gloved hand, but her eyes did not reflect the sentiment. She withdrew the hand swiftly, almost as soon as it had made contact with my own.

I cleared my throat, offered the usual platitudes and commented on the unseasonal weather, sweeping a hand towards the empty leather button back chair near my desk. She moved her skirts to the side and sat.

'As my letter stated, I am here to assess your suitability with regard to designing a family home by the coast. I should like to see some examples of your work and to discuss the possibility of a sizeable commission. At this stage I offer no guarantees, as I intend to interview several potential architects.'

'Certainly. Shall we discuss your requirements?' I took a sharpened pencil from my drafting board, walked to sit behind my smaller kneehole desk, and pulled a clean sheet of paper towards me. A permanent ridge of black across my fingernails from pencil dust and newsprint made me feel unusually self-conscious.

'I . . . *we* . . .' she corrected, but I'd already noticed the wedding ring as she slid her delicate white gloves off and rested them across her lap, '. . . have a plot of land near the sea, on the edge of my father's estate, and wish to commission a comfortable family residence.'

'If you could outline what you have in mind? Will it be your primary residence? How do you envisage the appearance and function?'

'I rather think it is for you to impress me, Mr Gladwell. I am not the architect.'

I shuffled in my seat. I was used to meeting with clients for preliminary discussions, but they were generally excited and enthusiastic about the prospect. She appeared disinterested by the whole thing.

'Are you aware of my previous work?' I asked, hoping she had at least apprised herself of my general style, the movement I followed, and its principles.

She shrugged and remained impassive. 'I was recently at the Bayldons', which I understand you designed, but I was so taken with the extensive grounds – they have installed a magnificent fountain in the water garden – that I paid the house scant attention.'

The Bayldon residence had been one of my first commissions. A large country house just outside the city of York for James Bayldon, who had made himself a considerable fortune by virtue of the confectionery industry – boiled sweets and chocolate treats. Like many of new money, he was keen to display his wealth and status, and was open to my ideas.

I sucked in a patient breath. 'Should you have occasion to visit it again, you will notice my preference for simplicity and honesty in both design and materials. Nature is a key element in all my buildings; the addition of motifs and murals to remind us of God's wonderful creation, and the extensive use of wood and stone in the interiors, which I am not afraid to leave in their natural state. The living world is full of miraculous things that lift the heavy heart and brighten the dullest day. Let us bring the outside in, I say.'

For the first time, she made prolonged eye contact.

'I did notice the use of an orchid motif in the glazed windows of the drawing room,' she ventured. 'It made me smile.'

'A particular favourite of Mrs Bayldon. She has recently built a spectacular glass conservatory to house her growing collection, I believe.'

She gave a brief nod. 'So you would use similar motifs in my house?'

'Mrs Marston, I would use motifs and themes personal to you. If you have a love of windmills or a passion for elephants, then I would include them in your property.' My grin was not acknowledged, but her interest had been piqued.

We talked briefly of gardens and it was apparent her knowledge was far superior to mine. Until recently, I had relied on the guidance of an old friend of my father's for the finer points of planting and garden design when it was required, but his eyes were failing now and his mind not as sharp as when I'd known him in my youth. The architectural element of a garden I was confident with, but which bushes might survive in an alkaline soil required more horticultural knowledge than I possessed. However, the subject had engaged the seemingly indifferent Mrs Marston, and I was content with that.

After we'd established her basic requirements, and I'd made some preliminary notes, she thanked me for my time.

'I must, of course, consult with my husband before this is taken any further.'

'Naturally.'

She stood to leave but sighed. 'For a wife must always consult her husband, but it is rarely the other way about. Yet my elderly aunt has the luxury of consulting with no one – a deliberate choice on her part not to marry, which one might consider an enviable position.' It was said without a smile, merely a raised eyebrow, but I detected a lighter side to the enigmatic Mrs Marston.

'At least marriage offers security and companionship. I don't think if I was born a woman I should choose the life of a spinster.'

'Ah, but marriage is rather like a game of chess, Mr Gladwell, with its strict rules of play, where you may and may not move. One must plan ahead and anticipate the reaction of your opponent, and sometimes you find you've fallen into a trap – a seemingly innocent move, only to find a valuable piece is taken. If you both stick to the rules you can have a decent game, but there is only ever one winner.'

'Unless you settle for stalemate,' I offered.

'Stalemate. Indeed. But then what a waste of time playing.'

She left at seven minutes to the hour – I know because I glanced at the mantel clock as she departed, keen to somehow hold on to her for those remaining moments but unable to prolong our encounter. Apart from her unguarded enthusiasm over the orchids and a brief conversation about planting, she appeared indifferent to every suggestion I laid before her. It was as though she'd made up her mind I was not suitable before we'd even met, and I wondered why she'd sought me out, if I was so obviously not to her liking.

Later that afternoon, I discovered she had inadvertently left a white lace handkerchief in the chair: a soft smell of bergamot and an elegant embroidered V in one corner. I tucked it into my breast pocket. I doubted she would return – she'd certainly given me no reason to think so. Yet even though our meeting had been brief, this lady had stirred something deep inside that no one else ever had. The handkerchief would be a simple reminder of that – for she was not, and would never be, mine to love.

Chapter 4
Present Day

The following day, as I was sprawled across one of the leather armchairs, feet dangling over the arm and flicking through Netflix, looking for something to fill the time as my purple toe polish dried, Mum walked in.

'Busy flat hunting?' she teased and handed me the phone. 'It's Wally for you.' But I'd guessed as much. He was the only person who ever spoke to me on the landline. Everyone else texted, WhatsApp-ed or Snapchatted. 'I told him you were staying for a couple of days and he wanted a word.'

'Granddad,' I gushed into the phone, sitting up in the chair and carefully resting my feet on the carpet. 'How's the garden?' I caught Mum's raised eyebrow as I turned away to indicate it was a private call. But the eyebrow was a whole other conversation she'd had without saying a word.

Walter was Brian's father, so *technically* wasn't my granddad. What bothered Mum was that I always called him 'Granddad', but refused to call Brian 'Dad' – even though he'd legally adopted me when he'd married Mum. I can't defend it – it just didn't seem right. Until I'd solved the riddle of my biological father, I couldn't bring myself to give anyone else that title.

'I bet it looks fabulous this time of year – all flowers and plants and . . . other leafy things.'

Granddad gave a slight chuckle, knowing my knowledge of flora and fauna was limited to grass and daisy recognition, despite his best efforts. 'I've not really been out there much, love.'

My warning light flicked to amber. Granddad's garden was his passion, and we'd hoped it would be his salvation after the unexpected death of Grandma last autumn. Surely this was the season when the garden needed the most attention? If he let the spring pass him by, a whole year of fruit and vegetables would be lost.

'Mum's started with ours.' I tried to sound upbeat and chatty. 'She's ordered plants for the window boxes, and the odd job man's been over to tidy our minuscule square of garden. He pressure-washed the decking and re-oiled it ready for the Pimm's season. You know how she loves her Pimm's?' I joked.

Granddad was quiet for a moment. 'Nothing's the same without Briggie, sweetheart. Even the flowers are mourning her. A lot of my daffs came up blind this spring, and a whole area of primroses succumbed to root rot after the unusually wet winter. Some days I just feel like the life has gone out of everything.'

'We all miss her, Granddad,' I said. He had no idea how much I missed her. How I'd give anything to have her back and live last summer over again. 'But she wouldn't want you to be unhappy. If you'd gone first, she'd still be cooking and preserving for England, and scrubbing the kitchen floor twice a day. There would be a Dorset Apple Cake on the table and she'd call us in for a fabulous home-cooked roast and then tell everyone off for coming through the back door with our shoes on. I'm certain she'd miss you every bit as much as you miss her, but she wasn't the sort to give up.'

There was a low sigh from the other end of the phone. 'It was the suddenness of it all that got me. There she was, as pretty as the day I'd first set eyes on her, dicing up onions for chutney. I went down the garden to collect the last of the green tomatoes and when I came back she was slumped in the chair. She'd upped and left me in those few minutes, love. Quietly and without warning simply slipped away ...' There was a pause, and possibly a shuffling of booted feet. '... I never even got to say goodbye.'

I couldn't find the right words, so waited for a bit, pulling at my bottom lip with my teeth. It was the appropriate moment for a hug, but you can't do that down the phone.

'Anyway,' he rallied, 'I wondered if you would like to come down for a visit? I appreciate it won't be the same, with Bridget gone and everything ...'

I felt them pull again: the dormant knots in my stomach that no one could untangle. Grandma had died without warning and I'd missed my chance to apologise.

'Especially as you were so poorly last summer,' he continued. 'She was heartbroken when your visit was cut short.'

She hadn't said anything to Granddad then. Perhaps it would be okay. And until last year they'd been good summers – despite Granddad's house being the weirdest house on the planet – or maybe because of it.

Brian's parents, Walter and Bridget, had lived most of their married life in this funny late Victorian house on the Dorset coast. Hawthorn Place had always seemed somehow incongruous to me, hidden down a stony, narrow track at the edge of the Jurassic coast in an area tourists had yet to discover. Bridget swore it was haunted – some pyjama-clad boy she'd seen on a few occasions back in the early nineties, clutching a shabby, one-eyed teddy and wandering around in the dark. But as he hadn't put in any ghostly appearances for a couple of decades, he'd fallen off my radar.

The house itself was enormous – six bedrooms, not including the attic rooms – and the exterior was a quirky mixture of deep red bricks and chunks of irregular flint, cleverly arranged in alternate squares like a chessboard. In many respects it was a hotchpotch of a building. The windows were different shapes and sizes, and there was a round tower at the far end. Inside, Latin phrases were dotted about, curious motifs decorated everything from the stairs to the windows, and it had the most peculiar room that wasn't properly either inside or outside.

But my childhood holidays with them had been the best. Two doting grandparents who encouraged me to run wild and free, and fed me enough home-cooked food to ensure I had the required energy reserves. For all the advantages of living in the city, the open spaces and freedoms of their lifestyle were price-less. Grandma let me roam: walk to the bay for a paddle, bike around the hills with a homemade picnic in my backpack, or just lose myself in one of the many bedrooms as I acted out games of make-believe.

'Of course, I understand if you have other things planned.' Granddad sounded hesitant. 'Or can't get the time off work. You're probably heading off to Magaluf or somewhere exotic with your friends. It was on the telly the other day – youngsters all cavorting about in bikinis with colourful cocktails in their hands.'

My spirits lifted as I suddenly realised that Granddad was a possible solution to my imminent homelessness. I could stay with him until Mum and Brian returned. Having soared to the ceiling, they then fell to the floor with a thud. Work wouldn't let me take four weeks' holiday, and a daily Dorset to London com-mute was impossible. Plus, as much as I adored Granddad, there was no Wi-Fi at Hawthorn Place and an appalling phone signal – one of the main reasons I'd struggled with my visits in recent years. It was a calamitous toss-up between having nowhere to rest my head and shutting myself off completely from the twenty-first century world.

'I'd love to see you, Granddad, but life is a bit complicated at the moment.'

'It needn't cost you much, love. As Briggie always used to say, the fresh air and the views of the sea are free. It would be great to have a bit of company. I know it's not as exciting as your life in London, but then perhaps visiting a lonely old man in the middle of nowhere isn't a particularly appealing prospect . . .'

Being used to Mum's ninja skills, I knew full well the simple addition of the word lonely in that sentence was deliberate. And effective. But the practicality of it all remained the stumbling block.

'I'd never get the time off work. I'm homeless, heartbroken and pretty skint,' I explained. But I realised as I said the words that the one thing I wasn't was heartbroken. I'd miss the life I had with Rupert, particularly the food, but our lives had become increasingly separate without me noticing. We'd settled into the jogging along together phase, having spent our university years so wrapped up in each other we barely came up for air. It wasn't anyone's fault, but the relationship had run its course, and after sleeping on it, I could see this more clearly.

'Then quit the silly job, which I happen to know you hate, and take some time out to get your head together – I believe that's the expression nowadays. Maybe pick up a temporary job down here. What do you say?'

It was certainly a short-term solution. Perhaps I could sell ice-creams. Or was it too early in the year for that? And Izzy could come and join me for a few days. The weather would be turning nice soon – May could take you by surprise and have you rummaging for the factor fifteen. Perhaps I could escape for the *whole* summer and totally reboot my life.

'I don't suppose you've got Wi-Fi yet?' I asked, knowing it was unlikely: he still struggled with the TV remote, preferring to stand up and fiddle with the tiny buttons along the edge of the screen. I, on the other hand, was bereft without it. I Googled everything, from the weather to calories in a chocolate bar.

'I'm afraid not, love. What does a seventy-seven-year-old widower want with all that skiing the net?'

Or maybe just until Mum and Brian came back from New York.

Chapter 5

There are only so many times you can say, 'Hello, this is Molly from Energy Solutions. How are you today?' without wanting to eat your own head. And there are only so many times you can have the phone slammed down in response before you start rummaging for the necessary cutlery.

My six-hour shift that afternoon had ended with me handing in my notice, with immediate effect. Granddad was right. I hated the work and most of my colleagues. Dorset was now my only option, despite the painful memories.

Mum was dashing about packing for their trip, and I only had three days before the arrival of the Americans. But I had some logistical obstacles to overcome. Neither Mum nor I had ever learned to drive, as having a car in the city was more of a liability than a necessity. And trains cost money. I wandered into the kitchen, earbuds in and belting out the words to a song by the Black Veil Brides.

'Molly!' Mum shouted, trying to make herself heard above my dubious vocals.

I tugged the buds out my ears and let them dangle over the edge of my Punisher T-shirt. Brian struggled with my love of Marvel, graphic novels and horror films, and it was another area where we were at odds. He'd always treated me like a little girl, never quite grasping the age-appropriateness of his gifts, perhaps because he was somewhat late to the parenting party. But just because I was small, did not make me a child. And when my tastes changed from pink to black, and from Disney to zombie, a perverse part of me enjoyed his discomfort.

'I don't think you realise how loud you are when you're plugged in. Wouldn't be so bad if it was in tune,' she teased.

I slumped on to the bar stool and forced a smile, not reacting to her words. Mum was cooking. Or rather she was preparing a colourful salad to accompany whatever was heating up in the oven.

'Something smells amazing,' I said.

Mum looked up from slicing red pepper and ripe avocado. 'Waitrose finest.'

'Nonna would be horrified,' I said. 'All those artificial additives.'

'I can cook when it's necessary, to impress Brian's clients or for family gatherings.'

Mum's culinary skills were top notch, rivalling even Rupert's, but then you couldn't be from the best southern Italian bloodlines and be mediocre in the kitchen. For the nine glorious years before Brian cramped our style, Mum made a proper meal every evening, even if it was just a simple pasta dish with a tomato sauce. Fresh ingredients and careful preparation, with her matriarchal mother watching her every move from two doors down in our cramped row of terraces. Nonna's standards were high, even though her income was low. And because Mum felt she'd failed as a daughter by getting pregnant out of wedlock, the least she could do was prove herself a proficient mother.

There was a pause. 'Don't suppose you thought to bring your empty coffee cups through, or your bowl from breakfast?' She tossed the rainbow of ingredients with her bare hands and sprinkled a handful of mixed seeds over the finished salad. It looked good enough to eat.

'Erm, no. I'll get them in a bit.' I cleared my throat. 'Have you done something different with your hair? It looks fantastic.'

'What do you want, Molly?' She slipped the oven gloves out from a drawer.

'Granddad has asked me to visit and so this afternoon, I quit my job. A couple of weeks at Hawthorn Place might be good for me. It would solve my immediate housing crisis.' I paused. 'I wondered if you'd lend me the train fare?'

'Brian will drop you down, I'm sure.' I was impressed how calmly she took the news of my unemployment, as she placed the foil container on the hob, and closed the oven door.

'Please stop pushing us together all the time. He's a bit full-on and I'd rather travel independently. He's not actually my dad.'

'Legally he is,' my mum pointed out. 'And emotionally. He's helped me to bring you up since you were ten years old, Molly. Your refusal to acknowledge that is heartbreaking for both of us.'

'But how can you expect me to accept Brian when the truth of my real father has been deliberately kept from me? I had to wait until I was eighteen to get my hands on a birth certificate that simply said "father unknown". What's the big secret? Why can't you be honest with me?'

'Do you think turning eighteen magically gives you all the answers in life?' she said. 'Being an adult isn't about how many years you've been alive, but more to do with your mindset, life experience and sense of responsibility. You are still my beautiful, clever daughter, and finding out who your father was doesn't change any of that.'

'Was?' I leapt on her choice of tense. 'Does that mean he's dead?' But she didn't so much as flick an eyebrow. It was the same game we'd played for years – me wearing my detective hat and her cooler than a frozen cucumber, giving nothing away.

'Married then?' I watched her face carefully for any indication these random guesses were getting warmer. Nothing. Just a sweet smile and a melancholy look about her eyes.

'He simply didn't want me, did he?' I sighed, as she walked around to my side of the kitchen counter and threw her arms about my shoulders.

'Do you trust me, Molly?' she asked.

I shrugged, noncommittally.

'You are overwrought at the moment, and looking for further reasons to be angry at the world. Please trust that I love you with all my heart, but this is something you have to let go. He will never be a part of your life. *Ever*. Be grateful for what you have, and don't look for answers that cause more problems than they solve.'

Brian wandered in, clutching my cereal bowl and mug from that morning. He put them on the worktop and slid out the dishwasher rack.

'Why do my two favourite ladies look so serious?'

'I've decided to stay with Granddad for the month,' I explained, not wanting to upset him by mentioning the real conversation. 'But I don't have the train fare.'

'I'll drive you, sweetheart. I was planning to pop down tomorrow anyway, especially as we'll be away for so long, so you aren't putting me out. Your mother and I are becoming increasingly worried about him, so it will be good to have a spy in the camp. After lunch suit you?'

27

Inwardly, I groaned. Three hours of sitting next to Brian in a car where he would spend so much time trying to say the right thing that I'd be embarrassed for both of us. Still, it solved my logistical dilemma.

'Thanks, Bri,' I said, as he beamed back at me, and I wandered upstairs to throw some stuff in my suitcase.

Chapter 6

I stood at the top of the steep stone steps and looked down into a dip of tree-shielded land. From the road you'd never guess there was a house nestled at the bottom. It reminded me of childish efforts to stop someone copying my work at school by covering the page – as if the trees were huge hands shielding it from prying eyes. In fact, the closest you could get a car was the main road above, where Brian's ostentatious Audi was now parked ahead of Granddad's ancient Fiat.

We clambered down the steps and my breath caught in my throat as I looked over to Hawthorn Place. With one foot on the bottom step, and the other on the ancient herringbone brick path that curled around the house, I felt as if I was standing over the meridian line in Greenwich. It was a point where I was in two places at once – two different worlds. I could never understand why flint and brick had been used for the house, when the surrounding landscape was awash with scars of pale stone, exposed through the green of the fields and hills. Portland was only a few miles away, famous for its quarries, and the obvious choice of building material. The property was odd not only in its construction, but also its location. It simply didn't belong here, even though I wasn't sure where it did belong.

'I could murder a cup of tea,' I announced, as I tumbled into the hallway and threw my arms about my dear old granddad. He looked slightly startled by my exuberance but I'm embarrassingly tactile. Probably the Italian in me.

I abandoned my shoes and hooked my rucksack over the quirky crenellated post at the bottom of the main oak staircase. Identical posts were dotted up the stairs, and always reminded me of tiny wooden castles in the air – all part of the charm and mystery of the house.

'I'll put the kettle on, love,' Granddad said.

'Molly is capable of doing that. You're not to run around after her, Dad.'

It wasn't said unkindly, but I still glared at him.

'I'll make it, Granddad. Sorry. You don't have to wait on me.'

'Nonsense, I bet you two are gasping.' He toddled off to the kitchen, as Brian parked my suitcase at the foot of the stairs and, neither of us commenting on the muddy trail over the cluttered floor, we followed behind. It was a similar story in the kitchen: piles of papers and accumulated dust, abandoned shoes and newspapers.

'How are you getting on with the microwave?' Brian asked.

'Grand, thank you. Not sure Briggie would be best pleased with me, but that bloody cooker has a life of its own. And there really is no point firing it up for one.'

'It's not an Aga, Dad. You don't have to light it and cart buckets of solid fuel across from the coal bunker any more. It's a simple electric cooker. Even Molly can operate one of those.' I stared at my feet, not convinced his faith in me was justified. 'Mind you, it took me long enough to persuade Mum the Aga was becoming a hazard,' he continued. 'The bottom door hung from one hinge.'

'I loved that old Aga,' Granddad said defiantly. 'The kitchen was always so lovely and cosy, and I could always warm me wellies in front of it.'

'Well, you've got radiators now, although goodness knows how you'd have managed if I hadn't insisted on dragging you both into the twenty-first century. Mum would have soldiered on until the end with oil lamps and coal fires.' Brian scooted a pile of envelopes across the worktop and got three mugs out the cupboard.

'Ah, she loved it. Never a shirker. That woman was up with the lark and to bed with the owl,' said Granddad. 'Every morning she strode down the footpath, along Back Lane and over the hill to the bay for her morning dip. Even in December the stubborn mule would launch herself into the icy sea. Start the day with a swim, she would say, to wash your cares away. Did you bring your cozzie, love?' Granddad asked, turning to me. 'I know how much you loved going with her. Be nice to see someone carry on the tradition.'

When I was younger, schoolgirl age, I went with Grandma on her early morning swims. Living in London, the sea was a novelty. I didn't care how cold it was. I dashed into the water with her, splashed about for as long as I could bear and then hobbled back over the pebbles, shivering, to the large canvas bag that held the bundle of towels. When I hit the end of my teenage years, I simply couldn't be bothered and now I wished for those days back. I could have roused myself and walked with her along the overgrown path, and we could have swum in the water and run for the bundle of towels together. But those later holidays with her, I'd slept in and Grandma had swum alone.

Brian persuaded Granddad into the garden whilst I took my suitcase upstairs to settle in. My first thought was to check social media. As I swiped my phone open, I remembered yet again how rubbish both the phone signal and 4G were at the house – probably something to do with it being on the edge of civilisation and down a huge dip. There was no connection, so I tossed the phone across the bed in frustration.

I unzipped my case and was surprised to find a pale blue envelope across the top, which Mum must have slipped inside before I left. She was always one for little notes; occasionally in my lunch box when I was having a tough time at school, reminders that she loved me when I went away on school trips, or Post-its on my mirror after one of my teenage outbursts.

Molly

I love you more than you can possibly know and I'm sorry that I keep stalling when you ask about your paternity, but I don't believe this is a conversation either of us is ready to have yet. When I return from New York we can talk about your biological father. Sometimes events must play out in a certain order. As Nonna would often say, 'to every thing there is a season' – her rigid Catholic faith a mystery to me but often a source of surprisingly incisive words.

Enjoy your stay in Summerton and see if this break doesn't help you to reassess your life. I hope your time away will help you recover from your heartache, and I know that if anyone can move Walter on from his grief, you can. I truly believe you need him as much as he needs you right now. Look after each other.

Mum x

Although she was finally promising me some answers, I'd still have an agonising wait, but in a way, I realised she was right about timing. It would be new starts for me all round when I returned, with work, romance and a clearer understanding of my genetic makeup. In the meantime, I could kick back and relax for a month.

I headed back down the main staircase but stopped at the half-landing to watch Granddad and his son together in the front garden. Brian was enthusiastically poking about in the borders as Granddad stood by, not participating. His garden and his wife had been his world. Now with the biggest and most beautiful part of that gone, he couldn't bear to carry on with the other. It broke my heart and made me determined to use my visit for good.

At six o'clock, Brian finally headed home and we climbed back up to the Summerton Road to see him off.

'You all right?' he asked, noticing me glance back at the house.

'Yeah,' I said. 'I was thinking of Grandma.' It was the first time I'd been back since the funeral and I knew it would hit me hard.

'Think of the good times, sweetheart. My spirits are always lifted when I return,' he said. 'It was such a smashing place to grow up. I was always fossil-hunting, den-building and playing down by the sea. Isolated but always full of adventure. And then I hit puberty and answered the call of the bright lights and bustling city life. I'm always pulled back, though. I can't survive without a regular top-up of sea air and open spaces.'

I smiled. Brian, momentarily surprised by some sign of thawing from me, smiled back.

'You'll be okay here.'

'I know,' I replied, kicking a loose stone with the toe of my Converse and avoiding eye contact.

'You're a good girl, Molly. You still have some life lessons to learn, that's all.' He patted my shoulder and slipped into the front seat.

'Give the wonderful Annetta my love,' Granddad said. He was the only person who still called Mum by her full name now that her parents had died. But Walter's Italian daughter-in-law always seemed exotic to him; a man who had only left the county of his birth once in his life, and that was to see his son get married at St Patrick's Catholic Church in the middle of London, on a wet December day.

As Brian's car disappeared into the distance, I decided to help Granddad find a zest for life again and make some solid plans for a brighter Molly future. The evening sky took on an orange hue and birds started up their own social media network as they sang across the treetops. We turned to descend the steep stone stairs and I hoped that despite being cut off from my internet lifeline, the time would simply whizz by.

'So, love, how about a nice game of draughts?' Granddad suggested.

Chapter 7
Percy Gladwell
1894

I did not take to Edward Marston much. By far the bigger man, he still felt the need to prove his superiority and his handshake was unnecessarily forceful. I resisted the desire to flex my hand and let my crushed fingers drop to my side.

'I understand you have already met with my wife, Mr Gladwell?' It was a rhetorical question. 'I have been informed that, without my knowledge, she visited these offices last week to discuss our building plans.'

I wondered how this meeting would go. Was he here to undermine his wife? Or was it a plan that had his approval?

'Yes, I had that pleasure. She outlined her intention to commission a large family residence by the sea. I believe she has connections in the area and clearly has a strong desire to escape London. She is, I could tell, a country girl at heart.'

Edward nodded and took both pipe and tobacco pouch from his pockets, packing the pipe, tamping it down and flicking a match. He had no regard for my time, nor indeed my weak lungs, as he lit up.

'Excellent. Excellent.' He blew a stream of smoke from his thin lips and it tapered towards the ceiling. 'Not that securing you was in any doubt, as I had already informed my wife you were my preferred architect, but it seems she felt it necessary to do some research of her own. Did she mention we stayed last summer at the Bayldons'?' He didn't wait for a response. 'The house had a vitality and a charm that I found most intriguing. Your clever use of yellow-brown sandstone and the endless ribbons of windows under the low-hipped roofs. Although my preference is the city, I was born a countryman and appreciate the skill of traditional crafts. Not for me the mass-produced and new. Besides, history maketh the man.'

It was manners, not history, but heritage was something Edward didn't have, so I charitably let his statement stand.

Prior to Edward's appointment, I had made discreet enquiries about him, curious to know of his background. Perhaps, if I am honest, keen to investigate Mrs Marston's choice of husband – if indeed there had been any choice in the matter.

Edward had made his fortune on the railways – not the building of the lines, for that was largely complete – but had instead inherited a large engineering works and was involved in the ongoing supply and repairing of rolling stock. The company had been established by his father, but in the decade since his death Edward had overseen substantial company growth. It was ironic to me that he spoke of supporting the craftsmen of this country when it was his livelihood that had gone some way to destroying it.

As international trade routes expanded and the railways dissected our land, goods were shipped far and wide in journey times that had previously been unthinkable. The building of factories continued, and mechanisation replaced honest working men on the fields and in the towns. Inevitably, we had witnessed a decline in quality of goods and working conditions, and a growing number of us refused to embrace these changes. Was it right that Welsh roof slate tiles should be used in areas where they did not belong? That fittings could be mass-produced in factories but resulted in inferior quality products? Or, conversely, items too perfect, so that each one produced was identical to the one before?

Right or not, being a part of our industrial advancement had enabled this wealthy young man to secure the hand of the enchanting Mrs Marston, but I doubted it was a love match. Edward's wealth was new money. His family name was not recorded in the annals of history. The marriage to Violet Marston brought legitimacy, and now he wished to design a country house because it was what those of his new-found status did.

'You have come to the right man, Mr Marston. Rest assured, I will be commissioning locally sourced, handmade items, from the timber and brick of construction, to the hinges and latches on every door. But be aware such items come at a price.'

He waved an indifferent hand in my direction, as another stream of smoke was expelled from his lips.

'Money, while not in limitless supply, is not my greatest concern. It is of the utmost importance Violet is happy with this house. She will be persuaded you are the best man for the job. My wife has an artistic soul and great sympathy for your movement, even though she was not as taken as me with the York house,' he continued. 'She thought it somewhat queer, preferring to spend her time roaming the grounds. But then it has always been hard to please our Violet.' He rolled his eyes and puffed at his pipe.

There was a stab to my heart as he talked of Mrs Marston's indifference. Not that this young woman was in any way qualified to judge my skills as an architect, but I was disappointed she found me lacking.

'My wife and I are very different people,' he said. 'I am up at five every morning, restless and pacing. She rises at nine. Whilst

I am constantly seeking meaningful pursuits and lively social engagements, she is sedentary, and seeks out nature, content to sit staring out to sea, or while away an hour dead-heading her precious flowers. The land we have secured will suit her well. She longs to be near her mother and brothers, and has fond memories of her summers along those shores as a child. Two years residing in London with me has only accentuated those feelings. I am city and she is country and coast.'

His pipe died and he removed it from his mouth, tamped it down and lit it once more, a fresh billowing of smoke surrounding his face. I stifled an involuntary cough.

'I have already apprised myself of your portfolio. The estate cottages at Bardenfield, the alterations made to the Steepleford parish church, and a growing collection of small country houses. Even my wife could not deny you made an excellent job of Steepleford; the west tower was a triumph. In your work, I see a simplicity and functionality that I find pleasing, yet an ability to embrace the imagination, which will doubtless appeal to the whimsy of my wife. I am more than satisfied and wish to go ahead with the project.'

'In that case, my first request would be to visit the plot to assess the landscape and amenities. I will consult my secretary and we can arrange a date that is convenient to yourself. We can then discuss function and aesthetics.'

'You misunderstand me, dear fellow. I will have very little to do with design and planning. I merely intend to provide the funds. I am a busy man, Mr Gladwell, and my business interests keep me in London. This house will be the primary residence of my wife, so it is she who must be consulted at every stage.'

I nodded my understanding and cannot deny my heart gave a tiny leap at the thought of further contact with the beautiful Mrs Marston.

'Then I will set about arranging a meeting convenient to your wife. It will be a pleasure to deal with Mrs Marston. She struck me as both intelligent and charming.'

Edward looked me up and down, narrowing his eyes. 'Do you have a wife, Mr Gladwell?'

'No.'

'Pity.'

'The thought of marriage does not appeal.' Although like every man with a soul, I earnestly hoped there would be someone out there for me when the time was right.

His eyes brightened. 'Ah . . . I see.'

Realising there was room for misunderstanding, I blustered. 'I am committed to my career, you see? I am—'

'You do not need to say anything more, dear fellow. You will do nicely. Besides, the temptations of some foppish young architect would worry me.'

I didn't need him to spell out that I was not the most eligible bachelor. My slender frame, weak chest and the pair of wire-rimmed spectacles balanced on the bridge of my nose were reminders I was no Adonis. Mrs Marston might have stolen my heart, but I would not steal hers.

'For I guard my possessions jealously, Mr Gladwell,' he explained. 'And always have. Take, for example, the horse I was given as a boy. It was a fine steed, but it didn't take to me. It bucked and reared, and I never felt fully in control. My younger brother had a way with him, and despite acquiring another more suitable mount, I refused to let my brother have that horse. You see – the horse was mine, even if I did not have cause to ride it.'

Was he really comparing his wife to a regrettable choice of horse?

As he made to take his leave, gathering his hat and cane from the corner, Mr Marston turned.

'Give Violet what she wants, down to every last detail. She must have no desire to come to the city and meddle in my affairs. I'm certain she will be quite content playing house, raising a litter of unruly children and growing silly flowers – as is her wont. I have my distractions in London. It is an arrangement that I will preserve at all costs. So much so, Mr Gladwell, that I am prepared to build her a house in order to do so.'

Chapter 8

Present Day

After politely declining Granddad's offer of draughts, I stood in the square hall of Hawthorn Place and realised how little things had changed in the eight months since Grandma's death. Her possessions were still dotted about, as if she was going to walk past at any minute, pick up a pair of abandoned spectacles and wander into the living room. But beneath the accumulated jumble, I was reminded yet again what a mishmash of styles it was. It had odd windows, none of which seemed to match, under a higgledy-piggledy assortment of high-pitched roofs. There was even a circular window in the front living room, which reminded me of cartoon submarines from my childhood. And then there was the round tower, like you might find on a castle, with a fairy-tale spiral staircase inside, and another, more formal staircase off the main entrance hall. When I was younger, I would run up one and down the other, in a never-ending loop.

There were other peculiar features that I'd not seen elsewhere: an upstairs window that was practically on the floor, mysterious Latin phrases over the fireplaces, and the inside really belonged outside – all exposed brick and wood. Everywhere I looked there were flower motifs. Five rounded petals of something I didn't recognise, carved into door panels and on various ceramic tiles on the floors and walls. It was a quirky house, full of history, and probably the sort of thing a more motivated person might have researched – beautiful in its way and yet somehow lost, as if the person who built it was ashamed of it – which I could never understand.

For a silent moment, I absorbed the curious atmosphere. It wasn't, and had never been, unsettling, despite being strange, really old and possibly haunted. But there was a sense of something undefinable about the house, almost as if Hawthorn Place had a heart and it was still beating.

On a whim, I climbed the main stairs in twos, and ran along the long corridor and down the curly stairs in the tower, like I'd done as a child. After this sudden burst of energy, I tipped my head back and looked at the disappearing spiral of steps that led up to the attic, reminding me of the fossilised ammonite shells found in the nearby hills. During the eighties and nineties Grandma rented it out as it was largely self-contained, but now it was full of clutter and cobwebs.

Sighing, I stood up and walked to the kitchen. Granddad was buttering a piece of toast, an opened jar of homemade jam next to the plate. In Grandma's lifetime, this room had always been immaculate and smelled of baking cakes and stewing soups. The food smells were absent now, apart from the slightly bitter aroma of burnt bread, and the work surfaces were untidy and dusty. 'You can't cook in a cluttered kitchen,' Grandma used to say. No one was doing any cooking, so perhaps it didn't matter. After all, you only needed twenty square centimetres of table to sort out a ready meal.

'You all right, love?' Granddad asked.

'I was thinking about Grandma. The house seems lost without her.' In my heart, I suspected the absence of her hustle and bustle meant the silence was playing a part in the atmosphere. She wasn't shooing me off the worktop to stop me sneaking freshly baked cookies, or persuading me to flick her ancient feather duster around rather than lying across the battered sofa waiting for my purple nail varnish to dry.

'Briggie loved this house but she was always convinced it held secrets.' He munched on a jam-laden triangle of toast.

'Oh? What sort of secrets?' That might explain its aura. I knew nothing about the place, except that it was Victorian. And really, really peculiar.

'Not rightly sure, but she often felt the house was trying to tell her something. The ghost of the little boy, the incongruity of the building materials, and all the messages and motifs. She even found something scribbled in the cupboard under the stairs that convinced her there was a love story at the heart of it all. At one point, she researched its history, but I'm not sure how far she got.'

This was news to me – not only that Grandma had tried to investigate this bizarre yet beautiful house, but also that there was a secret message in a tiny cupboard I'd never had cause to enter. How very Enid Blyton.

Granddad looked around the room and sighed. 'And you can bet she's looking down on me now, scolding me for all this mess. But then it was terribly selfish of her to leave me so suddenly.' His shoulders hunched slightly and he put a shaky hand up to wipe his watery eyes. I walked over and hugged him.

'There, there, love,' he said, reaching up and patting my hand. 'Don't you be starting. We can't bring her back with our tears. More's the pity.'

He pulled himself together, picked up a packet of custard creams and offered me one. I shook my head, and he tipped the contents on to the side of the large plate that held his jam-smothered toast.

'Help yourself to whatever you fancy. Want to watch some telly with me?' I shook my head a second time.

'I'm good, thanks. But you carry on.'

Intrigued by Granddad's throwaway line about a message in the under-stair cupboard, I returned to the hall. There was a full height coat cupboard and a smaller triangular door that filled the diminishing space under the lowest steps.

I flung open the larger door first. There was a brown Bakelite switch on the wall outside so I flicked it on to get a better look. Hand-forged high iron hooks were hung with musty old gardening coats, and the tiled floor was littered with shoes and boots. There was a large metal gun cabinet at the back, where Granddad kept his shotgun for the rabbits and the pigeons who were tempted by his spring greens. The cupboard smelled of garden and gun oil. I ran my hand down a weathered quilted jacket of Grandma's and felt nostalgic. It had been her odd-job coat, the one she wore to nip outside and collect a few fresh beetroot, or tip a bowl of peelings on the compost heap. My heart heaved. After inspecting every dusty nook and darkened cranny, I decided there was no message to be found.

I bent down to try the smaller door. It popped open easily enough but kept swinging back, so I had to put my foot against it to stop it closing. There was no light switch but then you couldn't walk into it – it was more of a hands and knees crawl. I used the torch on my phone to illuminate the space, and without the need for too much investigation, I saw a string of words, written in heavy pencil, across the wooden back of one of the lower risers.

Love will always find a way.

It was in old-fashioned handwriting – loopy and swirly – and the author had gone over the letters several times so that they were indented into the wood.

Not only was it a strange sentiment to scribble in your house, but also it was a very odd place to put it. I felt a shiver ripple between my shoulder blades. Grandma was right. There was a love story at the heart of this, and I was convinced that the house was trying to tell me about it.

After half an hour of wandering aimlessly like a ball in a pinball machine, I returned to the kitchen and walked along the narrow corridor that led to the utility. There was a beautiful row of stained-glass geese along the windows. Grandma had names for them all – Mother Goose was the largest and her trailing goslings were given silly names like teapot, eggcup and flip-flop – but I'd only been half listening as she'd sung her made-up song to remember the names. Why hadn't I paid more attention to her while she was still alive?

Despite the hour, I opened the back door, stepped into the garden and set off along the footpath to the cove. It had always been part of my ritual when I arrived, saying hello to the sea, possibly because we lived so far from the coast. The air always smelled salty and fresh, and the breeze was somehow more playful than back home – tugging me to places that needed exploring, sending me haring down hills or merely rippling gently across my body as I lay on the shingle, imagining animals in the clouds. I paused at the crest of the hill, memories swamping me and making my pilgrimage difficult. As if sensing my hesitation, a dancing gust caught me and swept me further along the cliffs, towards the sea.

Summerton itself was an inconsequential village on the south Dorset coast. It was a pretty sight with circling cliffs that embraced the bay – beautiful to look at but a nightmare to get to. And when you finally clambered down steep chalky paths and hopped across large white boulders and over the little stream that trickled into the sea, the going was slow as your feet sank into a mire of deep pebbles. Flotsam and jetsam hugged the tideline.

Colourful, even in the half light, but horrifying at the same time: a mass of plastic in its various non-biodegradable forms.

Catching that first sight of the sea always made my tummy roll over. I loved working out where the horizon finished and the sea began, and was overwhelmed by a sense of the vastness of it all. The never-ending ocean and the all-encompassing sky, sandwiching the world between them. There was no place in the city that ever made me feel quite like this.

I sat on the pebbles for a while, hugging my knees, pleased to be back but feeling the aching gap that Grandma had left behind. There were no wide arms to hug things better, no wholesome food, and no chance to make amends. A wobbly moon reflected in the water before me and I felt a shiver as I lifted my hoodie over my head and thought about my last visit. I'd been mean and I'd been unkind. But I was starting to realise everything she'd said that day was true.

'I'm sorry, Grandma,' I whispered. A gentle evening breeze picked up my words and carried them away – hopefully to a place where she could hear them. Even though last summer couldn't be undone, I could have been kinder and accepted that she was right. Instead, I'd yelled at her, rushing back to Rupert the very next day, feigning a mystery illness to save either of us having to explain the atmosphere.

And then, without warning, she'd left us and nothing could ever be made right again.

I sat for a little while longer, letting heavy tears fall to my knees, watching rivulets gather in the wide rips across my black jeans. My stomach constricted and folded in on itself.

I should have come down with her when she asked, I thought to myself, getting to my feet and turning back to the cliffs. I should have come with her and had one last swim.

Chapter 9

'Where have you been, love? I've been frantic!'

Granddad was pacing the path at the back of the house.

'I went to the bay to say hello.' All trace of the tears had gone. I didn't want probing questions.

'Right. Right,' he repeated. 'Only I was worried, see? Didn't know where you'd gone and it's getting dark.'

I wasn't used to accounting for my movements, being an adult. I was about to point this out but the concern on his face made me stop. 'Sorry. I should have said something.'

'Well, you're back now, love. That's all that matters. Just worried, see? Thought you might have fallen down a rabbit hole or something – slim thing that you are.' He chuckled at his own joke and raised an arm to usher me back into the safety of the house.

'That was an Alice, not a Molly,' I reminded him. 'Mind you, it might be fun to drop into another world for a bit of adventure,' I said, thinking that the possibility of anything remotely adventurous happening in this sleepy village with my aged and grieving grandfather was minuscule. We linked arms and walked back down to the house.

Because I couldn't get a phone signal, I resorted to Granddad's house phone to call Izzy before I headed to bed. It was in the hall, on the side table at the bottom of the main staircase, and stood proudly on a dated lace doily, bathed in coloured light from the rainbow-stained-glass panel beside the door. The handset was still connected to a base unit by a fabric-coated curly wire, and instead of buttons it had a rotary dial – a novelty to me when I was younger. I loved the feel of poking my finger into the numbered holes and hearing the whirring sound it made as the dial spun around.

'I told you it was win-win,' Izzy said triumphantly. 'He gets company and you get somewhere rent-free to reassess your poor life choices. Top up your tan and get Rupert out of your system by embarking on a passionate holiday romance with a hunky surfer—'

'I think you're confusing it with Cornwall,' I interrupted, hurt by the implication my current situation might be my responsibility. 'And it's hardly the height of summer. Not sure there's going to be many hot men hanging around this deserted backwater in May.'

She'd been completely behind my plan to stay with Granddad, having long since said that Rupert and I had run our course, but I wasn't sure leaping into bed with someone else was a necessary part of my healing.

'And I'm glad you chucked in that stupid job. You're capable of so much more, Molls. You just need to motivate yourself. Rupert fussed over you too much and you never had the chance to become truly independent.'

'I *was* independent.' I huffed down the line. 'It's not as if I was some unemployed loser still living at home. At least I'd got myself out into the world.'

'But had you, though? Rupert was all but a surrogate parent, and your job was only eighteen hours a week. I love you, hon, but you're still living in a Molly-centric bubble and clinging to the student lifestyle most of us left behind three years ago.'

'Oh, really.' I knew I sounded cross but couldn't help it. 'Easy for you to judge with your 2:1, steady job and cosy little flat. Life has been kinder to you. I'm homeless, penniless and unemployed.'

Izzy laughed. 'I worked hard to achieve all of those things, Molls. And you can have them too with a bit of effort – except for the degree, that ship has long sailed. Stop waiting for life to come to you. Go out and grab the things you want. Get a temporary job to help with your cash flow – babysitting is easy enough and you aren't committing to a contract. In the meantime, apply for decent graduate jobs, so that you have interviews lined up for when you return.'

'I can't job-hunt because Granddad practically lives in a sink hole. No chance of 4G. Even the mobile signal is ropey.'

'Stop making excuses and think outside the box. Get yourself into the nearest town and use the library computers. They have internet access.'

'Oh. Okay. I've still got a Summerton library card somewhere. Perhaps you could come down for a bit? I honestly don't know where to start.' Izzy was great at things like that. She often helped me fill out forms and pointed me in the right direction when I needed information. A true best friend.

'I've got to work, Molly. I don't have many holiday days left.'

'Next weekend? Just overnight? We can head into Weymouth and hit some pubs. Or even take in a film. There's a multi-screen Cineworld there.' Paying for it all was another matter, but then maybe I could tap Granddad for a loan – which I would absolutely, definitely pay back as soon as I started earning.

'I have responsibilities here. Besides, that band we saw last week have another gig in Shepherd's Bush on Saturday and I think I'm getting somewhere with the bass guitarist. He asked his mate if I was single.' She paused. 'I have faith in you. You've got this.'

We'd reached an impasse, so we chatted about other things for a while and finally said our goodbyes. Granddad shuffled past and said I wasn't to wait up for him. I kissed the soft wisps of silver hair on the top of his head goodnight and, with nothing better to do, climbed the stairs to bed.

The next morning I was woken up by light flooding in from the weird low window in my temporary bedroom. There was no reason to leap out of bed so I snuggled down and thought about Grandma's conviction the house had secrets. Did she mean something bad had happened here? Perhaps the pyjamaed ghost child had been brutally murdered or suffered years of torture at the hands of some madman and was waiting for revenge. Or did she mean the fabric of the house? The way it was built and all the curious motifs and quirky decorations? Why on earth would you put a window practically on the floor? It was almost as if it had slipped down the wall because it had been installed before the plaster had set properly. Like icing a cake before it's cooled down. (Which I might have accidentally done in Year Eight Food Tech.)

And then there was that sentiment in the cupboard. *Love will always find a way.* It was a message of hope – a promise that things would be okay. Maybe I should continue Grandma's research. Granddad would be pleased I was showing an interest in the place and, apart from Izzy's job-hunting suggestions, I didn't have much else to fill my time.

My tummy grizzled as I rolled out of bed. I intended to land on my feet, but got them tangled in the cellular blanket and ended up on my backside. Grandma would have plucked her own eyes out before she'd have embraced the duvet, but perhaps Granddad would be open to a bit of modernisation.

I wandered down the narrow hallway to his bedroom, my

room being halfway between what had once been the servant quarters and the main household bedrooms. His door was open, so I entered, to find the bed was made, but it was covered in piles of half folded laundry and abandoned wooden coat hangers that had surely sat there for weeks.

He'd always been an early riser and would have been up for hours, regardless of where he'd slept, but nowadays it was only to catch an early morning breakfast show on television. If Grandma had still been with us, she would have risen with the dawn chorus, walked down to the bay for a swim, put a load of washing through the machine, hung it out, baked four cakes, vacuumed the house and knitted a pair of bed socks by now. Thinking of her made me feel guilty. Perhaps I should make an effort to help with the housework while I was with Granddad. He didn't have the luxury of a cleaner like we did in London, so any mess I made he would have to deal with. And he wasn't exactly on top of the housework before my arrival. I promised myself I would pull my weight.

It was no surprise to locate Granddad in the living room. He hastily kicked a stray pillow resting by his feet behind the chair and ran a hand through his dishevelled hair.

'I made breakfast,' he said. 'It's on the table. Didn't like to wake you and thought you could do with a bit of a lie-in. Might need to make a fresh brew though. It's been there a while.'

'Thanks.' I smiled, noticing he was wearing the same clothes as the night before, but said nothing, and wandered through to the kitchen to find something to quieten my protesting tummy.

Not quite Rupert's smoked salmon and scrambled eggs, or Mum's blueberry and yoghurt pancakes, breakfast was more raspberry jam on toast. There was a thick brown Denby plate piled high with Granddad's efforts stood by a cold pot of tea, a knitted stripy cosy not up to the monumental task of keeping the pot warm for the several hours since it had been made. I poured myself a mug, complete with a filmy over-stewed surface, and zapped it in the microwave while I munched on some soggy toast. It was like drinking liquid metal, but quicker than brewing a fresh pot, and slightly preferable to Granddad's dodgy-looking instant coffee, so I downed it, noticing the fridge was practically empty apart from two pints of milk and some ready-meals.

After breakfast, I stepped out the back door to enjoy some sun. It took me a moment to realise how neglected everything looked. I'd headed straight for the footpath the previous evening and not appreciated the sorry state of the garden. Last summer, tall garden canes had stood proudly at the far end, lashed together with orange twine, a green screen covered in tiny scarlet flowers that grew into long, succulent runner beans. The huge, almost tropical leaves of some vegetable or another, possibly marrow, had draped idly over the edges of the path, and the high, frondy green carrot tops (which I might have once accidentally mistaken for parsley) danced delicately in the breeze.

Even though tiny plants were doing their best to push through the soil and grow anew, the borders were covered in rotting leaves, and dead flower heads bobbed about on the top of lolloping stems. Why had he abandoned everything and let this invasion of decay and neglect creep across his land? I couldn't tell the difference between the weeds and the plants that should be there, and didn't know what to clip and what to pull up. But I did know this was wrong. And it broke my heart.

I pulled at a handful of crusty flower heads, and tiny brown seeds exploded and scattered to the ground. Had I helpfully reseeded something pretty? Or inadvertently helped propagate an intrusive weed?

It was no good. I couldn't do this without his help.

'Granddad, shall we do some weeding?' I suggested, as I stepped into the garden room where he was flicking through the *Radio Times*, planning his entertainment for the evening ahead.

The most curious room at Hawthorn Place, if it even qualified as a room, was at the back of the property, accessed by the living room on one side, and the kitchen on the other. We called it the garden room but it was a sort of terrace inside the house rather than attached to it – as if a room had been scooped out of the middle. There was a bedroom above, which provided the ceiling, but it wasn't decorated like an interior room; instead the walls were the same brick and flint as the exterior. Second to the kitchen, I think it had been Grandma's favourite place in the whole house.

Despite a trellis partially covering the access to the lawn, garden detritus tended to blow into this space. Grandma had swept it out regularly, but I noticed a huge collection of dead leaves piled up by the back wall. Dusty cobwebs hung from the ceiling and it had a damp, mushroomy smell.

Granddad shook his head. 'Not today, love.'

He threw a few wistful glances towards the garden. In years gone by, it would have been him encouraging me to help thin out lettuces or gather up windfalls from the tiny orchard, depending on the season. I would be the one desperately making excuses or pleading with him to take me down to the bay with a crabbing line and a pot of bacon rind.

'Tell me when you want some lunch and I'll put some toast in,' he said as he picked up an inch-long pencil and circled a couple of TV shows. More toast. I was going to look like a white sliced loaf by the time this visit was over.

'And supper?' I asked, thinking that if the answer was anything remotely toast-based, I would walk back to London.

'Whatever is easiest for you, love.'

'Me? Oh. Right. The microwave lasagnes in the fridge then. How about veg? Have you got anything stored in the shed? Or bags of frozen?' Grandma was a great one for pickling, preserving and freezing.

Granddad shrugged.

'Is *anything* ready in the garden?' I was getting desperate. I may not be an active preparer of meals, but I was certainly an active consumer of them, and was used to a healthy and varied diet. I appreciated good food, and good drink, come to that.

'May's a funny month.' Granddad's voice was apologetic. 'End of the winter cropping, but a bit early for the summer harvest.'

'It didn't look like much was cropping to me.' I narrowed my eyes.

He looked away and chewed the end of the pencil. 'Yes, well, haven't felt up to it this year. I didn't get round to putting in the autumn onion sets or the spring cabbages. Brian helped me clear that top section, but I don't want to be fiddling about with seed trays and heavy double digging any more. There's no one to share it with. It's not the same. I can't cook for toffee, and I wouldn't know how to pickle or freeze if my life depended on it, so it would only go to waste.'

'We will need green in our diet, Granddad. *I* need green in my diet.' Playing the malnourished granddaughter card might make him buck up his ideas. If he wouldn't eat properly for himself, he might do it for me.

'There's some tins in that back cupboard. Have a rummage.'

Used to top notch cuisine, either as a result of the Michelin-star culinary aspirations of Rupert since we'd lived together, or from Mum's own fair hands or M&S when I stayed with her, I suspected our Sunday evening meal would be far from my usual fare. I slouched back to the kitchen to suss out the tinned vegetable situation, fully expecting our supper to be a couple of cheap fling 'em and ping 'ems, with a side order of tinned peas and a packet and a half of Crunch Creams to finish.

Chapter 10
Percy Gladwell

1894

'Charlotte Hamilton, may I introduce you to my son, Percy?'

I'd promised Mother I would be polite, but my heart had sunk as soon as she'd announced there was to be company for tea. I had nothing against the lady concerned, but it was yet another attempt by my mother to see me married and, in her mind, properly cared for. She didn't like me living alone and consistently moaned about my inadequate London lodgings, whereas I was only concerned that they were convenient for my offices. Most mothers worry about who might take care of their daughters, leaving their sons to fend for themselves, but mine was quite the other way about. And thus Miss Hamilton was the latest (and possibly oldest) woman to be paraded in front of me by my ever-hopeful parent.

'He's a highly successful architect with his own practice,' she added. 'A follower of the Arts and Crafts style, and his work is quite remarkable. His attention to detail and whimsical touches are a delight.' Mother was a huge devotee of my work, but then she had encouraged and nurtured my talent from the beginning.

Charlotte nodded. She was, I observed, a plain woman with serious eyes. The older Mrs Hamilton stood beside her daughter and physically pushed her forward as the introduction was made. My heart went out to the younger woman as her face flushed and she blustered her hello.

The immediate plan was to take a stroll along the esplanade and then, invigorated by our exercise, to return for a light tea in the small front parlour that Mother reserved for entertaining. And so, despite the gusty nature of the day, we embarked on a brisk walk in the afternoon sun.

'Shall we paddle?' I suggested. 'Feel the icy water on our toes and embrace the very feeling of being alive?'

'Hardly appropriate,' Mrs Hamilton muttered. I'd been warned that she was a religious woman who did not approve of anything approaching fun. No wonder her daughter looked so miserable.

Mother gave me one of her looks and I bowed my head. 'No, of course.'

The older ladies walked ahead and I fell in step with Charlotte, both of us struggling for things to say.

'Do you read?' I asked Charlotte, who at least had colour in her face now, although it was possibly connected to the supreme effort required to keep her hat about her person against the brisk breeze from the sea.

'Oh yes,' she exclaimed. 'Every day.'

'And what authors hold your interest? Dickens? Conan Doyle? Or Hardy – he is, after all, a local man?'

'Oh no. I do not read *those* kinds of books. Fiction does not interest me. But each night, for at least two hours, I study my Bible, and sometimes I read printed sermons on topics of interest. I am currently reading Ezekiel but find his visions difficult to interpret. Do you find the Bible an absorbing read, Mr Gladwell?' she asked. Our steps slowed and she looked up at me, still clutching at her wind-buffeted hat.

'Well, it is certainly, erm … long. But there are those who might argue the Bible comes under fiction …' I smiled, but the glare I received in return would dampen even Satan's furnaces. Perhaps it had been wrong of me to tease her about her faith – my own being somewhat shaky, as I preferred a more metaphorical interpretation of the Good Book. I moved the conversation on. 'Outside of your reading, perhaps you have other hobbies? Needlecraft? Sketching? Do you play an instrument?'

'None of those, sir, but I am heavily involved in the work of the church and it is very much my life. I will not set the world on fire, but I feel that I might do good in small ways. Even a tiny cog can be vital to the smooth running of the machine.'

Here was an earnest little thing. She was, like me, not one to walk into a room and arouse anyone's interest, and for that, I felt kindly towards her. But I sensed there was little else we had in common.

'Yet I fervently believe that everyone, Mr Gladwell,' and she reached out to grab my arm as she spoke, perhaps sensing my lack of interest, 'deserves to find love. There is, I believe, one person out there – one perfect match, one destiny – for all of us. We only have to hope that, by the grace of God, we will find them before it is too late.'

I turned to look at her then, her thin face and large eyes almost tearful, for it was the first and only point of that conversation that I passionately agreed with.

Chapter 11
Present Day

Sitting alone after supper in the cosy room (Grandma's name for the impressive front reception room with the round window and huge mitred brick fireplace), it struck me that I'd lost the ability to play by myself – funny as I'd spent so much of my childhood doing exactly that. Apart from my social media addiction, I didn't have any hobbies or interests; even Mum filled her time with voluntary committees and a love of art galleries. Without a boyfriend to do things with, I was lost. It was rather disturbing to think how easily I could fritter away an evening on my phone, tweaking and uploading photos to Insta, or messaging mates. I'd underestimated my reliance on technology and was about ready to knit myself a friend – if only I could knit, which I most definitely couldn't.

My thoughts drifted to Grandma, who'd always been busy making, mending and preserving. She had tangible things to show for her time, whereas all I had was a few extra likes on Instagram, or more views on my Snapchat story. I couldn't even ring Mum on the landline for a chat, as she'd be busy with last-minute preparations for their holiday. I was grumpy, bored and in need of a stiff drink.

When I returned home next month, Brian's nicely stocked wine cellar and drinks cupboard would be on hand. I knew which racks were strictly out of bounds – generally the dusty ones that contained wine he'd laid down to share with fellow connoisseurs or business contacts he wanted to impress. The stepdaughter who generally preferred a pint of real ale wasn't one of them. But he always kept in a selection of bottled beers for me, even though beer wasn't his thing.

'Don't suppose you've got any drink in, Granddad?' I asked, sauntering through to the living room.

'I could make us both a fresh brew? Or there's cordial in the pantry?'

'I was rather hoping for something with a bit more kick. It's been a long day . . .'

'Oh, alcohol.' He grinned. 'Well, let me see now. We never did buy anything fancy in, it was a luxury we couldn't afford, but the tiny cupboard under the stairs has a few bottles of the home-made variety. There's plenty there. Help yourself. Just remember the kick you're after might send you flying over the fence. I'm sure Briggie always overdid it with the sugar.' He chuckled and went back to his programme.

Was alcohol a luxury? Wasn't it a store-cupboard basic? Like bars of dark chocolate, artichoke hearts and kalamata olives?

I peered into the triangular cupboard. Several Canada Dry crates Granddad had liberated from a skip outside The Barley Mow pub years ago were stacked in piles of two or three, each one containing half a dozen bottles. I tugged at the nearest crate – *Elderflower Wine* printed in Grandma's efficient hand – and liberated a bottle. I stepped back into the hall and, as my foot moved, the door swung shut with a satisfying click.

I returned to the kitchen and hunted in the top drawer of the built-in dresser for a corkscrew. Another original feature of the house that stood out from the norm: a pale, wooden affair that met the ceiling and spanned the far end of the room, with spectacularly elaborate black iron hinges, each having the silhouettes of rolling waves along the length. After much tugging and twisting, the cork finally popped and I inhaled a curious scent of flowers and sickly sweet fruit. Not my usual tipple of choice, but any old port in a temperance storm. I poured a generous measure of the pale liquid into a glass tumbler. The first sip had me practically horizontal on the tiled floor, whilst my knees went for a skip around the kitchen by themselves.

I nodded my head slowly in approval. Okay – not quite what I was used to, but it was certainly going to help with the boredom. I swished the contents around in the bottom of the glass and took a sniff. Hmm . . . I was getting happy notes with undertones of hangover.

An hour later, I drained the last of the wine into my tumbler. The time had dragged, and it was only because I considered being in bed before ten lame that I stayed up. I peered in at Granddad, totally engrossed in the nine o'clock news, and decided to open another bottle. He said I could help myself. And just because I'd opened it, didn't mean I had to finish it. I could poke the cork back in and have the rest another day. I was going to need something to see me through the next four weeks. It wasn't going to be Wi-Fi, so it might as well be alcohol.

Wrestling with the knob to the smallest under-stair cupboard, I swung the door open. I was about to grab another elderflower when I wondered if there were any different wines. Something a bit sharper and less sugary – perhaps rhubarb or pea pod.

I got down on my hands and knees and tugged at a crate nearer the back, under the pencilled words about love. Ooh – dandelion. That might be more tangy and less sweet. As I reached over to check another crate, the cupboard door swung shut and everything went black.

'Dammit.' I shuffled forwards but there wasn't really enough room to turn around, so I continued backwards on my hands and knees and kicked at the door with my feet. The catch popped, light flooded the tiny space and I could see again.

Perhaps because I'd been drinking, there was a time delay to everything I focused on. One bottle of some pretty potent home-made wine and my brain was struggling with the panorama before me. The cupboard was empty. The wooden crates that I had just been rummaging through had totally disappeared. Inter-estingly, the handwritten *Love will always find a way* was still on the riser above – although it appeared to be in different handwriting.

I closed my eyes and opened them again. No crates. Just an empty space.

Had Grandma put some hallucinogenic substance in with the flowers of the elder tree as she'd whisked up the ingredients – or whatever it is you do to make wine?

I reversed out of the cupboard and stood up, brushing dust from the knees of my black leggings with my equally dusty hands. I gave a little cough and the dust motes circled my head, caught in the soft glow from the hall light.

I spun on my heels and my stomach flipped.

Everything was the same.

But it was all *totally* different.

The pointed arch doorways to the study and the living room were directly opposite me. The kitchen corridor was to my right, and the cosy room to my left. The stairs still had the quirky crenellated newel posts, and the solid oak front door dominated the square space.

But the walls had changed colour and were now a pale beige. Instead of Grandma's hand-knotted rug over wide polished floor-boards, the hall was carpeted in a rich terracotta. A modern black four-drawer cabinet stood next to the door, and an arty blue glass bowl filled with odds and sods stood on the top. To the right of the door, a huge pair of men's trainers were neatly paired beside a solitary ladder-back chair.

And yet, underneath the different décor, the thing that unnerved me the most was that the fabric of the house was absolutely identical to Granddad's, down to the tiniest flower in the stained-glass window and the unusual carved wooden doorknobs.

I blinked a couple of times but nothing changed, so I sat at the bottom of the stairs. Although I'd had enough to put me well over the drink-drive limit, I wasn't paralytic, but the room was a bit spinny and I felt slightly queasy.

There was a noise from across the hall. Granddad would sort me out. I stood up and walked over to the living-room door, pushing on it gently and peering around the edge.

My brain and my eyes had another battle where they violently disagreed with each other, because there in a black leather office chair, head down below the back of a computer screen, and tapping away on a keyboard at a gigantic office desk, was the head of a man.

And it sure as hell wasn't Granddad.

Chapter 12

The door made a low groaning sound, so I ducked back behind it before I was spotted. I hesitated in the hallway, straining to hear any noise that might indicate the stranger was going to come out into the hall and confront me.

Nothing.

The tapping of fingers on the keyboard continued, as did the beeps and buzzes from the computer, and Radio 4 played merrily in the background. I looked about me again. None of this made sense. How could I be in the house but *not* in the house?

Was I hallucinating, more drunk than I realised, or both? I put out my hand to touch the black cabinet. It felt real enough, and I knew Granddad didn't have one, but to redecorate and stage-set the house in the few moments I was stuck in the cupboard would be a feat even *DIY SOS* couldn't pull off. That left the wild and ridiculous conclusion that this was a parallel dimension, time-travelly thing. Equally preposterous.

News bongs came from the radio and I heard a repeat of the headlines I'd heard earlier on Granddad's television. So I wasn't in the future, and the humming computer suggested that I wasn't in the past. I heard a deep mumble as the figure spoke to himself, and the radio was switched off. There was a squeak of chair wheels and then footsteps headed towards the door. In

desperation, I launched myself back into the triangular cupboard, figuring it was the best and nearest place to hide myself,
and the tiny door clicked shut behind me.

In the pitch black, I craned my head forward to try and work
out if I'd been rumbled, but I couldn't hear anything. As I wriggled about to get more comfortable, my back brushed up against
something hard. Feeling in the dark, my fingers met the familiar
crates of homemade wine.

This was silly. What was I afraid of? The stupid man was in
Granddad's house, so he was the intruder, not me. He was the
one who had the explaining to do. I pushed at the door and
burst into the hall.

And everything was back as it had always been.

The next morning, suffering from the after-effects of the potent
elderflower and half a bottle of the dandelion, I dismissed the
odd incident of the night before as an alcohol-related vision.
Grandma had always joked that the homemade wine was dangerous stuff. Perhaps not such a joke after all.

It was definitely time for caffeine. Both Rupert and Brian
owned posh coffee machines that made magnificent coffee. You
put a little pod in, pressed a button, and after a few clicks a beautiful, barista-style coffee dribbled into your cup. Granddad's
supermarket own-label instant wasn't up to the same standard,
but I was nursing a slight dandelion-related hangover, so needs
must.

Granddad appeared at the door wearing the same shirt as the
day before, although it was decidedly more crumpled. I gave
him a questioning look.

'Fell asleep in the chair,' he mumbled.

'Oh, Granddad. Bet that was a rubbish night's sleep?'

'I've had worse, love. Bit of a stiff neck but serves me right.'

He glanced about the kitchen and his eyes fell on the table, covered in the remains of last night's meal. He rolled his checked shirt sleeves up his arms and reached for the first plate.

How awful of me. I should have cleared up, and now my poor, overtired Granddad was going to tackle the mess. 'Let me help. I'm sorry, I didn't think.'

'Don't apologise. I'm the host.'

'Hardly. I'm family. I should be pulling my weight.'

'I'm sure you're always on the go, rushing about, tidying up. You're here for a little break. Let me do it.'

'Erm, yes, but I want to help. Let's do it together.' Although my heart sank, when I remembered Granddad didn't even own a dishwasher.

A couple of minutes later, I discovered dried-on lasagne was a lot harder to shift than I'd expected. Despite using my fingernails and lots of hot, soapy water, the crispy bits were being particularly stubborn.

'Enough bubbles there, love?' he asked as I plunged my hands into a volcanic eruption of suds. I was used to dishwashers, or rather, I was used to Brian or Rupert managing dishwashers. Men loved their machines, and who was I to interfere? So how was I supposed to know the amount of washing-up liquid to squirt into the bowl?

'Very funny. Not sure Grandma would be impressed by my washing-up skills. She was always at the sink, elbows flapping and taps at full blast.'

'Not sure she'd be impressed at my domestic skills generally. We had our separate domains – see? Hers was the kitchen. Mine was the garden. Even when she sprained her ankle that time, she sat right there,' and he pointed to the lath-back Windsor chair in the corner, with its faded red velvet cushion, 'directing my every move and tutting at my incompetence'.

With a weathered hand, he picked up a bubbly plate from the rack and slowly wiped in a circular motion, over and over the centre, staring out of the window. The kitchen had a smashing view of the back garden. A rabbit hopped across the lawn, but it wasn't going to find any tasty treats in the barren vegetable patch. In years gone by, Granddad would have been straight for the gun cabinet, but now his eyes barely registered the interloper and he seemed lost in thought. Was he thinking of Briggie? The woman he'd never spent a single night apart from since their wedding day. The deafening silence as we worked only made me think of her more. There were many things she excelled at – baking, pickling, housekeeping and a general ability to both hustle and bustle – but Grandma was never good at silences, and so there hadn't been many when she was around.

As I tipped the last of the fluffy snow down the plughole, and Granddad placed a final smeary cup on the kitchen table with the rest of the dabbed-up crockery, the phone rang.

'Darling, I'm giving you a quick ring to see how you've settled in and check you got my note,' Mum said. 'We need to be at the airport for two, so I thought I'd ring you before we left.'

'Yes, I got the note,' I replied.

'Good. So we'll talk properly next month. In the meantime, you have an important job on your hands. Sorting out Walter is your priority. We're relying on you to work your magic and give that darling man a zest for life again. How's he doing?'

Suitably flattered by her covert motherhood skills, I sat on the bottom stair, winding the curly telephone wire around my finger, and staring at a stray clump of dried mud that had a definite welly boot tread shape to it. Boots inside would never have been allowed in Grandma's day.

'Not great. I'm pretty sure he lives on jam-smothered toast and the occasional ready meal.'

'We suspected as much. He needs more fruit and veg in his diet. And a damn sight less sugar.' She paused, waiting for me to say something.

'You could set up a delivery to here – if we're in a Waitrose delivery area.' Which I thought was unlikely.

'I could. But I'm not going to. I told you, you need to make your own way, Molly.'

'Gee. Thanks for the support.'

'But you do need to focus on Wally's diet. Start cooking some healthy meals.'

'You expect *me* to cook?' I halted my cord fiddling.

'Well, one of you is going to have to step up.'

'I would, but I really don't have the . . . ' – I was about to say time, but that would be blatantly untrue – '. . . skills.'

'It might be so left-field that it hits you on the back of the head as I launch it, but perhaps you could learn them, sweetheart?'

I let that one drop and moved on. 'I also think he might be sleeping in a chair downstairs and not using his bed,' I added.

'Go on . . .'

'He pretends that he's fallen asleep in the chair watching TV, but he keeps a pillow by the chair. And when I poked my head into his bedroom the other day I saw the bed piled high with laundry – several weeks' worth.'

'That we didn't know. But he definitely spends too much time glued to that television. What he doesn't know about *Loose Women* isn't worth knowing . . . That didn't come out quite right, but you get my drift.'

'I wish he'd get back out in the garden again,' I said. 'It's so neglected and covered in banks of nettles and . . . other green, stringy things. All those beautiful borders are being choked and suffocated by the wrong sort of plants. He's just cooped up in the house and seems to have lost interest in everything.'

'Then encourage him out there again. We all understand he's hurting, but he's only seventy-seven. He can't spend the next ten years hanging on to memories and not moving forward. Bridget would be furious. Wally loves you so much. If anyone can snap him out of it, it's you.'

Even though I knew she was employing her ninja parenting skills again, flattering me to do what she wanted, I felt momentarily puffed up. He really did love me. He always had, from the moment a shy ten-year-old girl was presented to him, hiding behind her mother, frightened of the strange house.

It had taken Mum several months to introduce me to Brian, never mind his parents, but when the wedding was imminent, we visited my extended step-family. Grandma stood in the kitchen, brandishing a rolling pin, with her wiry salt-and-pepper hair pinned up back then in a tight bun on the top of her head like a cottage loaf. Granddad noticed my wide eyes and knocking gawky knees, and took me to the garden, where he let me devour the contents of Bridget's biscuit tin while he tackled a big flowering bush with his snippers.

And since that moment, Granddad had never once been on my case, unlike his son, who spent the following fourteen years either questioning my every move or repeatedly asking if I was okay. Instead, Granddad and I often shared quiet afternoons in the dappled sun where a special bond was formed – me watching, him working. It was one of the reasons why I looked forward to my summers in Dorset and why I needed to rescue him now. It would be such a coup if I succeeded in pulling him out of this stagnation when Mum and Brian had failed.

'I'll see what I can do. Perhaps if I started digging the vegetable patch and getting out in the garden, he might join me.'

'What a brilliant idea. And perhaps suggest cooking together? You are clever. I have great faith in you.' There was a deliberate pause for me to absorb her words. 'It's not hard to make a proper pie or a simple pasta dish.'

'Like you make pies all the time and box them up in Waitrose packaging.'

'No, you're right, I don't do a lot now, but I used to. Remember? I'd make up trays of shortcrust pies filled with savoury mince, or batches of Bolognese sauce – freezing them in portion sizes?' I did remember. She'd been a wonder on a tight budget. A cold house and charity shop clothes, but always a hot meal and an atmosphere of love.

'I blame myself for not teaching you. Nonna tried, but you were too headstrong. I suppose we had it hard for so long that when Brian came into our lives, I figured we deserved a break. But with hindsight, I don't think I did you any favours, and now is an ideal opportunity for you to address that. Dig out some of Bridget's old recipe books? You're a bright girl, when you can be bothered to apply yourself.'

'I don't have the time to teach myself cookery.'

'I should think the one thing you have plenty of, stuck deep in the Dorset countryside with your seventy-seven-year-old grandfather and no job, my darling, is time.'

Chapter 13

'Thought we'd hit Dorchester this afternoon, love. I usually just stop at the supermarket, but you can wander into town if there's anything you need.'

Hoo-bloody-rah. I could get a decent signal and connect with the real world: the one that accessed the internet and involved more advanced methods of communication than smoke signals or homing pigeons. I'd taken a few photos of things blooming in the garden and it would be good to upload them. Maybe my Insta page could have a 'before and after' vibe, illustrating how I'd cheered up my granddad, pulled his garden around and turned into a whizzy chef. I could post some pictures of my triumphant creations. It couldn't be that hard to move on from pre-prepared microwaved meals (my uni staple) to creating my own haute cuisine pasta dish. As far as I could make out from watching Rupert, it was mainly a presentation thing. A few sprigs of parsley and a teardrop-shaped smear of sauce really transformed a dish.

Granddad only went into a big town once a week, and Mum had told me not to expect him to chauffeur me about, unless I was prepared to contribute towards fuel. So anything I needed beyond fresh air and sea, I had to sort that day, because he wouldn't be using the car again until the following Monday.

That was a lot of social media I'd have to cram in as we whizzed up the supermarket aisles.

'What do you usually buy?' I asked.

'Luckily, Briggie left me with a couple of jars of jam which should see me through 'til Christmas.' He opened the bottom door of the large dresser where about five hundred jars were stacked haphazardly. 'But I've been pretty much getting the same things every week since she went,' he said. 'Three loaves of bread, a pack of butter, four microwave lasagnes, six eggs, two tins of prunes—'

'Okay, I get the idea.'

'We could just double the quantities?' he suggested.

'Erm, yes. Or we could try something new? Vary your diet a bit? I'm not really a prunes girl, to be honest, and we could both do with some greens. I was thinking of an artichoke salad, perhaps to accompany a risotto or something? Maybe some pasta with spinach and asparagus? And fish – Mum swears by a weekly portion of oily fish to top up Brian's omega three levels.' Mind you, as much as I adored eating these foods, I wasn't confident with their preparation. Would I even recognise a raw artichoke in the vegetable aisle? Probably not, even if it had *I'm an artichoke* stapled to its, erm, green bits.

'Brian said I wasn't to spend a fortune feeding you, and reckoned if I doubled my usual grocery budget, that would be fair.'

'Which gives us?'

'Well, twice twenty is forty, but let's call it forty-five and treat ourselves a bit, eh, love?'

My eyes opened saucer-wide. I used to spend more than that a week on food at uni, and that was just for one. Okay, serious budgeting. I could do this.

Bloody, bloody, bloody Rupert.

After fiddling about for a couple of minutes in the car, while

Granddad went to collect the trolley, some choice vocabulary spewed from my very angry mouth. My phone contract had been cancelled, and I couldn't even ring my ex up to have a rant about it. We'd been together for so long that I'd forgotten he'd set me up with my last iPhone. How petty to cancel it just because we were no longer together.

I explained to Granddad that I needed to nip into my bank and would catch him up. Ten minutes later and the true horror of my circumstances were apparent. Even with my final wage due, I was shafted. I hastily cancelled my direct debits – Spotify and Netflix were no longer a priority, as without a phone they were useless anyway – but I still didn't have any money to set up my own phone contract. Dammit. Mum and Brian would be somewhere over the Atlantic Ocean by now – not that I expected them to bail me out, but it would have been worth a shot. Head down and shoulders slumped, I slunk off to find Granddad.

One aisle in and a quick tot-up in my head revealed we'd already hit twenty pounds, so I reluctantly returned the cherry vine tomatoes and the asparagus tips – shame, asparagus was lovely in a dippy egg. I thought buying fresh was supposed to be cheaper than pre-prepared. Frozen food seemed our only option, so we picked up some chicken pies and pizzas (how Nonna would have wept into her bowl of pizza dough if she'd seen the contents of our trolley) and an assortment of basic fruit and veg. Granddad threw in a few extra packets of biscuits, just in case. In case what? I wondered. The National Federation of Women's Institutes decided to hold their next AGM in his living room? Almost on budget, we loaded our shopping into the boot of the ancient Fiat and, because I had no money so there was no point in hitting the High Street, we headed back to sleepy Summerton.

*

Returning to Hawthorn Place, I decided I'd better learn how to deal with some of the food we'd purchased, and wandered into the study to look through the higgledy-piggledy bookshelves in search of culinary guidance. Even the seemingly straightforward bag of new potatoes I'd tossed in the trolley was a mystery to me. I had no idea if you boiled them for five minutes or fifty. There were no cookery books to be found, but I came across a wonderful old housekeeping guide from the late fifties, which I tucked under my arm because 'Linings and Interlinings', 'Footnotes on Darning' and 'Simple Homemade Table Mats' were subheadings I couldn't resist.

I met Granddad in the hall. He heard me approach and hid something behind his back.

'What are you hiding?' I demanded, with mock severity. 'Not more toast?'

Sheepishly, he pulled out an apple.

'But that's a great healthy snack. Why are you concealing it?'

'Not sure really. Probably because Briggie told me off for eating between meals. Fancied something green though.'

I nodded sagely.

'I let much of the orchard go to waste, although she'd picked some of the Bramleys and got a couple of bags of stewed apple in the freezer before . . .' He took a bite from the crisp apple to distract himself from melancholy thoughts. 'What I wouldn't give for a slice of her Dorset Apple Cake with a huge dollop of clotted cream right now.'

My mouth started to water, reminding me why I'd wandered into the study in the first place. I held out the housekeeping manual in front of me. 'Is it okay if I borrow this?'

'Of course, love. Take what you want. That old book was Briggie's mother's. I think she passed it on when we got hitched. You must be bored, eh, if I've driven you to reading that old tat? How to drain a radiator and make a rag rug.'

'I was actually looking for Grandma's cookery books but couldn't find any.'

'No, because they're kept in the pantry, you twit.'

Ah. That made more sense.

Who knew the pitfalls of rayon napkins? And the importance of laying out a fresh piece of soap in the bathroom when hosting a dinner party?

Snuggled up in a blanket on the sofa, I'd somehow lost an hour in the decidedly politically incorrect world of nineteen-fifties domesticity. I flicked through a book filled with grainy black and white photographs of various foods sticking out of half grapefruits on cocktail sticks, and detailed diagrams showing the best way to paint a wall. Despite the dated advice, there were clearly many aspects to running a house I hadn't appreciated.

There's no way I would admit it to Mum, but that afternoon I rediscovered the simple pleasure of reading – even if a chapter on managing your household budget wasn't quite as gripping as the dystopian novels of my youth. Somehow endless Twitter posts and reality TV star blogs weren't the same. At one point, I even bent down and sniffed the pages – a sweet, musky smell that reminded me of Granddad's shed. The paper had a soft feel, and was yellower than the bright, intrusive glare of a phone screen. Even the simple action of turning a page, and the swishy sound it made, was heaven. I'd been a voracious devourer of books until university made any form of reading a mind-numbing chore. Perhaps it was time to return to some escapist fiction.

I looked at my watch and realised I needed to think about dinner. I rifled through the large chest freezer, after Granddad's comments about the apple, and found a treasure trove of fruit, vegetables and various cuts of meat – although I still had no idea what to do with them. Eventually I resorted to our supermarket frozen chicken pies because at least they came with detailed instructions – although not detailed enough, as it turned out. Dinner was a disaster: overcooked broccoli and undercooked potatoes, with tiny burnt pies where we played hunt the chicken. Granddad's oven was proving more temperamental than me, but at least our evening meal didn't involve any more jam.

How I missed Grandma and her thick wedges of steak and onion pie, bursting with meat and delicious gravy. It made me more determined than ever to master the simple pie, so after attempting a bit of washing up, I padded down to the pantry to look for the mystical books that explained the ancient and complicated art of cookery. My arms goose-pimpled up and my socked feet felt chilly on the terracotta tiled floor. Grandma had told me that pantries were the forerunners of fridges, and this one was definitely like standing in a room-sized Smeg. My hand brushed over the cold marble slab that had always been used for butter and cheese but was now empty, and a draught blew in from the patterned zinc grate at the back of the worktop. I found a battered *Everywoman Cooking Compendium* (so old it only had about ten coloured plates) and a nineteen-eighties *Delia*, and carried them back into the warmer kitchen to browse.

It turned out cookery books weren't as scary as I'd imagined. The ingredients were listed clearly, and followed by a bullet-point method – although I'd never heard of cups as a measurement. (Glassfuls possibly, as a measure for the quantity of alcohol consumed during the course of the stressful food preparation.) The *Compendium* was the most worn: translucent, greasy smears and dark, crusty blobs where it had been spattered by ingredients. Pages were turned down and an assortment of rectangles cut from cereal boxes bookmarked particular recipes. I focused on this one, assuming it was Grandma's favourite, and I marked a couple of recipes in pencil.

The following day, I would attempt the fondly remembered steak and onion pie, as I'd noticed bags of stewing steak in the freezer, and it would be magnificent, with more than two scraps of meat floating around in a sea of gravy. And substantially fewer chunks of carrot.

Chapter 14
Percy Gladwell

1894

I could smell the bracing sea air, although we were some distance from the shore. It was completely contrary to the suffocating atmosphere in London – even the strength of the breeze seemed different. And there was so much sky. A vista of treetops and gentle sloping hills was, to me, as charming as the rooftops and spires of a busy city. It was, after all, Mother Nature's architecture.

The Marstons' plot was perfect; I had worried it would be a square of barren land and any planting would take time to establish. But there were several mature trees dotted about and the ground was sufficiently level not to require major re-landscaping. Before I'd even walked over to Mrs Marston, standing alone like an abandoned Dido, my mind was wrestling with ideas to assimilate the house into this beautiful setting; to make use of the trees and embrace the coastal nature of the site. Despite the inclement weather, she'd insisted on meeting me there to discuss the plans.

Her face flushed slightly as I took her gloved hand.

'Mrs Marston.'

'Mr Gladwell,' she said, removing her hand as soon as was polite to do so.

Gulls circled above us, squawking and crying, and autumn leaves swirled about her long skirts, dancing in the grass. She was in a fitted grey coat and her kid gloves were of a matching shade. The colour made her look fragile and pale, although her cheeks had a pink tinge. There was no smile from her lips and no attempt at friendliness.

I stood at the edge of the dirt track that ran down to the coast road, and began to assess how best to place the house in the landscape. It was important to have a bright southern aspect where I envisaged the main reception rooms. The house would be orientated off-centre to the plot, but symmetry and strict adherence to established rules had never been my guide. I took my sketch book from my leather case and started to make copious notes.

'The house will stand in this far corner,' she said, pointing to the only barren spot of land. 'With the best view across the fields, and away from the pond – which is a natural feature and simply must be preserved.'

To me it was more of a puddle: shapeless and murky, dominating the first quarter of the plot.

'My dear Mrs Marston, that would not work. The house cannot be the afterthought.'

'Nor the gardens, Mr Gladwell.' Her eyes were raised to mine in challenge.

'I agree. There will be a compromise, but let me first consider the practicalities of the build. The pond must be drained—'

'But think of the wildlife.' Her delicate face scrunched up in anguish and I wondered if she might stamp her tiny foot in protest.

'We can easily dig out another, one of your own design, and the plants and creatures will quickly re-establish. You will need access from the road, so the pond must go. I'm sorry.'

She nodded acquiescence but tugged hard at her bottom lip with her teeth.

'I should make it clear to you from the start, Mr Gladwell, that the garden will be as important to me as the interior of the house. It's only when severe weather dictates, that I retreat inside.'

'This parcel of land is sizeable, and even with a large property, there will be substantial grounds. We can work together in this regard. Indeed, my previous consultant on matters such as these is retiring, so I would value your advice when planning the garden.' I did not, as a rule, provide detailed garden plans but the landscaping was often undertaken at the building stage, and I saw a way to procure her involvement.

'As the client, Mr Gladwell, I believe it is I who has the final say.'

A childhood surrounded by women enabled me to understand and placate them, and make allowances for their emotions. Sometimes it was best to say nothing. Common sense would prevail.

'Can we at least save some of the trees?' she asked.

'It is my intention to save as many as possible. Why would I destroy the architecture that God has bestowed? A building is not separate from its surroundings. It should be integral to them.'

She looked at me intently through narrowed slits of clearest blue and studied me with interest.

'It's only a short walk over that hill to the cottage my father has let me use for the duration of the building work. It's small, but comfortable and convenient. When you have finished taking measurements, assessing wind direction, and establishing the acidity of the soil – or whatever it is you do,' she said, crossly, 'perhaps you would join me at the cottage and we can discuss matters out of this biting wind?'

Despite her words, her eyes twinkled. I nodded my understanding, unable to speak lest I laugh. Our gaze held for a fraction of a second and then she dropped her eyes and marched back to the cottage.

There was a roaring fire in the tiny parlour that Mrs Marston welcomed me into, and the improvement in temperature was most welcome. My fingers were numb from gripping the pencil and my neck ached from bending over a sketch book. A housemaid was adding another log to the crackling flames as we entered. My hostess requested tea and cake, and the girl scurried away.

'So, the property is to be a family home.' I waited for her to take a seat and then settled myself on a chair opposite, the heat from the fire starting to thaw my extremities. 'Would six bedrooms suffice? I am planning attic rooms to make use of the space under a tall gabled roof. These can be for staff or guests, as I plan a separate staircase ... but I digress.' As with all my projects, I was running before I could walk. Always my favourite part of a commission, where anything was possible, and before the restrictions imposed by engineering and practicality took over.

'Six bedrooms will be perfect as I hope, in time, to fill the house with children. I should like three or four – the nine children of our Queen seems somewhat excessive. Edward would be pleased enough should we have one healthy son; it is, after all, why all men of fortune take a bride. However, as yet ...' She stumbled over her words but rallied. 'We shall see if God is willing.'

The delicate nature of this conversation was awkward and the arrival of the tea tray spared further embarrassment. It was poured and distributed, and I thought of small children and nurseries, and then of Mrs Marston's passion for her gardens. How I had longed to see the outside views as a child, unable to run freely down the hills and climb trees like my siblings, and often confined to bed for inordinate periods of time. Instead, I'd waited patiently for my father to hoist me on his shoulders. If only the window had been lower. I added a hasty sketch of a dropped window to my notebook.

'May I see?' She stretched out a delicate hand for the book.

'It is merely details of the land and some initial thoughts. They're not ready to be seen.'

Her hand lingered in the space between us, her eyes expectant and wide. One could no more deny her than a child.

'These sketches are curious,' she ventured, flicking through my notebook.

'Is that a compliment, complaint or merely comment?'

My face was studied in earnest for the second time that day.

'Compliment. It's why I have accepted my husband's choice of architect, when I was so determined to use another firm. I have studied you a little further since we met at your offices. I was harsh to judge you on the Bayldon property alone. You were, after all, constrained by the requirements of the client, and perhaps the harsh Yorkshire landscape also?' Her finger traced the lines of the hastily drawn dropped window. 'A low window for a child. And here,' she turned the page, 'curious arched doorways . . .'

'Ideas are still forming in my head, but I was thinking of mitred fireplaces, making use of the local brick, and mirroring these with plain oak arched doors. I prefer my woodwork unpolished and plan to add accents of colour through the furnishings, floor coverings and wall-papers. William Morris is a master of design in this area – a scruffy, loud fellow whom I have seen lecture on occasion over the years, although his health is failing now.'

'Oh, I adore his wall-papers.' The sketchbook was closed and returned to me. 'When my mother redecorated her drawing room last spring, all the furnishings came from Morris and Co. He is a man with a great ability to bring the outside inside. My heart belongs in the long grasses, flitting insects and delicate petals, Mr Gladwell. Willow Boughs is a particular favourite of mine, but Mother selected his Sunflowers in blue to match the upholstery.'

I opened the sketchbook and made notes in the back. She leaned towards me a little.

'And what are you writing now? That I am a lover of long grass and butterflies?'

'These are details, madam, that are important to you, and so they will become important to me. As I have been commissioned to oversee the entirety of the project, I shall specify Morris for some of the decoration. It is important that you are satisfied with every detail, down to the last doorknob. As long as it is practical to do so, I will endeavour to meet your heart's desires.'

'Mr Gladwell,' she said, smoothing down her skirts, and reaching for the delicate rose-patterned cup and saucer. 'I knew you were the man for the job – *almost* as soon as we met.'

Chapter 15

Present Day

'I thought I might head to a library. Does the number sixteen still run into Weymouth from the top of the hill?' I asked Granddad the next morning.

'Not rightly sure, love.' He stood up, wandered out into the hall, and came back with a crumpled bus timetable. 'They've cut some of the services. I think they run quarter past the hour now.'

I glanced at my watch. I'd just missed one, so would have nearly a mind-numbing hour until the next bus.

'Any chance of lending me a twenty? I'll pay you back.'

'Ah, now that I can't do. Sorry, love.'

'Oh. Right.' Perhaps finances were tougher for Granddad than he let on. After all, he'd been practically living off jam and toast, and this enormous house couldn't be cheap to run. I immediately felt guilty for my earlier assumption that he could give me some financial help.

He saw my disappointment and put a gentle hand on my arm. 'If it was down to me, you could have whatever you wanted. It's not like I'm short. All those pensions and savings we paid into for years and now no one to share them with. I was told, you see, not to give you any money.'

'No, no, that's fine. It was wrong of me to even ask. I'll manage.'

Why were Mum and Brian so determined to make life difficult for me? I understood they expected me to be independent, but they could have given me a financial boost and let me enjoy my time with Granddad.

'You could walk into Summerton? They've got a small library behind the Co-op. It only takes about twenty-five minutes if you go the back way, down to the bay and along the cliffs.'

'Twenty-five minutes? That's an hour of my day wasted.'

'Bridget wouldn't have considered a lovely walk a waste of time, but then life seems to operate at a different pace for you youngsters. It's all rush, rush, rush. Her old bicycle is in the outbuilding. Not sure if the tyres are pumped up but I could dig it out if you like?'

'Bike? Right. Erm, thanks.'

Ten minutes later, I followed the path out the back of Hawthorn Place. It forked left to follow the footpath down to the bay, or right to meet the main road into the village. I took the right fork and it was bumpy going until I hit the smooth tarmac road, although it undulated more than Jason Momoa's chest, and there were muscles I hadn't even realised I possessed that were already throbbing and sore.

I'd barely made it up the first hill before I was forced to dismount and push the stupid contraption up the steep path. It was practically museum-worthy, didn't have gears and sported the most ridiculous basket on the front, which Granddad had proudly told me Bridget used to fill with dead rabbit and pigeon for market when they were first married. I felt like an extra on the set of *Call the Midwife*, except this episode was set in the Andes.

'Times were tough back then,' he'd said, as he checked the tyres. 'She inherited this big, old house from her aunt but we could hardly afford to run it. We briefly considered selling up, but there was something about the place that we both fell in love with. So every penny mattered and every shilling was spoken for.'

Times were tough now, I thought. For some of us, at any rate. Eighty-seven pence to my name. Not even enough for the bus fare. The only reason I was making the journey was to connect with the real world again. I still had my Dorset library card from a few summers ago when I'd been devouring the *Twilight*, *Hunger Games* and *Maze Runner* books faster than a book-eating, starved goat. I knew libraries had computers and Izzy assured me they were free to use for poor people. The thought of Wi-Fi spurred me on and I gave the pedals a determined push.

Summerton was large for a village but too small for a town. It hugged the coastline and sprawled along the contour of the bay. Granddad's end was sparsely populated but as you headed west, the houses became denser towards the centre. The sort of place you drive through on your way to somewhere else, or maybe stop off at for a pub lunch or afternoon tea in the café. Not the sort of place where you'd stay for a whole week. The beach was pebbles and awkward to access, and the amenities poor, but the clifftop campsite and the solitary B&B got by with travelling cyclists and ramblers – again, people passing through.

At one time, most of the buildings around the square were shops but now only a handful remained. Quite frankly, it was a miracle that the tiny library had survived. The village was still a pleasant place to be, however: a gentle hum of distant traffic, the scent of flowers on the breeze and a riot of spring colour. There was a small memorial: a simple Portland stone cross with the names of the Summerton fallen from both World Wars carved into the base. A beautifully maintained arrangement of four flower borders surrounded it, marking the points of the compass, and a wrought iron bench stood in front of the memorial, with a brass plaque in memory of some old chap who'd lived in the village and obviously done something bench-worthy. Gladstone, or something.

An hour in the library was enough for me to get myself online, search for temporary jobs (none of which were suitable), and moan to Izzy about the unfairness of life. I returned to the square and sauntered over to Rosie's Tea Rooms, all flowery tablecloths and old-person china cups, hoping they did a decent coffee. I was more of a Costa girl but the nearest branch was Weymouth and I wasn't cycling all that way for a flat white – my go-to coffee when things went pear-shaped.

I assessed the available seating. There was an elderly couple in the corner looking as bored as I felt, and I wondered if they did coffees to go. I didn't want to hang around in the Café That Time Forgot but was desperate for a decent caffeine kick. As I picked up the plastic-coated menu from the nearest table, with its curled and peeling edges and clumsy home-computer graphics, I remembered I didn't have enough money. Not even enough for a bottle of water. An older lady in a black uniform and frilly white apron came over to me, smiling.

'Erm, sorry, changed my mind.' I turned for the door, totally unused to the humiliation that came with being poor.

I wasn't stupid and knew not everyone was as lucky as me. I'd lived in a three-storey Georgian town house in west London, with a twice weekly cleaner, until I'd moved in with Rupert. And then he'd overseen most of the housework, as his standards were somewhat higher than mine. Money had never been a worry for me until now, but I was still humble enough to remember life before Brian.

Mum had been a single parent holding down a low-paid job, and my maternal grandparents, Nonna Carmelita and Nonno

Benito, provided the wrap-around childcare needed either side of the school day. We lived in a row of tiny, rented terrace houses in Clapham, and money was always tight. When my grandparents arrived in this country in the late nineteen-fifties, Nonno got a job as a labourer and Nonna spent all her life cleaning for wealthy people who didn't particularly care if her English was abysmal as long as she picked up their dry cleaning in her own time.

They never asked for much in life, which was just as well, because they never got much. All they wanted was a child, and even that was almost denied them. Mum was a miracle baby, born when Nonna was in her forties, having been told she would never be able to conceive without medical help – and Nonna's strict Catholic faith ruled that option out.

But when I was ten, after a year of dating, Mum married Brian, and his most redeeming quality was his generosity. He had plenty of money and, to give him his due, he always shared. But now he'd refused to even toss me that lifeline and let me fester on the scrap heap of poor people again, after Rupert's calculated decision to move to greener, more culinary-compatible pastures.

I stood outside the café, the smell of filter coffee drifting out to mingle with the earthy scents from the earlier rain, and my mind turned to Tassimo machines, Pimm's on the balcony and restaurant quality meals. Perhaps I'd taken Rupert for granted – and the endless supply of warmth, food and shelter. How did people manage when they had to think about every purchase? Worrying if they even had enough money for a cup of coffee, when access to caffeine was surely a basic human right?

Seemed I was about to find out.

I glanced across at The Barley Mow. Pubs were always looking for staff. I propped the bike against a large wooden barrel of dying daffodils and walked through the dark green double doors, the pubby smell of fried food and stale alcohol hitting my nostrils as I entered.

'Monday, Thursday, Friday and Saturday evenings, plus every other Sunday lunch,' the bald man behind the bar said, as he wiped the rim of a pint glass with a white cotton tea towel and ducked down to place it on a shelf under the counter.

That was a bigger commitment than I was hoping for. I still had a granddad to save and only needed twenty pounds to set up my own phone contract.

'Erm, do you have one day a week? Preferably Monday to Friday?'

'I'm running a pub, not a drop-in centre,' he said. He looked me up and down, taking in my thin, small frame. 'You're what? Eighteen?'

'Twenty-four,' I said.

'Ah, you look a lot younger. Really looking for school-aged kids at the moment.'

'But surely I have more life experience if I'm older? And I've done bar work before.' For nearly a whole day when I was at uni, and until I'd baulked at lavatory duty. But he didn't need to know that. 'And I have a degree.'

'Bully for you, but the hourly rate goes up when you turn twenty-one, see?'

I didn't see. Being a more mature candidate was a good thing, surely? And I'd quite rightly get more money than a spotty sixteen-year-old schoolkid for the same amount of work.

'Look, love, the wages bill is my biggest expense. Can't cut the food budget so I have to make savings with the staffing. Sorry, but I'm looking for students.'

I slumped out of the pub and grabbed the bike, not looking forward to the cycle ride home. How could I be too old for a job at twenty-four? And clearly over-qualified. But at least Mum couldn't say I hadn't tried.

With the end of the tarmac road in sight, exhausted and sweaty, I reset the pedals and pushed off towards the footpath. Time to catch my breath and enjoy a bit of sea breeze through my tufty hair. As the houses petered out and a landscape of undulating hills stretched before me, I saw a hunched figure walking ahead. The last section of road came to a dead end in a large turning circle, and I was freewheeling at a steady speed. It felt like I was about to take off into the sky like Elliott's bike in *E.T.*, especially as there was plenty of room in the front basket for a small extra-terrestrial life form.

Keeping the figure in my eye line, I focused on the wobbly handlebars for a split second, just as the dozy pedestrian stepped out in front of me. The ancient brakes were slow to operate, and the combination of loose stones and minimal friction resulted in an almighty collision. The bike swung from under me and skidded in a large semicircle – almost worthy of a dirt-track bike stunt. I stuck my feet out but toppled away from the bike, skinning my knees as I struggled to balance.

'You stupid maniac!' shouted the hunched figure. His mobile phone skimmed the pavement and came to a slow halt as we stared at each other in a moment of silence.

'You stepped out on me,' I yelled. 'You weren't even looking.' Had I been that obsessed with my phone? I wondered. Funny how I didn't miss it now that it was denied me. It was sitting abandoned and useless on my bedside table, whereas before it had been all but glued to my palm.

'Yeah, well.'

'A sorry would be nice. Look at the state of my knees.' Tiny droplets of blood had come to the surface. They were going to scab up like a primary schoolchild's legs after a vicious break-time game of tag.

'If my phone is damaged—' The young man's nostrils started to flare.

'If your phone is damaged, it's your own stupid fault. You were looking at your phone and not where you were going.'

He grunted and walked over to retrieve it. 'Butter side up. You're lucky – just a bit of scratching to the case.'

'No, *you're* lucky, sunshine, because if this bike had buckled there'd be more than a bit of scratching going on.'

After a few more moments of staring hard and trying to be the first to out-scowl the other, we finally let our eyes drop.

I heaved the bike upright and started to push it towards home.

'Nice bike,' he said from behind, in a tone that suggested he thought the opposite.

I swung around to see his hand back on his mobile, a lazy thumb sweeping over the screen as his eyes flicked between me and the device. His smile was lopsided but that somehow made it more attractive, and a clump of hair swung across one eye – almost as a counterbalance to the smile. He looked me up and down.

'Smashing pair of legs though.'

I swung one of the aforementioned legs over the crossbar and gave him my best evil glare as I pushed off. Only when I was sure I was out of sight did I allow the glare to morph into a grin.

With one unanticipated collision, things in sleepy Summerton were suddenly looking up.

Chapter 16

Feeling pleased with myself for remembering to take a bag of stewing steak out of the chest freezer the previous evening, I prepared to embark on the manufacture of The Pie. Armed with Grandma's cookbook, I decided to fortify myself with a small glass of something before commencing my challenge – the first stage being to make pastry. Uncorking the bottle of homemade wine from the Sunday evening, I was disappointed to find there was barely half a glass left, so I decided to grab another one before my hands got all floury.

As I reached to the back of the small under-stair cupboard, the door clicked shut again. I shuffled about and finally managed to reverse and push the door open with my feet. Light entered the tiny space and my heart thudded to the floor like a dropped bowling ball. The crates had disappeared and the hallway had changed.

Again.

Okay, so perhaps the previous cupboard incident hadn't been the result of a hallucinogenic home-brew. I'd only had a sip of the dandelion and was a damn sight more sober than last time.

I crawled out of the cupboard and stood in the house that was Granddad's, but definitely *wasn't* Granddad's.

It was the same terracotta carpet, the same black cabinet and the same pair of neatly paired trainers as my trippy experience two nights ago.

The small door swung shut behind me as I walked towards the familiar front door, the floor bathed in streams of coloured light from the identical stained-glass panel beside it – a rainbow over a landscape dotted with flowers.

'Nothing like letting yourself in.' An extremely well-spoken, low voice came from behind. It wasn't said unkindly, but quietly and with a degree of amusement.

I spun around to be greeted by a tall, red-haired man with the orangest, sproutiest beard growing from his pale face. He could have been an extra from *Braveheart* if he hadn't been wearing a pale blue shirt and jeans. And really dodgy corduroy slippers.

There was a flash of grey hair either side of his temples and the delicious smell of expensive aftershave exuding from every pore. Quite a slender man, the beard was the widest thing about him. He stood like an orange yeti, or a stick of carrot-flavoured candyfloss.

'Erm, I . . . erm . . .'

The stranger gave me the once-over – taking in my casual, predominantly black clothes, spiky hair and chipped black nail polish. He sighed and ran a hand through his wild, dark red mane.

'I didn't hear you knock, but then you're early. At least it proves you're keen. Please, Holly, come through.'

How could he possibly have been expecting me? And how did he know my name? Well, nearly know my name.

'Molly,' I said.

'Sorry. I was sure you said Holly. My mistake. You should have corrected me yesterday. I must have said it a dozen times.'

If he'd met me yesterday, I would have remembered. And

told him my name wasn't Holly. Was I in one of those bizarre dreams where nothing made sense, but no one challenged it because it was a dream?

I followed him through to Granddad's living room – except it was set out as an office. Staring at his distinctive hair, I realised that it was the same man who'd been sitting at the computer from my surreal experience the other night.

He gestured for me to take a seat and tucked himself behind the wide desk. It was a huge L-shaped affair, with a black glass top and chrome legs. Not particularly attractive, but possibly functional. There were three computer monitors alongside each other but seemingly only one keyboard. Bit overkill, I thought. Perhaps he was an online gamer. One of my uni friends had been into PC gaming and had a similar set-up in his room. Each to their own.

As I sat down, I took in the furnishings. Although Hawthorn Place was stuck in a time warp, its dated furniture suited the house better than the modern pieces in this weird parallel dimension. Two silver metal filing cabinets stood along the side wall, there were bold abstract prints along the walls in frameless picture frames, and a low bookcase was bulging with folders and professional-looking periodicals.

He rolled the office chair along so that he was no longer facing the plethora of screens, but instead was sitting in the gap opposite me. I felt like I was at some sort of job interview.

'You come highly recommended.'

Oh, I *was* at some sort of job interview.

'Do I?' My eyes swivelled slowly from side to side in confusion. For what, exactly? I wondered.

'Yes, and it's the only reason I'm considering you. As Mrs Gammell is your godmother, you are fully aware of my situation. I'm a very private person and I want to keep it that way.'

He shuffled some papers in front of him and then drummed his fingers on the glass top of the desk as he ordered his thoughts.

'Like I said on the phone yesterday, it's a Girl Friday-cum-housekeeping sort of job. Keeping the place tidy and doing all the running around jobs that involve contact with people in the town.'

On the phone? Okay, that might explain the name confusion, but I'd never spoken to this man before in my life – never mind on the phone. He obviously thought I was someone else. Holly probably. Whoever she was.

'Look, I think there's been some kind of—'

'We said nine pounds an hour, so for two shifts of three hours that's fifty-four pounds a week, cash, with the option to extend your hours if the arrangement suits. I only wanted a face-to-face today to check we were both happy and give you a quick tour.' His eyes flashed briefly towards my black nails but quickly returned to meet my eyes. 'It's a formality really. After all the things we talked about, you sound ideal.'

I wriggled about in the seat and avoided his eye. My brain, however, held on to the fifty-four pounds this stranger was dangling in front of my impoverished, can't-even-afford-a-proper-cup-of-coffee face. And then I thought about how Rupert, Brian and even my mum all thought I was a total domestic klutz and needed looking after. Surely, I could keep a house tidy and run a few errands? Hell, for fifty-four pounds I'd do it naked, wearing bunny ears and a smile.

'So, erm, starting when exactly?'

'Tomorrow? Or whenever suits.' He started shuffling through a pile of papers. 'As you know, I'm based here, so you can do the hours to suit yourself. It doesn't even have to be the same days each week. Obviously you've got to work it around your studies, but you said Friday afternoon was mainly study periods, so

I thought that could be the daytime jobs – going to the town, that sort of thing. And then an evening to suit you. When term finishes we can adjust accordingly.'

'Right,' I said, pulling at a hangnail with my teeth. 'Right,' I repeated, my mind doing a few quick sums and trying to join some scattered dots. 'That sounds fine.'

'We're done then, as we obviously covered most of the details on the phone, so shall I show you around?' He placed the papers together in a neat pile and placed his hands on the edge of the desk, ready to stand.

'Perhaps we could go over a couple of those details again. Just for the sake of clarity?'

'Like what?'

'Oh, erm, all of it might be a good idea. You know, just to check we're both *totally* happy.'

He frowned and rubbed his hand across the great orange hedgerow on his face. I half expected a couple of startled sparrows to fly out.

'Well, it's basic cleaning and housekeeping, but your cooking skills might come in handy. I *absolutely* never entertain, with the exception of my parents, who insist on visiting to check I haven't done anything stupid, and that I'm eating properly, blah, blah, blah. You know what parents are like? And then the running around stuff: going to the post office, emergency trips to the baker for chocolate cake ... and so on.' His hypnotic eyes flashed briefly and I think he smiled. The beard certainly wobbled about a bit.

I nodded my head slowly and tried to look thoughtful, but I was totally at sea. In fact, I was so at sea, there was no land in sight. I was floating about in a huge ocean of bewilderment with clouds of doubt overhead. But the money kept dancing about in front of me. Fifty pounds a week was two hundred for the whole month. Not a fortune, exactly, but enough to get my mobile contract restored and have a few beers at the pub. Maybe I could make some friends or explore Izzy's holiday romance idea – after all, I'd established there was at least one attractive man in Summerton. And, let's face it, how hard could the job be? It certainly couldn't be any harder than cooking, and I was sort of getting to grips with that – The Pie was bound to be a triumph. Cleaning was basically tidying up and vacuuming. Not that I'd had much practice with either activity, but I was trying to help out with Granddad, so I felt qualified.

My top leg bobbed up and down over my lower knee and I made a decision.

'That sounds fantastic. I can do three hours tomorrow evening, plus three on Friday afternoons.' If this was a silly dream, then accepting the job didn't affect anyone. If it wasn't a dream and Granddad really did have a freaky portal in his cupboard, I had to hope it would continue to work.

'Brilliant.' He got to his feet. 'Now for a quick tour.'

I nearly blurted out that I was familiar with the layout of the house, but that would take some serious explaining. Either he'd think I'd been snooping around, or I'd have to run the whole dodgy cupboard thing by him. I nodded.

We walked out to the hall. It still wasn't Granddad's: not a hand-knotted rug or lace doily in sight. I stared hard at the triangular cupboard door, praying it would continue to offer me a way back to the new job I had accidentally acquired.

'This is the main living room.' He gestured to Granddad's study. 'No need to go in there, certainly not to begin with. I barely use it. I'd like you to focus on the kitchen. It's in a terrible mess.'

I followed him across the hall and he pointed to the cosy room. 'That's my home gym. Another room you can largely avoid. It's not like you need to dust a running machine.' He took me down the corridor to the kitchen, which was more modern than Granddad's but not in a good way; it felt like a betrayal of the house. However overpowering the fitted dresser was, it was right for Hawthorn Place and the period. The white fitted kitchen before me was anachronistic. And very untidy.

'As you can see, things have rather got on top of me.' We both surveyed the mess.

'Looks kind of homey to me,' I said, thinking of my general lifestyle standards, and how I was definitely an excessive clutter and possessions sort of person, rather than the minimalist neat freak my mum had become. But then Rupert had mentioned my untidiness as one of the reasons our relationship had ground to a shuddering halt.

'I'll try and get that bin emptied before you come, and tackle some of the washing up. Sorry, I've been, erm . . . distracted, and then it reaches a point where I struggle to get stuck in. I sort of zap and run.' He pointed at the microwave, smothered in papers.

'It's okay.' I plastered a huge fake smile across my face, determined to become the best Friday housekeeper, or whatever he'd called it, on the planet. Assuming I was actually still on the same planet. 'Leave it all to me. It's what I'm best at.' I sounded more confident than I felt.

'I don't think there's any need to show you upstairs today. Eventually it would be handy if you could strip the bed and vacuum up there but I'm only using the one bedroom. The house is phenomenally big for one person but my parents moved out to be nearer my grandmother a couple of years ago and the timing was, erm . . . convenient for me to move in. I needed to escape London and be on my own, even if it was into a house built for ten people. There are *two* staircases, for goodness' sake. How pretentious is that?'

'But the spiral stairs are cool.' He looked at me and frowned.

'Erm, Mrs Gammell told me about them. They're in the round tower.' I realised the mysterious Holly hadn't been in the house, so I'd need to be careful what I said.

'Of course. Obvious really. What else could be in there? I used to pretend I was a knight fighting dragons in that tower when I was little . . .'

'Me too! I mean, that's exactly what I *would* play on a spiral staircase. If I had one. Which I don't, but I could imagine that I had. Curly stairs are very castle-y.'

He nodded, seemingly deep in thought, as I jiggled about on the spot. My earlier three cups of tea had finally caught up with me.

'May I use your loo?'

'Of course. There's an en suite in the gym. I had it put in so I could shower after a workout without traipsing upstairs. These old houses weren't built with adequate bathroom facilities. I'll be in my office. When you've finished, come and find me so we can swap contact details. I have your home number, obviously, but a mobile will be handy, and you'll need mine, in case of emergencies, like forgotten homework or a hot date.' He smiled.

'Um, I don't have a mobile at the moment.'

'A seventeen year old without a mobile. That's got to be a first.'

Seventeen? I tried to conceal my horror, but I'm certain my eyes flashed wide. Unfortunately, there was still something of the adolescent about me, being small and slim, with less chest than a pirate robbed at knifepoint, but it explained the homework reference – he thought I was still at school. How he couldn't see an intelligent and driven twenty-four-year-old woman before him, I didn't know, but now was not the time to point out his error.

'It's not through choice. But I'm getting it sorted.' As soon as you start giving me some glorious cash and I can get the contract reinstated, I thought. 'I can give you the number though.'

I slipped through his home gym, Granddad's cosy room, and immediately noticed the same Latin inscription above the arched fireplace and identical round window. This room also felt wrong, converted into something so modern in a house with so much history. An expensive black rowing machine, long treadmill, futuristic-looking exercise bike and an assortment of scattered weights all stood on squares of black rubber matting. The look was finished off with a wide screen attached to the wall – presumably for him to watch TV as he went on his ten-mile run, or whatever he did with the scary-looking Meccano-like machines.

When I returned a couple of minutes later, I glanced out the window next to the front door, the gap between the rainbow and the flowers being clear glass, and noticed a young girl walking up the path to the house. It was the first time I'd looked outside, and it was now apparent that however freakily the interior of this house resembled Granddad's, the exterior was completely different. There were no rolling hills in the distance and I could see acres and acres of sky. The property wasn't in a dip; it was in a flat and open landscape.

The pale-faced blonde girl approached the front door as a reproduction station clock on the wall behind me bonged out six chimes.

This must be Holly. And she was coming for my job: the best chance I had to reinstate my phone contract and buy Granddad some plants for his vegetable patch. This would ruin everything, and it was not happening on my watch.

I opened the front door as quietly as I could, and spoke in a low whisper.

'Holly?'

'Yes. Hello.' She stuck out a hand. 'I have an appointment with Mr Brooker at six o'clock.'

'I'm afraid to inform you the job has gone.'

'Gone? But I only spoke to him yesterday.'

'Sorry and all that but a better candidate came along.'

Her shoulders slumped and she looked so dejected I nearly reached out and gave her a hug.

'A better candidate. Who?'

'Um, me actually.'

Holly looked me up and down in disbelief. 'Oh.'

The poor girl looked so crestfallen I nearly gave her the job back, but then remembered my need was greater than hers. Probably. 'But you were a strong second choice. Should I not have been available. I mean, you practically had it until I came along. You were very much in the running . . .' I needed to stop gabbling. It was the guilt.

'I didn't realise there was anyone else interested. He gave me the impression he was desperate. Our tiny town on the north Norfolk coast, in the middle of nowhere, isn't exactly a teeming pool of enthusiastic and available workers. Most of the locals are retired, and so many of the houses in the village are holiday lets and unoccupied for half the year.'

My eyes nearly popped out of my head and I was tempted to waggle a finger in my ear, just to check I'd heard her correctly.

Because I thought she'd said we were in Norfolk.

Chapter 17
Percy Gladwell

1894

'For someone who spends his life designing such arresting and grand houses for wealthy clients, and who takes great pains to specify every detail from the window latches to the floor tiles, you live in decidedly modest conditions, Percy,' Mother scolded.

She was in London for the week and we had plans to see Wilde's latest offering at St James's Theatre that evening. It was a shared love of ours and it was always a joy to entertain my beloved mother.

'Just look at the state of these window-curtains.' She shook them and a flutter of dust leapt from their folds and into the sunlight.

My previous lodgings had been noisy and increasingly expensive – the landlady forever charging for some *little extra* that I considered a necessity, and my shirts had a tendency to go missing on a regular basis. But I was happy at Mrs Cooper's – a woman who confessed she had little time for religion, but who proved herself to be more Christian than many of the ladies who sat in the front pews of a Sunday and spouted Bible verses at every turn. Herself a widow, Mrs Cooper offered rooms in her West End home only on personal recommendation, and admitted her cooking skills were basic, but she was honest in her dealings and kindly in her attentions. The arrangement suited me well and was convenient for my Great Marlborough Street offices. I worked long hours and merely needed a meal at the end of the day and somewhere to rest my head.

'How can you be happy in this single room, with a small table for working and barely two seats to entertain? The practice is doing well and you can easily afford to rent a little property of your own.'

The room was larger than many and had good light from the windows, with its cheery southern aspect. It was, however, over-furnished, with a proliferation of rugs, mahogany furniture and rather too many amateur pictures hanging on the walls. But it contained no less than three bookcases, and that alone had sold the room to me on my first viewing.

'It's clean and comfortable, Mother,' I said, 'if a little dusty. Besides, I don't have time to run a household.'

'It's easy enough to hire a young girl or, better still, get your-self a wife.' She saw me roll my eyes but ploughed on regardless. 'Charlotte seemed very taken with you . . .'

In the five years since Father passed away, Mother had become increasingly meddlesome in the affairs of her children. Unfortu-nately for me, each of my siblings was now settled, leaving me as her pet project. It came from a place of love, but she had an onerous task on her hands – I had no great fortune, only the promise of a burgeoning career. I was of medium stature, needed spectacles to see beyond the end of my own nose, and was losing my hair a little at the temples. She had adjusted her hunting ground accordingly, and now seem determined that as long as the woman in question was of suitable moral standing and could cook, she would suffice.

'Miss Hamilton was nice enough, but I found conversation difficult and she is decidedly too . . . righteous for my tastes.'

'You don't need to regularly converse with the woman, just marry her. Honestly, Percy, she's in no more position to be choosy than you. She's fast approaching spinsterhood and would, I'm certain, be realistic enough about the arrangement. You need someone to look after you and she needs a husband.'

I smiled then at her candid review of the situation. 'Oh, Mother, I do admire your dogged perseverance.'

'So you'll see her again? I may arrange another meeting when you're next in Weymouth?'

I nodded and hugged the diminutive lady before me, and was rewarded by one of her delightful smiles. Charlotte had been innocuous enough and Mother was right. I would never attract the attentions of anyone comparable to Mrs Marston and should be content with Charlotte Hamilton.

Chapter 18
Present Day

Holly walked away, her shoulders all slumpy and her feet dragging along the path, and I felt awful. I'd stolen her job and now had to pretend to be wispy and capable like her, fudge a knowledge of cleaning and cooking to live up to her ridiculously accomplished domestic talents and, to top it all, pretend to be seventeen – when in reality I was a much more mature twenty-four year old, with seven more years of life experience and accumulated wisdom.

I closed the door behind Holly, again noting the flat landscape and distinct lack of Purbeck Hills. Was I really in Norfolk? Could the cupboard have transported me across seven counties in a microsecond? It was all very *Doctor Who*, albeit a bit less phone-boxey and distinctly more cupboardy.

'Did I hear voices?' the red-haired man asked as I returned to the office. His voice was like thick treacle – smooth and packed with sugar – and made him seem like a kindly uncle, or a slimmer, more ginger Father Christmas.

'Erm, I was talking to myself. Sorry – I do that sometimes.'

He frowned. 'You'll remember what I said about needing a peaceful environment though, won't you? It's one of the reasons I thought you might be suitable – Mrs Gammell said you were a quiet child. And please, call me Rory.'

I wasn't sure I liked the 'child' bit, but then, with those flashes of grey hair and penchant for corduroy, he was probably approaching fifty, so anyone under twenty-five would seem like a child to him. And being so much younger than him, I would feel uncomfortable calling him by his first name.

'Yes, of course, no talking. Quiet as a mouse. No problem. You won't hear a peep from me. I will be a silent and diligent worker. I won't make a sound. Absolutely promise.'

'Hmm.' He narrowed his eyes. 'So, what time tomorrow, assuming you are happy with everything?'

'Erm, ten-ish?' I wasn't an early riser, so that would give me time to down a couple of inferior instant coffees and get myself looking vaguely presentable, assuming my commute to work remained under three seconds.

He frowned and scratched at some of the ginger fur on his face. 'I thought you were at school during the week, apart from the afternoon we already discussed – or am I wrong?'

'No, silly me. I wasn't thinking. Of course, I'll be at school, erm, learning things, so maybe after school? Five?' I didn't want this job to eat into the weekend and any potential socialising – not that any was going on at the moment. But persuading Izzy down, or the odd trip to The Barley Mow for a swift half – especially if I was soon to get my hands on some hard cash – might soon be a possibility. 'Then I can move both days to the daytime when school breaks up for the summer.' Although I would be long gone by then. This was a smash-and-grab job – purely to solve a temporary financial crisis and give me something to do other than play draughts with Granddad for the next month.

'That works for me. I've let the house go a bit since Mrs Gammell stopped coming at the start of April, so the first few sessions will probably involve quite a lot of hard work to get things back round.'

'No problem. I *love* hard work.' I gave a big, and what I hoped was enthusiastic, smile. 'I'll see you tomorrow at five.'

He stuck his hand out and I noticed a dusting of auburn hairs across the back of his fingers. The leather straps and bangles that adorned my wrist jangled as he shook it firmly. Probably a middle-aged man thing – shaking on a deal. I retracted my limp fingers and he stood up to escort me to the front door.

'It's okay, I'll see myself out,' I said, as I was fairly certain he wouldn't be expecting me to find my way home via the under-stair cupboard.

'What's cooking?' Granddad asked as I poked the potatoes with the blade of a knife to work out if they were soft enough to mash.

Two hours after returning from my unexpected job inter-view, massively relieved the cupboard had done its thing, I was so hungry that I was contemplating neat spoonfuls of home-made jam. No wonder people bought ready meals, if it took this long to produce a decent meal from scratch.

'Homemade steak and onion pie.' Not wanting to run before I could even crawl, I was serving it with simple mashed potato and peas.

'Smells good. Got to be better than the supermarket effort we had the other night.'

I hadn't really thought about pastry before; what it was or how it was made. I guessed it was flour and some other mystical ingredients that turned a dusty old powder into a delicious crispy crust, and I remembered Grandma with her hands in deep mix-ing bowls, with sticky dough plastered over her fingers. Turned out pastry was basically flour, butter, salt and a splash of water – not such mystical ingredients after all. Although I wish I'd known to factor in chilling time – and not just for the stressed-out cook.

I assumed you made pastry and then it was good to go, but apparently not.

The resulting pie tasted okay but looked a complete dog's regurgitated breakfast. Although making pastry was relatively simple, cooking the damn thing was a whole other ball game. The crust had collapsed into the middle of the pie and I had a soggy bottom. *And* the mash was lumpy, but even I couldn't cock up frozen peas. Granddad licked up every last morsel, although that was probably more to do with it being practically nine o'clock before the poor guy was fed than my expert culinary skills.

Tomorrow it was back to a microwave lasagne.

Chapter 19

Funny how having a job motivated me the following day. I woke at eight, unusually early for me, and practically bounced out of bed, nine whole hours before my first shift. I had a plan and a purpose, and both felt good.

Because there was a distinct possibility that my newly acquired position was a figment of my imagination, I'd decided to follow Izzy's advice and advertise for babysitting work in Summerton as a back-up. How hard could it be? As long as they weren't *actual* babies (who terrified me with all their crying and leaking of various substances from various orifices) it would mainly involve watching some late-night TV, and maybe checking on their softly sleeping bodies from time to time. It still rankled that people thought I wasn't capable of looking after myself; imagine how impressed Mum and Brian would be if I was actually responsible for another human being.

I set off for the library and felt strangely proud of myself for cycling further up the hill towards Summerton than last time. Previously, I'd clambered off Briggie's boneshaker next to the post-box but, almost as a challenge to myself, I kept going another fifty metres, even though it was like cycling through custard, and made it as far as the wooden gate that fenced off a field of sheep. Next time, I would make it to the top. Rupert dumping me had been a good thing after all. I was even exercising.

After some quick online research at the library, I cobbled together a postcard-sized advert to offer my services as a babysitter and felt sure I'd soon be inundated with calls. People were crying out for childcare.

Capable and trustworthy 24-year-old graduate seeks babysitting in the Summerton area.

£7 per hour. No under-threes. Weeknights preferred.

Still without a functioning mobile, I added Granddad's landline as my contact and booked out a couple of YA titles and some graphic novels to help with the long and boring evenings. The Co-op let me display my advert for free and, feeling on top of the whole adulting thing, I leapt on the bike and prepared to cycle home.

As I headed towards the coastal path, I noticed a paste table covered in trays of seedlings for sale at the end of one of the modern bungalows. I hopped off the bike and rested it against the stone wall. My backside was starting to ache from sitting on the uncomfortable saddle, and my legs were glad of the temporary respite.

I couldn't identify any of the plants. They were all tiny seedlings with small green leaves – although even my untrained eye could see the leaves were different shapes: some spiky, some rounded, and even some that looked like wispy blades of grass.

'Can I help you, dear?' A sing-song voice made me look up and a thin, older lady tottered out of nowhere and across the driveway.

'Erm, I wanted to buy some of these for my granddad. Are they vegetables?'

'All the pots are labelled and the prices are underneath in red. What are you looking for? I've got runners, tomatoes, spring onions . . .?'

I picked up a small brown plastic pot and read the label. *Moneymaker. 20p.* The irony of a plant that could grow money wasn't lost on me.

The lady stood next to me and dropped the glasses balanced on her head down to her nose. She bent forward to read over my shoulder.

'Good choice. A nice all-rounder tomato with lovely flavour. Indoors or outdoors?'

I wasn't really sure what she was asking, unless she was one of those confused old dears who had no clue who she was, what year we were in, or where we were currently standing, so I hesitated.

'Are you going to grow them in a greenhouse or plant them in the garden?' she clarified.

'Oh. I don't know. Granddad has both – not that he's doing much with either.'

'If he's got a greenhouse they'll do better in there. Tomatoes originate from South America – a much hotter clime – so they'll ripen faster in the heat. How many would you like?'

I rummaged in my pocket for the eighty-seven pence and studied my open palm, just in case the money had magically bred and given birth to a few pound coins.

'Erm . . . four?'

'Tell you what. Take this tray. They're a bit on the small side. I was late getting the seeds in this year. Blasted bunionectomy put me out of action for weeks. I'm only just back on my feet.'

I handed over all the change and shook my head when she tried to give me the surplus seven pence.

'Thank you. I'll be back for some of the others when I've got more money.'

'No problem, dear. Hope your granddad gets a good crop from them. Are you a gardener, too?' she asked.

'Not really, but I'm hoping I can learn from Granddad.'

The biggest smile spread across the old lady's face. 'I got my love for the garden from my grandmother. She was late marrying, but by the time she met my grandfather, a penniless and somewhat dour vicar, she'd established a reputable nursery. My older sister and I often used to help her pot up seedlings when we were younger.'

'I don't have any siblings,' I said. 'But then I guess you don't miss what you've never had.'

'Sometimes you don't miss the thing you *did* have,' the old lady said cryptically. 'My father died when I was four, but my mother did such a good job of bringing us up, I never felt we suffered from the lack of one. Besides, my grandmother once confided that he was a bully who was rather too fond of the drink and we were probably better off without him – a harsh thing to say but it always somehow took the edge off it all.'

I couldn't help but draw comparisons with my own situation. Was Mum right? Would finding out about my dad bring more trouble than joy? I hadn't considered that my father might not be a nice person. Perhaps Mum and I had been better off alone in those first few years. Nonno and Brian, in their own ways, had helped to fill that gap.

'I'm Jean, by the way,' and she stuck out her thin hand, which I shook. 'If you are coming this way again next week, I'll have some more seedlings for sale. Do stop by.'

And she floated over to a flower border, where I spied a gardening knee pad, and continued the weeding she had obviously been doing when I'd pulled up.

With the tray of seedlings balanced in my basket, I continued home. I headed along the road and then veered off on to the footpath that overlooked the bay, when I heard a 'Hey!' from behind.

I applied the brakes and turned to face the good-looking lad who'd launched me into the stratosphere a few days earlier. I put a hand across my eyes to shield them from the glaring sun and, suddenly self-conscious, ruffled my spiky hair and tugged at my retro Nine Inch Nails T-shirt.

'Hey, it's the current British Motocross champion.' He stuck out a friendly hand. 'I'm Harrison.'

'Hey, it's the kamikaze pedestrian,' I said sarcastically, and then I shook his hand. 'Molly.'

'Yeah, sorry about the bike thing. How are the knees?'

'Scabby.' I'd put my favourite black ripped jeans on to cover them up, despite the warm weather, not wanting to look like a clumsy six year old. 'How's the phone?'

'Scratched to buggery but I'll claim on the insurance – say I was in an accident, which is factually correct. Maybe I can wangle an upgrade.' He looked me up and down. 'So, Molly, are you a local girl?'

'For a while.'

His eyes went all twinkly and my knees went all wobbly. 'Thought I didn't recognise you.'

'I'm staying with my granddad. I usually visit for a couple of weeks in August, but I've come earlier this year and am spending a bit of quality time with him. You?'

'Yeah, I'm local, but looking to escape this place as soon as possible and see something of the world. Just sorting out stuff first. Y'know?'

'Travel the world, like a gap year?'

He pulled a packet of Rizlas and a gold pouch of tobacco from the inside of his jacket pocket. One foot was placed on a bench that faced the breathtaking view, and he stuck a filter tip between his lips as he started to roll a cigarette.

'Not into that whole uni thing.' He held a paper between his finger and spread a pinch of tobacco along the fold.

'So you work?' I asked, realising I'd slipped into Molly-world again and forgotten that not everyone had my academic opportunities, or even wanted them.

After rolling it backwards and forwards a few times, he licked the edge, sealed it and offered it to me. I shook my head. He shrugged, tapped the end on his knee and placed it between his lips.

'Great hair. It's kinda fierce.' The end of the roll-up wobbled up and down as he talked. He took a lighter from his pocket and flicked the wheel. A small yellow and blue flame erupted and he bent over to light the end. Tobacco smoke flooded my nostrils as I breathed in.

'Thanks.' I noticed he'd avoided my question about work, but I didn't care either way. I was only asking to make conversation. I watched him inhale, and saw his shoulders rise and relax as he blew out a stream of smoke. After my teenage dabblings, and apart from the odd undergraduate joint, I hadn't ever been a smoker, but he was making it look extremely sexy. All very nineteen-fifties and James Dean – especially as Harrison had more than a passing resemblance to the tragic film star.

He ran a hand through his droopy fringe and gave me a cheeky wink. My scabby knees trembled again. There was something about this guy that really flipped my trip switch.

'Anyway, I've got to head back,' I said. It didn't do to appear too keen, despite the sudden power surge.

'Catch you in the pub sometime?' he said, as I adjusted the pedals and tried to make cycling look a graceful and sexy activity.

'Maybe,' I said, and freewheeled down the first gentle slope towards home.

Chapter 20

That evening, at one minute to five (the shortest commute to work I'd ever had) I climbed into the under-stair cupboard. I told Granddad I was going out for a couple of hours, although I was half expecting to come crawling back out after five minutes of sitting in the dark and feeling a complete idiot.

The door clicked shut and I groped about for the wooden crates. Good – they'd gone. It meant this bizarre phenomenon was increasingly unlikely to be a figment of my bored, and therefore possibly over-active, imagination. I leaned towards the door to see if I could hear noises, because the last thing I wanted to do on my first day in my new job was surprise Mr Brooker by bursting out of his under-stair cupboard as he wandered idly across the hall.

It was silent so I crawled out, relieved to find it was the same *different* house as before. There was no sign of my new employer, so I made a hasty dash for the front door, twisted the ornate brass doorknob (weirdly identical to Granddad's in every way) and slipped outside. Unlike the dry, if somewhat gusty, Dorset weather I'd left only moments before, it was raining wherever this was. The underlying temperature was still pleasant but big, bulbous raindrops were falling on my bare arms and summer clothes. My hair started to clump and tiny rivulets ran down my face. I rang the doorbell.

'Good evening, Mr Brooker,' I forced the biggest, happy to be at my new job, enthusiastic employee face as the door swung open.

'Rory is fine. You make me sound old.' But I struggled to think of him by his Christian name, especially as he rather reminded me of my A-level history teacher and was considerably taller than me. 'Come in. You're getting wet, Holly,' he purred in his soft, unhurried voice.

'It's Molly, actually.'

'Sorry, I don't know why I've still got Holly in my head.'

As I stepped over the threshold, I noticed him look me up and down. Perhaps I hadn't thought through the appropriate clothing for a cleaning job. A simple black linen dress and knee-high tartan converse boots probably wasn't what he was expecting. And he must think me a total nutcase to have turned up to work in the rain without something waterproof to protect me. Oh well, I'd dress more appropriately next time, assuming I managed to pull this whole Friday Girl thing off.

'I need a bit of head space and it's been a stressful day, so I'll leave you to it. Knock on my office door at eight and I'll pay you.'

'Right. Absolutely. I'll start on the, erm, dusting straight away.'

He frowned and his dark auburn brows met in the middle of his furrowed brow – the only bit of skin visible on his face.

'The dusting can wait. Could you start on a general tidy up of the kitchen, please? I know it's awful, but I've left things to build up as I knew you were coming, and you did say you were used to chaos and mess – having such a large family.'

'Did I?'

'On the phone.'

'Oh ... no problem. Yes, our house is chaotic and an absolute pigsty with all those, erm, siblings running around. Well, maybe not a pigsty because obviously I do tons of tidying and cleaning, but it would be if I didn't, because of all the people ... I mean, we're practically three to a bed, top to tail and no space to fold a cat, never mind swing it ...'

Mr Brooker frowned. I was gabbling again when all he wanted was quiet. And I was telling lies, which didn't sit easily with me, but I was overcompensating for the guilt I felt stealing another girl's job.

'I'll hit the kitchen like a hurricane.' I coughed. 'That sounded wrong. A quiet hurricane that leaves neatness and order in its wake, not destruction. After all, you're the boss. For nine pounds an hour I'll do *whatever* you ask ...'

There was an awkward silence and I stared at my booted feet.

'Well, you know, within reason.' OMG. Could I possibly be any more embarrassing? I needed to stop talking.

'Right.' Two tiny patches of skin where his emerald eyes looked out flushed red. 'I'll be in my office. Please keep noise to a minimum. I appreciate you can't vacuum silently, but no banging or shouting. And try not to disturb me unless it's an emergency. I didn't have a great night's sleep and I'm exhausted, but then, as my mother would tell you, I've never been a good sleeper. Restless baby, sleepwalking child and angst-ridden teenager. My nights are just as disturbed now I'm older, although for different reasons.'

'I'm a ten ... erm, eight hours a night girl, myself.'

'I envy you that. I'm lucky if I get three hours in one stretch.'

No wonder he seemed so withdrawn and distant. There was no way I could survive on so little sleep.

I headed for the kitchen and stared at the task ahead, noting

117

the only real difference between Hawthorn Place and this one was the décor. Although Granddad lived in a bit of a time warp, it suited the house. Not that I think you should live in a museum, but if your house has serious history, it's in keeping to have lovely old furniture and vintage knick-knacks about. Mr Brooker's was the house of the modern man, despite the obvious historical features, and I wasn't sure the two sat together comfortably.

This kitchen was fitted, whereas Granddad's was largely free-standing units and the gigantic dresser. Solid granite worktops and white plastic cupboard fronts surrounded me, with far too much chrome for a property that celebrated natural materials, like brick and wood. Lots of upmarket gadgets were dotted about, including a bright red and silver coffee machine (which made my heart skip) and others I didn't recognise, with jug attachments and long black leads.

Despite the professional-looking kitchen equipment, Mr Brooker was clearly in the same camp as Granddad: Ready Meals 'R' Us. The chrome lid of the stylish free-standing bin had a pepperoni pizza box and a Chinese sweet and sour carton poking out. Okay, emptying it was the priority, although I'm ashamed to admit, I couldn't recall having ever changed a bin in my life.

I pulled out a few of the plastic, softly gliding drawers looking for the appropriate bags, and found a roll of black sacks under some pristine scarlet oven gloves. I knew kitchen bins took white bags, but I wanted to get stuck in and impress my new boss. If it took twenty minutes to locate the right colour, I'd be behind and I didn't want to lose this job on my first day.

Wrestling with the overflowing bin, I gave the bag a final heave upwards, only for it to split and the rubbish to cascade over the kitchen floor. Red drippy sauces oozed from tins and seeped over the tiles. Cardboard packets slid in various directions. And a black banana skin landed apart from the majority of the detritus – daring me to step on it as a perfect comedy end to this whole horrible situation.

Stupid man shouldn't have let it get so full. It wouldn't have happened if he'd emptied it before everything got wedged in. It wasn't rocket science to keep on top of the household chores. Rupert managed it.

Yuck. Disgusting. Now what?

I rummaged about in the cupboard under the sink until I found some Marigolds and knelt down to gather up the mess, trying not to gag at the sour smell and gloopy containers.

The mop and bucket were in the pantry – one of those red-handled affairs with a square of yellow sponge on the end. I'd seen adverts where similar mops slid effortlessly over grubby monochrome floors, leaving sparkly clean paths in their wake, but this mop held all the water until I pressed it to the floor and then released it in an almighty flood.

Turning back to the bucket, I slipped in the huge puddle and landed with a thump on my backside. I bet the banana skin was laughing on the inside. That was going to bruise, especially as I didn't have a lot of padding. I used a whole kitchen roll to soak up the water, so the recently emptied bin was now half full of soggy paper. Two steps forward, one step back.

The horrific backlog of washing up was my next task. Plates and bowls were stacked haphazardly, and tea mugs had the black rings of dried tea inside. Surely one of these shiny white units concealed a dishwasher? It was only old people like Grand-dad who washed up by hand, and I'd learned the hard way that you don't leave dirty dishes overnight unless you have a blow-torch handy. Mr Brooker needed to learn the same lesson. Actually, if he owned a dishwasher, he had no excuse.

Luckily, the fourth cupboard door concealed the sought-after appliance. I pulled out a rack of clean dishes and huffed as I unloaded them on to the minuscule strip of clear worktop, feeling more cross by the moment. Honestly – why didn't people finish jobs properly?

With a full to bursting dishwasher merrily chugging away in the background, I tidied up papers, and wiped accumulated crumbs and dust. There was a tangle of charger wires knotted behind the microwave, but un-crocheting electrical cable wasn't part of my remit, so I left well alone.

Exhausted, I sank on to my bruised bottom as I tried to figure out how I'd lived to the ripe old age of twenty-four and not known any of this stuff. Especially as for three years at uni, and nearly a year with Rupert, I'd lived away from home. But then the joy of shared student accommodation was someone else always got fed up first, usually Izzy or one of the lads. Offering to treat everyone to a takeaway or a few beers if I didn't have to participate in the clean-up worked wonders. But now it was just me and the mess, and I couldn't buy my way out of the situation. Resisting the urge to cry, I stood up, ploughed on and got lost in my work until the dishwasher finally beeped.

Great white fluffy clouds of bubbles blobbed out on to the floor as I opened the door, and my new boss picked that exact moment to walk in.

'I'm not checking up on you. I just popped out to make a cup of . . . oh.'

His gaze was firmly fixed on the small cascading snowstorm erupting from his dishwasher.

'Problems?' he said.

'I, erm, well . . . yes.'

'Good grief, girl. What did you put in there? Laundry detergent?'

'Um, washing up liquid.' His expression told me that was the wrong answer, but surely that was what it was for? Washing dishes.

'My mistake. I didn't show you where the dishwasher tabs were. You should have asked.'

'But you said not to disturb you,' I said, seizing my chance to shift the blame, my voice going up half an octave. 'So I improvised.'

In a final lazy volcanic heave, a large clump of white fluff splatted to the floor – as did my hopes. This job had been as short-lived as my spell at the bar, where I'd also not lasted a day. Tears that had been threatening to appear all evening finally trickled down my cheeks and hung from my chin.

'I need this job. Please don't fire me. I'll try harder. It was just a bad day and things kept going wrong. I'm so sorry . . .'

He looked startled, as men often do when confronted with full-on female emotions, so I coughed out a dramatic sob for good measure. Wringing the hem of my grubby, and rather soggy, dress between my hands, I gave my best abandoned, half-starved kitten-in-the-rain face.

'Don't worry. I know you need the money.' He walked towards me and for a moment I thought he was going to pat me on the head. 'Everyone has bad days – I should know.' His eyebrows met briefly in the middle of his face and then parted just as quickly. 'Start afresh next time. It's fine. And actually – it's sort of funny. It looks like a scene from *Frozen* in here, but I'm afraid I won't be launching into song anytime soon.' He smiled a gentle, kind smile that reached his eyes and made them twinkle.

Walking over to the kettle, which was now on a clear section of worktop, he flicked it on.

'I have rather thrown you in at the deep end. Mrs Gammell has only been gone a month and I've let the house deteriorate. I don't cope well with mess – ironic, as I'm the one creating it. Do your best to clear up the bubbles and then come to me for your money.' He noticed the abandoned bucket by the corridor. 'It won't take long with the mop.'

'Erm, about that, I'm having problems with it. I think it's faulty.'

'Really?' He picked up the mop, pressed a lever halfway down the handle and the sponge folded itself in half as all the excess moisture ran back into the bucket. Ah. So that was how it worked.

'Seems okay to me, but I can order a different one online if you're used to something else?'

'Oh, no, it'll be fine. Perhaps I wasn't squeezing it hard enough.'

He sauntered out into the hallway with his tea and I gave the mop a withering stare . . .

Five minutes and one dry floor later, I stood back and assessed the kitchen. It wasn't quite showroom standard, but I was proud of my achievements. I found Mr Brooker in his office and he handed over the glorious, hard-earned cash. I resisted the urge to kiss it.

'Right,' he said. 'Thanks for today. Let me see you to the door . . .'

Chapter 21

Percy Gladwell

1894

As promised, I returned to Weymouth and Mother accepted, on our behalf, an invitation to the Hamiltons'. They lived the other side of the harbour, in a modest Georgian property that had little to recommend itself apart from its symmetry.

After a splendid tea, the mothers engineered, with a distinct lack of subtlety, that Charlotte and I should be separate from the gathering to allow for private conversation. After a few moments of stilted small talk, she sighed and looked across at me.

'I know I'm not an interesting person,' she said, quite out of the blue. 'And I realise that I am ungainly and ordinary-looking . . .'

'Not at all, you are—'

'Mr Gladwell, please don't.' Her eyes were serious. 'Let us just talk plainly and dispense with unnecessary niceties. I am honest and hard-working – let that be enough. The truth is I don't want to spend my life alone, or worse still, be the spinster daughter whose only role is caring for elderly parents in their dotage. Tell me what you admire in a lady and let me be that thing.'

'Don't try to be someone you're not to please another,' I said. 'Find a hobby that interests you and nurture it. I'm certain it will make you altogether more content. You mentioned earlier that you're often bored, so you must look for something to fill your time, like reading, or sewing, or perhaps even gardening.' I thought of Violet Marston and her love of the outdoors.

'Yes, yes.' Her eyes became animated and she gave a little clap. They were pretty eyes, I noticed and, even without her earlier assertion, you only had to look into them to see they were honest. 'Oh, Mr Gladwell,' she said, after another awkward pause, 'I can't tell you how happy I was that you requested to see me a second time,' as if the invitation had been my idea.

'You are good company, Miss Hamilton,' I said, my impeccable manners sometimes creative with the truth. 'Why would I not be pleased to meet with you again?'

Charlotte's eyes narrowed. 'Promise you won't play games with me, Mr Gladwell. I do not have the energy, nor more importantly the time, and so ask bluntly now if you can ever see this becoming more than friendship?'

I was surprised by her directness but admired her courage and so answered honestly.

'I think we are very different people, Miss Hamilton, but I also think we are both quite lonely. My mother is correct; I work too hard and my job has taken over my life, but I don't intend it should always do so. The coming year promises to be extraordinarily busy. Commissions are coming in at a rate I hardly dared dream possible, and I am still training up a new apprentice, Freddie, which takes a large proportion of my time. I plan to enter the design competition for the Berryford Institute, which would further my career dramatically should I win, and I am finally starting to earn a respectable income. My business *must* be my focus this coming year, but I promise to turn my attentions to . . . other matters in due course.'

I recognised then that I'd been holding out for that one special person to come into my life and steal my heart so completely that I would know with surety she was the one. What I had not considered was that, should I be lucky enough to find her, she might not be available. Meeting Violet Marston had made this all too apparent.

'Then you do not rule out a possible engagement in the future?'

'No, my dear Charlotte, if I may call you that? I think perhaps we should get to know each other better over the coming months, and I promise nothing, but most certainly do not rule it out.'

She promptly burst into happy tears at my words. With my arm about her shoulders in some feeble attempt to offer comfort, her mother had happened upon us and read decidedly too much into the situation, clasping her hands together and giving me the broadest smile.

I'd tried to be honest regarding my intentions, but the affectionate embrace her mother gave me as we left made me wonder if this would be accurately relayed to Mrs Hamilton after my departure.

Chapter 22

Present Day

I stared in horror at Mr Brooker's closed front door, and wondered how on earth I could make the two-hundred-mile journey back to Dorset before Granddad raised the alarm – assuming Holly was correct about this being Norfolk. I couldn't even ring for help as I hadn't bothered to bring my mobile with me, it being next to useless until I could reinstate the contract. Mind you, Mr Brooker's house was quieter than an empty public library in a power cut, so a bit of music would have livened things up. Perhaps I would charge it and bring my earbuds next time – he could hardly complain about my music if he couldn't hear it.

So what were my options? A train journey would take hours, and I was damned if I was going to waste my precious wages on a train fare which probably wouldn't even take me as far as London. I needed to get back inside the house – more specifically, back inside the cupboard.

Clutching the rolled-up notes and loose pound coins in my hand I realised I had nowhere to put them. How dumb not to have brought a bag, or at least a purse, with me. But then, people don't generally take personal belongings with them when they nip under the stairs. At least the rain had stopped and there was enough warmth left in the day to make it a pleasant evening, because my damp dress was starting to feel uncomfortable and clingy.

Feeling more and more of a lemon the longer I stood there, I walked over to the garden gate. I didn't want to be found loitering on his doorstep, so I stepped out of sight to assess the situation, following the brick path, noting it initially had the same curves and bends as Granddad's. However, this path was considerably longer and met with a tall iron gate, whereas in Dorset it met the bottom of the stone steps from the road above. Mr Brooker's house was set in more substantial grounds than its twin and somehow seemed to embrace its position and draw attention to itself.

Lifting up the heavy black gate latch, and noticing that the sign said Acacia House, I swung the decorative gate towards me. It contained a clever silhouette of a tree with flat, black, fern-like leaves fashioned as hinges, and was mitred at the top like the fireplaces and doors inside the house. Did that mean an acacia was a tree of some kind? It would make sense, since Granddad's house was Hawthorn Place. The next time I visited the library I would investigate the houses in earnest, as the dormant historian inside me was starting to stir. With the scribbled words under the stairs and the cupboard a very real connection between two houses hundreds of miles apart, I was beginning to suspect a romantic link. *Love will always find a way* – had love found its way through a cupboard that defied logic and science? The gate squeaked as I closed it and stepped out into a single-track road.

Along the road were several small cottages of the same flint and brick construction; although they weren't as grand as Acacia House, flint was clearly local to wherever this was. This house was in context. It embraced its surroundings and made use of local materials. Granddad's, however, was an oddity when compared to all the beautiful pale Portland stone houses in his village.

There was a salty, fish-based smell in the air. As a screeching keow-keow echoed in the sky, I realised I was near the coast. It was all very familiar, yet somehow subtly different, maybe because the landscape was so open.

My rumbling stomach joined in with the tuneless orchestra above. Okay. Prioritise. Find some food, sit down (if my bruised bottom would allow) and take stock.

Ten minutes later, and with my bare legs dangling over the edge of a concrete sea wall, I was basking in the late evening sun, and eating hot fat chips from a cardboard tray. Tiny rivers of sharp vinegar ran into one of the corners and the chips alternated between salt-encrusted and totally unseasoned. I tried not to burn the roof of my mouth with my impromptu supper and pondered my situation. I'd never in my life been so conscious of exactly how much money I had – or more precisely, didn't have. It was an unpleasant feeling.

The Tourist Information Centre had closed hours ago, but I peered at the various displays in the window of the free-standing booth and worked out I was in a small town called West Creeching which, as Holly had rightly announced, was somewhere on the north Norfolk coast. When I asked about public transport, a passer-by told me there hadn't been a train station in town since the fifties, and all Norwich-bound buses stopped at six. A vague memory of branch line closures popped into my head from a twentieth-century Britain module I'd taken at university. Perhaps I could read up about it again on the internet? History was much more interesting when you didn't have to produce a reasoned twelve-page essay at the end of it. And I could Google West Creeching and see if there was an obvious connection with Summerton – a family link or a marriage. The two houses being so identical was freaky – in some ways more freaky than the method of transportation I'd accidentally discovered between them.

So, if returning home using traditional methods wasn't an option, I'd have to gain access to the cupboard again. After a few minutes, I had a plan, but it was hardly worthy of a top MI5 operative. I'd sneak around the back of Acacia House, creep into the garden room and through the kitchen. If I was discovered, I'd pretend I'd forgotten something.

Successfully negotiating a commando run to the back of the house, with only one minor stumble when my toe caught a loose brick in the paving, I took a peep through the office window. I was surprised to find Mr Brooker still working, staring at one of his multiple screens and jotting something down on a notepad. They didn't look much like gaming screens; they were full of writing and columns of figures. He clearly worked from home doing something numbery. I ducked back down and crept along to the garden room.

To my horror, both the kitchen door and the back utility door were locked but, to be fair, it was already getting dark. I returned to the front of the house and spotted that the submarine window into his home gym was open. All those years of hurling myself down the flumes at the local water park were about to pay off.

As my flailing legs propelled me into the orifice, I managed to wriggle my inelegant body through. It occurred to me my back-up story of forgetting something would be less convincing if I was discovered half in and half out of a tiny window. There was a rip as my dress caught on the latch, but I slithered gently into the room, my foot catching the edge of some piece of gym equipment as I did so. There was a crash as the whole thing tipped forward and fell to the floor.

Damn. He'd have to be stone deaf and living in Zimbabwe not to have heard that. I stood the machine upright, ducked into the en suite and waited for him to come storming in to investigate – which he duly did.

There was much muttering under his breath as he threw open the door to the gym, and I heard him walk around, questioning what had made the noise.

'. . . damn sure it came from here . . .' he muttered.

My heart started to thud so alarmingly in my chest, I was convinced he'd be able to hear it. Then the door to the en suite swung open – with me cowering behind it.

Don't come in, don't come in, I repeated in my head. A pretend seventeen-year-old recent employee who he was already clearly having doubts about was not going to last long in the job if she was discovered lurking in his loo.

To my great and everlasting relief, he seemed happy nothing was amiss, and the door closed.

'. . . always was an odd house . . .' and his voice drifted off out to the hall.

After about five minutes, assuming the coast was clear, I crept out into the corridor and back into the cupboard. The door clicked shut and my hand met with the familiar crates.

I really had to find a better solution to my commuting issues.

Chapter 23

'Come on, Granddad. Look lively. We're going to sort out that vegetable patch of yours.' My sloppy grey jumper sleeves were yanked up to my elbows and I was standing between Granddad and the television, determined not to be brushed off this time.

'It's a bit late to start sowing things now. Maybe next year. Maybe when things aren't so raw.' He tipped his head to one side, trying to see past me and catch the domestic drama playing out on the screen.

'Surely there are still things you can plant? It's only May. Quick-growing things like . . . I don't know, cress?'

'That doesn't grow in a vegetable patch, you ninny. Besides, I think I'm getting too old for all this, Molly. I appreciate your concern, but my gardening days are over.'

'Nonsense. I met a lady yesterday who must be your age or even older and she's still gardening.' I suddenly remembered the tomato plants. 'Actually, I've got something for you,' and I popped out through the garden room to retrieve the tray of seedlings.

'Moneyspinner?' I returned with the tray.

'Ah, Money*maker*. Good choice. They look like they need a drink – poor buggers.'

'Sorry. I forgot about them. They've been sitting in the bike basket all night.'

'They'll be fine, love. I'll let them soak for a bit and then transfer them to some bigger pots.' I was encouraged by his offer to take over their care but proceeded gently.

'You can grow them in the greenhouse or the garden,' I said knowledgeably.

Granddad smiled. 'Normally I'd have had some seedlings of my own by now, but, well . . . you know.'

'Life goes on though and it's not too late to get things in. You could at least tidy up the dead bits from last year?' I collapsed into an armchair and ran a frustrated hand through my hair.

'It's no good me trying to pretend everything's dandy. I miss her, love. I miss her so much. I'm useless without her. The house is a complete mess, my cooking abilities are minimal, and I don't even know how to iron a shirt. I've been so bloody lonely, so it's been truly wonderful to have another human being around the place. Brian and Annetta have been very good. They're down at least once a month for a weekend, but it's almost worse than no company at all. When they go, this big, old house feels even emptier than before.'

Granddad wasn't a man particularly given to emotion – too many years with Grandma, who didn't condone that sort of thing – so when I saw tears forming, it affected me more than I was expecting.

I stood up and walked over to this grieving old man. Bending over his shoulders, I put my arms around him and squeezed tight.

'You're having a good holiday, aren't you?' Granddad looked up at me. 'I know that it's not as exciting as the city, but you're having a rest and a break from it all?'

Break from what? If I was honest, I did even less at home than I was doing here.

'Well, Wi-Fi would be a bonus, you haven't exactly embraced

the twenty-first century, and the house is a bit quiet, but I *love* spending time with you. I'm having a marvellous time. The best. One of the most . . . relaxing holidays I've ever had. It doesn't have to be all cocktails and nightclubs. Peace and quiet can be just as . . . erm, thrilling.'

'That means the world to me,' he said, squeezing my arm, and I felt my heart constrict as though he'd reached up and squeezed that too.

'It's okay. I'm not going anywhere just yet. I'll stay here for as long as you need me. We can sort the garden, plant seeds and things, and harvest them when they're done. Anyway, I've got a part-time job now, so maybe I'll hang about for a while.' The words tumbled out, not properly thought through.

He smiled and patted my hand, resting on his shoulder. The tears swelled some more, burst their banks and fell to his polyester-trousered knee.

'Oh sweetheart, I didn't know you'd got a job. How wonderful. Does that mean you might consider staying for the whole summer? That would make me a very happy man.'

I nodded, because to do otherwise would break his heart. Getting a full-time job and re-joining the real world would just have to wait. Granddad was more important.

He settled down to watch an afternoon quiz show and I made him a cup of tea. Well, it looked vaguely tea-coloured and he didn't complain. I'd been here less than a week and things were dragging more than a limping man with a broken leg. What was I going to do in sleepy Summerton for the *entire* summer? The job with Mr Brooker was only six hours a week, and even with my shoddy maths, that still left about a hundred and sixty hours to fill. Games of draughts and sprinkling a few seeds over the vegetable patch weren't going to keep me busy until the end of August.

I decided it was time to throw myself into researching the house. It was intriguing; all the symbolism and mystery, especially since I'd discovered its identical twin two hundred miles away. And maybe I could get some gardening manuals to work out what Granddad should be up to at this time of year. Alan Titchmarsh was a gardener, wasn't he?

It was an embryo of a plan, so feeling a bit more upbeat, and after working out the time zones, I gave Mum a quick ring – largely to prove I was on top of the whole situation. I'd only spoken to her briefly the day she'd landed, not wanting to bug her on holiday. Plus, since my conversation with Jean, I was feeling more charitable towards her and her parenting decisions. I wasn't going to let her off the hook for twenty-four years of silence on the subject of my paternity, but she was right, it wasn't a conversation to have over the phone.

After hearing all about Ellis Island, the Guggenheim and their trip up the Empire State building, I told her about The Pie, the job with Mr Brooker and my efforts to find babysitting work.

'I'm not sure looking after children is part of your skill set, darling. You visibly panicked when our neighbour handed you her newborn at Christmas.'

'That's babies and I specified none of those. Older kids will be fine – you can talk to them. And anyway, they'll be sound asleep. I'm only there in case the house catches fire or the parents get a flat tyre on the way home. Easy-peasy.'

Mum made an 'mmm' sound that implied there might be more to it than that, but I moved the conversation on.

'I'm not having much luck getting Granddad back outside. He still prefers *Come Dine with Me* to "Come Dig with Me".'

'Perhaps if you made the first move he'd feel guilty and up his game?' If this was an insight into her ninja parenting, she might need to rethink her strategy, because twenty-four years of watching others cook and clean hadn't exactly spurred me into action.

'I guess it's worth a try, especially as I've somehow managed to commit to staying the whole summer. That's an awful long time without Wi-Fi.'

'An impressive sacrifice on your part, indeed,' she said.

'Can I come back home afterwards?' I asked. 'Just to sort myself out? I promise to start flat-hunting and looking for a decent full-time job when I do.'

'Of course. We missed you when you went to live with Rupert.' She emphasised the *we*, but I doubted Brian mourned my absence. He had Mum all to himself, which is probably what he'd been planning since I was nine, even though he'd done a fantastic job of pretending otherwise. But it was all show, surely – it had to be.

'Great, because I *really* miss the Tassimo.'

There was a brief snort. 'I'm afraid we don't miss you using it. I was forever taking out your empty pods, running the cleaning cycle and filling the water tank.'

I didn't even know there was such a thing as a cleaning cycle. To clean what? I always used a fresh mug.

'Perhaps you can buy yourself one now you're earning?'

'I don't think my salary will stretch to coffee machines just yet.'

'I have faith in you, sweetheart. When one door closes . . .'

. . . A tiny triangular cupboard door opens up a whole world of mystery, I thought to myself.

'So what do all these Latin words above the fireplace mean?' I asked Granddad as I lay sprawled across the threadbare sofa in the cosy room.

I'd nearly finished the first library book. It was like being back home or in Rupert's flat on my days off – three hours lying on a sofa all afternoon – except I had no likes or retweets to show for it.

'*Ego semper tecum sum quamquam procul absumus*' danced before me. There were a lot of words for a small area of wall, but somehow aesthetically they worked, although I couldn't even begin to guess what they meant.

'It's about love but I can't remember the exact translation. Never did anything as fancy as Latin at school. But after our conversation the other day, I remembered Briggie finding a box of bits relating to the house not long after we'd moved in,' Granddad continued. 'It was under the bottom stairs, tucked out of sight, and she came across it by accident. It was only old photos and letters, but she reckoned it was to do with the original owner.'

My book slid to the floor with a thud as I sat upright. *Only* old photos and letters – a fantastic source for an historian. Which I practically was with my degree and everything.

'Do you know where it is, Granddad?'

He scratched his head. 'Can't remember seeing it for years, but I know she wouldn't have thrown it out. She was fiddling about with it for days, reading the letters and asking the villagers if they remembered anything about the house. Apparently, an older gentleman had it before her aunt, but he had no children, so when he died, it went on the market and that's how it came into Briggie's family.'

My heart heaved. Hawthorn Place was a family home, so full of love and hope. It wasn't built for one person. 'Such a shame Grandma's aunt never married,' I said, wondering if the only child to ever live in the house had been Brian.

'There's the tragedy, love. She *was* married, right before the war – some well-to-do chap from town. It was his money that bought the house, and then he was killed on the battlefields of

France. There were no children and she was so grateful when her only niece looked after her in her later years that she left Briggie the house and her life savings – although most of the money got eaten up by the death duties. We'd only been married a year ourselves when she died and were lodging with my parents at the time.'

I shuffled on to my elbow. Had they told me that before? I couldn't remember. 'Great timing for you then. Inheriting this at the start of your lives together.'

'It was and it wasn't. It was a ridiculously big property for us to run and we found it really hard at the time. That first winter we practically lived in the kitchen because we couldn't afford to heat the rest of the house, but we found plenty of ways to keep warm . . .'

I blushed at the implication and tried to get the conversation back on track. 'And did Grandma find anything out about the solitary man?'

He shrugged. 'I'm not really sure. Trouble was, I never listened properly. You know how it is? I sort of switched off and gave the occasional nod. Briggie loved the place, though, right from the first day we moved in. Said it had a magical feel and, a bit like you, was curious about all the fiddly bits and what they might mean. She never even minded about the little ghosty boy. Said he looked harmless enough.'

I'd forgotten about its haunted history, which somehow didn't fit with the romance of the place. This was a house full of fun and love, not a house of sadness and trapped spirits waiting to pass to the other side.

'But I do remember there being lots of references in the letters to plants, because she quizzed me about it all,' he added. 'Although,' he paused and scrunched up his face, 'I seem to remember them not making much sense – everything too random and jumbly.'

'So where is the box now? *Think*, Granddad . . .' I resisted the urge to lean forward and grip his shoulders.

'Oh Molly, there's so much clutter about, I wouldn't know where to begin.' He cast an embarrassed glance around the room and his eyes rested on a stack of old newspapers balanced near the fire. 'Perhaps I need to have a bit of a sort out, but I couldn't bear to move anything after . . .'

'It's okay, Granddad.' My shoulders dropped. I didn't want to pressure him into anything. I picked up the library book, placing it carefully on the small side table.

'I still can't decide if it's worse to keep looking at all her things, painful reminders that she's not going to walk through the door and huff about the state of the place, or bundle up her possessions for the charity shop. If I get rid of everything, will the memories start to fade? Am I wiping her out? When I look at her wooden sewing box I think of her tutting at the state of my gardening trousers and it makes me smile, but her toothbrush in the bathroom brings me to tears almost every night, without fail.'

'Maybe there's a compromise? Maybe together we can go around the house and decide what can go and what can stay. Have a bit of a sort-out?'

'Okay.' He sighed. 'But if we're going to have a spring-clean, we'll need to get our roller skates on because it's nearly summer.' He chuckled and then pulled back to look me in the eyes. 'I know I keep saying it, but it's wonderful that you're here, Molly. I'm starting to feel I can face things again.'

Getting Granddad to tackle the clutter was a great first step, but it was tinged with guilt. I now had an ulterior motive – I wanted to get my hands on that box.

'When she did all her research, did she find a link between this house and another one?' I asked. 'Perhaps a house in Norfolk?

Were there any connections between here and that part of the world? Can you remember *anything* that Grandma discovered?'

He shrugged and I cursed myself again for not having questioned Grandma when she was alive. I was slowly being drawn into the history of the house, but it was too late to question my most valuable ally. Granddad was frustratingly vague.

'Apparently there used to be a mural in the bedroom you use. Animals and plants all over the wall – Briggie remembered it being there when she was little, but it got painted over by her aunt when she turned that room into a guest room. And I'm pretty certain Briggie worked out who the architect was, but damned if I can remember the fellow's name. He's got some memorial in the village.'

'Where?' I asked, sitting upright again, and practically ready to run out to the bike and speed-cycle into Summerton, despite the hour. How silly of me not to think of the architect.

He shrugged. 'Sorry. No idea. But the house is a special style of building – particular to that period. Let me think . . . Arts and Crafts, she used to say.'

'Arts and Crafts. What does that mean? It's made of sticky back plastic and fuzzy felt? Although I can quite believe it was designed by a four year old – all muddled and random.'

But as I joked, I thought about the house in a more sensible way. Yes, it did seem a jumble, but it wasn't when you thought about it properly. It was like looking at an abstract painting and dismissing it as amateur, when the artist had been Royal Academy trained. All the elements worked and it was much cleverer than it first appeared when you understood what you were looking at.

Perhaps I needed to brush up on my architectural knowledge. Or rather, acquire some.

Chapter 24
Percy Gladwell
1894

'I now have in my mind the basic layout of the house, so we need to consider the decoration and more personal details that will make this house your home. We must talk about the things that matter to you: your interests, your loves, your hopes, your desires.'

I had engineered a second visit to the seaside cottage of the enigmatic Mrs Marston within the month. Freddie, my promising if somewhat clumsy apprentice, was delighted to be allowed to survey the site unwatched by his master. Equally, I was delighted to have an interview with my client alone. Winter was fast approaching but the day was unseasonably warm, and she asked if I minded sitting in the gardens of the cottage. I remembered her desire to be outside whenever possible, and decided there was no reason the interview could not be conducted al fresco.

There was a scattering of orange and yellow leaves across the lawn, but we were in a sheltered spot, under an arbour covered in a tangle of barren branches. Birds were calling to each other and there were only a few smudges of cloud in the sky above.

'Am I to be subjected to a quiz?' Mrs Marston asked.

She looked vivacious in a dress of palest green, and totally at one with her surroundings. The breeze fanned my notebook open and I moved it to my lap to better control the pages.

'If you could enlighten me as to how you might spend your time once the house is completed, I can decide the best placement of various features within it. For example, should you be keen on embroidery, I will ensure there is an area with adequate light. If you plan to entertain regularly, the size and layout of the dining room will reflect this . . .'

'Do you wish me to supply you with a detailed biography?' She was teasing, but there was still no smile or light about her eyes.

I took the question at face value. 'If you would be so kind.'

'Then prepare to be bored, for I have lived a very dull life indeed.'

But every detail that she conveyed, every childhood tale and passion that she shared, helped me to understand her, and to know her more intimately than I had dared hope. A woman with four older brothers and consequently a rough and tumble childhood, whose father had a family name that went back to the time of William the Conqueror, but whose estate fortunes had declined in recent years, as had those of many in the countryside these past two decades. But most importantly, Violet Marston was a woman who had grown up beside the sea, appreciating its freedoms and rugged beauty – who enjoyed the simple pleasure afforded by a walk across the fields or along the shore, and who nurtured and relished the flora and fauna that surrounded her.

'We talk of frivolous things, Mr Gladwell. You are fully aware my greatest passion is my garden and you have heard about my embroidery and love of baking. What more can you possibly need to know?' She raised an eyebrow in anticipation and placed her hands together on her lap.

'Do you read?' I enquired, for reading was a passion of mine.

'Yes, silly things. Books that you would not have heard of and hold no interest for an educated man such as yourself.'

'Try me.'

A pink hue flushed across her cheeks and her eyes dropped to the clasped hands. 'In my youth I enjoyed the novels of Ouida, but I would not admit this to Edward. He would heartily disapprove. In fact, I am embarrassed now to have admitted such to you.' She looked puzzled. 'And I am not sure quite why I did.'

'They are frivolous and romantic, true, but also entertaining. *Under Two Flags*, *Idalia* – both I remember with fondness.'

'You have read her?' She leaned forward and then, realising her eagerness, adjusted her position. There was a squawk from behind as a blackbird dived headlong towards a tabby cat prowling along the hedge – although it was too late in the year to be protecting fledglings. I smiled at the bird and Mrs Marston's incredulity.

'Indeed, I read all sorts as a child. Despite numerous siblings, my childhood was largely solitary due to ill health.'

She raised a questioning eyebrow.

'When I was five I had rheumatic fever and nearly died. I pulled through but remained a sickly child. My mother became terribly protective of me and is convinced to this day my heart might give out at any moment. It's true there is a murmur, but I do not feel her cosseting was strictly necessary. I do not smoke, and I do not exert myself, but I still plan to make old bones.' I smiled. 'But being limited in my activities, more due to her fussing than necessity, led me to find other pastimes. One of which was to steal my mother's reading materials when endless Latin and Greek bored me.'

For the first time, something warm flashed across her eyes, so fleeting I could hardly pin it down. She clapped her hands together, bringing them to her lips. So I stumbled on, anxious to hold her interest.

'Take *Under Two Flags* – how can you not feel moved when Cigarette throws herself in front of the firing squad to save Bertie? But then not smile inside as she takes several pages to die and utters such eloquent and dramatic prose as she does so?'

'Escapist nonsense though,' she sighed.

'But just because a thing is not intellectual or is frivolous doesn't mean it has no merit.' I shuffled forward on my seat. 'Consider the drawings of my seven-year-old niece, Millicent. She sketches houses for me, knowing my profession, and they are abstract and fanciful. There is naturally no observance of engineering principles and they could not be built in the real world. But they are charming and you find yourself wishing perhaps they could be. A roof made of peacock feathers? Rainbows painted across exterior walls? And who would not want to have a rope from their bedroom window to launch themselves from the sill and land with aplomb in the petunias? I'm sure I would drop to the ground every time with an enormous smile on my face.'

'Perhaps, then, the skill is creating a compromise between what we want and what we can have. Is that how you operate, Mr Gladwell? Do you strive to create that balance between aspiration and achievability for your clients?'

'A house must be comfortable and practical, undoubtedly, but let it also be glorious. I wish my clients to sit in any aspect of a room and be pleased. A window is a necessary thing to provide light, but let us also make it beautiful. Let us capture that light and let it pass through a rainbow of colours so that it transforms into something magical as it falls the other side.'

'Oh yes, I should like a stained-glass window.'

'Then you shall have one, and perhaps I will place it next to the front door so that every time you enter a rainbow of colours will fall at your feet as you enter, and you shall think of Millicent and smile.'

There was a brief meeting of eyes and hers were sparkling, adding something bewitching to her already ethereal beauty.

'And perhaps, Mr Gladwell, I shall plant petunias to remind me of your desire to launch yourself from a window.'

We spent a pleasant afternoon chatting as Mary, her maid, topped up the teapot and kept us supplied with cake. Freddie returned a little after three o'clock, having dutifully completed the list of measurements I had requested but somehow managing to lose his pocket measure on his journey back to the cottage. I don't think we even noticed that Freddie had joined our little tea party, but then I am certain his focus was on the array of cake and not our conversation.

'I adore fairy tales,' Mrs Marston ventured, slipping another slice of cherry cake on to my tea plate. 'I like escaping to worlds that aren't real. My world is so dull that I think it is sometimes good to leave it behind for a while.'

'And which fairy tales do you enjoy the most?' I asked.

'*Sleeping Beauty* and *The Golden Goose* – I have an inexplicable love of geese. You think that funny, Mr Gladwell? I caught your fleeting smile.'

'No, indeed I do not.' My mind was racing with crenellations and other simple motifs I could incorporate to surround her with fairy tales and romance. And geese.

'I appreciate they can be vicious creatures, and I have absolutely no experience of keeping them, but in the new house, I think I shall. They have funny faces and make excellent guard dogs.'

'And taste exceptionally good with sage and apple stuffing.'

'You *are* teasing me,' she said, and I responded with a feigned look of innocence. 'But you're right, they do taste good with sage and apple.'

And the soft look about her eyes finally made it to her lips, which curved into a small smile, turning an already beautiful creature into a thing of perfection. This was no ordinary woman. This was a magnificent woman in ordinary circumstances, but the fire and passion would have to surface at some point and I dearly hoped I might be around to witness it. But, I asked myself, how long could I, in all good conscience, drag out the planning and building of this house? For the completion of the project would likely mark the end of our acquaintance.

She reached out a hand, as if to touch mine, but it was withdrawn again at the last minute.

'You understand me so much better than Edward,' she sighed.

And that was why, I reflected, he did not deserve her.

Chapter 25
Present Day

The next day I cycled back into Summerton, getting almost to the top of the hill before being forced to clamber off. Small victories, like my cycling aspirations or getting Granddad to sort through Grandma's belongings, were now the biggest things in my world.

I wanted to hunt down the memorial Granddad had mentioned. With no obvious stone angels spreading their wings across the misty grey sky, or any Arc de Triomphe-style structures towering above the horizon, I asked a passer-by who suggested the little bench by the war memorial. I raced across the square and crouched over the brass plaque – shining bright in a sudden burst of sunshine through the parting clouds.

In loving memory of Percy Gladwell.
An architect of great renown,
A friend to Summerton village,
And the holder of my heart.

I'd been expecting something more dramatic than an unassuming wrought-iron bench – a bench that I must have sat on hundreds of times in summers past, tying up the laces on my Kickers or sucking away at an ice lolly purchased from the Co-op with my pocket money. But I felt a massive thrill at finding the first piece of the puzzle and noted down his name.

I headed to the library, feeling more motivated than I'd ever been as an undergraduate, and logged on to one of their computers. I quickly realised I was looking for the Arts and Crafts *Movement* – a trend in design and decoration during the second half of the nineteenth century. Artists, writers, designers and architects all reacting to the rapid industrialisation sweeping the country, and consequent inferior quality of mass-produced, machine-made items. They pushed for a return to traditional craftsmanship, convinced that when people had pride in their work and could remain in their rural communities (rather than travelling to the big cities to work in factories) the social and moral decline of the country could somehow be reversed. As I scrolled through the images, I could see that Hawthorn Place was heavily Arts and Crafts-influenced.

William Morris was the founding father of the movement and the name was familiar to me. I'd seen his designs on bags, bedding, notebooks and even mugs over the years. When his Red House came up on a link, I noticed little round windows not unlike the one at Granddad's, and a similar random jumble of roof tops. This house, designed by Morris and the architect Philip Webb in 1859, was one of the first examples of the Arts and Crafts style.

Next, I Googled Percy Gladwell. Because it was a fairly unusual surname, the top entry was a Wikipedia article about a nineteenth-century architect. Bingo.

Percy Samuel Gladwell, RA FRIBA (5 May 1865 – 13 November 1937) was a British architect known for his work in the Arts and Crafts style.

Early life

Percy Gladwell was born in Weymouth, Dorset, to Elizabeth and John Gladwell. He was one of four boys and two girls. As a child he suffered from rheumatic fever and was educated at home by his mother. He attributed his initial interest in architecture to her.

After showing a flair for architecture and design, he trained at the Kensington School of Art (became Royal College of Art, 1896) and was subsequently articled for three years to the architect Richard Norman Shaw. In 1892 he established his own practice in Great Marlborough Street, London. He was a contemporary of Edwin Lutyens and a good friend of Charles Robert Ashbee.

Notable works

Notable works include Highgate House in Cumbria, Bayldon Manor in York, and Carmarthen Hall in Carmarthenshire – recently acquired by the National Heritage. He also undertook the repairing and extending of numerous parish churches throughout the country, and is remembered for his quirky country houses and the unusual loggias in his early works.

After a failed suicide attempt in 1896 (citation needed) and subsequent health struggles, Gladwell withdrew from public life for seven years, returning in 1904 to win the prestigious Fairfax Prize with his design for Kingsway Grammar School, near Bristol, which many consider to be his finest work.

Private life

Notoriously a private man, Gladwell's suicide attempt fuelled rumours regarding his sexuality, as Ashbee (a known homosexual and fellow member of the Arts and Crafts Movement) was a lifelong friend. Gladwell never married and spent much of his later life in his beloved Dorset, becoming a generous benefactor for numerous local projects, including the design and build of several social housing initiatives. Although he consistently – and somewhat unusually – refused to undertake lucrative commissions abroad, he successfully revived his career to become one of the most highly regarded architects of the early twentieth century. He passed away in 1937, at his home in Summerton, after a short illness.

Although the article hadn't stated as much, I was now certain that Gladwell was the solitary man who'd spent his life at Hawthorn Place. I couldn't believe there was another house in Summerton where he might have ended his days. And somehow the mystery of the house fitted with the mystery of this local figure. Given that the Victorians couldn't even say 'homosexual' without passing the smelling salts, the stigma of his sexuality could have easily led to a suicide attempt.

If Gladwell had been gay, that would also explain his unmarried status and lack of children. And going back a hundred years, any romantic partners would have been kept secret. This all made sense. The bench had been donated by a lover, but not one who could be open about their relationship. I felt sorry for the man – both men, in fact – and thankful times had changed.

An advert for National Heritage properties in the county popped up in a sidebar and I realised that Bickerton Manor, not far from Weymouth, was an Arts and Crafts house. It didn't have any connection with Gladwell, but I decided that seeing something in the flesh, or stone in this case, would increase my understanding so much more than dry online research. I noted down the details and, clutching a biography of William Morris and an Alan Titchmarsh book on growing vegetables, I left the library.

Stopping at the hardware store, I purchased a few packets of seeds, horrified a tiny paper envelope containing a few microscopic seeds could be nearly two pounds. Then I paid some cash into my bank via the post office. One more wage packet and I could reinstate my phone contract – although interestingly I wasn't missing it as much as when I'd first arrived.

As I coasted down the hill, my eyes scanning the road ahead for sexy, reckless pedestrians, I thought more about poor old Percy Gladwell and the two houses. If Hawthorn Place was Arts and Crafts, why wasn't it built from Portland stone? One of the overriding principles of the movement was sourcing local building materials and supporting the skills of local artisans. I had to assume his decision to build the house was therefore linked to Acacia House. Far from helping me to understand why it felt so out of place, my research only made everything more of a mystery.

As I wheeled the bike up Granddad's path, I noticed the tray of tomato seedlings. Sitting in the direct sun and deprived of water, they'd withered and died. The brittle compost had shrunk away from the sides of each compartment and the drooping stems had collapsed like stray threads of abandoned cotton.

As I picked it up, Granddad appeared at the back door. He saw it in my hands and looked guilty.

'Forgot all about them. Sorry, love.' He peered over the edge of the tray. 'They're goners. Chuck 'em on the compost heap. *Neighbours* starts in five minutes. Want to come and watch it with me?'

'No thanks. I'll bring you a cup of tea though.'

'That would be smashing,' and he shuffled back inside.

This was ridiculous. He was addicted to mindless daytime television and not even out in the fresh air long enough to water a few seedlings. And then I thought of how I'd spent my days before arriving here, and the irony wasn't lost on me.

Chapter 26

The next shift at my new job was more successful and decidedly less soggy. Because Holly had Friday afternoons off school, I undertook my microscopic commute after lunch and dressed more appropriately: faded green cargo trousers and a white vest top. I felt like Lara Croft about to raid some serious tombs, and somehow this motivated me more.

My first task was to work through a long list of things Mr Brooker needed me to do in town. I had parcels to take to the post office (it appeared most of his shopping was done online and these were largely returns), there were a few items to pick up from an electrical store, and he fancied some fresh cream cakes from the bakery. I hoped being out and about in West Creeching wouldn't lead to the discovery of my fraudulent pilfering of Holly's job, but he knew me as Molly, and the town was large enough for a degree of anonymity.

As he'd lent me his front door key to let myself back in, I also stopped at the engravers and got a spare key cut so that getting home wasn't such a trauma if he decided to show me out again. Aware that what I was doing was probably illegal, I justified it by promising myself I would only use it to get home and not for any untoward snooping. As soon as the summer, and my job at Acacia House, was over I would dispose of it.

Back at his house, I knuckled down and had a productive afternoon. My newly acquired knowledge from Grandma's housekeeping guide suggested vinegar, water and newspaper worked wonders on smeary windows, so I put it to the test. I was keen to try toothpaste as a silver cleaner, but Rory hadn't yet requested I set to work on the family plate. I got out my phone, still without internet access but able to play my stored music, and popped in a pair of earbuds, mindful of his middle-aged desire for peace and quiet.

As I swung around the kitchen, now a dab hand with a squeezy mop, Rory walked in. I popped one of the earbuds out.

'Erm, would you mind?'

I looked blank. 'Would I mind what? Mopping faster?'

'The singing – if you can call it that.'

'Sorry. Didn't realise I was.' I'd been shouting out angry (and rather sweary) song lyrics.

'I know I seem like a boring grown-up to you, but I must stress again my request for peace and quiet, Molly, and you are *much* noisier than I anticipated. A bit of gentle Radio 4 in the background is about all I can manage. Nihilist and somewhat obscene rap songs are a bit much.'

'No problem. If peace and quiet is your thing, I'll try to respect that.' I looked suitably contrite.

'I'm not sure it's my *thing*, but it's certainly what I need right now. When you're older, and understand all the pressures life brings, you will learn to focus on what's important. Self-preservation is my thing right now. It's all about priorities. They used to be money, my career and a side order of hedonism, but things change . . .'

'Like your taste in footwear?' and my eyes darted to his slippers.

'They are extremely comfortable,' he huffed, and then looked down at his feet. 'But you're right – if I'd had a crystal ball at your age and seen this future vision of myself, I would have baulked. Guess these things just creep up on you without you noticing.' His face scrunched up and he sniffed the air. 'Have you been eating fish and chips in here?'

'Oh, the vinegar. I cleaned the windows.'

'What's wrong with the glass cleaner under the sink? It smells far less . . . chip-shoppy.'

'Sorry. I was embracing traditional methods because . . . ' – I didn't have access to Google to get my back – '. . . because modern cleaning products are packed full of nasty chemicals and I'm embracing the environmentally friendly.'

'If you're going to cart my dirty dishes down to the stream and wash them with strips of yucca, I don't want to be billed the extra hours.'

'No, I . . . oh, you're joking.'

He almost smiled but stopped himself, as though he couldn't give himself permission, and then disappeared into his lair for the remainder of my time, only reappearing at five o'clock.

'Time's up, Molly. How have you got on?'

'Erm, I might have accidentally broken one of the espresso cups.' I held up a teeny-weeny handle.

He sighed. 'Don't worry. I appreciate your honesty. And you did manage to keep *relatively* quiet. We'll take that as the achievement for today, shall we? Baby steps.'

Relieved breaking a cup wasn't a sackable offence, I smiled. 'I'll see myself out.'

The following few days whizzed by. The weekly pilgrimage to Dorchester on Monday had resulted in a fully reinstated phone contract (hoorah), yet I was still avidly consuming my library books. I brushed up on Alan's gardening tips, bookmarked recipes in various cookbooks, and gorged myself on YA fiction – dystopian worlds with hunky but damaged heroes. My shifts at Rory's were relatively disaster free, and Granddad and I started working through the house, slowly sorting out Grandma's possessions. I initiated a three-pile system: go, keep and undecided, which were really items to go but which I understood he couldn't part with quite yet.

Granddad stepped through the front door, returning after mysteriously disappearing for most of Saturday morning, and I'd taken the opportunity to do something to lift his spirits whilst he'd been absent from the house.

'Surprise,' I said, spreading my arms wide to draw attention to the hall floor I'd swept, the broom still in my hand. A grubby trail remained through the centre, which obviously needed more than sweeping to shift it, but at least all the dust and hair was gone. It was amazing how much had accumulated under the hall table and in the corners. I even found a long-dead mouse. The unexpected satisfaction from cleaning Mr Brooker's house was proving a drug, so I was applying my newly acquired housekeeping skills to Hawthorn Place.

'Oh, love, thank you. It looks so much more welcoming now. And I've got a surprise for you too.'

'Ooh, chocolate?'

'Better than that.' His dark eyes twinkled.

Was there anything better than chocolate?

'Don't tease. What is it?'

'Seeing as you're going to be staying for a while . . .' Ah, yes, my hasty commitment to remain in this buzzing metropolis for the whole summer. 'I got to thinking how I could make that more fun for you, so I snuck off to town and took myself into one of those Apple shops.' Great, he was about to regale me with a detailed list of further groceries he'd purchased in an effort to satisfy my desire for green. 'There was a lovely young girl who was very helpful and very patient, because I don't know much about all this technology nonsense. And the upshot is I've bought myself one of those tablet things.'

'You've bought a *tablet*? An electronic one, that connects to the internet and everything?' The broom handle slipped from my hands and clattered on to the floor.

'Uh-huh. After you mentioned Wi-Fi would be a bonus, I decided to drag myself into the twenty-first century. Briggie would have tutted and told me there was nothing wrong with the old ways, and listed all the dangers, probably imagining we would get hacked up or our identities would be sold to pirates, but then she's not here, so I thought I might begin to explore the world beyond my front door without her. Not that it doesn't mean I don't miss her every waking second, but having a young 'un about the house reminds me that life goes on.'

There was a slight flaw in Granddad's otherwise genius and very welcome plan.

'But you don't have an internet connection. It will be next to useless without that.'

'All sorted.' He crossed his arms and puffed up his chest. 'I rang BT yesterday while you were at work and played the helpless old pensioner card. They told me a technician will be with us within ten days to install the . . . whatever it is. Apparently our speed won't be great, but it will be enough. So hopefully by the end of next week I'll be on the interweb and surfing with the best of them.'

The biggest, happiest, preparation-for-social-media-selfies grin spread across my face. 'Got to hand it to you, Granddad. That certainly counts as a surprise.' And as far as I was concerned, a good one. With a job up my sloppy sleeve, actively touting for others, and internet access only days away, I felt the most upbeat I'd been since arriving.

'I might need your help though, setting stuff up and operating the buttons and things. Although the young girl said it's all stroke-screen nowadays.' He chuckled to himself. 'Not even any keys to press. Isn't technology marvellous? My father would have thought he'd wandered into some kind of phantasmagorical dream if he'd been around today.'

I nodded in sympathy. Phantasmagorical experiences were a speciality of mine.

Chapter 27
Percy Gladwell

1894

As winter took a firm hold, the nation could only pray that it would not be as severe as the last. Mother, who always embraced the seasonal traditions with unbridled enthusiasm, managed to gather all of us, including her five grandchildren, on Christmas Day for the first time since Father had passed six winters ago. I have never seen her look happier, as we all sat around a tree adorned with glowing candles, and sang carols.

We ran into the Hamiltons at church, the Sunday before I returned to London. I generally found church tedious and had hoped to get away early, but Mother begged me to accompany her, and her motive quickly became apparent.

'You look in splendid health, Miss Hamilton,' I said, as we stood under the early Gothic doorway, watching our breath condense before us as we spoke. There was more colour about the woman now and she seemed animated and enthusiastic as she tugged at my sleeve and pulled me to one side.

'I have been thinking about your words since we last spoke. I do not wish for much,' she said, when we were out of earshot. 'I want a home of my own, away from Mother, and someone to care for, other than Father. I do not need new dresses or big hats.

I do not need feigned devotion and insincere words. I have spoken to Cook and am attempting to master some basic skills, and have purchased Beeton's *Book of Household Management* to this end.'

'Quite a thick tome,' I commented. 'With that and your Bible, you are truly set for life.'

'Please don't mock me, Mr Gladwell, simply because my interests differ from your own.'

I was again reminded that not everyone is open to teasing, although Mrs Marston seemed to rise to the occasion. I pulled a suitably contrite expression.

'I know that my life is small and my wants simple. I do not aspire to design monuments or great houses. For me, learning how to bake a fruit cake or pluck a fowl is enough.'

I looked at her for a sign that she was in jest, but she was in deadly earnest. I studied her face, open and honest, and wondered if I could learn to love her, or at least make her happy. And I thought perhaps I could. Mother was right – I needed someone to look after me and to offer a distraction from work.

'I have also decided,' she gushed, 'to take myself outside more and learn about the garden. Cooking and gardening are useful interests, don't you think? Should I ever have a home of my own to run. When the weather improves, Father has said I may have my own plot, and I thought perhaps flowers and vegetables.'

I felt uneasy again. It was as if she had taken it upon herself to acquire a range of skills deemed suitable for matrimony and it was now her sole objective to become my wife. She had made assumptions based on my words that I had not intended.

'I have a busy year ahead, Miss Hamilton,' I reminded her, 'and several important projects underway. As I mentioned before, perhaps twelve months hence, when Freddie has been trained up and I have paid some of my loans, I might be in a position to . . .'

I saw it form – a tiny tear in her left eye, that tumbled down her cheek and landed on her lap. She looked across at me and smiled, her whole posture more self-assured, and confident.

'Yes, and I will wait, Mr Gladwell. I will gladly wait.'

And somehow, I found that I had promised Charlotte Hamilton something I might not be able to deliver.

Chapter 28
Present Day

'So, hon, can you make it?'

Izzy had rung me on the landline and was pushing me to return to London for a house party in Shepherd's Bush on the first Saturday in June, still under the assumption I was returning home in a fortnight. I knew nothing about the party, which had apparently been discussed and planned on Snapchat for days. I felt completely out of the loop; the installation of Wi-Fi couldn't come soon enough.

'Change of plan. I'm staying with Granddad for a bit longer. Funds are still too tight for me to leap on a train back to London, I'm afraid. But I have managed to find part-time work down here.'

'Ooh – do tell. Executive cream tea taster? Or surfboard waxer for a bunch of hot Australian dudes?'

'I'm in *Dorset*. Will you stop muddling your West Country counties, Iz? Anyway, it's not that exciting and it's only temporary. I'm a sort of PA for some neurotic bloke who works from home.'

'Oh yeah. And what does a *sort of* PA do?'

'Erm, posting stuff, and tidying, and organising things for him.'

'Like what? Last-minute plane tickets for international conferences? Booking five-star hotels for his entourage? Ordering necklaces from Tiffany as a birthday surprise for his girlfriend?'

'Not exactly, more domestic organisation. Like the dishwasher and laundry.'

'So a PA who cleans around the toilet bowl and empties the bins? I'd love to know how that's working out for the girl who paid me to do most of her share of chores at uni, and the only time she ever tidied her room was when she emptied it to leave at the end of the year. I love you and you are my best friend, but I think Rupert had a point.'

I wriggled and uncrossed my legs, tugging at a hangnail with my teeth. 'I think he probably did too. But I'm working on it and Mr Brooker seems happy enough with my domestic skills.'

'So is this Mr Brooker good-looking? Wealthy? Single?' she asked.

'It's not like that. He's like a middle-aged yeti – all orange hair and comfy slippers. I don't know about you, but that certainly doesn't tick any boxes for me.' Although he did have beautiful eyes, deep and unfathomable – a bit like his voice.

'What does he do, exactly, that he needs a PA?'

'We haven't got that far yet. Something with computers and numbers.'

Izzy's tinkly laugh echoed down the phone. 'You don't even know what he does for a living? Some PA you are . . .'

Barely had I put the phone down to Izzy when it rang again. 'Molly Butterfield?'

'Yes . . .'

'My name is Catherine and I'm ringing about your card in the Co-op window. And, although I've never seen quite such a restrictive advert before,' the caller chuckled, 'you happen to fill all my criteria – just. Tommy is three. I'm looking for someone to cover my yoga on a Tuesday evening and my Spanish lessons on a Thursday.'

'I'm your girl . . . woman.' This was perfect. One little

three year old who would hopefully be sound asleep. Totally easy money.

'If you'd like to pop over for a very brief informal interview, we'll take it from there.'

Feeling on top of the world, and finally cycling to the top of the hill without having to dismount, I Google-mapped my way to the babysitting interview with my mobile data, only to be greeted by three bouncy, hyperactive children as I rang the doorbell of a pretty, pale stone, semi-detached house at the far end of Summerton.

'Erm, I thought you only had a three year old,' I said, as Catherine showed me down a narrow corridor to a sunny but minuscule conservatory at the back of the property. This, I quickly worked out, was the children's playroom, because it was littered with colourful plastic hazards, like bright yellow construction vehicles that moved from under you when you accidentally stepped on them.

'Are you okay?' Catherine smiled, helping me back to my feet. I nodded. My bottom was going to bruise. Dinosaur legs were terribly jabby.

'She's funny. I like her,' said the youngest and grubbiest of her offspring. 'Can we keep her?'

'Ah, I mentioned my three year old, Tommy, because you specified no under-threes, but Oliver and Amber are five and seven respectively. Is that a problem?'

'Absolutely not. I *adore* children. Couldn't eat a whole one though.' I forced a smile and Oliver, a freckly, cheery-faced boy, gave a huge fake laugh at my very lame attempt at humour.

'It's two hours both nights. I'll only be down at the village hall so can get home quickly in a real emergency, but I can't see any major issues. Do you have much babysitting experience?'

'Absolutely heaps,' I said, fingers crossed behind my back as I leaned forward, trying to come across as enthusiastic. I'd lied through my teeth to get Rory's job and I was coping okay, so I was pretty sure I could manage a few little kids. 'Will they be in bed when you leave?' I asked hopefully.

'Tommy goes at six, and I need to leave about five to seven. The other two will be pyjamaed and bathed, so it should just be a quick bedtime story and supervising teeth.'

'Excellent.' I looked across at the girl, who was staring at me with intense, chocolate brown eyes, dark ringlets dangling across her face. How could a seven year old make me feel so nervous? She knows, I thought. She knows and is going to make me pay. I wriggled uncomfortably in my seat. Catherine turned to deal with Oliver, who'd got his finger stuck in a fidget spinner, and I stuck my tongue out at her. Ironically, this made her smile and move closer.

Tommy thrust a fire engine at me and I started raising the cherry picker, putting a plastic yellow fireman inside and doing a silly voice.

'Do you have a reference I could follow up?' Catherine asked.

Damn. I hadn't thought about that. Of course she'd want references if she was leaving me in sole charge of the most precious things in her life. I wondered what sort of reference Energy Solutions would give me.

'Erm, I'm not local. I'm staying with my Granddad at Hawthorn Place for the summer, so I'm not sure—'

'Wally Butterfield?' I nodded. 'Oh, you must be his granddaughter – I should have guessed from the surname. I knew Bridget very well. She was very fond of you. Often used to talk about your holidays with them, and I know she looked forward to your visits for weeks. Such a tragedy.' She put a comforting hand on my arm. 'We'll skip references. The job is yours if you want it, to start the week after next?'

'Yes please,' I said, the mention of Grandma almost bringing me to tears.

Walking down the path from the house and texting Izzy *Just call me Molly-two-jobs-Butterfield*, I was surprised to see Harrison in an opposite front garden, peering out from under the bonnet of a clapped-out Ford. In his overalls, the top few buttons undone to reveal he was shirtless underneath, he looked like a male calendar model.

'Thought I recognised the bike. Can't be many of them still in existence,' he said, as I latched the little gate behind me and threw my rucksack into the front basket.

'It's a classic,' I replied. 'Like an Aston Martin or a Lamborghini.'

'So is the Trotters' van, but I wouldn't fancy my chances in a head-on collision.' There was a flash of darkness across his face for a moment, as if he'd said something he shouldn't have.

'I think you'll find you only had a superficial scratch to your phone,' I said, thinking back to our collision. 'I had all the physical injuries. Anyway, no one is asking you to ride it. It suits me just fine.' I tossed my head in a nonchalant manner and hopped on my *classic* bike.

'Hey, if you're not busy this evening, perhaps we could hook up?' He wiped an oily hand on an equally oily rag, taking a sudden side road with the conversation.

'Maybe. I might wander down to The Barley Mow later. I'll see how I feel.' I shrugged.

'Yeah. I'll probably stick my nose in about eight-ish.'

'Might see you there then. If nothing better crops up.' And I pushed down the pedal and started to freewheel away.

Woo-hoo. I had a hot date with the Summerton stud.

Chapter 29

'Granddad, I've done all the washing up and taken some mince out the freezer for later,' I said, popping my head into the living room. There was a shepherd's pie recipe I wanted to try. Pastry pies had proved too much of a challenge, but mashed potato ones might be manageable.

'Thanks, love. Maybe I'll peel some veg in a bit.'

'Your hair looks great,' I said, hoping to get him on side. He put a hand to his thinning hair and smiled. 'So, anyway, I wondered if you'd like to take a trip out with me this afternoon to look around a local National Heritage house?'

He shook his head. 'I'll pass, love, if you don't mind. Not up to speaking with strangers today.'

Bang went my chance of a lift then. I trudged out to the study and hunted for an old *A–Z* I remembered lying about. Google Maps had deserted me again as soon as I'd descended into the dip and the Wi-Fi had yet to be installed. After referring to the scale, I worked out eight miles was just about feasible to cycle, and embarked on the longest cycle ride of my life to Bickerton Manor.

It took nearly an hour but would probably have taken a more cycle-y person half the time. Just a few short weeks ago I would have laughed at the prospect of that much exercise, but somehow I managed it.

The Manor cost fourteen pounds to get in, which I thought was extortionate, despite being informed I could return as many times as I liked within the next twelve months. Great in theory, but my aching buttocks and throbbing calves had already approached the union rep and were considering strike action.

However, the house was worth every hard-earned pound. It was a beautiful example of turn-of-the-century Arts and Crafts architecture. Standing astride the bike, I took some photos of the exterior on my iPhone, noting it was built from pale Portland stone – *local* stone. It was a large L-shaped building with no obvious symmetry and strange, protruding windows at the front of the house. I wondered what the correct architectural terms were for these features.

The property was built on a mound, raised above the surrounding landscape, and wide shallow steps led to an impressive arched entrance tucked in the crook of the L. It had the feel of a property that had evolved over time, but the information sheet in the entrance hall explained it was deliberately designed to give the impression it had been around for centuries.

Inside the main hall, rustic flagstones overlapped with a timber floor as you went from one wing to the other, as if an earlier Tudor building had been extended. Clever. There was an abundance of oak: oak panelling, solid oak furniture and dark-stained oak parquet floors. Upside-down hearts were cut out from flat banister rails and chair backs, reminding me of the pansy motif that graced Granddad's curly stairs. Like Hawthorn Place, the fireplaces dominated the rooms, large hearths in deep recesses with simple mottos above, like *If you seek his monument, look around*.

Each room contained a helpful and chatty volunteer to enlighten you further if you had any questions. Some knew more than others, but all had access to a set of notes which they could refer to when they had particularly inquisitive visitors. And I was definitely one of those.

A silver-haired older guy called Michael, who had a nostalgic whiff of Brut about him and wore a burgundy waistcoat, spent a long time with me in the impressive entrance hall. He was a retired history teacher, so once I started to show an interest, his tiny black eyes became so animated they bounced about in his head like Mexican jumping beans.

'It was the last great period for building English country houses. Bickerton is lucky to survive. Many were demolished – increased taxes and the ripples from the First World War. In fact, Bickerton came close. Acquisitioned during the Second World War, it was returned in a very sorry state, but the family passed it over to the National Heritage in the fifties rather than see it disintegrate further. Have you been upstairs yet and seen the stunning original wallpaper in the master bedroom?'

I shook my head, but would make a point of seeking it out later. He reached for the folder but didn't need to open it as he continued to spout facts and figures at me in abundance, and I was pleased my previous research meant I was able to hold my own in the conversation.

'I've been researching an Arts and Crafts architect, Percy Gladwell,' I said. 'Have you heard of him?'

'Ah, a local boy. Yes, he was active during this period and was born somewhere near Weymouth I believe, but he spent the majority of his life in London, where he had his practice. I came across him when I was looking at churches for a local history pamphlet. He worked on two that I know of in the county, and they were done extremely sympathetically – quite a master of his craft. There might even be one of those yellow plaques at the house he was born in.'

Goodness. I hadn't realised he was famous enough for a

yellow plaque. Perhaps Granddad could get one for Hawthorn Place. After all, Gladwell spent over thirty years there.

'He was quite a reserved character by all accounts. There was very little information about his private life. Quite a big name, along with Lutyens, Voysey and Shaw. He had some sort of breakdown in his thirties, I think, and his health was always poor, but he returned with a vengeance and most of his best work was done in the early nineteen-hundreds.'

'So if he was a big Arts and Crafts advocate, why would he design a flint and brick house in this area when Portland stone was the local building material?'

The guide chuckled in a patronising manner. 'He wouldn't, my dear. At Steepleford parish church, he went out of his way to secure an authentic reproduction bell when repairing the west tower, and he insisted on long straw thatch on a property in Bridport, when water reed was becoming more popular else-where in the country. He would hardly build something that totally contradicted his principles.'

Suddenly, although I didn't know why, I realised Percy had deliberately kept Hawthorn Place a secret. Building it in a dip made sense – away from the road and under the cover of a can-opy of trees so that people wouldn't find it.

'Perhaps I got that wrong,' I said, backtracking. 'Silly me. I'm thinking of a house on the Norfolk coast that he designed. It's got a beautiful flint and brick chequerboard façade. Not on this scale, of course, but still really quirky. There's a funny room inside the house that doesn't have an outside wall but is open to the elements.'

'Ah, yes, I've seen a similar loggia by Gladwell in Northamp-ton. They didn't really take off, I think light was an issue, but it was a bold design and he is known for them. Do you have an interest in architecture, young lady?'

'No. Yes. I mean I'm interested but I don't know what I'm

looking at. There's so many bits of the building I don't even know the proper names for, like the pair of sticky-out windows I noticed above the main door when I came in.'

Michael chuckled. 'A lack of knowledge is easily remedied, my dear, if you have an enquiring mind and a love of reading. I'll jot down some books you should investigate. You'll need to start with the basics.' He handed me a piece of paper. 'And they are called oriel windows.'

Upstairs, the master bedroom had a beautiful leafy wall-paper in shades of green with the occasional lighter leaf, which cleverly gave the design a sense of depth.

'Morris's Acanthus paper,' a voice said from behind. I spun round to see an older lady, grey hair in a ponytail and wearing a twinset and pearls. Honestly, everyone that worked here looked like an extra from a BBC Agatha Christie production.

'Ah.' I'd never heard of an acanthus. Guess it was a type of plant.

'The bed is original to the house,' she continued. 'As is some of the bedroom furniture, but many of the other items, such as the crewel work bedspread, are contemporary and were sourced elsewhere.'

'It's beautiful,' I said, not quite understanding the nature of *cruel* work – perhaps it was done by prisoners or slaves.

'Hand-embroidered. Would have taken months. See the daf-fodils around the edge?' I nodded. 'Well, there's a tragic tale associated with this bedspread. It came from a lady jilted by her fiancé at the altar, and daffodils symbolise unrequited love. Apparently, she never got over it and this was on her bed until the day she died.'

'So the daffodils were like a nineteenth-century version of an emoji?'

'Sort of.' She smiled as if considering this analogy. 'The

language of flowers was embraced by the Victorians and each flower represented a different sentiment. We all know red roses symbolise romantic love, but oak leaves symbolised bravery, the snowdrop hope, and so on.'

'So giving a bunch of flowers had a coded meaning?'

'Exactly.'

Two hours later, having absorbed the history and beauty of the Manor, I cycled very gingerly home, pondering the cryptic nature of symbols and motifs – and how it might all relate to Gladwell's design of Acacia House and Hawthorn Place.

Chapter 30
Percy Gladwell
1895

Mrs Marston had arranged to travel to London for the day and was due at my offices at two o'clock. Consequently, my toilet had taken longer than it should: the asymmetry of my moustache perplexed me and I fussed over my collar like one of the foppish young architects Edward Marston had been so anxious his wife should avoid.

It had been several weeks since our last meeting and I was looking forward to her arrival with both fear and delight. I never felt this restless meeting Charlotte. What was it exactly about Mrs Marston that flustered me so? I paced like a caged beast as the wretched mantel clock almost went backwards.

It had been a dull morning; not only were the skies overcast and heavy, but my spirits were gloomy. Progress on many of my projects was frustratingly slow, hindered by an unbelievably harsh winter. The country had suffered much: collieries were forced to close and coal could not be transported on frozen canals. Rail lines were disrupted, goods trains overturned, and infirmaries were overstretched. It seemed only skate-makers and undertakers profited. But, now that the adverse conditions seemed behind us, I hoped work could soon commence on the

Marston property in earnest and, next winter allowing, the house would be complete by the spring of ninety-six.

Finally the hour arrived and Mrs Marston was shown through by Freddie, who still hadn't mastered his necktie, but had at least not toppled any inkwells over that morning. I spread the drawings before her.

'It was good of you to see me at such short notice.'

'Mrs Marston, it is always a pleasure. Please take a seat.' I rushed to the armchair and fiddled with the cushion. 'I have been finalising the plans as we discussed,' I gabbled, like a nervous schoolboy. 'Your landscaping ideas for the garden have been incorporated; the irregular-shaped pond and the terracing by the house. I have been busy acquainting myself with the available local materials and where to source them. I took the train to the site again only last week to this end.'

As she leaned across the desk to inspect the drawings, I caught her scent: hints of bergamot, ambergris and jasmine. So much more sophisticated than most ladies of my acquaintance, and indeed Charlotte, who splashed lavender over every article they wore. I settled myself opposite and picked up a pad to make notes, should she desire any alterations.

'You should have called in, Mr Gladwell. I would have been pleased to see you.' Her hands traced the lines of the floor plan. 'It has been a lonely season for me, despite the rugged beauty of the landscape, the white coverlet of never-ending snow and the drama of the sea. I lost some of my more delicate plants to the extreme weather, but I hear they held skating festivals on The Serpentine and the Thames again. Even Edward purchased some skates – most unlike him to participate in such frivolous activities, but then perhaps he has friends who encourage such behaviour . . .'

It was possible, then, that it had been Mr Marston I'd glimpsed in Hyde Park last month, but it had not been Violet Marston clutching his arm and skating at his side.

Not wanting to meet her eye, I began a sketch of her face for want of a distraction, tilting the page away from her.

'Has Mr Marston not been with you?' I enquired.

'He came for a short spell over the Christmas period, but his business interests kept him in the city.' She twisted the gold band around her finger without looking down at it.

Keen to change the subject, I asked for her opinion on the plans before her and she took the time to examine them more closely.

'Much of your design is charming. However . . .' she began, seeking out the front elevation. My heart sank. 'I wrestle with the irregularity of the windows. Each one is different and the roof is a jumble.'

'And you find such conformity in your gardens, Mrs Marston? Do you require that all your flowers should have the same number of petals? That each bush or tree should grow to a specified height?'

'Of course not. You're being ridiculous, Mr Gladwell.'

I gave her a moment, feeling my point had been made, and let her have adequate time to absorb my words. I changed the subject.

'I will be visiting the site again soon to meet with a local flint knapper. I have worked in flint before but the effects I wish to create with the façade need a degree of skill above mere laying and pointing.'

'Yes, I am quite taken with the alternating squares of flint and brick. The house will look very dramatic and imposing.'

'I had in mind a chessboard when I designed it.'

Mrs Marston's eyes flicked up to mine, and then almost as quickly returned to the page. 'You miss nothing, Mr Gladwell.'

'Details are an important part of my profession. With the addition of an ornate doorknob or a bespoke hinge, you can transform a door into something quite unique. It ceases to be merely an object of necessity and becomes a thing of beauty.'

I let her examine the drawings some more, whilst I continued my sketch, unaware I was being watched.

'I understand you always take notes when we meet, Mr Gladwell, but your intense study of my face and repeated reference to your notebook, suggests that is not what you are doing now.'

My guilty eyes fell to the page. I'd been caught. It was only a simple pencil portrait I could look back at when the commission came to an end. Perhaps I would find it nestled between the pages of an old diary, gaze at it and think, I knew that lady once.

'It's nothing. Accept my apologies for I can assure you, you have my full attention.'

'May I see?' She put out one of her tiny hands, palm upwards. Powerless in her presence, I passed the sketch over.

'Oh, but Mr Gladwell, I do not think this is a good likeness. You have idealised me. I am not quite such a beauty and I am aware my nose is crooked. But you are a proficient artist. I'm impressed.'

Any words that might have served me well in the following moments floated from my head and drifted out of my reach.

'May I keep it?'

'Of course,' I said, and carefully tore the page from the binding. Her face was so etched on my mind that I could easily do another from memory.

'Perhaps I should commission you to paint the mural for the nursery,' she teased. 'I have decided upon a large oak tree on the back wall that has branches reaching around the whole room, even into the cupboard. There will be birds nesting, squirrels leaping from the boughs, and hedgehogs rummaging around the roots. I had an idyllic childhood and am determined to provide a nurturing and loving environment should we be blessed with children.' She broke out one of her rare smiles. 'Was your childhood a positive one, Mr Gladwell?'

'Very, and when I think of my parents, I always think of love. Unconditional and ever-evolving love. Theirs was a love match that both sets of parents allowed because it was financially and socially convenient to do so. My eldest brother followed nine months after the nuptials, almost to the day, and Mother produced siblings at regular yearly intervals until they decided their family was sufficient.'

She raised an eyebrow at my last statement but said nothing.

'My father was an academic,' I continued, 'and spent long periods at home when he was writing and researching his papers, so had an unusually active role in our upbringing. I hardly ever remember him being cross, despite our best efforts. Even when Charlie smashed a ball through his beloved glasshouse or Emily steadfastly refused to kiss a maiden aunt, he could not bring himself to punish us. "God has seen and He will administer the necessary retribution in His own time," he would say. Two days after the glasshouse incident, Charlie was struck down with measles, so we naively believed he was on to something.'

The smiles that had seldom materialised in our early acquaintance appeared more regularly now. She had let down her guard and decided she no longer had to pretend in front of me. On this occasion, she even giggled. Charlotte would not have found my irreverent humour amusing.

'And then, as I have mentioned before, I was struck down with rheumatic fever, yet I hadn't put a tennis ball through a window or been rude in front of guests. It left me weak and I wasn't sent away to school like my brothers, my mother in constant fear she would lose me. I have never clambered on to the back of a horse and ridden over the hills, unlike Charlie, who now lives for the hunting season – his aim considerably improved since the tennis ball incident. Instead I took to books and drawing, and my mother encouraged my sketching. In good weather, I cycled about the countryside, often stopping to draw the churches and grand houses. I became fascinated by the construction and design of these buildings and my parents saw the potential for a respectable career.'

'They sound wonderful, both loving and supportive,' Violet said. She looked momentarily distracted. 'It is so very important to bring children into this world surrounded by love.' She toyed with the gloves resting across her lap. 'And yet, in so many marriages, it is the one thing that is missing. Make sure that you marry for love, Mr Gladwell. Find a woman who stirs something inside, who you would do anything for and who is the day to your night. Do this, or don't marry at all.'

And as her words stirred something inside me, and her sincere face made my heart accelerate and my pulse race, I thought of poor Charlotte and wondered if I could ever truly love her in the way Violet Marston described.

Chapter 31

Present Day

Back in Summerton, I launched myself into a hot bath (the shower at Granddad's was a perished rubber affair that you pushed on to the taps and not an appealing option) and got ready for my date. Although I'd abandoned my childhood love of pink and frilly for the black and the dramatic, it still took me ages to get ready for a night out. It was almost harder to achieve the I Don't Give a Flying Fig What You Think of Me look, than the How Gorgeous Am I? that Izzy managed to pull off.

Sometimes I missed my glorious childhood hair, the way it would coat my shoulders and swish as I walked. Other days the relief of a tangle-free ruffle with my fingers was liberating. I slipped into a pair of black leggings and a long slate-grey smock, to give me a bit of width so I didn't look like a windscreen wiper. I finished with a liberal application of black eyeliner. If he was expecting a girlie girl, he was going to be disappointed. And anyway, I reminded myself, I didn't give a fig, flying or otherwise.

I spied Harrison outside the pub half an hour later, his scruffy T-shirt stretched tightly across his chest and his hair still flopping over one eye, and I felt a flush of desire. I wondered if his attractive but indifferent appearance had taken as long to achieve as my own.

He abandoned his roll-up when he saw me approach and

ground it into the gravel of the pub driveway with the heel of his boot. I wheeled the bicycle down the path and leaned it up against the whitewashed stone wall. I still didn't have a bike lock but doubted anyone would steal Briggie's boneshaker.

'Smokin',' he said, casting his eye over me.

'No thanks ... oh, you mean me.' The stubborn side of me realised my ungirly look worked for him. But then I wasn't into being fake. This boy needed to know who I was from the start. And as Mum always said, anyone who took me on deserved what they got.

I shrugged my small leather rucksack from my shoulders and pulled out my purse.

'First round is on me. What's your poison?' I asked, determined to show him I was an independent woman as I strode towards The Barley Mow. My final wages from Energy Solutions were now in my account, and with two jobs to my name, my finances were finally on the up. I held the heavy door open for him and tried to appear more confident than I felt. The smell of sharp cider drifted from the interior, and a cold pint of draught Guinness called to me.

We sat at a small circular table by one of the bay windows, Harrison impressed that I was a pint drinker. I sat opposite him, totally unable to control my furiously spinning stomach. Even looking at him was enough to make me almost pass out with lust and I felt thankful there was a table between us to hold me in check.

'Makes a change from the girls I know, who drink endless bottles of Prosecco or variations of pretentiously flavoured gin,' he said, nodding at my drink. 'Nice to be with someone who appreciates a good pint, and doesn't insist on buying in halves – like they aren't going to end up drinking the same amount anyway. And don't tell me it's because a pint glass is too big or heavy for their dainty little hands – I know how much girls' handbags weigh.' He took a gulp of his bitter and gave me an intense stare.

'If I'm honest, I got into the habit to annoy my stepdad. He thinks beer is unladylike, so it's a reaction to his outdated ideals. Besides, after about six months I actually started to like the taste.' I shrugged. 'But then Brian is always on my case, stressing about where I'm going, who I'm with and what I'm doing to my body.'

'Stepdad? Hey, don't knock it. At least you've got someone watching out for you. My dad lives two streets away from me and I haven't seen him in four years. When no one cares what you're up to, there's a danger your behaviour ramps up just to get attention. And sometimes that behaviour has consequences ...' I thought he was going to elaborate but he tailed off.

I was starting to realise I might have been harsh on Brian. Plus, I'd never thought about how my relentless quest to discover the truth about my real father might affect him. I was implying he'd done an inadequate job, filling the gap left by a man who hadn't stepped up to the mark for whatever reason. In reality, Brian had been a good stepdad. I'd spent years grumbling about his constant monitoring of me, but Harrison's situation made me think. Surely my behaviour towards Granddad was exactly the same? I was monitoring him: checking what he was eating, constantly on his back to take better care of himself, and begging him to return to his garden. If my actions came from a place of love, perhaps Brian's did too. I back-pedalled.

'He's not that bad, I guess, but he's always mollycoddled me – appropriate given my name, huh?'

Harrison smiled a crooked smile, the left side of his top lip curling up. 'You don't look like the sort of girl who needs coddling.' He raised a lazy eyebrow under his drooping fringe. Sweet Lord. Bits of me I thought I'd left behind in London tingled like mad to remind me they needed attention. 'You look like an up-for-anything kinda girl. Someone who grabs life by the balls and runs with it.'

'Maybe.' I tried to return the nonchalant look and hoped it made me as sexy to him as his almost indifference did to me. 'If I'm with the right person.'

He finished his bitter and chewed on his bottom lip. He had lovely lips. Very full. And potentially very kissable.

He leaned forward over the circular table between us and kept unbroken eye contact. 'If that's a challenge, you're on.'

My tummy flipped and I picked up my Guinness to take a few sips as a way of avoiding an answer.

'So when shall we do some serious ball-grabbing then, Molly Coddle?'

'Whenever. I have a summer job as a PA for some guy that works from home. It's only part-time but I've also picked up some babysitting. That was what I was doing when you saw me the other day.'

'Oh, Cathy. Poor woman. Selfish husband went off with the nurse from the GP surgery.'

'How awful, but I guess all men are suckers for a woman in a uniform.'

'Hey, what's with the gender assumption? The nurse was a bloke.' Poor Catherine, abandoned with three little ones, but she wasn't throwing any pity parties and seemed to be getting on with life. The yoga and Spanish were proof of that.

'So what do you do,' I asked, 'when you're not entertaining vintage-bike-riding, mollycoddled summer visitors?'

Harrison finished his pint, putting it back on the table and spinning the glass around a couple of times. 'Had a rough ride recently,' he said. 'Lost a friend and it knocked me. Then I had an accident at work. Did for my back and I'm waiting on a claim, so I'm just a loveable, penniless drifter waiting for something to anchor me down.' Despite the humour, there was a lost look about him. 'I could really do with some mollycoddling of my own.'

My heart heaved for the troubled man before me and I paid for the next two rounds without a second thought. Normally, I wouldn't have noticed nor minded, but my funds were diminishing rapidly.

We'd both managed to inch around the table during the course of the evening, so that I was all but on his lap by the time last orders were called. He finally threw his arm around my shoulder and the plasma globe of my body shot bright blue tendrils of light towards the points of contact.

'Let's go for a spontaneous moonlit stroll down to the beach. We can stargaze. It's a pretty amazing view – lying beneath a sky full of stars and realising how mind-blowing the universe really is.'

'You are joking? It's pitch black and really cold this time of night.'

'Where's your sense of adventure? Has your Up For Anything got up and wandered off? Or am I not the right person?' Another penetrating stare. Oh, there was no doubt he was the right person. He was a man who intrigued and excited me in equal measure. 'Anyway, I have a torch and supplies.' He gestured to the rucksack by his feet. Not as spontaneous as he was making out then.

I shrugged an okay and we left the half-empty pub, Justin Bieber playing for the umpteenth time on the digital jukebox – enough to make me evacuate by itself. I was desperate to be alone with this man, but not so keen on the proposed long trek into the darkness to do it. We headed along the main Summerton street and down the footpath that led to the bay.

One of the reasons Summerton wasn't a huge tourist attraction was because the beach was quite a distance from the road, and most holidaymakers are innately lazy when it comes to their beach-to-car proximity. The brisk fifteen-minute walk around the fenced-off military training area was a long haul for a beach that was basically gravel. There were no toilets or cafés, so it was only for the most determined of visitors or the canny local fishermen.

The bay was sheltered by the raw-edged cliffs that swept protectively around it, and a bank of pebbles fell sharply down to the sea, so those brave enough to swim found that two metres in the water was waist high. It was a nightmare to walk across in bare feet, but perfect for sea fishing, as occasional shoals of unsuspecting mackerel swam straight towards the waiting night fishermen, following sand eels to the shore.

I'd come up this end before with Granddad but not for a few years and, although I'd been rather squeamish at the catching and dispatching of the fish, I loved watching him cast his line out, as I sat on an old towel with a picnic and a Thermos of cocoa prepared by Grandma. If we were lucky and the fish were in, he prepared them on the beach and cooked them over a small open fire. It was my job to collect driftwood and sticks for kindling. The juicy, smoky fish was delicious mopped up with a hunk of Grandma's homemade bread.

My tummy rumbled at the memory as I trudged behind a striding Harrison, who was only visible in the moonlight and he was wearing a faded yellow tour T-shirt from some band I'd never heard of. The man in the moon looked as fed up as I felt, and the breeze rushed across the open fields and swirled around me as it persuaded me onwards. We climbed up a grassy slope and paused on the brow of the hill, where I could sense the enormity of the ocean stretching before me from the ripples of light reflected in the water.

Following the beam from his torch, we scrabbled down the steep bank and over the large tumbled rocks that lined the edge of a burbling stream that ran into the sea. Harrison wriggled out of his rucksack and pulled a small picnic blanket from the top. He tossed it on to the stones and then placed the rucksack in the middle to weigh it down.

'Right. Last one in's a total girl.' And he lifted his T-shirt over his head.

'I hope you're joking,' I said, peering into the gloom to see who else was on the beach. In the distance, I spotted the dim glow of a Tilley lamp. Other than that it appeared deserted.

'I thought you were out to live life for every moment. Or were you just saying that to impress me?' He looked disappointed and I felt churlish.

'I don't have my costume.' There was no way I was going to get naked in front of someone I barely knew. Not yet, anyway.

Harrison bent forward and slipped his jeans down to his knees. He reached out his hand to my shoulder and steadied himself, then shook each leg off as the jeans fell to the blanket. There was enough light from the sulky moon for me to assess his lean, muscular body and hairless chest, as he stood upright, sporting a black pair of Calvin Klein's. Perhaps Izzy hadn't been so wide of the mark with the holiday romance after all.

'Naked or pants. It's up to you, but last one in definitely gets the beers next time,' and he slipped off the tight boxers and strode confidently into the sea, his firm buttocks highlighted by the reflected moonlight.

Bloody cheek, I thought – like he'd bought any of the drinks so far. And then I realised he was talking about a potential second date. Could he be into me as much as I was into him? Feeling buoyant, I tugged off my clothes and hobbled after him.

*

183

Bobbing about in the freezing black English Channel, I regretted abandoning my clothing. Whether it was courtesy or indifference, Harrison had kept his back to me as I'd dashed into the waves. It wasn't like the August sea, by which time three months of hot sun had raised the core temperature by a few degrees. The icy water was biting into my skin and causing physical pain.

I let out a shrill, girly squeal that I didn't seem to be able to rein in.

'You're so dramatic. Man up, woman,' Harrison said.

He turned and looked at me hugging my body tight, teeth chattering and my head shaking uncontrollably.

'Portlanders take a dip on New Year's Day – it's tradition – so I don't know why you're whingeing in May. Move about a bit more. You'll soon warm up.' And he flicked a handful of salty water in my face.

I ducked my shoulders under the dark waves and kicked my stick-thin legs like mad to keep warm, returning the dousing with a sweep of the arm as I went down. A mini water fight broke out. Leaping and thrashing about, I didn't even notice we were moving closer to the shore, and my tiny satsuma-sized breasts were now above water level and exposed – my skin like the dimpled peel of the citrus fruit they resembled.

The biting sea breeze whipped around my exposed body and water lapped at my waist. Even in the sulky light, Harrison's eyes were drawn to my hip, now visible above the water level. He stood still and bent closer.

'Wicked,' he said, pointing to the small swirls of black ink along my knicker-line. 'Didn't figure you as that sort of girl.'

'Why does having a tattoo make me a *sort*?' I was indignant and defensive.

'Not sure, just not what I expected from Molly Coddle. Ah,

I get it.' He looked thoughtful. 'More rebelling against the evil stepdad?'

'No.' I frowned. 'It was done for me.'

'It has special significance then?' he challenged, the waves continuing to buffet our waists.

I struggled to answer, because the painful truth was I hated it. I hated the inky blackness of it, the creeping tendrils of a flower I didn't even recognise over my virgin pink skin. I hated myself and the reasons I'd had it done. Not to embellish my body or because the design had any deep meaning, unlike Izzy, who had a small butterfly on her ankle to remind her of a beloved grandparent. It was done to spite, to shock and to make a point. A more extreme (and permanent) version of cutting off my hair. Anything undertaken with those motives was never going to end well.

'It's kinda cute,' he said. 'Like you . . .'

My shaking was now of epileptic proportions. Harrison stepped closer and a low wave hit his back, splashing up behind him. He put his long arms about me and drew me close. I felt the warmth of his skin on mine and our bodies moulded together.

Cute wasn't the word Grandma had used when she'd seen the tattoo: irresponsible and disappointing were her choice of adjectives. It had fuelled the building crescendo of our argument last summer – another reason I could hardly bear to look at the damn thing.

'You're such a wispy little creature,' he said, head bowed down so that his lips were in my hair. 'Let's get out of here and I'll see what I can do to warm you up.'

I was still shaking uncontrollably as he steered me to the shore. I ouched and ooed up the pebbles, collapsing with relief on to the blanket.

With juddery arms, I reached to my right to grab my abandoned clothes, but he placed his hand on mine, preventing it from reaching the dress.

'This is a skin-on-skin survival situation,' he said, and he leaned across me, lifting his free hand to stroke my hair. His head came towards mine and I tilted my face upwards to his. Our lips bumped and I could taste the smoky tobacco. His mouth was warm and his tongue insistent – a kiss instantly so powerful that all the mercury shot from the top of my thermometer.

I pulled his head closer to mine and felt the urgency as I pushed myself towards him. Lost in the volcanic eruption of my desires, I was surprised when he pulled back.

'Hey, steady, tiger.' He kissed the tip of my nose. 'We've got the whole summer. I'm not here to rush anyone,' and he threw a crumpled towel over to me.

I rubbed myself down and hastily dragged the smock over my damp body. The leggings were a nightmare to pull on, like a schoolgirl wrestling with her tights after a swimming lesson. Harrison had already wriggled into his jeans and settled next to me, both of us with our knees drawn up to our chests, looking out at the pale reflection of the moon wobbling about in the dark sea. There was a gush of water running up towards us over the stones and then the hiss as it rolled back to the ocean, dragging stray rolling pebbles with it.

'Here, put this on.' He tossed me a scrunched-up fleece from the rucksack and I pulled it over my wet hair. It was several sizes too big, but this was perfect as I could slip my knees under the front of the jumper, my dark purple toenails poking out the bottom. He shuffled his lean frame closer and threw a casual arm about my shoulders, rubbing the top of my arms to keep me warm. It felt good. I leaned my head on his shoulder.

'I'm still working through a lot of stuff,' he said, out of nowhere, but perhaps as an apology for brushing me off.

'It's fine,' I said, my body violently protesting that it most certainly wasn't fine, as it bubbled back down to a gentle simmer.

'Summerton is suffocating me,' he said. 'Bad memories, complicated situations . . .' His voice trailed off for a moment. 'And when I sit here looking across the sea, it fuels my desire to travel – to find out what's beyond our sight line.' He sounded thoughtful and unusually serious.

'I've seen quite a lot of the world.' I felt smug. Here was a topic where I could hold my own. 'I've been to America a couple of times, south of France, Spain, Italy of course, and the Maldives.' I hugged my knees tighter to my body. Summers in Dorset were a given, but slightly more glamorous family trips abroad had been scheduled every other school holiday: Easters in the sun to cheer us up, Europe for Mum to visit galleries in the autumn, and even a Christmas Day in Florida.

All these trips were post-Brian, obviously. I only recalled one holiday pre-Brian and it was in a static caravan in Lincolnshire. We went with Nonna and Nonno. I remembered the giant blue rabbit wandering around the complex, trying unsuccessfully to engage with small children, and tiny bedrooms with about ten centimetres of space around the beds. Nonna had a stroke not long afterwards, and lingered, an impaired version of her former self, for another three years. When she finally left us, Nonno followed within months. Nothing dramatic – just old age and loneliness, I guess. Sad but somehow inevitable. They lived hard lives and simply wore out.

'Family holidays?' Harrison asked.

I nodded.

'So hotels and tourist areas?' he said dismissively.

I nodded again, not adding how luxurious they were. I suspected he was more a flint and steel, survive on a dead squirrel and handful of berries type of guy. Recommending a five-star seafood restaurant or listing galleries worth visiting in a particular city wouldn't interest him.

'I'm talking about proper travelling. Backpacks and hostels. Living and working in the provinces – not swanning about in the phoney world presented to ignorant tourists. Talking to the natives, seeing the dirty side of town, understanding the social and economic pressures they are under, y'know?' He looked at me with serious eyes, barely highlighted by the pale moon. 'Working to earn my keep.'

As he struggled with that concept in this country, I wondered how that would pan out for him.

'Have you always had this wanderlust?' I asked.

'Possibly, but that friend I mentioned was the catalyst. Wiped out in a head-on,' he said, turning back to look straight ahead and not blinking. 'Not long passed his test and gets hit by some drunk-driver going too fast around a blind corner.'

'Oh, I'm so sorry.' I reached over and placed my hand on his knee. His flippancy was, I suspected, his way of dealing with it. To talk about such a tragic event in any detail would open a wide gateway of hurt that would be difficult to latch closed again.

There was a prolonged silence that spoke a thousand highly emotional words. This was a huge deal, something Harrison would never get over. And I could understand how losing someone so close, so young, might make you reassess your priorities. It was easy to drift along in life with the assumption that we had time – time to do things, see things and experience things – and it wasn't always the case.

'So, I'm living life for Ben,' he finally said, his voice cracking as he said his friend's name. 'He often talked about travelling – but then he talked about so many things that he'll never get the chance to do. So out of the whole sorry mess, I'm determined to live for the here and now.' He tore his eyes away from the sky-line, looked back at me, and I realised they were brimming with unspilled tears.

'You'll need money,' I pointed out, trying to move away from his heart-breaking revelation. 'The airfare to your first destination, initial accommodation, emergency funds?'

He wiped the back of his hand across his eyes and sniffed all emotion away. 'That's the only thing holding me back. Waiting on that compensation claim. Need to get some cash behind me and then I'm off.'

'Off where exactly?'

'Wherever the wind blows. Maybe start in Australia and then drift back across Indonesia and India, and finally up through Europe. You can't say you've truly lived if you haven't travelled. If the money comes through, I'm thinking end of August.'

Oh, so whatever this thing was between us, he clearly didn't view it as permanent. Yet I'd felt an undeniable chemistry as soon as we'd shared that mercury-spurting kiss. I looked across at the silhouette of his face against the sky, and wondered why I felt so gutted by this news. After all, I was only a temporary visitor to this village myself.

Chapter 32

Over the next couple of weeks, partly to clear my head, and partly because it made me feel alive, I began taking early morning walks to the bay. Although my icy experience with Harrison had put me off swimming until the sea warmed up, I witnessed some spectacular bonfire-like sunrises to the east, and sat in silent contemplation, thinking of Grandma and missing her so badly. I did a few more shifts for Mr Brooker and continued to work my way through gardening, cookery and architectural books – sometimes with a bottle of homemade wine, sometimes with an enormous mug of tea.

Harrison proved frustratingly difficult to pin down. Despite making plans to meet at the pub the previous weekend, he'd cancelled at the last minute, saying something had come up but choosing not to elaborate. And with Mum calling to say they'd landed back in the UK safely, but very vague as to whether the Americans had enjoyed their stay, I realised we were now into June. If I didn't take garden action with Granddad soon, our window of opportunity would close for the year. The theory was fine; now to indulge in the practical.

I took Alan outside with me and stood him by the vegetable patch, propping him open at the chapter on preparing the ground. Next, I wrestled with the warped shed door and looked for a spade. There was a row of garden implements resting against the back wall, all clean and shiny. I remembered Granddad telling me how important it was to look after your tools, to keep them sharp and well-oiled to stop them going rusty. Many a sunny afternoon he'd sat on the low brick wall sharpening some blade or another, his walnut skin soaking up the sun's rays, totally at peace with his surroundings. Now he spent his days glued to a TV screen, agitated by the state of the world, or lost in mindless daytime TV, and I wanted the old Granddad back.

Several things looked spade-shaped, so I grabbed the biggest one with its taped-up wooden handle, thinking the bigger the spade, the quicker the job. I carried it outside and tried to sink it into the soil at the bottom edge of the patch. It was tougher than I expected, especially as we'd had some dry days recently and the ground was hard. I heaved it out and tried again, this time putting my foot on the top as I'd seen Granddad do, but it wasn't going anywhere and the angles seemed wrong somehow. Reluctant to admit defeat before I'd even started, I took a calming breath and persevered. After ten minutes I'd got no further than an elderly marathon runner who'd collapsed at the starting line. All I'd achieved was scraping the top few centimetres of soil. Alan would not be impressed. I was supposed to be double digging – I was barely single digging.

Okay, think. Perhaps if the soil was wet, it would be easier.

After fiddling about with the yellow plastic hose attachment and jiggling it over the end of the outside tap, I turned it on as far as it would go. There was a gurgling sound, so I wandered back to water the concrete soil that was causing me so much grief.

The pulsing water started to flip the pipe violently from side to side, so that it resembled a tortured animal in the throes of death. And then it spun one hundred and eighty degrees, showering me in a freezing jet of fierce water. I screamed but continued to rush towards the flailing pipe, arms outstretched, partly to protect myself but partly in the vain hope I might be able to grab the writhing end.

'Molly? Molly? Are you all right, love?' Granddad's concerned voice came from the back door.

'Yes,' I squealed, as I finally pinned down the pipe and pointed it towards the ground. 'Hose pipe issues.'

He appeared beside me and took one look at his bedraggled step-granddaughter and started to chuckle. 'Is it time for your annual bath?'

'I was watering the vegetable patch.'

He frowned. 'But there's nothing in there.'

'I thought I could soften up the soil and dig it over, but I'd have more joy with a limp shoelace.'

Granddad peered at the small lake where the water was still puddling, unable to drain through the baked soil, and then looked at the abandoned spade. 'Well, if you were trying to dig it over with that, no wonder you weren't getting anywhere.'

Was he implying I wasn't strong enough for the big spade, or what? I gave him a blank look.

'It's a shovel,' he explained.

'Shovel? Spade? What's the difference?'

He bent over to pick it up and began dusting bits of dirt from the edge. 'A shovel is for scooping and lifting. See these raised sides and the angle of the handle to the blade? It won't cut through soil like a spade, which is straight.'

No wonder I felt like I was tripping over myself as I dug. 'They looked the same to me.' A big blob of water dribbled down my face in place of tears I was on the verge of shedding.

'Let's turn the hose off, love. All you're doing is making a mud bath for pigs and small boys to play in. And there aren't any around to enjoy your efforts.'

When he returned I was slumped on the wet grass, the hose end limp in my hands. He sat down, shuffled next to me and put his arm about my very soggy shoulders.

'I was going to surprise you and put in the seeds that I got from the hardware store.' I sniffed.

'Oh, love. I'm pathetic, aren't I?'

His voice cracked and I looked up to his craggy face. His brow was knitted together and his thin face looked pinched. 'She'd be after my backside with a rolled-up newspaper if she was here. "You lazy bugger," she'd be shouting. "Get off your arse and stop feeling sorry for yourself."'

He stared across the garden and focused on the row of butterfly-covered buddleias (a plant I could now happily identify) covering the steep bank that hid the horizon. I let my head slump on to his shoulder and reached over for his weathered hand. I wrapped my fingers around his and gave them a tight squeeze.

'I'm reckoning I need to get off my lazy chuff and dig this over or they'll be no veggies for me this year. Shall we do it together?'

And five minutes later, armed with proper spades, we began the back-breaking task of digging over Granddad's neglected vegetable patch.

Granddad turned a corner in his grief and my life settled into a routine. Mr Brooker largely left me alone once he'd let me in, trusting me to do my hours and let myself out.

'I'm not a people person, not any more, and I'm generally happier if I don't have to deal with human beings,' he explained.

'Including me?' I said, feeling a bit put out.

'It's not personal, but yes. Ideally, I'd like you to dip in and out unseen.'

'Like a housework fairy?'

'If you like,' and there was a ripple of beard as he smiled. 'I can always leave a note if I need you to do anything in particular. You're a churchgoer after all, Molly, so I think I can trust you.'

I snapped my mouth shut quickly before he noticed my shock. Bloody Holly – if I hadn't actually met her, I would swear he was making her up, basing her on a cross between Mother Teresa and Mary Berry.

'Amen,' I responded sombrely, putting my hands together in prayer at the last moment, and then blushed. Where had that come from?

After he'd insisted several times that I call him Rory, I finally began to think of him as such. Being on first name terms made him seem less intimidating and, although he largely stayed out of my way as I worked, our chats when we encountered each other (usually at the Tassimo) became friendlier and less formal. I was trusted with additional tasks, like booking the window cleaner, or sorting out a plumber to deal with a drippy tap. And he asked me if I was happy to include more household duties now the house was tidier, mainly laundry, to include washing, drying and ironing his clothes. I tried not to panic as I agreed. So the following shift I was greeted by a bright red plastic basket of dirty laundry in the middle of the hallway.

'So sorry to interrupt, Rory.' I poked my head around the door to his office.

'Yes?' He looked up.

'I made you a cup of tea and looked out this lovely plate of Hobnobs . . .'

His eyes narrowed. 'Do you want something?' Was I really that transparent?

'Erm, now you come to mention it, your washing machine is totally different to ours.' Probably. One of the few tasks Granddad had been forced to master after his wife's death was the washing – although I use the term *master* loosely, as the dirty laundry from my floor periodically disappeared and returned a couple of days later as a crumpled heap at the foot of my bed. 'Would you mind running through it quickly? I don't want to shrink all your trousers or turn your pants pink.'

He sighed and pushed his chair back. 'I'm pretty sure most machines are standardised. A forty wash is a forty wash.' He took the proffered tray and put it on the edge of his desk. 'I think perhaps you exaggerated your domestic skills when we first spoke, don't you?' I avoided his eyes and he led the way to the utility.

'What don't you understand exactly?' He had his hands on his hips as we stood in front of the Hotpoint. 'I take it you know what the big round hole in the front of the machine is for?'

'Ha. Ha.' I glanced across in case my retort sounded rude. I chewed at a thumbnail. 'This pull-out bit has three compartments. What's that all about?'

He threw me a puzzled look and then pointed to each in turn. 'Powder, fabric conditioner, and pre-soak. Although I usually buy liquid capsules which you put straight in the drum. And then select the appropriate programme with this dial. Press start, unless you want to do time delay – but I'm on standard electric. Really, Molly, I can't believe your machine at home is so very different.'

My leg was wiggling as it tended to when I got agitated. 'Ours is really old because we're so poor.' My lies were lame and embarrassing but still they tumbled out like coins from a slot machine. Remembering my dated housekeeping guide, I blurted out, 'It's a twin tub.'

'Good grief, Molly. I didn't know they still existed. Right, if that's all, I'll go back and have that cup of tea – assuming it's still hot. Your money is in the usual place. I trust you to leave at eight. Please try not to disturb me again. I'm done for today and I'm expecting a phone call shortly and don't want interruptions. It's my . . . it's personal. And later I'm going to have a session in the gym. I've ordered some more pods for the coffee machine; we seem to be using quite a lot between us.' There was a pause because we both knew who'd been whooping through them. 'They're in the cupboard above the kettle.'

I returned to the utility and tried to decipher the hieroglyphics on the clothing labels. Some were straightforward but what on earth could a triangle with a cross through it mean? Don't wash this item in Egypt?

I should have studied the laundry section in the housekeeping guide a bit better. Working the machine was only half the problem, I knew you had to sort the washing into groups, but groups of what? Colours? Sizes? Country of origin? I was desperate not to ruin any of Rory's clothes. They were expensive labels and I'd be totally stuffed if he deducted the costs of any damaged laundry from my already meagre wages.

The bright idea of nipping back for the housekeeping book came to me as I stared at a pile of Rory's rather sexy Emporio Armani trunks, surprised he wasn't more of an M&S cotton briefs man, like Brian. Two minutes later and I'd undertaken the necessary four-hundred-mile round trip. Jules Verne had nothing on me.

Although dated, the book contained a helpful chart explaining the washing labels. Most of Rory's laundry was casual shirts and trousers, and some sportswear (not forgetting the Armani trunks that I couldn't seem to get out of my mind). They were all suitable for a forty wash and didn't need pre-soak – probably because he never went anywhere to get the clothes dirty.

I put on the first load and was left with a couple of white items in the bottom of the basket; sports socks and a T-shirt. I remembered his towels were white so grabbed them from the downstairs shower room in the home gym. I meant to collect fresh towels from the airing cupboard but, after dumping them all in front of the merrily spinning machine, I got distracted.

Now that I was largely on top of the downstairs rooms, Rory asked me to give his bedroom a quick dust and vacuum. It felt weird entering this private space – a place he undressed and slept in. I gathered up some empty coffee cups, flicked the duster about, and ran the Dyson around. It was a very masculine space – muted blues and greys. I'd expected him to have the master bedroom, like Granddad, but he was in my room – well, the parallel version of it.

There was an aftershave bottle on the sleek white chest, so modern it didn't appear to have any handles, just recesses where you pulled out the drawers. I picked up the aftershave and sprayed some on to my wrist. I left it a moment to dissipate and then sniffed. My tummy flipped. It was a male scent; a bit cinnamony, with a dash of grapefruit and an afterthought of leather. And yes, it made me think of Rory, in the same way the smell of fresh bread always made me think of Grandma.

I'm not a nosy person but I started a discreet rummage. It wasn't prying, merely trying to get to know my enigmatic employer better. I slid the top drawer open and cast a quick eye over the underwear and socks, and then walked over to the fitted cupboard and pulled back the doors. The interior was hand-painted and totally took my breath away. Branches of a tree crept into every nook, and tiny woodland creatures played about in the boughs. It was enchanting and part of something much bigger – I could tell by the way the mural was cut off at the edges – and must have covered that entire back wall. I remembered Granddad talking about the mural in Hawthorn Place and how it had been painted over to accommodate modern tastes. From the fragment remaining, I could see how magnificent the entire thing must have been.

One side of the cupboard was cubby holes containing folded jumpers and T-shirts, and the odd shoebox. The other had a row of shirts and trousers hanging from a wooden rail. A high shelf at the top held a jumble of carrier bags and plastic storage boxes. As I went to close the doors, something caught my eye, peering out from behind a box. It was a large, tatty teddy with an eye missing. The traditional sort, with articulated limbs and rough, slightly threadbare fur.

My heart leapt a little for Rory. He was a great big, orange Viking invader of a man, but this was a poignant reminder that he'd been a little boy once. And the fact he was sentimental enough to hold on to a clearly beloved childhood toy was endearing. Even in a gruff Viking.

I closed the cupboard and returned downstairs, lugging the vacuum behind me. The first load of washing was flung over a ridiculously difficult to assemble airer because it was too late in the day to hang it outside. Perhaps I'd ask Rory if we could move my sessions to the morning. Holly must have finished term by now, and I was getting up earlier and embracing the day more. I loaded a second wash, which Rory would have to sort.

It was only as I plugged my earbuds in that I realised what a twit I'd been. I could have used my mobile to look up all the complicated washing instructions. Perhaps I'd been too long without technology, because it hadn't even occurred to me. If I asked Rory for his Wi-Fi code, all future domestic queries could be solved by the swish of a screen, and I wouldn't look such a total idiot.

It was getting on for half eight. I'd totally lost track of time and was running late, so I collected my money and walked out into the hall, trying to work out where Rory was lurking before I climbed in the cupboard. I could hear the shower hissing away as I passed the gym. He'd obviously finished his workout and was freshening up.

As I headed for the front door there was an alarmingly loud yelp and lots of foul words bellowed from the echoey shower, so I returned to the gym to see what the shouting was about, and caught the tail end of the rant.

'. . . are the bloody towels?'

The door burst open and, out into the hall, every bit as shocked as me, leapt a totally butt-naked Rory.

Chapter 33
Percy Gladwell
1895

Spring arrived and the practice was taking over my life – at least Mother grumbled it was.

'You've lost weight,' she commented as I returned from my brief and bone-chillingly cold paddle in the sea. She sat on a covered bench on the esplanade promenade, wrapped in fur and velvet and, out of respect for my father, still predominantly in black.

She'd already tutted at my recklessness for entering the sea out of season, but until you have lived in a city, the malodour and relentless noise of London so suffocating, it is hard to appreciate how entering the ocean, feeling the bite of the icy water, and letting the wind whip about your face is a cleansing and necessary thing.

'I've been busy, that's all. I'm perfectly well.'

'Too busy, Percy. I haven't seen you since Christmas. You used to visit far more regularly. I would have thought you might have other reasons to come to the county now. Charlotte eagerly asks after you every time we meet.'

'Charlotte expects nothing from me at the moment. I made it clear that the practice would be my focus this year, and only after that would I be thinking about marriage.'

I dried my feet and nestled beside her, the shelter affording some protection from the chilly breeze, and glanced across at the colourful clock tower, a relatively recent addition to the seafront. It was four o'clock and we needed to head back.

My mother raised her eyebrows. 'Charlotte expects *everything*,' she said. 'And rightly so. I don't know what you are playing at, Percy, unless you have hopes of another?'

I shook my head. Realistic hopes and fanciful dreams were not the same thing at all.

'Mrs Hamilton was overheard at the drapers last week enquiring about suitable fabrics for a wedding dress, and her father has made several references to our soon being family when I've encountered him at church. You may have not given Charlotte a date, or even made a formal proposal, but I can promise you she ardently believes you have an attachment.'

The final plans for the Marston residence were spread over the desk. Freddie had proved more than capable with his execution of the detail drawings, so I had allowed him to work on some of the decorative elements by himself. I remembered the thankless years of standing at a board copying plans by hand, repeatedly dipping my pen in the ink to produce perfect copies of another man's designs. It was laborious and repetitive work, and I'd knocked over far more inkwells than Freddie, but it didn't do to tell him that. The lad had promise and still held me in awe, so I was happy to let that state of affairs continue a little longer.

Mrs Marston flicked through the drawings, the essence of which she had seen on her last visit, but all elevations and floor plans had now been completed.

'The chequered façade is going to tie in beautifully with that row of workers' cottages down the lane.' She studied the plans.

'You have put so much of me in this house. It is full of whimsy and insightful touches . . .'

'I am rather given to whimsy. It was probably reading more Ouida than was good for me.' I smiled. It was a gentle tease, designed to befriend rather than alienate.

'I, too, rather like whimsy, Mr Gladwell. It is eminently preferable to the alternatives.'

I suspected Edward Marston was not a man given to flights of fancy, and my heart went out to her as I continued to elaborate on aspects of the design.

'The house has been orientated to maximise the sun and her journey throughout the day. The pantry and larder face north, to keep them cool, and I have incorporated a marble slab in the larder, for butters and meats, and zinc grills to the outside, allowing air to circulate. The kitchen has a western aspect, and I have specified unusually deep windowsills to enable the ripening of fruit by the late sun of the day. Here is the terracing we talked about to add interest to the garden. I shall leave the detailed planting of the orchards and grounds to you, however, for your knowledge is far superior to mine in this field.'

Mrs Marston gave me a shy smile. 'I adore sunsets. Undoubtedly the best part of the day. There is a warmth to them which lifts my heart – the gentle goodnight kiss of the sun as she disappears below the horizon,' she said.

I tried not to let thoughts of metaphorical kisses distract me and continued to summarise the design.

'The woodwork will remain honest and unpainted throughout, and any joints or methods of construction will be visible.' I was keen to explain any aspect she might find wanting. 'Colour is supplied by the furnishings, tiles and floor coverings. We can finalise these together.'

'The use of red brick inside the house, as well as on the exterior, is charming.'

'Yes, herringbone brickwork around the principal fireplaces – the rich reds of the bricks on the mitre arches adding to the feeling of warmth. These arches are also found on the downstairs interior doors, and I have continued the herringbone to the paths. See? A trail of brick to lead you to the door.'

Her head gave a slow nod, but there was something amiss. I could tell by her expression, but I resisted interrupting her, letting her small, pale hands glide over the sheets as she wrestled with something in her mind. A delicate finger traced the line of a wall and the circle of the tiny pivot window.

'Can I be honest?'

'Of course.' My stomach rolled over.

'The majority of the design is perfect. I love the geese, I know they will make me smile as I walk down the corridor, and the violet motifs give me an ownership that will last beyond my own lifetime. The crawling window is adorable – how I can just imagine a small child rearing up and peering through. These are thoughtful details I had hoped for, and recognised you were capable of delivering, Mr Gladwell.'

'But?' I said.

'I see before me a beautiful house and gardens. They are original and have an unnervingly personal touch – clever elements within each that complement and contrast with each other. You have converted me to your way of thinking and I feel foolish not to have seen the beauty in the asymmetry of your earlier designs. But I shall either be inside, looking longingly out, or outside, no longer connected to the house. I had a fancy for there to be a point at which I was both. That there would be some way to bring the outside inside.'

Her point was valid. I had deliberately shied away from a

conservatory, rising in popularity since cheap steel had enabled such structures. In doing so, had I failed her? I attempted to defend myself.

'But throughout our correspondence, I have considered the planting of the garden most carefully. In fact, I am much obliged to you for the extensive horticultural knowledge imparted since our last meeting, and in your detailed letters of the past month. I have selected various naturalistic Morris wall-papers, as we discussed. "Chrysanthemum" and "Marigold", with their exuberant scrolling foliage – stylised yet not formal.'

'Yes, they are glorious reminders of the beauty found in nature, but they remain merely that – reminders.'

'And see here.' Undeterred, I pointed to another sketch. 'We have this solitary poplar lined up with the half-landing window to give the illusion of a painting, the window framing it perfectly as you walk down the stairs. It is Mother Nature's obelisk. This was a direct result of your influence, whereas before I might have included a stone structure. Surely this is a pleasing combining of the two?'

'You are too defensive. I was merely wondering – oh, this is remiss of me and I ought to have suggested it earlier – but perhaps a covered terrace or recess of some description would be possible? Can we somehow let a portion of the garden invade the floor plan of the house?'

She picked up a pencil, and checking I did not object, started to sketch her idea on a sheet of foolscap from the corner of my desk.

I watched her small fingers as she made neat strokes across the paper. Yes, it could work. One of the reception rooms could easily be sacrificed to this end. It would involve substantial reworking of the drawings, but the overhang of a second-floor room would give a space underneath that was neither truly outside nor inside. Instead of a conservatory invading the garden, her idea was a simple reversal of roles; the garden could invade the house, like a loggia. I pictured perhaps trellis work and low gates opening into a space that would remain open to the elements. I pulled out my sketchbook and picked up the pencil she'd abandoned.

She moved behind me and leaned over my shoulder; the smell of her floral perfume was intoxicating and I felt the pencil falter under her keen eye. Taking her initial sketch a stage further, I experimented with a standard elevation. The exterior walls would follow into the space, and one could sit at the back, looking out as if through an enormous invisible window, and still feel the breeze dance over one's skin and smell the flowers beyond.

'Yes, yes, that is exactly what I envisaged. Can it be done?'

'For a price. Everything comes at a price.'

'Yes,' she agreed, and her eyes moved to look at some distant point the other side of my offices. I followed her gaze but there was nothing of note to engage her attention. Her head dipped slightly. Her face was so near to mine that I could almost feel the heat of her skin. There was a silence that neither of us broke for a while, and for the first time, I no longer thought of her as Mrs Marston, but Violet. She did not belong to him. She belonged to me.

Out of nowhere, and without a thought for Charlotte, I wanted to kiss her then – to turn and pull Violet's soft lips to mine, to be the man I was certain Edward was, forceful and uncompromising. Did she feel it too? Neither of us moved and the moment dragged on for an eternity but I, of course, did nothing. She was married and Charlotte had every right to hope that we might have a future together. I cleared my throat and focused.

I allowed my rapid heartbeat to return to normal before daring to speak.

'I shall come to visit again, if I may?' I ventured. 'Before the month is out. And I shall have the revised drawings. And you shall adore them.'

I finally turned and looked up at her. She smiled and our eyes locked.

'Mr Gladwell . . .'

'Please.' My voice cracked a little. 'Percy.'

'Percy, you are offering me a flickering light in an exceedingly dull world.'

Chapter 34

Present Day

In less than a nanosecond, my super quick appraising gaze took in a surprisingly fit and youthful-looking body. It was sturdier than Harrison's – the shoulders were broader – but he was still a slim build. His muscles were more defined, from all that time spent in his home gym, and there was a generous sprinkling of auburn (and I'm being polite) hair over various parts of his anatomy. And then I felt embarrassed for thinking slightly sexual thoughts about someone his age. I cast my eyes downwards and Rory's hands went straight to his ginger dangly bits, but a fraction too late for me to unsee what had been seen.

'What the . . .? You should have left half an hour ago. Why are you still here?' He inched sideways towards the cupboard.

'Sorry. I lost track of time. Here – let me.' We went for the cupboard door at the same time and bumped heads. A flurry of 'sorry's ensued. I reached for a clean towel, handed it to him and spun around to preserve what little was left of his dignity.

'I thought you'd gone,' he muttered. 'The shower's been playing up recently – boiling hot then freezing cold. I leapt out but the damn towels had disappeared.'

'My fault. Sorry.'

'No, I'm sorry for my foul language and the X-rated strip show. Oh God, please don't tell your mother. She'll tell the vicar, or worse, my mother, and then I'll be in hot water.' His eyes expanded at the thought.

'Better than the cold water you've just leapt from.'

'I'm not laughing, Molly.'

He looked awful: pale and worried. We were both adults, but he didn't know that.

'Honestly, it's no biggie.' My mind flashed to my earlier view, and my head tipped slightly to one side. Actually, it was a biggie but he clearly wasn't in the mood for jokes, so I bit my lip and tried not to laugh at the situation.

Two naked men within a fortnight. I'd definitely had my quota for the month.

'I'm off to Dorchester this morning if you want to catch a lift. I want to visit the garden centre,' Granddad said, finishing the last of his scrambled eggs with mashed avocado.

Garden centre? I did a slightly clumsy but very exuberant victory dance in my head. The old Granddad I knew and loved was back, which meant I had succeeded where Brian and Mum had failed.

'I'd love to come along. Maybe we can pick up some seedlings rather than trying to start from scratch. And it's not too late for runners and salad crops.' Goodness – I almost sounded as if I knew what I was talking about. 'If we go via the main road into Summerton, I know where there might be courgette plants. Just don't mention the tomatoes . . .' I said, remembering Floaty Jean.

Ten minutes later, we pulled into a lay-by near her bungalow. There was a fresh assortment of pots and trays for sale. Granddad wandered over to the table and began looking through the plants.

It wasn't long before the front door opened and Jean stepped out. She still appeared to glide up the drive rather than walk, as if she had umpteen encyclopaedia volumes balanced on her head.

'Good morning,' she said, raising a hand to shield her face from the sun. 'Are you the gardening granddad?'

'Has my granddaughter been telling tales out of school?' Granddad looked amused and continued sorting through the pots. 'Which variety is this?' he asked, holding up one of the courgette plants that was getting too big for its pot.

'Supremo – lovely flavour and they have a good resistance to cucumber mosaic virus.'

'Actually, I'll take the lot,' he said, waving his hand over the table and rummaging for his wallet. 'Good sturdy plants that I'm sure will do marvellously in my plot.'

'I reckon you're in there, Granddad,' I said, as we loaded the trays into the muddy boot of his Fiat.

'Don't be silly, Molly. Not everyone is on the lookout for a relationship. Anyway, no one can replace Briggie.' But I noticed he glanced in the rear-view mirror as he sat in the driving seat, and adjusted his wiry hair.

We had a successful morning at the garden centre, but unexpected summer rain put paid to any plans for planting that afternoon; it was too fierce and would pummel anything we put in the ground. By teatime, the rain cleared as suddenly as it had appeared, which was a bonus as I finally had another date with the Summerton stud at six.

'So I'm thinking truth or dare?' Harrison took a swig from the beer can and passed it to me.

In contrast to my evenings out with Rupert, who had invariably taken me to fashionable restaurants and wine bars, this was another open-air affair, and the venue was Gladwell's memorial bench.

I shook my head.

'C'mon, Molly Coddle. You've got secrets, haven't you?' He wiggled an eyebrow and looked interested. 'Because it's only fun if you have.'

I gave a resigned shrug. 'Okay.'

'Great.' He rubbed his hands together. 'You first. Truth or dare?'

'Truth.'

He studied my face intently and then raised a curious eyebrow. 'First time?' He didn't need to specify first time doing what. With that tummy-turning look he was hardly asking me to talk about the first time I rode my bike without stabilisers.

'Caleb Parker. Upper sixth. We'd been seeing each other a few weeks and then his parents went on a Caribbean cruise and left him in the house. I told my parents I was staying over at Izzy's. It was . . . nice.'

'Nice? Oh, come on, I was expecting you to be underage at least. Aren't all you middle-class darlings doing the pool man behind daddy's back, while he pays for ballet classes and thinks the only time you spread your legs is at horse riding lessons?'

'How old were *you* then?'

'Fourteen.'

I choked on my mouthful of bitter. 'Fourteen?' I was still trying to persuade Brian to buy me a pony at that age. Harrison's observation was disconcertingly close to the truth; the lure of a horse had been greater than any boy. 'Who with?'

'You don't get to ask questions. I can decide truth or dare, and I choose dare.' Damn. I had a great question lined up about why he'd cancelled our previous date at the last minute. What on earth could I dare him to do? I was pretty certain nothing I could think of would make him bat so much as a gorgeously dark-lashed eyelid.

'Okay. See that lady over there?' A rather plump, middle-aged woman was struggling along the street with two bags of shopping, looking harassed and fed up. She stopped to put the bags down and flex her hands, wiped her brow with a baggy sleeve and carried on.

'I want you to give her a kiss. I don't care what you say to her or how you justify it, but that poor princess needs cheering up and you can be her prince charming.'

'And that's the most challenging thing you could come up with?' He was already on his feet and adjusting his hair. 'Watch and learn, babe. Watch and learn.'

I was too far away to hear anything as Harrison engaged the woman in conversation, but her face went from flustered to flattered. Smooth talker. After a couple of minutes she rummaged in her shoulder bag and got something out. It was difficult to see as the light wasn't great and Harrison's back was to me. Then he put his hands on her shoulders and went in for the kiss. Not the quick peck on the cheek I'd envisaged, but full-on mouth-to-mouth, tipping her back slightly like you see in the movies. It went on for longer than I liked but they both resurfaced for air and there was a bit more chatter. Finally he walked back to me and the beaming woman scooped up her bags and continued on her way.

He leapt up to sit on the back of the bench, his feet on the seat, and handed me a piece of paper.

'Got her number as well. Just in case, y'know?' He winked and I couldn't help laughing. He was as bonkers as a box of frogs on speed, but it was certainly never dull with him. Not like with the orange yeti – all 'keep the noise down' and 'I don't do people'. I couldn't imagine Rory agreeing to this game.

I looked up at my date, half in shadow and half bathed in the early evening sun. Sinewy muscles strained at the sleeves of his old T-shirt and a sprout of dark hairs was visible through the rip in his jeans.

He slid to the seat and took a can of supermarket beer from his rucksack, and there was a click-pffft as he pulled back the ring. After several deep gulps, he balanced it between us.

'Molly Coddle, you rock my world.' His breaths were heavy and strangely sexual as he focused on my lips.

I realised he was serious, even though the words were a bit cheesy. I looked down at my hands and then back up at his intense, chocolate brown eyes. His head was tilted so his fringe slid slowly across his left eye and he tossed his head back to shake it away. God, he was good-looking. I wet my lips with my tongue and tried to swallow, even though my mouth was as dry as a month-old loaf of bread.

Harrison leaned in and there was a waft of tobacco – a strangely attractive smell my mind had connected to this intoxicating man. His long fingers grasped my neck and guided my face closer to his. My eyes fluttered and then closed as he leaned in, and I felt the warmth of his breath on my face. Slowly at first, his lips moved over mine and teased the skin – the gentle tugging of our lips and the increased throbbing of my pulse making me feel dizzy. He shifted his body slightly and his other hand slid behind my back, and then a powerful territorial kiss from nowhere. Frantic fingers wove through my short hair and our bodies pressed together so tightly I thought I might pop out the other side of him if he squeezed me any harder.

I hadn't been sure earlier how I really felt, but at that moment I wanted him so badly that I would have agreed to anything and everything, right next to the Summerton war memorial, in the middle of the village.

His bruising kisses stopped and he rested his forehead against mine. I risked a peep and his dark eyes were almost too close for me to focus on.

'Your place or mine?' he whispered.

I thought about Granddad for a moment.

'Definitely yours,' I replied.

Chapter 35

There's nothing like tip-top sex to put a spring in your step and an extra thrust in your kitchen dance moves.

'You seem perky. Even perkier than usual,' Rory said, as I bounced into the kitchen clutching the shower head from his downstairs en suite.

I now had the Wi-Fi code from Rory and had searched for temperamental shower heads, only to discover water temperatures can fluctuate wildly when they fur up. Rory had found a packet of descaler in a cupboard.

'Well, y'know?' I shrugged. Ugh, I sounded like Harrison. 'I might have acquired a boyfriend over the weekend.' Cue mahoosive grin.

Rory's mouth stopped mid-biscuit-nibble. 'Boyfriend? That's, erm . . . great.'

'I know – right? He's absolutely gorgeous. And funny.' Plus, there was a vulnerable side to Harrison, one he had only hinted at when he talked about the death of his friend. Underneath his laid-back façade, he cared passionately about things, including, I hoped, me.

'Local lad?'

'Pretty much. He lives the other side of Summerton.'

I jiggled the head about in the descaling fluid, watching the small white specks of limescale float from the pin-sized holes and drift to the bottom of the jug. The nasty chemical smell hit my nose and I sneezed.

Rory frowned. 'Summerton? Where's that? I thought I knew all the villages around here.'

'Oh, erm, he was born in Summerton, Dorset, but he's local now. Lives up near the caravan park as you head out to East Creeching.' Were there houses up by the caravan park? Probably.

'Don't let him distract you from your studies,' Rory said. My chest rolled. Please don't let him start preaching at me like Brian.

'No, absolutely not,' I promised. I didn't have any studies so Harrison wasn't a distraction from them.

'Someone from school?'

'No, I, erm . . . met him in the pub . . .' Was that the wrong answer for church-going, holier-than-thou, under-legal-drinking-age Holly? 'When I was having a meal with my mum.'

'Oh, he works at the Cock and Bottle?'

'No. He's, umm . . . between jobs.'

Rory's eyes narrowed. 'Unemployed? Promise you won't let someone who doesn't have any personal ambitions stop you from achieving your potential.' Mr Silent and Untalkative was being unusually inquisitive.

I let the shower head slide back into the Pyrex jug and turned to face him. 'I promise. But please don't make him out to be some loser. He's got all these fantastic plans to travel the world and experience new things. He's great fun. Always laughing, joking around and generally enjoying life.' I didn't need to add unlike you.

'Right. Fun. Right.' And he stomped out through to the garden room with his tea and remaining biscuit, where he sat silently staring at a clear blue sheet of sky for the next hour.

*

Rory found me later, squirting blue liquid under the toilet rim. I'd always wondered why the bottles had bendy little duck-shaped heads. Now I knew.

He cleared his throat. 'I meant to say earlier, the other day . . . me towel-less in the corridor . . . you know that was a total accident?'

'Please stop apologising.' He'd said sorry a gazillion times when it happened.

'I feel awkward. What with you being so young and everything. I don't want to end up on some register of dodgy blokes. This sort of thing can ruin careers. Not that I've got a career left to ruin . . .'

'Honestly, I'm not going to mention it to anyone. It was my fault for not replacing the towels. Anyway, I'm hardly a child . . .'

'At the risk of sounding patronising, technically you are. You're not legally an adult in this country until your eighteenth birthday, regardless of the law on consent. I appreciate you've been forced to grow up much faster than most girls your age since your dad died, but you are still only seventeen.'

Oops. Yes, Holly was still at school. I must try to remember I wasn't actually me. It was only some time later that the part about her dad being dead hit me in the chest like a taekwondo kick. How bad did I feel for stealing her job now?

The much-coveted Wi-Fi was finally installed at Granddad's and I was once again connected to the twenty-first century, although it was interesting that my love affairs with Snapchat and Instagram were fading. After an hour scrolling through my feeds trying to work out what I'd missed over the last few weeks, the conclusion was not very much, unless you counted endless pouting selfies, numerous photographs of restaurant meals, and a continuous stream of cats simply being cats. I realised I'd been part of this but that I didn't want to be any longer, and couldn't think of anything interesting to say. My friends weren't going to get involved in enthusiastic discussions about when to use fabric softener.

'Where do I put the batteries?' Granddad wandered through as I uncorked a dusty bottle of pea pod, waving his tablet at me.

I set up the charger, sat with him at the immaculate kitchen table (go, me!) and went through the basics. There were some essential apps to install and then I encouraged him to have a play. It was slow to begin with because he was too handsy and the screen kept disappearing, but he persevered.

I took a big gulp of the pea pod and Granddad looked up at me. 'Is that stuff any good?'

'Certainly does what it says on the tin,' I joked. 'Sorry. I should have offered you a glass.'

'Nonsense. I'm capable of getting one for myself. Haven't felt like drinking on my own, but you're here and I can think of nothing better than having a cheeky homemade wine with my best girl.' And he shuffled to the dresser, got out a tumbler and helped himself.

'Cheers.' We clinked glasses.

'To Briggie,' he half-coughed. 'And her devilish wine-making secrets.'

'They needn't be secrets. You've got the entire world at your fingertips now. Go into the search engine, type *homemade wine*, and you have access to an infinite number of resources. Google is your friend. You can ask it anything.'

'I'm more interested in this Facechat that people keep talking about. How do I get on that?'

'You want to go on Facebook?' I asked, somewhat intrigued. 'Why not?'

Why not indeed? I had one surprising and funky Granddad.

The evening passed quietly, both of us glued to our respective screens. I was frantically scribbling research notes down, and Granddad had somehow stumbled across YouTube. He was now on his second tumbler of wine and giggling away to himself.

Acacia House came up in a local history blog for West Creeching where notable buildings in the town had been catalogued. The description noted its Arts and Crafts features but also gave me names and a date – the house was built for Violet and Edward Marston around 1896.

There were various dated photographs of the interior. Rory's office was set out as a living room, with dreadful seventies brown curtains and a garish orange swirly carpet, but no sign of his monstrosity of a desk. I skim-read the details of each room, but I was more excited about the Marstons. Had the house been their love letter to each other? A light bulb pinged above my head and I Googled violets, the flowers, and realised both houses were full of *violet* motifs, not pansies, as I'd initially thought. (It was something to do with how many of the petals pointed up.) Romantic old Edward had filled his house with violets for his wife. It lifted my heart, while I considered another thread to the story.

Since my Wikipedia discovery that Percy had possibly tried to take his own life, I'd worked out a rough timeline that, if anything, deepened the mystery. The alleged suicide attempt was 1896, the same year Acacia House was completed, and then he disappeared until he won some architectural prize in 1904. I discovered Hawthorn Place was completed around the turn of the century – slap bang in the middle of Percy's career gap. Violet and Edward had clearly been a young couple in love (the Latin inscription above the fireplace confirmed that), but I still couldn't work out why the architect would have been compelled to build a replica house three years later, in completely the wrong part of the country, tucked out of sight and going against all his abiding principles.

And then there was the cupboard – this powerful, inexplicable link between the two houses and, I had to assume, the two sets of occupants. I thought about the handwritten words, *love will always find a way*. Was there a love story here that I hadn't considered? Could it be that there was an unrequited and forbidden love between Percy and *Edward*? My mind toyed with a possible scenario – a besotted Percy, spurned by Mr Marston, tries to take his own life and then builds Hawthorn Place as a tragic memorial to the unobtainable object of his affections?

Granddad started taking pictures of me with his camera app, which was distracting, so I stopped my research and showed him how to turn the camera around for selfies.

'Wish I'd had this last year. I could have taken some pictures of Briggie to look back on.'

'I have some photos of her on my phone. Here, I'll send them to you.'

'And I can look at them on this?' He looked astonished. 'That would be smashing, love.'

The first one pinged through – a shot of her standing by the veg patch in her apron, holding a basket of harvested goodies. 'Blimey, love. It's like she's here again,' and he caressed the rosy face of the woman he adored, whichever celestial sphere she was on. Or smart device, come to that.

It was touching to witness. You could see by his expression that he was looking at the most precious thing in the world to him. His eyes were at once so full of joy to connect with this woman again, yet brimming over with a desperate sadness and aching loss.

Five minutes later, I discreetly left him alone, tears streaming down his cheeks as he scrolled through my gallery of photographs – his lips wobbling as he tried in vain to control his heartbreaking emotions.

'Put the bloody remote control down,' I yelled.

'Umm . . . Molly said a red word,' Oliver announced solemnly.

It was the evening of my first babysitting shift and there were already more children out of bed than when Catherine had left fifteen minutes earlier. Although settled and, according to his harassed-looking mother, *nearly asleep*, Tommy had raced downstairs the moment the Yale lock clicked shut and she shot up the path to be all bendy and chant 'Om' at a hall full of other premenopausal women.

I wasn't tech-savvy at three, but a dinosaur-onesied Tommy had run into the living room, gone straight for the remote and started playing a totally inappropriate episode of *Riverdale* at full volume. I was trying to get to grips with voices for some cute kids' book called *The Gruffalo* – Amber complaining the mouse didn't have the same funny accent as on the previous page – when all hell broke loose. Ten minutes of screaming children, me chasing a surprisingly nimble Tommy about seven times around the circumference of the living room, and Oliver deciding now was a good time to kick a football about.

After my less than polite request for Tommy to relinquish the remote, I realised a red word was not a good thing, and I'd lost control of the situation.

Google is my friend, I repeated under my breath. Ignoring the noise and occasional missile, I searched for what to do when your toddler misbehaves. My eyes scanned the bullet points: afternoon naps (too late), keep calm (also too late), praise the good behaviour (what good behaviour?) and finally distraction.

'Tommy, look, there's a scary monster hiding behind the sofa,'

I said in a loud voice. He stopped leaping from chair to chair, but the TV was still drowning everything out.

'There's nothing there,' Amber said knowledgeably, peering over the back. I shot her an evil glare.

Emperor's New Clothes moment. 'Or is there?' I said, trying to sound mysterious. 'It has a clever chameleon-like camouflage. You need to have the right sort of brain to see it. Some people are smart enough, and some people aren't.'

'I can see it,' said Oliver. 'It's got boggly green eyes and *fifteen* legs.' His eyes were wide.

'Clever boy,' I said, remembering the bullet points.

'Oh, *that* monster,' Amber said, crossing her arms.

'Can't see,' said Tommy, pushing everyone else out of the way with his little T-Rex arms. I took the opportunity to discreetly swipe the remote from his chubby fingers and press the power button. Amber watched as I placed it on top of the high bookshelf, and her omniscient eyes narrowed. Damn and blast the perspicacity of a seven year old.

'You haven't finished the story,' Oliver whined, and I flopped into the nearest armchair, confident I had regained a degree of control.

Four Julia Donaldson books later and all three children were still clambering over the sofa next to me, but apparently still mega-engaged in my reading. Seems I had a talent for storytelling. Who knew? Cries of 'more' followed the final page of every book – Amber helpfully bringing an armful down when I announced bedtime because we'd run out of stories.

It was only mid-*Guess How Much I Love You* that I noticed Tommy had fallen asleep. His hot, pink cheeks pressed up against the sofa arm as heavy breaths came from his dribbly lips.

'Amber, can you be a big girl and help me get Tommy into bed?' I asked. 'I don't even know where his room is.'

Her little chest puffed out and she instructed me to follow her. Five minutes later and our mission was accomplished, with Tommy snuggled under his duvet, still out for the count. It was now gone eight, and I had two wide-awake kids most definitely not tucked up in bed and asleep. I wouldn't get the opportunity to read the historical architecture books I'd optimistically brought along, for what I'd wrongly envisaged would be an evening of easy money.

I discreetly searched for *winding kids down for sleep* on my phone. Music, bedtime stories and keeping still were listed. Keeping still? What was I expected to do? Staple Oliver to the floor?

'We're going to play sleeping lions,' I announced.

'Boring,' said Amber.

'Really?' I feigned surprise. 'Because the winner gets an *enormous* chocolate bar, which I will bring when I babysit next time.' Assuming Catherine ever let me in the house again.

Chapter 36

'I'm not working today so could you help me sort out the office?' Rory asked. 'I know you usually run the vacuum around but it smells very insidey, and I'm starting to remember how much I like things smelling outsidey.'

'No problem. I'll fling open some windows.'

There was something different about my boss and it took me a while to pinpoint that it was the clothes. He was in a pair of slim-legged chinos and a tight, long-sleeved sweater. He might have even trimmed the beard. It looked sharper. And on his feet were a pair of brown leather mule-type slippers. He never did short-sleeves, I noticed. Even in this hot weather.

'Are you expecting visitors?' I asked.

'You should know by now I'm a miserable old loner who never leaves the house. You're about the only person I ever see, apart from my parents. Why?'

'No reason.'

'Right, we need to sort through this clutter. My therapist . . .' He paused. 'My head is a bit muddly at the moment and a tidy working environment will help. Can you grab some black sacks?'

'Absolutely. And I *promise* not to sing,' I said, keen to show Rory an enthusiastic, capable and quiet employee.

He paused. 'Goodness, what has it come to,' he mumbled, presumably to himself, 'when I stop a bright young girl from singing as she goes about her work?'

I said nothing, because my music was hardly on a par with the upbeat, lyrically optimistic songs from the Disney musicals, but then angry music always made me feel better, so it had the same result.

We worked companionably together. He began sorting and filing, and kept adding to a growing pile of recycling. As he emptied shelves, I cleaned them, ready for him to replace the contents. There was no need for conversation.

Without the iPhone, which I felt would be rude in front of my boss, I accidentally started humming 'Teenage Dirtbag'.

'Interesting key changes, Molly.' I knew I couldn't sing in tune but never felt that should stop me expressing myself through music. 'Did you say you sang in Saint Martin's choir?'

'Did I? Oh, I do. Yes, that's me. Every Sunday I sing my little heart out to glorify God and all that. Love it. All those harmonies and archipelagos.'

'An archipelago is a small group of islands, you wally.' He smiled through the beard and my tummy capsized. 'Arpeggio? Allegretto? Altissimo?'

'Something like that,' I muttered, feeling daft, but our eyes met and both sets twinkled to acknowledge my error was amusing.

There was something – a moment – and then it evaporated into the cloud of Mr Sheen as I sprayed the top of a white bookcase and forced myself to focus.

I gave all the surfaces a good dust and helped him move one of the filing cabinets nearer to the desk, biting my lip every time I thought of a conversation opener, in a bid to be the perfect, silent worker he thought he'd employed. How he could spend all day in total silence was beyond me.

'Why do you need about fifty screens?' Oops. That one just slipped out.

'Three.'

'Okay, why do you need three screens? Are you into gaming? Like, an X-Box tester or something?'

'No, not gaming – trading. I need to keep an eye on several newsfeeds.'

'You deal in stocks and shares?'

'No, I'm an FX trader.'

'Like special effects?'

Rory tutted at my ignorance, which was doubtlessly rein-forcing his perception of me as a naive child. I didn't like him thinking of me in that way. I wanted him to respect me. I wanted to shout out that I had a degree. That I was sexually active and had been since I was Holly's age. And that I was going places – and not just to Bickerton Manor on a rusty old bike. But I didn't.

'I buy dollars and sell Euros, working with small amounts to minimise losses. Big sums mean big wins, but it's more risky and you can lose the lot. I don't need that stress any more. I make enough to get by.'

'From home? I thought that was a city job? Lots of men in sharp suits standing in a big circle on the trading floor, looking up at a screen shouting into your phones, "Buy coffee, sell oil," and getting angry when the price drops by nought point four pence.'

'I used to be one of those, although I've always dealt in cur-rency, but it was on someone else's behalf before. And now I work for myself.' He turned his back on me and heaved a pile of magazines from under the redundant desk in the far corner.

So Rory was a burnt-out currency trader. That explained the isolation and the penchant for silence. I placed some loose pens back in their pot and moved a tangle of wires to the side to dust the back of the desk.

'You have to follow the markets every day then?'

'Yes.'

'And work out all sorts of clever formulas to decide if the values are going up or down?'

'Look, I don't want to be rude but I'm not a great conversationalist.'

'Sorry.'

'No, I'm sorry.' He stopped rifling through the magazines and stood up. 'I've been isolated for too long, but it's been a difficult journey. Perhaps I'll tell you about it sometime – as a salutary lesson about the dangers of being a grown-up. I'm going to dump all this in the recycling and then sit outside for a while. There's a glorious sunset forming and I can drag a chair out of the garden room. Best thing about that room – the sunsets.'

'Let me help. I've finished in here,' I said, as I tried to exit the room gracefully, and promptly tripped over the vacuum hose.

Together we carried the heavy piles of paper out to the recycle bin. It took several trips, plus the black sack of shredded sensitive information.

'That feels good,' Rory said, as he let a pile of *Economists* slide into the bin. 'I know clutter makes me worse, but I've never been a tidy-minded person.' Worse than what? I wondered. This was obviously connected to the therapist slip earlier. It must have been a big burnout.

'Your herb garden could do with a weed. That mint is rampant,' I pointed out, keen to share my recently acquired gardening knowledge.

'I have a gardener, but she mainly mows the grass and cuts back the trees and bigger bushes. Since she slipped a disc, everything's looking a bit overgrown.'

'You could do it yourself, until she recovers. Some fresh air might do you good?'

Rory narrowed his eyes. Perhaps I'd overstepped the mark – the invisible one between employer and employee. And then I remembered getting agitated with our cleaner back in London when she helpfully suggested I should try 'a leedle bit harder to get a job' after I'd graduated.

'Good point. I spend too much time inside. Years of watching my pale skin in the sun, I suppose.'

'I guess gingers are more prone to skin cancers, but if you use sun cream and wear a hat, you'll be fine.'

'It's *not* ginger. It's auburn,' he said, as he let the lid of the recycle bin fall rather sharply and walked back to the house.

'Ginger,' I whispered under my breath.

'Is that why you shut yourself in a room to exercise, when you live in such a beautiful part of the country?' I continued, following him through the back door. 'Because I'd much rather be jogging along an open coastline than staring at a TV on a wall – especially this time of year. You don't have to be out in the full sun; early mornings and evenings can be the most beautiful parts of the day.' I chose not to add that I'd only recently made this discovery myself.

'My lack of enthusiasm for being outside is unconnected. And, if you don't mind me saying, not really your business.'

Fair enough. Exactly what I'd said to our cleaner, only less politely.

'Coffee?' he said as we walked back through the utility.

'Of course. I'll get right on it.'

'No, I meant, would you like to join me in the garden room for a coffee? Unless you're in a hurry to get home?'

'Oh. No, I've got time. That'd be great.'

*

Mr I-Need-Total-Silence was in an unheard-of chatty mood, so I found myself telling him how I'd been sucked into my architectural research after noticing a connection between his house and Granddad's, as we sipped our caramel lattes.

'And history is my thing,' I said, before remembering I was a seventeen-year-old A-level student and not a twenty-four-year-old history graduate. 'Well, my hobby really. In those quiet moments after all the cleaning and cooking I do at home.'

'You are a surprising girl. I don't know how you find enough hours in the day.' There was a pause. 'Especially now you have a boyfriend.' His eyes fell to the low table between us and he suddenly seemed engrossed in the twiddly leaf pattern on the tea tray.

'When something interests me, I get motivated. I've even translated the phrase above the fireplace. *Ego semper tecum sum quamquam procul absumus* – I am always with you, even though we're far apart.' I thought the phrase apt considering the two houses technically were *very* far apart.

'I'm impressed. I didn't think Latin was taught in schools nowadays.'

'It isn't. Not at my school anyway. I looked it up. Granddad's house has the same inscription. The houses are bizarrely identical.'

'Really? Perhaps they were built by the same builder.'

'Designed by the same architect actually.' I wiggled my eyebrows knowledgeably.

Rory sat up straighter and leaned forward to place his empty mug on the tray, eyes wide and interested. For the first time I felt important. I had something to say and Rory wanted to listen. I cleared my throat.

'Percy Gladwell was part of the Arts and Crafts Movement – William Morris and all that. This house was built in 1896 for a young couple called the Marstons, when the movement was really taking off.'

Rory looked impressed. This was how I wanted him to look at me: in awe, respecting me and seeing me as an equal. Not treating me like a child.

'Arts and Crafts?' He looked quizzical, so I gave him a brief history lesson on the movement and its principles.

Rory stroked his beard. 'You must tell me what else you find out. I've always been fascinated about the place, ever since I was a kid. I know it's been in the family for a while, but I'm not sure quite how long. I'll ask my parents.'

'I will.' I took a smug gulp of coffee.

'Great. And on a complete tangent, but while I think of it, Mum said one of her friends in the village was looking for a dog-walker. It would be extra money. You might even know him – old Mr Pickersgill?' I shook my head. 'The hours are flexible. And I remember you saying how much you adored dogs.'

'Oh yeah. I *love* animals. We've got hundreds at home. Including loads of dogs, obviously.'

He shook his head. 'Your house must be manic – all those people *and* animals,' he joked.

'Yes, we've got cats, dogs, pigs, goats, snakes, and erm … fish.'

'Pigs? Get a couple of elephants and a pair of giraffes and your house will be like Noah's Ark,' he joked. 'Okay, I'll pass on your number.'

'Great.' And I gave a fake grin and put up both thumbs, like the teenager I was supposed to be.

Twenty minutes later Rory decided it was time to check on his numbery screens and insisted on seeing me out.

Through the stupid front door.

Chapter 37
Percy Gladwell

1895

'Thank you for making the journey out to West Creeching, Percy. I'm so rarely in London nowadays. Edward frowns upon it and, to be honest, I find the train journey tedious.'

Having greeted me and seen me through to the parlour, Violet insisted that I addressed her with her Christian name – the formality of Mrs Marston no longer necessary since she now regarded me as a friend. How my weak heart had fluttered and my resolve to remain professional had been put to the test. Friend was a state of affairs I was more than content with, especially since she had been so indifferent at first, and anything more intimate would never be attainable.

Outside of work, Violet and Charlotte consumed my thoughts in equal measure. After many restless nights, I'd accepted that the young Miss Hamilton would indeed make a suitable wife. Frequent updates from Mother and occasional letters from Charlotte herself informed me that she was earnestly preparing herself for married life. She asked nothing of me, nor indeed mentioned our conversations, but had taken my words at face value and thrown herself into various activities – ironically, considering Violet's passion for nature, the growing and cultivating of flowers was now Charlotte's particular favourite.

But it was Violet who had been stealing into my unconscious and dominating every dream.

She motioned for me to sit.

'The more I am in the city, the less I wish to return. Even the coats of the sheep grazing in Regent's Park turn black with time. I look at them and feel the longer I am there, the blacker I become on the inside. I wish to gaze upon white sheep, Percy, hear the wind rampage through the trees, and smell the salty sea air, rather than listen to the incessant clatter of hooves across cobbled streets, the shouts of traders and unnerving horns of the coachmen. The commencing of the building work cannot come soon enough, for then I will have little reason to head to the city, and an infinity of reasons to stay.'

Her monologue complete, she looked to me and sighed. I cleared my throat.

'You are curious, then, to see what I have done since our last meeting?' I slid the top sheet from my portfolio. 'I wrestled with where to place your suggested recess. My natural instinct was to make it south-facing, but remembered your favourite part of the day was the sunset, and that evenings are a perfect time for reflection and contemplation. Instead it faces west, next to the kitchen, which equally does not suit the extremes of north or south.'

'Oh, it's perfect.' She clasped her delicate hands to her chest in delight.

'Light may be an issue,' I warned. 'But then I think we should play with this. Being surrounded by the dark flint and red brick-work will create an almost cave-like feel, and then it opens on to a veranda, here.' I pointed to the drawing.

'I adore it, Percy,' she said. 'You are truly a man of great

231

talent. And one of the few I have met who listens to our gender and takes us seriously.'

The revised plans having met with her approval, she poured a second cup of tea for us both. Mary opened the window to let in some cooling air and our talk returned to the joy of our surroundings.

'I heartily agree with your earlier assertion – there is something quite addictive about the sea air,' I pronounced, still floating from her effusive praise of my work. 'I grew up just outside Weymouth. Although the landscape is markedly different to your patch of the Norfolk coast, there is something familiar and consolatory about being near the ocean, be it here or my home county. I return when work allows, as my mother retains an apartment on the esplanade. It is my refuge when city life starts to smother me. London offices are a necessity for a successful architect, but a place by the sea or in the country is equally vital – for the feeding of the soul, if nothing else.'

Violet smiled, something she was doing more and more in my presence. I noticed how her hand was not withdrawn so hastily from mine any more, and her conversation was increasingly personal. She was interested in me as a friend, not just a business acquaintance, and this change towards me was most welcome.

'Dorset is not a county I have visited. One of my brothers studied the fossils there for a time, when he was younger. An important coastline for geology, I understand?'

'Indeed it is, but as an architect rather than a geologist, I can assure you it is so much more. Weymouth, for example, was originally two towns that over time have become one. It is heavily influenced by the harbour; even in the centre, away from the sea, you are aware of the masts and rigging that invade the skyline between buildings. The smell of the sea and the cries of the gulls overhead.'

Violet looked amused. 'And do you analyse all the places you visit in such a manner?'

'Of course. I have a natural curiosity about every town and city. Each one has a unique story of evolution.'

'I can tell you think of Dorset fondly. It's how I feel about West Creeching. I have so many good memories here that to leave it, even for short visits to London, feels like abandoning a friend.'

'I agree and have always supposed I would return one day – back to my roots. And my memories.'

'You must. You should always build your house where you feel most at home. Surround yourself with beautiful things and beautiful people, a wife and family . . .'

Perhaps it was an opportunity to mention Charlotte, but I said nothing.

A photograph standing on her mantelpiece caught my eye. I'd noticed it on previous visits, but the nature of our conversation had made my subconscious seek it out. Violet and Edward on their wedding day: he was seated with one hand on the arm of an ornate, almost throne-like, carved wooden armchair, and the other across his knee, holding a pair of white gloves. She stood by his side in a long white dress, blossom in her hair and a floor-length veil cascading down her back. Her hand was on his shoulder, and her eyes full of hope . . .

I was violently returned to the room by her abrupt change of subject.

'So what other magnificent projects do you have up your sleeve? Where in the country will your work take you next?' Her eyes were alive and her cheeks had a healthier, more animated glow – even during our short conversation her colour had returned.

'I've arranged to visit a site near Carmarthen next month, and am excited about the prospect of working with limestone again. True to my impatient nature, I am already planning playful Gothic carvings and Freddie has been contacting local stonemasons to this end. There is currently a collection of small agricultural buildings on the land, and I am keen to see if any of the materials can be salvaged. They have a history and it would be wonderful to include that in the build.'

'A new challenge?'

'Yes, but a bleak landscape. Since I lost my horticultural consultant, the garden will prove difficult . . .' I sat back, fiddled with my teaspoon, and waited for her to take the bait.

'Perhaps you would like me to make some suggestions?' she ventured.

I played my hand slowly, although I was not a particularly proficient card player. A propensity for honesty had always been my downfall. 'If you could, that would be truly wonderful.'

She smiled then.

'Perhaps a continued correspondence between us after the completion of the house would be in order? You can be my unofficial advisor in matters of garden design,' I suggested.

'I would be honoured.'

The breath I'd held in was released slowly, and the idea I'd pinned my hopes on was accepted. All I had asked of God, kneeling at my bedside for these past months, was to continue some form of contact, even if it was only through correspondence.

It seemed He had granted this.

Chapter 38
Present Day

I kicked at some loose stones and dragged my heavy feet towards the unmade road that led to West Creeching. Rory's key was in my pocket, but I could hardly loiter in his front garden until it was safe to sneak back in. As I rounded the corner of the high street, heading for town, I saw a figure I recognised. It was Holly. I remembered her pale face and dejected posture. Apparently she wore it all the time, not just when she'd lost out on a job to a surprise rival.

I looked for a doorway to duck into or a tree to skulk behind, but she'd seen me.

'Hello again,' she said. 'Aren't you the girl working for Mr Brooker?'

'Yeah, sorry about that. Again. I'm Gemma.' I stuck my hand out to introduce myself. Gemma was one of the students who flat-shared with me and Izzy at university and was the first name that popped into my head. I couldn't tell Holly I was Molly – it would just sound like a ridiculous coincidence, which of course it was.

'It's okay, I'm not mad at you. I was a bit gutted at the time because I needed the money, but I've picked up a weekend cleaning job at a local B&B, and some occasional waitressing. They help with my travel expenses into Norwich – the bus fare is horrific – as Creeching Secondary doesn't have a sixth form.'

I swallowed hard but justified my previous actions in my head because I needed the money too.

'What are you studying?' It was lame but I couldn't think of anything else to say. How's church? would have been worse.

'Halfway through my A-levels, but we break up soon. This year has been so full-on, I'll be glad of the holidays.'

I immediately sympathised. 'I remember that feeling. And then I did a degree, so ended up with another three years of study.'

'You're a graduate? Wow. The job market must be tougher than I thought if graduates are reduced to cleaning jobs.'

Arghhh. Why had I started with the lies? My default setting was honesty but now I'd contradicted everything I'd told Rory, including my name. What if they met and started talking about me? Thank God he hardly ever left the house.

'Yes, well, it's not a career move, but needs must. Have a fabulous summer holiday. Erm . . . bye then.' And I scampered away before I got myself into any more trouble.

I killed some time in Creeching but eventually headed back to Acacia House, and crept around the back of the property to double check Rory was safely immersed in trading activities before entering through the front door. But as I rounded the corner, I stopped abruptly, because he was kneeling by the overgrown chequerboard herb garden and weeding away. Thrilled that he'd taken my advice on board, I slipped back to the front of the house, unlocked the door and returned home.

Because I was earning more now, I started to contribute to Granddad's weekly shopping budget, meaning we could splash out on some decent food. So when we next hit the supermarket,

I insisted on adding some luxuries, like vine-ripened tomatoes, fresh asparagus and a big tub of tiramisu – which made me think of Nonna, even though she had always been at pains to point out it was a relatively recent Italian phenomenon and not a traditional dish.

'There's some pretty fancy stuff here,' Harrison commented, as he sat in Granddad's kitchen watching me unpack everything.

'I'm half Italian,' I said. 'It's a given that good food is an important part of my life.'

'And the other half?' he asked.

I shrugged. 'Mum has never said. But I'm not sure it bothers me as much as it used to.'

In those few short weeks with Granddad I'd changed so much. I'd learned more about life and what my priorities were by being forced into a situation I'd initially resented. The desperate need to ascertain my paternity had been a lost and floundering me trying to find out who I was as a human being, but I was learning the answer in ways I hadn't anticipated. The cleaning job proved I was hard-working (much to my surprise); the sticky situations I kept finding myself in demonstrated a quick-thinking, problem-solving side to my personality; my keen interest in the two houses highlighted my motivation and ability to research independently. I was confident – holding my own with Harrison – and I'd discovered that a caring side lurked under my indifference. I knew I would do anything to make Granddad happy and was proud of myself for putting him first – a totally new experience for me. Finding my real father wouldn't change any of this.

After dealing with the shopping, I dragged Harrison to the beach, painfully aware Granddad was slow to warm to my new boyfriend. He hadn't said anything unkind, in fact, he'd done the opposite – but when you know someone well, you realise they are saying the things you want to hear and not necessarily what they believe to be true. Knobbly pebbles dug into my back as I stretched out on the blanket, and I watched the wispy clouds trot by, ushered along by the breeze.

'Don't suppose you could lend me some cash?' Harrison asked, lying beside me and shielding his eyes from the sun.

'What makes you think I've got any more than you?' I asked.

'You've got about fifty jobs.'

'Three, if the dog walking comes off. And I'm hardly pulling in megabucks. They're part-time jobs for teenagers. I'm twenty-four. I need a career.'

'Whoa. An older woman.' He shuffled on to his elbows. 'I thought you were like me – about to hit your twenties. Didn't realise you'd slipped headlong into that decade. But it's cool. Your age doesn't have to define you, y'know?'

'Thank you. I *do* know.' Was he implying twenty-four was old? 'I'm still young and carefree.'

He bent forward and planted a gentle kiss on my forehead. I looked up at his shadowed face. There was a lot about Harrison I didn't know. He had secrets – I was sure of that. But there was something about his eyes that was fragile. This young man had things to prove and hurts to heal. If only he would let me in, I felt sure I could help.

'Prove it. Come and meet my friends tomorrow for a spot of surfing.'

'Love to,' I said, with more enthusiasm than I felt. Being upright on dry land was enough of a challenge. This surfing was not going to end well; I could feel it in my, as yet unbroken, bones.

Chapter 39

We spent the following evening at The Barley Mow, where I met some of Harrison's friends, and began to feel more positive about our relationship. I clearly meant more to him than a casual fling if he was introducing me to his inner circle. They were a friendly crowd and made me feel welcome.

After last orders, we headed to the car park, and I was relieved that the aforementioned surfing hadn't come up. It had been a pleasant evening without any need for reckless leaping about in ice-cold waters.

Outside, the last of the daylight was sinking towards the horizon, leaving smudges of plum and apricot behind. I could smell sickly honeysuckle from a nearby garden, and a bat swooped over our heads, silhouetted against the sky. Harrison lit up. No one else smoked, but a couple of the girls vaped and strong citrus scents vied with the honeysuckle.

'Time to surf?' Harrison's best mate, Liam, asked, and my heart sank.

'Now you're talking,' he replied.

'You can't surf in the pitch dark. You'll drown,' I said, and everyone sniggered. Did they think I was a party pooper? There was fun and there was stupid. A weird feeling flopped around my tummy. I was obviously missing something.

'Stop hyperventilating, Molly Coddle. We aren't about to dive in the sea. We're not that dumb. We're heading to the woods.' Harrison threw a casual arm about my shoulders and steered me towards Liam's car.

We piled into various vehicles and the designated drivers took us the short distance to Summerton Wood, about two miles out of the village. It was pitch dark, away from the glow of the houses, and the trees were a fuzz of shadow and moon-glow. There was a clearing as we pulled off the road, probably a car park for visitors, but at that time of night it was a deserted open space. Liam drove his car to the far end and we got out and stood in an expectant cluster.

'Lessons from the master,' Harrison said, as he leapt up on to the car roof. Liam put it into gear and pulled off slowly. He wasn't going particularly fast, because there was only about fifty metres of track before he turned and began a gentle loop. Harrison stood, like an airshow wing walker, arms outstretched and concentrating on his balance.

Right, so it was *car* surfing. Standing like a total pillock on the roof of a moving vehicle.

The car completed a circuit and came to a slow halt next to us. Harrison bent down and put out a hand.

'You're up next, Molly.'

'What? No.'

'Don't leave me hanging, hon.'

'Molly! Molly! Molly!' everyone chanted.

Nothing like peer pressure to force your reluctant hand. I put a tentative foot on the bonnet and Harrison heaved me up to the roof. Liam's grinning face disappeared back inside the car and I felt myself lurch forward. I adjusted my stance so that feet were hip-width apart and focused on not falling off.

Was I really standing on a moving car, after a couple of pints of Guinness, at the edge of a dark wood?

'I'm impressed,' Harrison whispered into my ear. 'Thought you'd wimp out. I can never get any of the other girls up here. They think it's too dangerous.'

'It *is* too dangerous,' I replied.

'Yeah, well, sometimes you have to live for the kicks, to remind yourself you're still alive.' His voice cracked slightly and I knew this need was connected to the death of his friend.

He stood directly behind me and reached forward to hold my hands in his.

'Do *not* turn this into a naff *Titanic* moment,' I warned.

'Now you've said it, it's gotta be done.' I should have known better than to suggest anything to him that sounded remotely like a dare.

I was still wobbly, but his strong frame leaned into mine and he gently lifted my arms so that we stood like Kate and Leo. For all my fear and trepidation, it felt good. Adrenalin pumped around my body so fast my insides resembled a Moulinex blender. High up and breathless, I was on top of the world.

We started to creep forward, and I prayed Liam wouldn't suddenly put his foot down and accelerate, but then the second worst scenario played out. He braked. Not hard, but enough for both of us to lose our balance.

I stumbled forward and let out a scream as my feet slid down the windscreen. My flailing arms tried to catch something, anything, to stop my fall, but there was nothing. I tumbled over the bonnet, rolled to the ground and ended up, like a dog, on all fours.

'What the hell?' an angry Harrison demanded, unbelievably still standing on the roof. My skinned hands stung and my knees felt bruised and sore. I looked back over my shoulder. He parkoured sideways, one hand on the roof as his body twisted to the side over the passenger window, and landed on his feet.

'Something ran out in front, mate.' Liam opened the driver's door and slid out. 'I think it was a fox. You okay?' he called to me as he swung it shut.

'I'll be fine.' I flexed my fingers. My left wrist hurt badly but I didn't think it was broken, just twisted where I'd fallen.

Liam and Harrison stood face to face. It was like something from the wild west. I half expected one of them to draw a pistol. There was a moment of silence. Was this the calm before they beat the hell out of each other?

'Now *that* was a good craic,' Harrison finally said. 'Did you see my impressive dismount?' He bobbed his head and looked to his rapt audience, spreading out his arms at the flutter of applause. He bowed and lapped up every clap and whoop.

There was the buzz of a phone and Harrison fished his mobile from his pocket, putting it to his ear.

'Don't sweat it. I'm there, babe . . . ten minutes . . . Nothing I can't drop. It's no biggie.'

The group were milling about and daring each other to be next. Illuminated by the sidelights of the car, I slumped to my bottom, waiting for Harrison to come over to his crumpled and bruised girlfriend. One of the girls realised I was still scrabbling about on the ground and walked over to help me. By the time she'd helped me to my feet, Harrison was long gone.

As we piled back into the cars a while later, I sat next to the helpful girl who'd rescued me from the dust, but as she wittered on about how long her Snapchat streak was, the sleepover she was going to next week and her latest Kylie Jenner lip kit, I realised we had little in common. My life was no longer Molly-centric. I had bills to pay and people other than myself to think about.

The talk turned to her unreliable boyfriend and here I could sympathise.

'Pinning Harrison down is like nailing custard to a sponge-cake ceiling,' I said. 'Look how he's dashed off tonight, without a thought for me.'

'Abby does rather click her fingers and he comes rushing, but then he's always been so good with the kid.'

The car came to a halt outside the pub, and I turned to her in the half-light, my mouth wide open.

'Shit. He hasn't told you. Forget I said anything. It's not important.'

'What on earth have you done to your hands?'

Two days later and the scabs were really impressive. Rory noticed my injuries as I passed him a coffee.

I pulled the cuffs of my black shirt down and tugged at my bottom lip. 'It looks worse than it is. It's only a bit of scratching. Harrison and I were car surfing and I sort of fell off.'

Rory stopped mid-Tassimo.

'Car surfing?' He slammed the espresso cup down on the worktop.

I nodded, my stomach knitting into a tight tangle. Honesty is not always the best policy.

'As in idiotic, juvenile adrenalin junkies standing on moving vehicles like total nutters?'

I nodded again, but slower this time.

'You stupid girl. Kids die doing that every year, their thought-less actions putting not only their own lives at risk, but also the lives of other road users. Not to mention the poor emergency services who have to scrape the bodies off the tarmac. I'm sur-prised at you, Molly. The longer I know you, the less you resemble the girl I thought I'd employed. Don't tell me – it was your boy-friend's bright idea? Actually, don't answer that. I don't want to know.'

'We were only driving round a car park and we weren't going very fast,' I said, crossing my arms.

'Fast enough to hurt yourself. You're lucky it's just a bit of scabbing and not a broken arm. Or worse. Foolish child.'

I bristled at being referred to as a child, but considered his words.

'You're right. It was stupid but it seemed fun at the time. And everyone should have a bit of fun in their lives . . .' Our eyes met but mine fell to the floor first and I almost whispered the last bit. 'Sorry.'

'Yeah, well, pray about it lots on Sunday and I expect all your sins will be forgiven,' he snapped, as he launched the empty pod into the bin, slammed down the lid and walked out of the room.

Razzle (who calls a bullmastiff Razzle?) was a lot bigger than I'd expected. I was hoping for a dainty Chihuahua or cute, wide-eyed King Charles. Stocky and packed full of muscle, he pulled at the lead and I was jerked forward. Quite frankly, he scared me witless, but I was bluffing my backside off, as Rory had assured Mr Pickersgill I was an expert dog handler.

'Bye then,' I called as I was tugged out of view, stuffing the proffered handful of small black plastic bags in my pocket. 'I'll be back in an hour.'

I hadn't really thought about where to take Razzle for his walk, but I needn't have worried. Razzle knew exactly where he was going.

He yanked me out of the housing estate and towards the coastal footpath. I'd not been this far out of town before, as most of Rory's errands were in the centre. The Creeching coastline was totally different to Summerton. There were no rolling hills or deep dents of land, just flat sweeps of grass and stunning panoramas of the North Sea.

'Dogs aren't allowed on the beach in June,' an indignant woman informed me, as Razzle sniffed his way over the low sea wall and nearly tugged me with him to land face down in the sand.

'Sorry. I didn't realise.' I pulled at the lead and managed to persuade him to keep to the pavement as I headed for the open countryside behind the parish church.

What I would previously have dismissed as a boring old building, and walked by without a first glance, never mind a second, was now a thing of beauty and rich in history. I'd always considered architecture a dry subject but could appreciate the church was a masterpiece in three-dimensional art. I knew it was Norman, having learned about the distinctive arches and windows from that period. The technical skill, the aesthetics and, in this case, the phenomenal age were mind-boggling – and it still stood, dominating the skyline, and lording it over its neighbours.

Razzle didn't appreciate the construction or the history, and was nose down, apparently unable to walk in a straight line. Points along the route of no obvious significance seemed to attract his snuffling nose. With his frustrating habit of stopping every four steps, our progress was slow. I looked at the hound in front of me and wondered how I'd managed to acquire three part-time jobs that pretty much covered all the things I didn't like or had no experience of – cleaning, children and animals.

I gave a weak smile to a passer-by as Razzle stopped by a wonky gravestone and refused to budge. Adjusting his position, he crouched down in a squatting position and focused intently.

Oh no.

Unable to bring myself to look at his deposit, I started to walk towards the gate into the field.

'I hope you're going to clear that up,' the man called. 'There's a hefty fine if you don't.'

Oh well, another life skill to put on the CV.

Chapter 40

'You'll never guess what I came across in the bedroom last night?'
Granddad appeared, clutching a dusty cardboard box.

Did I really want to know what my seventy-seven-year-old
grandfather had found in Grandma's knicker drawer?

'That old box of house stuff you seemed keen to rifle through.
It was tucked behind some folded linens at the bottom of the
wardrobe.'

Almost ripping it from his hands, I put it on the kitchen table
and peered inside. A small bundle of letters sat at the top, each
one addressed to Mr Percy Gladwell Esq., and all tied together
with a faded green velvet ribbon. I picked them up, slipped the
first letter out, and unfolded the delicate page.

It was dated 1895 and it contained quite formal and detailed
plans for planting the garden at Acacia House. It was signed by
Violet Marston and her tone was friendly and businesslike. The
letters weren't in any way romantic, but I suspected Percy's
heart was imminently to be broken by her husband.

There were seventeen letters in total, largely covering the
period when the house had been built, with the last one dated
1896 – the year of Percy's suicide attempt and subsequent
withdrawal from life. They were full of gardening references

and horticultural advice that I didn't understand, so I re-tied the letters and looked at the other items in the box.

There was a collection of loose black and white photographs. Several were portraits of an elegant Edwardian woman. She had a long, graceful neck, her hair in a simple chignon, and was wearing a single strand of pearls. From the backdrop, it was clear the photograph had been taken in the formal surroundings of a photographer's studio; her posture was upright and stiff, but her eyes were more carefree. They twinkled at the camera, as if she knew something the photographer didn't, something bubbling underneath the starched and elegant clothes.

I knew it was Violet before I even turned the first photograph over. It had to be. In looping handwriting she had written *With love, V.* Nothing else.

There were some family groups with the same woman at the centre of them all. A tall, bearded man stood beside her, his hand on her shoulder, and two small boys sat at her feet. My heart did a slow flip in sympathy as I looked through the remaining contents.

There was a small leather volume of poetry, two old, heavy books – a *Flora Symbolica* and a novel called *Under Two Flags* – some loose sketches of Acacia House (I only knew because the gardens were different), and a small lace-trimmed handkerchief with a pale blue embroidered *V* in the corner. A handful of childish sketches, by her sons, no doubt ... pretty buttons ... a pressed flower ... a piece of knapped flint ...

It was then I began to wonder. This small but precious box of tokens was obviously treasured if Grandma had found it hidden away at the back of the tiny cupboard. And, let's face it, you don't hang on to someone's handkerchief unless it means something. These items were treasured by Percy and they were largely linked to Violet – not Edward. Perhaps my assumption about his sexuality had been wrong. Perhaps he'd been in love with Violet but she'd not been able to return that love. The more I thought about it, the more it made sense. Silly old Wikipedia had jumped to the wrong conclusion. Violet had been happily married to Edward, they'd had two sons, and poor old Percy, bereft, had tried to end his own life. It suddenly seemed obvious to me why he had built Hawthorn Place: if he couldn't have the woman he loved, he could build a replica of her house and imagine himself near to her.

And, of course, tuck it out of sight so that no one would ever know.

'I'm totally not the jealous sort but I'm curious, when you disappeared after the car surfing, where did you go?' I asked Harrison, a few days later. We were in Granddad's garden, now a tidier, thriving idyll in contrast to its former self.

'Hey, why the inquisition?' His face scrunched up under my questioning gaze. 'I was helping out a mate.'

'A mate you call babe?'

'Yeah. A mate I call babe.'

'Okay, but you keep disappearing home early or telling me you're busy at odd times, when I know damn well you aren't working.' I sighed. 'If you're seeing somebody else, just tell me.'

'Honey, if I was seeing someone else, I probably would tell you.' I didn't like the probably, or that seeing someone else wasn't potentially a big deal. 'However, since you've brought the subject up, I need a favour,' Harrison said, reclining in a wooden-framed, canvas-covered, stripy deckchair. Granddad had unearthed a pair of them from the back of the shed, muttering about how in his day young men worked for a living.

I folded my arms across my chest and stared at the verdant vegetable patch as if my precious crops were going to grow and ripen before my very eyes.

'I haven't got any money,' I lied. 'I gave my last cash to Granddad for petrol.'

'It's not money. It won't cost you anything, just a couple of hours of your time.'

I narrowed my eyes, wondering where this was going.

'Because you're so popular with Cathy's kids, I told Abby you'd have my little Freya for a couple of hours next Monday morning. I said you wouldn't charge because it's helping a friend. I'm taking Abs to the hospital for a thing. Not a great place to take a little one.' He shuffled his wallet from his back pocket and flipped it open to reveal a cute picture of a rosy-cheeked toddler with jet-black ringlets and a smile that would melt any disgruntled girlfriend's heart – if she wasn't about to go ballistic at the news her boyfriend had a child with another woman.

'Oh. My. God. You have a daughter?' *Finally* his admission about Abby, but only because he needed a favour. The cheek of it. Volunteering me to look after a daughter he hadn't even seen fit to mention, *and* expecting me to do it for free.

'Sort of.'

I was horrified. 'How can you *sort of have* a daughter? Either you do or you don't.' This was typical of Harrison. Refusing to take responsibility. 'Just because it doesn't suit your carefree, float-on-the-breeze, wild and wacky lifestyle. You can't be a dad some of the time and a bloody great big kid the rest. Honestly, you really take the chocolate-covered biscuit.'

'She's not mine. Chill out.'

'I . . . I don't understand.'

'When Abby found out she was pregnant she was seeing a couple of guys. I was one of them. There was this period of a few weeks when none of us knew who was the daddy. I don't mind admitting, I was worried at the time. Anyway, turned out

250

to be some loser who shot off faster than a NASA rocket when she worked it out. And I felt sorry for her – on her own at sixteen with a kid – so I stuck around and did what I could to help. Bit of babysitting, that kind of thing.'

Wow. I wasn't expecting that. He did have a conscience under that *whatever* façade.

'Sorry, I assumed . . .'

'It's cool. Lots of people do. Abby appreciates it and Freya's such a sweetheart. Sometimes I wish she was mine, perhaps I'd have made different life choices, but Abby and I wouldn't have lasted. She's not my sort, y'know? Bit high maintenance. But we jog along as mates and I promised I'd always be there for her and Freya.'

'Except when you're thousands of miles away, finding yourself on the other side of the world.'

'Yeah. Except for then.' He scraped at a flake of peeling varnish on the arm of the deckchair and looked across the garden. For a moment he was thoughtful, and then he spun back to me. 'So can I tell her you said okay?'

'I suppose so.' How could I possibly refuse after the sob story?

We sat together, me with my head back, looking up at the clear, uncluttered blue sky, as he swiped open his phone and flicked through pictures of faraway places.

'Did I tell you that Granddad's house is one of a pair?' I said.

'Hmm . . .' He wasn't listening, now that he'd got what he wanted, but it didn't matter. I was sorting things through in my own head. Talking out loud helped me clarify things.

'An architect built one for a wealthy young couple at the end of the nineteenth century on the Norfolk coast. This is an exact copy, to the extent I believe Norfolk building materials were shipped down here to ensure everything, down to the last hinge, was identical.'

251

'Identical to what?' Harrison was half-listening, but the phone held the majority of his attention.

'A house up in Norfolk. Grandma found some letters years ago that show it was a collaboration between the architect and the lady of the house. I'm wondering if he was secretly in love with her – even though she clearly adored her husband. An unrequited love that he never got over.'

'That's probably why it's covered in all those ridiculous hearts and flowers then. Look, there's a working holiday scheme in New Zealand that lets you stay for up to a year if you're between eighteen and thirty.' He waved his screen at me. 'Fancy it?'

'Are you listening to me?'

'There's nothing holding us back, Molly Coddle. We're as free as leaves in the breeze. And you said your cleaning job was a drag.'

'That's not exactly what I said. I mentioned Rory was a difficult man, but I've got to grips with it now and it's not so bad. Rory's really . . .' What were my feelings for that ginger recluse? '. . . nice.'

He put the phone on his lap and leaned forward. 'So what's he like? You're always going on about him.'

'Middle-aged. Quiet. A bit sad really. And I don't go on about him. Much.'

Harrison's posture relaxed slightly. 'Where did you say his house was again?'

'Less than five minutes from here,' I said, choosing my words very carefully, not wanting to tell a lie or be too specific. 'It's convenient and pays better than minimum wage.'

'But if you only do six hours a week, it's not a proper job.'

'It's six hours a week more than you do,' I huffed. 'Plus, I do the babysitting and dog walking. It all adds up.'

'I'm incapacitated. Back injury. You know the story.'

Story being the appropriate word. Not so incapacitated he couldn't frolic about in the sea, ride on the roof of a car, or partake in some pretty athletic sex.

'Anyway, enough talking.' He leaned forward and bent over my chair, his lips in my hair, working towards my ear and tugging at my earlobes with his teeth. Thoughts of the athletic sex returned to the forefront of my mind.

I forgot all about the house, Rory and Granddad, and focused instead on Harrison and the tantalising things he was doing with his hands.

Chapter 41

Percy Gladwell

1895

Mother came to town for a week in June and brought Charlotte along, as the rather sheltered Miss Hamilton had never visited the city before and Mother was, I think, glad of a travelling companion. The days that I was working, the pair visited all the usual tourist attractions, and the weather was favourable enough for them to walk along The Serpentine, as they were hopeful of catching a glimpse of the Queen – the park being a favourite of Her Majesty.

On the Saturday, the first full day I was at liberty to spend with them, I suggested the theatre as a pleasant way to spend an afternoon.

'I am sorry for the Wilde scandal,' I said, after flicking through *The Times*. '*The Importance of Being Earnest* was a triumph and I should have liked you both to see it.'

Charlotte gave an audible gasp. 'Wilde is a sinner of the very worst kind, who deserves no endorsement, and I am disappointed in your praise of him, Percy.'

'I merely express my admiration for the play,' I said gently. 'I pass no judgement on his private life.'

'This cannot continue,' she said, in an uncharacteristically confident manner. 'You must consider how your bold opinions will affect me when we are together. There are some sentiments suitable for a good Christian and some that are not. I fear there is a lot about your lifestyle that will have to change in the coming months, Percy. A comedy, indeed.' She tutted. 'Whatever next? A burlesque show?'

Mother looked at me then – a woman who had always encouraged magnanimity towards others and embracing a variety of life experiences, not all of which God might necessarily approve. I often wonder if that was the point she regretted her meddling and stubborn insistence that Charlotte would make a satisfactory wife. For my part, I remained unsettled and confused. How could a simple request for more time to assess our relationship have become a definite proposal in Charlotte's mind? Although I had warmed to the idea of marriage, I still had yet to make any formal offer.

'Besides, I am possibly more suited to a drama,' Charlotte concluded. 'I can never quite see the humour in comedies.' She smoothed her skirts and looked agitated.

I caught my mother's eye but said nothing. For the first time, I began to worry that a marriage without humour was not a marriage at all, but a sentence.

Work was well under way on Violet's property as summer swept us up in her arms. The practice was growing and I took on a further apprentice to help me keep on top of the increased volume of work. Freddie was sent to West Creeching to oversee the groundworks and I was kept busy with the Carmarthen commission.

'This arrived for you, sir.' The new lad appeared in my office doorway with a large brown paper parcel, nearly dropping it as he handed it over.

Mother and Charlotte had returned to Dorset the previous

week: Mother unable to bring herself to embrace me as she departed, doubtless feeling guilty for the tangled mess of my love life, and Charlotte merely standing on the platform and nodding her farewell, almost certainly convinced any form of pre-marital physical contact would outrage God and condemn us both to hell.

I opened the proffered parcel and found inside a beautiful cobalt blue, gilt-embossed edition of the *Flora Symbolica* with a handwritten inscription on the first page.

A Rosetta stone for my hieroglyphs. V.

Although it was a kind thought, and a volume I would treasure purely because it was a gift from Violet, I wasn't sure why I would need to know in such detail the language of flowers, but I smiled at the Rosetta stone reference. It had been mentioned in a novel we'd both read and had naturally led to a conversation about how this ancient civilisation had consumed our nation for most of the century. My fingers traced the flowing lines of her words and the volume was not more than a yard from me for the remainder of the day – anything to imagine she was near.

We corresponded regularly and I lived entirely for the small cream envelopes in her delicate hand being passed over to me by Freddie. Initially, our letters were confined to her advice regarding gardening aspects of my new commissions, and to her planned planting at the house – which, despite several discussions, she had yet to name.

Through Violet, I started to acquire a deeper understanding of horticulture: the thoughtful use of colour themes in different areas of the garden, and planning ahead for the seasons when each plant would be at its best. She talked of her ideas for a south-facing summer border and a clever chequerboard herb garden to match the façade of the house, and her use of water-colour sketches gave me a sense of the completed designs.

I finally returned to West Creeching in the late summer. The builder was a curious fellow, who spoke with such a broad dialect that I sometimes had difficulty understanding him, but he was amiable and extremely competent. I tried my hand at flint knapping, always keen to have a better understanding of the materials and finishes I specified. Although the progress on site was slower than anticipated, I was satisfied; I'd chosen the craftsmen well. They had hundreds of years of experience between them and genuine pride in their work. No machine-made products could produce such quality finishes, such raw and honest work.

I took my time, inspecting and questioning, even though I could not wait to visit Violet at the cottage, rather like a gift that you delay unwrapping, because once unwrapped you cannot go back and live through the thrill of anticipation a second time. After a hearty lunch, purchased down by the harbour, I undertook the ten-minute walk to her house.

I was conscious of an invisible hourglass with tiny grains of sand trickling through one chamber and into the other. It lurked on the periphery of my mind every waking hour. This is how I measured the time I had left with Violet, and the bottom chamber contained considerably more sand than the top.

'Did you receive my gift, Percy?' she enquired as she directed me to a chair. She looked thinner than I remembered, and slightly peaky.

'I did indeed – thank you. A glorious volume from which I'm sure I will learn much.'

'Mind you use it,' she said, looking at me in a curious manner. 'The language of flowers is a beautiful and symbolic thing.'

'Of course, it is greatly treasured already.' She smiled at that. 'And in return, I have a small volume of poetry for you,' and I handed her a leather-bound book of verse that I'd purchased in London with her in mind. 'It begins with a medieval poem that always manages to move me to tears. I hope you find it equally stirring.'

I handed her the book and she opened it at the first page.

'*To VM from PSG*,' she read aloud. I'd kept the inscription simple. 'What does the S stand for? Simon? Stephen?'

'Samuel.'

'A solid biblical name.' She turned over the pages to the first poem. '*For weal or woe, I will not flee To love the heart, that loveth me . . .*' she began.

'Read it later,' I begged, 'after I'm gone.' We locked eyes and she nodded her understanding.

'Is it you I have to thank for the recent Hertfordshire enquiry?' I asked, as she settled herself in a low upholstered chair opposite me and I took my seat.

A little pink flooded to her unusually pale cheeks. 'Edward and I were invited to some self-important industrialist's large country manor last weekend and I took the opportunity to recommend you for their planned extension. It would be quite a coup should you be able to secure it, Percy.'

Mary, the epitome of discretion, placed a tray on the side table and withdrew. I glanced at my pocket watch, working out how long I had in Violet's company before I needed to leave for the London train.

Violet poured us both tea and cut two slices of cake. It smelled delicious – a hearty fruit loaf for a hearty day's work.

'How is Edward?' I asked, feeling remiss not to have enquired after her husband upon arrival.

'He is busy.' She didn't meet my eyes. 'Affairs in London

continue to occupy much of his time, but he tries to come up at least once a month, and occasionally we stay with friends, like last weekend, but it's always for the furtherance of the business and I generally find the company dull.'

'And self-important.'

Her cheeks coloured and the corner of her delicate mouth twitched. 'But much of the time, I am alone. Don't misunderstand. I'm happy in this beloved county, but it is a shame Edward's . . . work keeps him tied to the city so.'

What an awful excuse for a marriage. Although I didn't feel the same powerful draw to Charlotte as I did to Violet, I would never leave her abandoned in a far-flung corner of the country – however beautiful that corner might be. But then we both knew Edward had other demands on his time, and they weren't all business related.

We discussed the house, and then the recipe of the cake, although Violet's remained untouched, which was unusual for her. I stood to stretch my legs and wandered to the window. The sky was haunting. Dark clouds had moved overhead, as if to remind me there were gloomy days to come. Days when I would no longer have cause to visit Violet Marston. I stood for some time contemplating this, until she crossed the room to share the aspect, but her shoe caught on the rug. I saw her struggle with her balance for a moment and was swift to catch her before she fell.

Time stood still for those brief seconds that I held her in my arms. No words were spoken by either party, but we held such a glorious interchange with the one, unbroken look that we shared. A grain of sand from the hourglass was suspended in mid-air between the two chambers. Time allowed us a precious second that stretched over what seemed like minutes. Words can bluster over emotions, bodies can shy away from the thing you are pulled to, but eyes will always expose the raw truth, even if the owner does not want you to know that truth. I studied her lips then, as I am certain she studied mine. I noticed them quiver, heard her breaths deepen, saw them part slightly wider. She tore her gaze from mine, but it was too late. I knew.

When holding her was no longer viable for either my back or propriety's sake, I pulled her upright and we parted.

Her shaking hand was placed on the mahogany tilt-top table that stood upon the offending rug.

'I am a good Catholic, Mr Gladwell.' For that one moment she reverted to my surname, distancing herself from me. 'And I take the vows I made before God very seriously.'

'I know,' I whispered.

I did not dare add Violet, or even Mrs Marston.

Chapter 42

Present Day

A couple of contented weeks rolled by. Harrison and I hung out a lot – warm afternoons on the beach and fun evenings down The Barley Mow – and I saw more of Rory as he spent less time in his study, instead following me about, increasingly chatty and interested in the world outside his multiple screens.

'You're so lazy,' I said, as Rory joined me in the utility and tossed a damp towel into the laundry basket.

'How can I be lazy when I've just done an intensive half-hour workout?' He'd come straight from his home gym, and looked unexpectedly appealing, sporting the Just Out of the Shower look.

'Yes, in your own home, but do you ever leave these four walls?' I wanted him to share my newly discovered joy of being outside and distancing myself from technology. My spirits were lifted by my walks down to Summerton beach, or even simply pottering about the garden with Granddad.

'Generally, no, I avoid going outside.'

'That's madness. You live in such a beautiful part of the country, all sea air and open landscape, perfect for running or cycling. But you shut yourself in this big, old house and don't interact with anyone.'

I grabbed the peg bag, and opened the washing machine to

pull the damp clothes into a plastic washing basket. It was a gusty day and with any luck this load would be dry before I left.

His voice got unexpectedly teacher-firm. 'No, Molly, I don't. But you know nothing about me and so aren't in a position to pass any comment on my lifestyle choices. You have absolutely no idea what I've been through.'

I knew he'd been through something difficult – his previous slip that he was seeing a therapist suggested as much – but I'd hit a raw nerve and didn't want to pry or make him feel uncomfortable.

Instead, I focused on the wet washing, but as I bent forward, I felt my scarlet top ride above the waistline of my black and white graffiti-style leggings, exposing my right hip and my unwanted artwork. I hastily tugged the top down, but it was too late.

'You've got pen all over your . . . oh my God, it's not pen . . . Is it real?' His brow was furrowed and his nostrils flared.

'It's not something I'm proud of, okay? But it's not worth getting in a tizzy about.'

'Did this Harrison persuade you to get it?' He started to be a bit shouty, which was really unlike him. 'Did you lie to them? Tell them you were eighteen?'

Ah yes, it was illegal to get tattooed as a minor. Oops. Again.

'Don't tell me not to pass judgement and then do the same to me.' I started to be shouty in return, which sadly was *exactly* like me.

'Don't speak to me like that, young lady. You need to make considerably better life choices, starting with the drop-out boyfriend and your dangerous pranks. You're a bright girl, Molly. That much is obvious. You have an enquiring mind and a willingness to learn. Look how you've applied yourself to researching the house. I can see you going to university and coming out with a good degree.' I gulped. 'But you have no career plan beyond finishing your A-levels. You're not at all what I expected from Mrs Gammell's recommendation, and I can only think this Harrison –' he spat the name out as if it was a contagious disease – 'is the one pulling you down.'

I was livid. How dare he lecture me?

'Just because you're older than me doesn't mean you can boss me about. You're not my father.' Although there was a part of me that considered every man over fifty was a potential candidate. He glared at me and I glared back even harder. Then I picked up my duster and stormed out.

Moments later I heard Rory enter the living room behind me. I didn't turn around but carried on my frantic dusting, the yellow duster flicking madly about with no purpose, so that the dust floated up in crazy swirls and settled in the same place. I gave an angry squirt of the furniture polish and then coughed because I hadn't realised the nozzle was pointing towards my face.

'I had no right. I'm sorry.' His chocolatey voice was low and gentle, giving me pause for thought.

'No, I'm sorry. I had no more right to pass judgement on you than you did on me,' I said, turning to face him. 'I was trying to help in my cack-handed way. I thought a bit of fresh air and meeting people would be good for you. As for the tattoo, it was *my* mistake. No one else's. I had, erm . . . false ID. You can't blame the tattooist. I did this silly thing to my body, and I have to look at it every single day, to remind me of my stupidity.' I shrugged and hoped he could see I was being genuine.

He locked eyes with me – a strange look that I couldn't decipher, but that disconcerted me.

'You're not the only one,' he said, and rolled up both sleeves to reveal a criss-cross of white bumpy scars across his wrists, and I was shocked that Rory had self-harmed in the past. Goodness. I'd really stumbled across a whole can of wriggly worms and spilled them over the carpet. It certainly explained why I'd never seen him in T-shirts.

He rested one hand on the back of the sofa and sighed. 'I had a breakdown – not a term used by the medical profession, but that's what it was. There was a lot going on in my life at that time. I'd just come out of a difficult relationship, was drinking heavily and surviving on very little sleep, but the pressures of my job were the tipping point. I'd wrongly equated happiness with material success, and hadn't noticed the mounting pressure and my increasing inability to cope. The headaches, the stomach ulcer, the insomnia ... I didn't know how to ask for help, until one day I stopped functioning. I remember hiding out in the men's cubicle at work for several hours until my boss came looking for me. He took me back to my desk, helped me to collect what I needed, and insisted he didn't want to see me again in the office until I'd been to my GP. I thought he was going to fire me, but instead he said to take all the time I needed. Perhaps he'd seen it coming: the weight loss, social withdrawal and random outbursts of temper ...'

I processed the information as he paused, perhaps considering how much he wanted to share.

'It was a long road to recovery. There were days when I couldn't even get out of bed, and I'm not exaggerating. Even that simple task was a massive deal when I did it for the first time. Things you don't even stop to think about, I had to work at: getting dressed, eating properly, eventually having a purpose to my day by working again ...' His body language became defensive as he crossed his arms, and his features sank even further into that mass of ginger and grey.

He rubbed at his temple.

'Oh, Rory. I had no idea.' I flung my arms about him, employing the family philosophy that a hug helps with most things. He froze for a moment, doubtless stunned by the young girl about his waist, but then he patted my shoulder and I felt the warm buzz of his skin on mine.

It occurred to me that hugging your boss was inappropriate, so I let my arms drop to my sides.

'Sorry, my Italian side coming through. We're embarrassingly tactile.'

He raised both eyebrows as he took a step away from me.

'I didn't realise you had Italian heritage?' he said, perhaps keen to change the topic of conversation.

'My mum's parents were post-war immigrants from Puglia. Can't you tell by my Mediterranean colouring? If I hadn't had a hissy fit a couple of years ago and cut off all my hair, you'd see it more.'

'I thought your mum was fair-haired?'

Dammit. Holly was photobombing my life again.

I cleared my throat. 'Yes, well, genetics can be a bit random.'

'True enough. No one can work out where my hair came from.' He ran a hand through his orange mane. It badly needed a trim. How did he manage things like haircuts? You couldn't order them online, but then judging by the state of it, he probably did it himself.

'No one else in your family is ginger?'

'It's *not* ginger. It's auburn.'

'As in a packet of auburn biscuits? Or the famous dance partner of Fred Astaire – Auburn Rogers? Run, run, as fast as you can,' I chanted. 'You can't catch me—'

Rory put up a commanding hand. 'Enough! I get the picture.' But he was smiling, really smiling, and I was pleased we'd moved on from his distressing revelation. It was something I would give more thought to later, but in the meantime, my tummy leap-frogged my heart as I picked up the polish again.

'Anyway, must get on.' I rubbed at the coffee table like mad, just to make sure it was thoroughly polished.

'We're good, Molly?'

'Absolutely. I'm sure neither of us meant anything unkindly.'

As he slipped back into the hall, I thought about the accusations he'd levelled at me. I *was* drifting in life, like Harrison, and didn't have a plan. Strange as it sounded, I wanted Rory to be proud of me. Perhaps I had a bit of a father complex and Rory was slipping into that role, but then it was hardly surprising since mine had never been on the scene.

Granddad came bounding into the garden room, where I was sitting immersed in the *Flora Symbolica*, feet curled under me. I'd found an inscription inside referencing the Rosetta stone, and I was feeling particularly smug for realising it was the key to deciphering her letters. After a couple of hours, and with a notebook and pencil by my side, I realised that Violet was a woman trapped in an unhappy marriage in an era when wedding vows were sacrosanct. There was no other conclusion to draw but that Violet and Percy were in love; even her house name confirmed this. Acacia meant secret love, and poor old Percy, building this house a few years later, had named it after a tree that represented hope. Two people who couldn't be together, but he'd held on to that one emotion that keeps us from spiralling into total despair. It was tragic.

'Monty Don re-Twittered me!' Granddad announced, and I closed the book to give my darling grandparent my full attention. He was nearly as addicted to the tablet as he had been to the TV. Out of the frying pan and into the social media time-suck.

'And I've got forty-two followers now. Not exactly Lady Gogo proportions, but I'm making new friends all the time.'

'Virtual friends,' I pointed out. 'How about some real-life ones as well?' The problem with being such a devoted couple was Grandma and Granddad hadn't needed anyone else to make them happy. All very well until one of you selfishly bows out of the game at the kitchen table. Granddad knew a lot of people in Summerton – inevitable after living there for so many years – but there wasn't anyone he could nip down to The Barley Mow with for a swift half, or take to the garden centre – apart from me, and I wouldn't be in Dorset for ever.

'Thought I might give lasagne a go. Great recipe on the You-Tube. And I've been Goggling ideas for the veggies come harvest time. Did you know you could roast broccoli?'

'How about *Googling* housework?' I teased. 'I've been helping you in the garden. You can help me around the house. We could tackle the attic tomorrow?' I was determined to leave him with an uncluttered house at the end of the summer – which suddenly didn't seem so far away.

Where were the days going, I wondered? I was cleaning, babysitting and dog walking, even though most of my money was going on nights out with Harrison. I'd looked after Abby's daughter, Freya, for the hospital appointment, and tried not to mind when he asked if I could have her again the following week. Izzy and I talked often, especially now I had access to the internet, but she was as reluctant to abandon the new guitarist boyfriend as I was to head back to the city.

I retired to the garden room with a glass of pea pod, to watch one of the spectacular sunsets – well, the bit of it that I could see over the top of the trees. My brief falling out with Rory put me in a contemplative mood, and I thought about Grandma's similar reaction to the tattoo, and how it had been the dramatic finale to our quarrel last year.

Although I'd always spent several weeks with Grandma and Granddad over the summer when I was younger, as I hit A-levels and university, it became more of a duty visit. Don't get me wrong, I enjoyed spending time with them, but it meant sacrifices on my part, the lack of Wi-Fi being the biggest, and a couple of weeks without Rupert, which I also found hard. So the holidays to Dorset became shorter. Whereas I would stay with them for most of August when Mum first married Brian, my last visit hadn't even lasted a week.

It was on the second day that Grandma casually mentioned my unemployed status.

'When I was your age I'd been working at Pickering's for eight years. Nearly fifty hours a week on poor money and not much time for socialising. When I came home, I had to help around the house, and my mother took half my wages for board and lodging.' It was a comment out of nowhere. Perhaps she was merely reflecting on days gone by, but to me it stung. I sat at the kitchen table, bored and belligerent. Mum had also been on my case and I was missing Rupert desperately. I'd have been more enthusiastic about a mini-break in Kabul than trundling down to Dorset and it showed.

'Please don't start the everything was so much harder in my day routine. I'm really not in the mood,' I snapped. Grandma looked shocked. I wasn't usually that blunt with her, so I tried to justify my reaction. 'Things are different nowadays, Grandma. Jobs aren't as easy to come by. It's not like I haven't tried.'

'There was unemployment in my day too, but most jobless people don't have access to the unlimited funds of the National Bank of Brian. I hear he recently paid for expensive festival tickets for you and Isobelle, and didn't get so much as a thank you. You've always treated him badly, Molly, and it has to stop.'

She picked up the lump of dough and threw it back on to the floured board, kneading and stretching as she talked.

I thumped my hand down on the table and stood up, wanting to storm out in a highly affronted manner – which I would have done without so much as a blink at home, but I had more respect for this slightly intimidating old lady.

'Oh. My. God. Has Brian been telling tales again?'

'Now you just steady your knickers, my girl. Brian didn't mention those things to me, your mother did. He always makes excuses for you, although heaven knows why. You have to let him in. He's my son and he's a good man.'

By teatime, an enormous homemade cheese and bacon quiche with a crunchy side salad and hunks of freshly baked bread smothered in butter temporarily smoothed everything over, but Grandma and I said very little to each other during the meal.

The following day there was further friction when I rolled downstairs mid-afternoon. I'd been up late watching some late-night horror film, in the days before you had to mud-wrestle Granddad for access to the TV.

'You've missed lunch, young lady. And the best part of the day. I was disappointed you didn't join me for the morning swim.' Grandma was surrounded by freshly baked goodies, cooling racks covering every available surface and the pervading sweet smell as addictive as Marmite. The floor was washed and her old-fashioned wooden-handled mop rested against the back door with all its thick grey bits of string draped across the bucket. The neatly stacked crockery from a recently eaten meal waited to be returned to the heavy dresser at the far end of the kitchen. She'd been up for hours and done the work of a hundred housewives in that time. My day was just beginning.

'I used to look forward to your visits so much because I had company on my swims. It really is the most beautiful part of the day, Molly. Perhaps tomorrow?'

'Yeah, maybe.' But I think we both knew me rising early was unlikely. Funny how doing nothing was so exhausting. Again, I felt got at. Again, I felt that she was on my case rather than being understanding about my situation.

By the end of the day, tensions were running high. I remember my grunting answers, heavy sighs and eye-rolling, and she bore it all without further comment. Granddad was largely oblivious to the atmosphere, especially as Grandma was smiley and cheery every time I came into a room. But the fuse had been lit, glowing and crackling along the fuse wire, until the eerie moment of silence before the bomb exploded.

Her final crime was to walk into the bathroom – I'd forgotten to lock the door and she was bustling about, collecting laundry. Her eyes were instantly drawn to the black swirls of the small flower across my hip.

'Oh, Molly. What have you done?' Her disappointment was palpable as she dropped the bundle of dirty sheets to the floor. 'Ruining your beautiful young body and perfect skin?' Her bottom lip trembled. 'Rather irresponsible and somewhat disappointing.'

'Don't impose your outdated values on me – it's my body. You're as bad as Brian – trying to turn me into some twisted image of a perfect daughter he's carrying around. Well, I've got news for you both: I'm *never* going to conform.' I pushed past her and went into my room to sulk.

By the end of the day Brian had dutifully collected me after I'd feigned some mystery illness and demanded to come home.

She stood at the top of the steep stone steps, her ample frame shrinking as we pulled away. There had been no cheery wave or all-embracing hug to remember her by. I briefly thought of asking Brian to stop, of leaping out and running back to my no-nonsense, omniscient grandma, hugging her tightly and apologising for being such a brat. Instead, I returned my gaze back to the road ahead and swallowed hard.

And I never saw her again.

Chapter 43

'When you go out on the Razzle ...' I looked blankly at Rory, not understanding what he meant. 'The dog walking,' he explained. 'Do you meet many people?'

He was paying me, counting out the notes as he lingered in the doorway, and seemed reluctant to let me go.

'Not really, especially if I do it in the evening.' Having a key meant my dog walking didn't have to coincide with my shifts at Rory's any more, but that day I'd linked up the two. I had a small window between both jobs to grab something to eat in the town and was due at Mr Pickersgill's at half past. 'I take him along the cliff path. You should see the view.'

'I've lived in Creeching all my life, Molly. I know what the cliff view looks like.'

'Ah, but when *exactly* was the last time you took in that particular heady sight?'

He blushed like an embarrassed child and then shrugged as he looked me in the eye, his foot toying with the edge of the entrance mat. 'In about twenty minutes?' he asked hopefully.

'You want to come out on the Razzle with me?' That was unexpected, and my heart did a muted victory dance. I was proving somewhat of an expert at liberating old men shut up in their houses. First Granddad, now Rory.

'I wouldn't put it quite like that,' he coughed.

'Okay, as long as you don't expect a share of my wages.'

Rory hung back at the gate while I knocked on Mr Pickersgill's front door and collected the dog. As soon as Razzle saw me, his tail wagged so frantically that it whacked both sides of the narrow hallway, waiting for his elderly owner to attach his lead. I looked back at Rory, half expecting him to bolt, but he also waited patiently.

'Come on, boy. Let's go.'

When he was clear of the door, Razzle jumped up and put his paws on my thighs. A big dog, I had to steady myself on the fence post. He knew full well I was his passport to freedom.

Rory kindly closed the gate as I was pulled through, and Razzle yanked me off towards the coast.

'Wait for me,' Rory called as I shot up the road, arm outstretched and baggy T-shirt flapping behind me.

'Tell that to the dog,' I called over my shoulder, as my arm was nearly forcibly removed from its socket.

Once on the church footpath, Razzle slowed down and was more or less walking to heel. Or, more accurately, hip. His square head and bulging eyes turned to ask if I would let him off the lead, but that wasn't going to happen as I was worried about him running off or darting into the road.

'Do you want to take him for a bit?' I offered.

'I'm fine.' Rory looked alarmed at the prospect.

I took a sneaky look at my companion as we picked up our pace and headed away from the bustle of town. If only he'd get rid of the damn beard. Most of the eye-watering ginger was on his face, and perhaps he had a point about his hair being nearer to auburn.

We approached a stile and Rory put a supporting hand on

my back as I climbed on to the wooden step – the warmth of which seeped through my T-shirt and made me feel protected and cared for. From nowhere, memories of Brian guiding a younger me through doorways and catching me leaping from walls came to mind. The problem with not knowing the truth about your father was that you saw paternal behaviour in every-one. Not that Rory seemed as father-figure-like as when I first met him.

Threading the lead under the stile, I hopped over the top as Razzle wove his way between the posts. We stood silently for a moment, the hyperactive dog pulling for me to continue, as we gazed out at a dark sea, rolling out to meet a blurry hori-zon. There was the smell of freshly mown grass, where a path through the field had been cut for walkers, seasoned with the salt from the sea. To our left, the playful sun kept popping out from the clouds, searing us with blasts of intense heat, and then came a noticeable drop in temperature as she hid behind drift-ing clouds again. A tiny boat bobbed about near the spit, a brilliant white sail in a canvas of deep blue, and a flock of gulls circled over a patch of ocean to the right, probably following a shoal of unlucky fry as they swam inland.

A low gushing sound made me look at Rory, and I realised he was letting out a hearty breath. His eyes fluttered shut for a moment. This was why I'd been so desperate to get him outside. To help him remember. And possibly help him forget.

'Got to be better than staring at a silly TV on your gym wall?' I said.

'Yes. It really is.' It was wistful. I looked up and realised he was watching my face, but his gaze quickly returned to the sea.

Razzle gave a gruff bark. Too short to see over the hedge and too dog to appreciate the view, he was eager to sniff every tree, bench leg and cow pat between here and the far end of the field.

And undoubtedly add a few scents of his own to the mix. I patted my pocket to check I had the poo bags and wrestled with the lead as he strained to get free.

'Aren't you going to let him off?' Rory asked.

'No way. I'd never get him back.'

'The trick is to be firm. He's a good dog. I remember when John first got him and took him to puppy classes. He's big and full of doggy beans, but he's not disobedient. And anyway, this field is enclosed.'

'If you're sure . . .'

'Come on, Molly. You're the one with dog experience.'

So I set Razzle free. A streak of bounding joy, his muscles rippling as he ran and both ears flying behind as he raced down the slight slope towards the far end.

'If only we could be more like dogs,' Rory said. 'Satisfied with the simple pleasures in life.'

'It's human to aspire, to crave more than we have. And natural to want to achieve and succeed.'

'Maybe. But sometimes all you crave is to run down a hill as fast as your legs can carry you, unhindered and free.'

'Be my guest,' I said, gesturing to the rapidly diminishing Razzle.

'I'm not in that place yet,' he said. 'And sometimes I wonder if I ever will be again.'

We walked and chatted companionably as Razzle burned off an excess supply of energy. An elderly couple in matching Pink Floyd T-shirts were walking along the path with a clipped poodle-like dog in tow.

'Razzle.' Rory called the dog to heel with surprising authority. To my relief, the dog bounded over with huge expectant eyes, his tail wagging so madly it looked like a triangle. My boss shot a wary glance at the advancing couple.

'Come on then, boy.' He retrieved the tennis ball from the mesh pocket of my rucksack, and pulling his arm back, threw it to the deserted side of the field. Razzle was off faster than a startled burglar, followed by a more restrained Rory. Ball firmly between his jaws, Razzle finally stood at Rory's feet, and let himself be petted.

'Your boyfriend really loves that dog,' the approaching man said.

'Oh, we're not a couple.' I felt my face flush and I tugged at my T-shirt. Surely if they were going to mistake our relationship, it would be father and daughter, rather than partners. But then as I looked over to Rory, bending to ruffle Razzle's fur with a frenetic hand, he looked younger than I remembered. I'd initially assumed he was Brian's generation, but it was amazing what a bit of colour in your cheeks and an unguarded smile could do for a man. Ignore the grey and he might pass for this side of forty.

When the couple had moved on, Rory returned.

'Sorry, I didn't feel like . . .' His voice tailed away.

'It's okay. I understand.' I put out my hand to his arm. 'You'd think dog walking would be a solitary activity, but it seems you are automatically part of some sort of club, like when you're a mum and everyone stops to ask the baby's name. You've got a dog, they've got a dog – dog-related socialising is fair game. But I'm sure no one would accost you running, in case they got trampled, especially if it was antisocial hours before most people are up, like eight o'clock.'

'Eight isn't early. You say the oddest things. But maybe I will give the running a go. At an antisocial hour, like *six* o'clock.'

'And shaving off the beard would help.'

He frowned.

'Drag factor? It must be like running into the wind with an open parachute attached to your face.'

'Hey, don't knock the beard. I've become rather fond of it. They're all the rage. And I like to consider myself a young man about town.' He pulled a faux-sexy face and stroked the ginger monstrosity rather too seductively for my liking.

'Except you're rarely about town. And not young,' I added as a cheeky rejoinder.

'Depends what you define as old. I can assure you, as the years pass, your definition changes. When I was your age I thought twenty-five was old.'

'Oi! I'm twenty . . . in a few years,' I blustered. 'Anyway, old is like fif-six-seventy,' I said, not wanting to offend him by getting too close to the truth.

'Great. That means I've got about forty years to enjoy my youth.'

Apart from his maths being seriously dodgy, and out by at least a decade. I patted him playfully on the arm. 'You'd better start soon then, or you'll run out of time.'

Nothing was said for a few moments. He returned his gaze to the vast ocean ahead of us and then took another sideways glance at me.

'Yes, Molly, you're probably right.'

'Please say no if it's not convenient, but how do you fancy earning some extra money?' We were heading back to Razzle's house, our speed determined by the dog.

My eyebrows did a slow, curious glide up my forehead.

'Depends what you want me to do.' Oh dear, what other superior life-skills had Holly bragged about that I was going to have to live up to? Juggling with flaming batons? Give a solo performance of Bizet's *Carmen*? Or something more domestic – whipping up a Michelin-starred five-course meal?

'Help me with a dinner party?'

The five-course meal, then.

'After all,' Rory continued, 'you do most of the cooking for your family because your mum works.'

Bloody Holly. Was there anything she didn't excel at? I was about to politely decline, but my cash flow was getting low and I couldn't afford to lose my phone contract again.

'Erm . . . okay, but don't get your hopes up. I'm no part-time sous chef. It's just egg, beans and oven chips for my siblings.'

'Come on. You're being overly modest. How about that project you did in Year Eleven? You said Food Tech was your best GCSE – a grade eight. You told me you loved baking – or was that another exaggeration? Did you mean opening Mr Kipling packets?' He grinned.

He was expecting more than egg, beans and chips then. Not that I was even confident of producing that. Mastery of The Pie had still evaded me.

'I do enjoy baking. Absolutely love it. All that yeast and bowls of dough. In fact, I made a Dorset Apple Cake only the other day . . .' Which was true. It had cheered Granddad up no end, despite the burnt bits. Plus, Google was now my best friend. It would be fine.

'It doesn't have to be complicated and I'll pay extra. I appreciate Saturday night is a big night for you youngsters. Even though you're not old enough to be hanging around in pubs, I'm sure you drink cider in the bike sheds, or whatever the modern-day equivalent is. Rhubarb gin shots behind the vape store? I'll pay you to come over, set the table, prepare the food and so on. I can order the ingredients in. It's not like I can't cook, more that I don't want to. Not any more. And then you can help clear up afterwards – load the dishwasher and tidy up?'

With Harrison infuriatingly vague about any plans beyond the next five minutes, I was tempted.

'Dinner party?' I queried. 'Isn't that a bit ... sociable for you?'

'Maybe dinner party is an exaggeration. It's my mum's birthday next week and, typical mother not able to let go of her son, all she wants is to spend it with me. Yeah, I know, she must be desperate. So, I wondered –' he dropped his eyes – 'with all the extra expense having a boyfriend incurs, if you'd like to get paid for cooking us a meal? It's only the three of us but I'm sure you could produce something far exceeding any of my shoddy efforts.'

'Erm ...' I had to get out of this one somehow.

'I can add what you need to my internet delivery – just give me a list. And we can set the table nicely and make her feel special. What with preparation time and clearing away, you'll probably take home another seventy pounds.'

Or should I give it my best shot? Seventy pounds was extremely appealing.

'That's an expensive meal,' I ventured.

'Not really. There was a time when I wouldn't think twice of a thousand-pound bill for a couple of us heading into the city on a Friday night.'

'You're joking – right?' Mum and Brian enjoyed eating out, but there's enjoying a romantic dinner at a Michelin-starred restaurant and being totally ripped off. In fact, I was so shocked I stopped walking, despite Razzle pulling at the lead.

'That's city traders for you. Top the evening off with a couple of bottles of vintage champagne at four hundred pounds a pop to celebrate a good day on the markets and it starts being silly money.'

He could see my open mouth and saucer-like eyes expanding. Even Razzle knew this was serious stuff. He stopped yanking at the lead, gave a funny whine, and sat like the obedient dog he most definitely wasn't.

'Fuuu ...' Angelic Holly wouldn't swear, so I didn't. '...

279

Funny how money doesn't matter when you don't have to worry about it running out.' As I said this, I remembered Brian had accused me of something similar when he'd cut my allowance the year after uni. That and Grandma's words had been the catalyst to taking the telesales position. But instead of pushing myself to get a better job, I'd drifted along, letting Rupert take care of me. But I was hungry now – to succeed and achieve greater things. When I returned to London and Granddad was back on track, I'd be looking for full-time work and, hopefully, a little flat of my own.

'I figured it's what bonuses were for. And to keep Maryanne in the style to which she had very much become accustomed.' It was the first mention of what I assumed was a significant other in Rory's life and I didn't like it, even though she was clearly long gone. 'Look. I don't do restaurants any more, and not just for financial reasons, and Mum deserves more than beans on toast for her special day. You need the money and I don't want the hassle of cooking, or the cop-out that is a takeaway.'

'Okay. When?'

'Saturday.'

'As in *this* Saturday? Three days away?'

He pulled an apologetic We've-Forgotten-the-Crackers-Grommit face. It was surprisingly cute on his furry face. Like a gigantic teddy bear apologising for tripping over the blanket and spoiling the picnic.

'Oh, you're out with Harrison on a hot date, aren't you?' He shuffled his foot back and forth along the pavement.

'No, I'm not, actually. He's more of a last-minute, if-he's-free-he'll-see-me kind of boyfriend.'

'Nice guy,' Rory said in a tone which implied he thought Harrison was anything but.

Chapter 44

Percy Gladwell

1895

I recognised Edward immediately. He was coming out of the Devonshire as I crossed St James's Street. He looked up as I called his name, frowned and studied my face.

'Oh, you're my architect fellow. Gladwin?'

'Gladwell.' I put out my hand and he crushed it with his own.

'Funny I should bump into you. I popped up to see how the house was coming along recently and it's looking good, old chap. Spent a bit of time with Vi. Got to keep an eye on my investments, you understand.' He winked at me, the ambiguity of his statement hanging in the air.

'And were you pleased?' I asked.

'Violet seems happy enough, which is my main concern. Tells me it will be called Acacia House – not that I care what she calls the damn place, but I'm guessing she'll be planting an acacia tree now.'

Violet and I had discussed names on a few occasions, and I wasn't surprised that she had chosen something from nature. I remembered the tree as having bright yellow flowers, which I thought suited her personality well.

'The build is solid and impressive, Gladwell. Good job. She

has, as I feared, filled the interior with lots of mawkish and frivolous nonsense though. Since when has she been into damn Latin? Feel a bit bad really. That quote about us being far apart, all the hearts and over-sentimental nonsense she's included. Guess the old gal misses me more than I thought, eh? But I'm looking forward to entertaining there from time to time. The hunting is always top notch in that part of the country and, although her father's estate is buried in debt, he has some jolly fine partridge drives on the land. Do you hunt, Gladwell?'

'Not actively, but I enjoy a good hunt ball and have occasionally shot for pheasant. Not really my thing though.'

'Good, good.' Edward's eyes were darting around the street, looking at anyone but me. He had no real interest in my answer and was obviously keen to be on his way. 'Builder fellow said looking at a late spring finish. Should be a nice little retreat for me, and a place for Violet to pursue her domestic ambitions. Quite frankly, she's been a happier person since I agreed to the house. I doubt you will have noticed, Mr Gladwell, women and their moods not being of particular interest to you, but she's become quite amenable. Seems to have lost her edge somehow.'

A hansom pulled up alongside us and a couple got out, Edward tutting at the puddle water that splashed his shoes. I felt I should correct his implied accusation.

'I think you have mis—'

'And damnably pretty when she makes the effort. What with all the distractions in town, I'd forgotten quite how much. Anyway, must dash. Need to get across town. Meeting an old friend at three.' He winked at me and my stomach rolled. 'Good to see you, old boy. You keep making our Vi happy and I'll keep signing the cheques.' And with that he tipped his hat and strode off towards Piccadilly.

Later that evening I thought about Violet's insistence I paid attention to the volume she had so kindly sent, and pulled it from the shelf near my bed. She had said nothing to me about calling the property Acacia House. It was not a tree we had talked about for the grounds and I wasn't aware of any special meaning it had in her life, yet I knew the naming of the property was something she took seriously.

I slid the heavy volume on to my lap and opened it at the index, my finger tracing down the A section, and read the significance of her choice, my heart beating out a fast rhythm as I read the words.

Acacia, Yellow . . . Secret love.

Chapter 45

Present Day

Having agreed to cook for Rory's parents, I spent several hours flicking through Grandma's cookery books and researching recipes online. I knew a considerable amount about food, I realised, having spent my life surrounded by highly competent cooks. I'd simply never put any of it into practice.

It needed to be easy but impressive – pasta was the obvious answer. I remember Nonna saying that the key to good Italian pasta, proper pasta, was the sauce. The secret was simplicity and the quality of the ingredients – special Roma tomatoes fresh from the market, a firm onion, plenty of garlic and some seasoning. None of this chucking in a slug of leftover red, a splash of Worcestershire or a diced red pepper – the student fare I'd often witnessed Izzy prepare. Nonna also moaned that the English never used enough water or salt to cook their pasta. I still remember her, floral apron around her ample middle, stirring an enormous pot, dipping her own mother's wooden spoon in, and purring '*Magnifico*' as she tasted it.

In many ways Nonna was similar to Bridget: both serious about their cooking, and very particular about their ingredients; old-fashioned matriarchs who loved their husbands, but also kept them firmly in their place. They had only met twice: once before Mum married Brian, and at the wedding, naturally – on both occasions Nonna was post-stroke and in a wheelchair. Mum said the two women were too alike to ever be firm friends. Perhaps they detected too many similarities to follow up a friendship. And Nonna's English was never great, even though she lived in England for more years than she lived in Italy. She was forever muttering obscure Italian phrases under her breath – always disconcerting because I never knew what she'd said. Despite my heritage, and because Mum had been embarrassed by her parents and their lack of English as a youngster, neither of us had really picked up the language – another wasted opportunity in the life of Molly Butterfield.

I scrolled through various websites of Italian food, but as glorious as a good tomato sauce was, I wanted the meal to look more impressive. Rupert was forever saying 'Presentation is everything', and I'd picked up a few things from him – the importance of garnishes, use of colour and even the choice of plate. I settled for Mushroom Lasagnette – one of Mum's specialities. It would look great served with a side salad. If it was important to Rory that the meal should be special, then somehow it was also important to me.

My mobile buzzed but the signal was still poor and cut off before I'd answered it. Harrison's name had briefly flashed up, so I rang him back on Granddad's landline.

'I'm thinking let's take in a band on Saturday. Meet you at The Barley Mow at eight?'

'A job has come up last-minute. I can't make it,' I explained.

'Hey, if we're together, you need to be there for me, y'know? Can't you cancel? I've blagged free tickets.'

'You've cancelled on me before now. Anyway, it pays good money. You know, the thing that buys your pints up the pub.'

I heard a huff down the line. 'So what's the job?'

'Helping Rory host a dinner party.'

'I thought you were the cleaner?'

'PA. He needs my help. And I expect it to be a late finish.'

'What, just you and him?' He almost sounded jealous.

'Don't be ridiculous. He's entertaining and I'm helping prepare the food. He's only using me because there isn't anyone else.'

'And you're cheap.'

'Yes,' I acknowledged. 'And that.'

As I stirred the *besciamella* I sensed Rory creep up behind me. His shadow fell across the pan and I could see a blur of orange in my peripheral vision.

It was an unexpectedly hot July Saturday. Weather forecasters had been caught out by a particularly stubborn system of high atmospheric pressure refusing to budge and a mini heatwave ensued. Not the best conditions for a prolonged duration in front of an oven, but I'd been at Rory's since five and was soldiering on. All the ingredients were stacked neatly in the middle of the clear kitchen table, or on an allocated shelf in his huge, silver Smeg fridge. There was a glorious buttery smell pervading the air and the comforting sound of a bubbling pan.

Rory's parents had been introduced when they arrived at six: Clive and Miriam. Facially, they both had a strong resemblance to Rory – there was no doubting his parentage – but neither had the extraordinary ginger hair; in fact, Clive's hair was snow-white.

'I came to offer you a *small* glass of Prosecco left over from the aperitifs for when you finish cooking – emphasis on the small, young lady. I'm not so old that I don't remember the joys of pre-age drinking. I'll leave the bottle here for you to pour yourself one later, as Mum's moved to the Barolo now.'

I'd suggested Aperol spritz before the meal, in keeping with the Italian theme, and the Prosecco was from that. Mum had embraced her heritage more as she grew older, particularly the cuisine, and I'd attended the odd dinner party where she'd showcased her ancestry.

Rory waved the opened bottle at me and placed it next to the hob. I could have snatched it and glugged back the remaining contents in one go. I felt hot and bothered. A good slurp of alcohol would help relieve the pressure of all this entertaining.

'Is the sauce supposed to have lumps?' he asked, peering over my shoulder.

'If you want to cook this meal, be my guest. I don't loiter over your shoulder when you're selling truckloads of coffee beans in Argentina and buying up shares in British Telecom.' I stirred the small pan of what looked like watery cottage cheese or badly mixed wallpaper paste, with the odd cremini mushroom bobbing about.

'I deal in currency, not commodities,' he chuckled, 'as I've told you many times before.'

I turned to him, waving the fluorescent green spatula in a menacing fashion, and he put up his hands. He looked quite smart in his casual long-sleeved shirt. I was used to seeing him in more slouchy, can't-be-bothered-to-leave-the-house-type clothes.

'Okay, okay. I'll leave you to it. It smells good. I was only asking.'

'Well, don't.' I returned to my sauce and poked it a bit. The sooner the great hairy Yeti got out of my face, the sooner I could turn to my old buddy Google.

'Go and talk to your parents. After all, it's you they've come to see. You can't leave the birthday girl alone,' I said.

He rolled up the corner of his top lip. 'We've caught up with all the family gossip, but I suppose you're right, it's just I've heard it all before. It will be the same set of probing questions, the same helping of parental concern and the same worried glances exchanged over the table.'

I put my hands on my hips. 'If you stay in here, I'll make you grate a kilo of Parmigiano-Reggiano. It's either that or take the starters through . . .'

'No problem. I can take them.' And he picked up the tray of bruschetta I'd been about to distribute before I noticed the worrying texture of the sauce. As he left, he stole a piece of tomato from the bowl of freshly chopped salad and flipped it up into the air, catching it in his open mouth. Quite a feat when there was so much beard obscuring the entrance.

When I was certain he'd gone, I slid my phone from my pocket and frantically searched for the answer to my culinary catastrophe.

To save a lumpy béchamel sauce, press it through a sieve with the back of a wooden spoon and then reheat, or blend with a stick blender.

'Bingo.' See, everything was going to be fine. Google *was* my friend.

Okay, sieving was harder than it looked. And when you are balancing a tea strainer (the only thing Rory possessed that was sieve-like – the holes in the colander were too big) over a Pyrex bowl and squashing drips of white sauce through it, sometimes pasta boils over. The cooker hob was covered in bubbly, white, filmy water and the lasagne sheets looked less al dente and more al duvet.

Adrenalin pumped around my body. My brain focused and I acted with superhuman speed and incisiveness. There was plenty of lasagne left, so I could cook another batch. But the sauce was beyond redemption, *and* I'd used all the shallots and mushrooms.

To add insult to near fatal injury, the panna cottas hadn't set. Granddad warned me they were too adventurous when I was planning the meal, but I was certain they were exactly the sort of thing perfect Holly could whisk up in her sleep. They sat in their ramekins, liquid and defiant. Aargh. Perhaps I could pop them in the freezer for a bit? However, the main course was my immediate problem.

Then I remembered I had two tubs of wild mushroom fresh pasta sauce in the fridge at Hawthorn Place – two hundred miles (or twenty seconds by cupboard) away. Perhaps I could cut the lasagne sheets into slices, like a kind of fettuccine. Thank God for Granddad embracing the healthier, slightly more affluent lifestyle and abandoning the toast. I cleared the decks (pushed everything up the far end of the kitchen), got a fresh saucepan from the cupboard, filled it with water, set it to boil, and dashed for the stairs.

'What are you doing back, love?' said Granddad, as he caught me head down in the wood-effect Indesit fridge in his kitchen. 'I thought you were working late?'

'Just nipped back for something. Won't be long.' And then I noticed he had a plate piled high with several slices of toast, coated in a thick layer of raspberry jam. Seems he'd been caught out as much as me. 'You said you were going to cook something,' I whined.

'Oh, erm, just some toast to be going on with. I like toast . . . and all that fancy stuff you've been buying. I like that as well . . . I'll rustle up something more substantial later.'

Hmm.

We locked eyes for a second and then both decided it was best not to question each other's behaviour.

'See you later,' I said, scooping up the tubs of sauce. Just as I was about to close the door, I noticed the tiramisu wedged under a savoy cabbage, and thrust it all into a bag for life.

'This mushroom sauce is delicious,' Miriam said. 'Rory told us you were a good cook. What's the flavour I can taste in the background? Thyme? Marjoram?'

'I couldn't possibly say,' I said, tapping my nose. Because until I looked at the label on the tub, I didn't have a flipping clue.

'I thought you were cooking lasagne ...' Rory's puzzled face was endearing and I wanted to squeeze his little pink cheeks.

'Aha. That's what I wanted you to think ... Anyway, the fettucine has been cut from the lasagne sheets. It's how my grandmother did it. Excuse me, I have to attend to the dessert.' I tried to sound mysterious and made a hasty dash for the kitchen.

Right, now to transfer the tiramisu into glasses – pop a sprig of something on the top and make them look homemade. I took a gulp of the Prosecco to help me focus, and dashed out to Rory's recently weeded herb garden to snap the top off something that looked green and sprig-like – noticing how much love and care Rory had invested in reviving it. Each square now contained a different herb – some trimmed back and tamed into submission, and some newly planted. I snapped the tops from the thyme (one of the few I recognised) and rubbed it between my fingers. It had a subtle, slightly minty smell and I hoped Rory would be inspired to not only cultivate these plants but also cook with them.

The sky was dark, confirming the earlier warnings that a heavy summer storm was on its way. There was a thick quilt of darkness with a pale grey light peeping out around the edges. The breeze whipped up and I shivered, despite the suffocating heat, before scurrying back inside.

I found three matching, elegant wine glasses in one of the wall cupboards and managed to scoop out the dessert and slide it into the glasses more or less disaster-free as Rory walked back in.

'Good grief, Molly. The kitchen looks like a student flat after an all-night party,' Rory held a tray of empty plates in front of him. I hastily slid the nearly empty bottle of Prosecco (oops) behind the coffee machine and threw a tea towel over the tiramisu container.

'You can't make an omelette without cracking eggs,' I replied, hands on hips.

'Or produce an excellent four-course meal without trashing my kitchen?'

He thought the meal was excellent. The warm glow inside me wasn't only from the drink. I'd been carrying around a house-point chart in my head for the last few weeks now, awarding them to myself when I got praise from Rory, as if he was the teacher I wanted to impress. I added a couple of shiny gold stars to the effort column.

'I'll bring the dessert through in a minute,' I said, keen for him to leave my workspace, and he took the hint.

Five minutes and a final slug of Prosecco later, the thyme-sprigged wine glasses were arranged on a small tray. They were sliding about as I walked down the hall, so I held it firmly in both hands and tried to push the door to the dining room open with my bottom. Collapsing into the room and showering everyone with mascarpone and coffee-flavoured ladyfingers would not get me any further stars – gold or otherwise.

I paused as I heard Rory's agitated raised voice. He was usually so calm and gentle when he spoke that his tone surprised me. I didn't want to barge in on a family quarrel.

'Because we worry,' his mum replied.

291

'There is absolutely no need. I'm fine. You are fussing over nothing.'

'Rory –' her voice was gentler now – 'you know how much we love you. And it's hardly nothing when two years ago I received a phone call at work to tell me you'd tried to take your own life.'

Chapter 46
Percy Gladwell
1895

Violet was due at my offices at ten. I'd been surprised to receive her message as she was a reluctant traveller and rarely came to London. She had an appointment in the city later that day, the nature of which she did not divulge, but I was delighted that this afforded her a reason to call. We had little to discuss regarding the plans, but we both knew this was not the real reason for the visit. Our relationship had strengthened through both our time spent together designing the house and our correspondence. Nothing had ever been spoken, but I felt her letters had increased in intimacy.

The longer I paced the rug, however, the more I started to question whether I had foolishly been reading more into her words than she intended, such was my desire for our relationship to be greater than architect and client.

Her gift of the *Flora Symbolica* had led me to believe that her letters contained a simple code, and that the naming of the house was deliberate. Her correspondence often began with a paragraph of her thoughts regarding the garden at the cottage, but the random selection of plants made no sense unless interpreted through the language of flowers. She invariably wrote a more reasoned second paragraph detailing planting she had decided upon for Acacia House; her genuine plans for the gardens.

She had spoken of the crimson polyanthus (the heart's mystery) and her regret the ivy (marriage) had strangled her borders at the front of the cottage, saying that she could not in good conscience remove it but would plant around it, hoping these plants would take root and grow taller, to overshadow the ivy. The periwinkle represented friendship – it would detract from the invasiveness of the ivy, growing stronger so that she need not look upon the ivy any more, even though she could never completely eliminate it.

There was no ivy at the cottage. How else was I to interpret these words? I'd been slow, but the book had been her way of establishing a method of communication that was exclusive to us. That she should even consider such, was a compliment in itself.

Besides, the moment we'd shared when she'd tripped on the rug had said everything her words could not. How many times had I played it over and over in my mind? Seeing her today would tell me everything I needed to know, and then I feared I would have to end my understanding with Miss Hamilton. Even if Violet could never be mine, I could not marry Charlotte now.

An hour after she was due and I was highly agitated, watching the hands jerk a steady journey around the face of the clock. I was certain she would have sent word had some other event taken priority.

'Frederick,' I bellowed down the hall when eleven chimes rang out.

'Mr Gladwell?' The young lad came scurrying up the corridor, brushing dust from his cuffs and tucking a pencil behind his ear.

'Have we had word from Mrs Marston yet?'

'None, sir. I was expecting her at ten. The paperwork you requested is all laid across the desk in readiness. Did she not come?'

'No, she did not.'

And I knew deep inside that something was terribly wrong.

Chapter 47

Present Day

With my bottom pressed against the dining-room door, I froze. It wasn't polite to listen in on other people's conversations, but I was stunned to hear Rory had tried to take his own life. I'd assumed the scars on his wrist had been self-harm after our previous conversation, distressing enough, but I hadn't considered they might be the result of a serious suicide attempt. No wonder he'd shut himself away from everyone and everything. I straightened up and tried to stop the glasses toppling over.

'It was a very worrying time, son, and we felt the miles between us very keenly. I hope you know that we'd be there for you again in a heartbeat, should you ever need us for *anything*.' He stressed the last word. I couldn't see Clive's face, but I knew it would be saturated with concern and love. Rory was lucky to have two such supportive parents. As was I, I realised.

'I don't want you worrying about me. I was ill back then, Dad.' Rory's initial agitation had gone, and his tone softened. 'It was the dramatic culmination of numerous factors – misguided ambition, the self-destructive lifestyle, a complicated love affair and sheer physical exhaustion. I should have got help sooner, I know that now, but as soon as I did, I began to take back control. Yes, it's been a long road to recovery, but I can assure you that those feelings have long gone.'

'You mustn't mind us checking up on you. You are, and will always be, my baby,' Miriam said.

'I appreciate that you worry, but it was two years ago. The therapist is happy with me, and I've worked really hard to address my issues. You have to trust me when I say that I'm getting on with my life.'

'Are you though?' his mum questioned. 'Are you getting on with your life, darling? I understand recovery doesn't happen overnight, but perhaps you're ready to try some new things now?'

Miriam began to address Rory's lack of social life and suggested numerous activities her son could engage in, each one dismissed by Rory. The conversation, however, was now much less sensitive.

'Dessert,' I announced, barging into the room.

'Smashing,' Clive said. 'Tiramisu, if I'm not mistaken?'

'I don't remember any of those ingredients on the list,' said Rory, peering at the contents of his wine glass.

'I brought some bits from home,' I said. 'Last-minute change of plan.' If only he knew how last minute. 'It's a new recipe. Tell me what you think. My siblings seemed to like it.' Oops. Having decided to keep all lies to a minimum, it was embarrassing how often the fibs slipped out.

'Yes, Rory told us you come from a big family,' Miriam said. 'How many of you are there?'

Damn. See, this was why it was better to keep my silly mouth shut. I was getting in deeper and deeper water. What had Holly told him?

'There are five of us.' That sounded about right; enough to be a handful but not Dickensian proportions. 'I'm the eldest, so I've had to look after them a lot over the years because my mum works really long hours now that she's a single parent.'

'Molly is great with kids and babysits for a family.' Ooh – who handed him a pair of pompoms and a *Go, Molly* T-shirt? I felt a warm glow as I basked in Rory's praise. 'She's also walking Razzle for old Mr Pickersgill. A regular Nanny McPhee.'

A Nanny McPhee who was winging every new chapter of her life, and was a bit rubbish at most of it.

'And you're still at sixth form, my son tells me?' Miriam said. 'Eighteen in September. He'll have to up your hourly rate.' She smiled. 'What are you studying?'

'Oh, the usual.' I placed a dessert in front of her, not liking the way the conversation was going.

'Economics and sociology for a start,' said Rory. 'Don't know why you're being so coy, Molly. And was it business studies?'

God, I really hoped not. I didn't have the first clue what that subject involved. How to set up a shop and a hundred and one ways to sell oil to the Arabs?

'So, where will this all lead, young lady? What do you see yourself doing career-wise?' Clive spoke before I could answer.

'Erm . . . I thought perhaps . . . sociologiser . . . or erm . . .'

'The poor girl obviously doesn't want to talk about school. Leave her alone.' I threw a grateful look at Rory's mum, especially as she then deftly changed the subject. 'Rory said earlier you were asking about the house?'

'Yes, I've been researching it. So quirky.'

'Ah, the house.' Clive put his napkin on the table and shuffled into a more comfortable position, throwing one leg over the other and leaning back. 'It's been in Miriam's family for as long as anyone can remember, but I really must look further into that. I started investigating the family tree and then life got busy. We must quiz your uncle more before he loses his already scattered marbles – after all, the old boy is getting on,' he said to his wife.

'So you grew up here?' I asked Miriam.

'I did, but I don't think I appreciated it until I was older. Guess I assumed everyone had Latin phrases on the walls and stained-glass panels in the windows. This house is a total delight everywhere you look – the adorable crawling window in the nursery, for example.'

A crawling window – it had been referenced in the local history article, but I hadn't understood it. Obvious now I thought about it. That was why it was so low, to let children see outside, and it being a bedroom between staff quarters and the main bedrooms made sense as a nursery. But then there was a lot about the houses that was childlike. The castle theme on the newel posts, and the curly stairs in the tower. They hinted at fairy tales and escapism.

The investigation of the two houses was so dear to my heart, that I told the Brookers everything I knew. That their house had been commissioned by Edward and Violet Marston not long after their marriage, was designed by Percy Gladwell, and that coincidence of coincidences – my grandfather lived in an identical property in Dorset. Clive, in particular, was fascinated by the movement and impressed that I knew so much about the subject.

'Molly has an impressive knowledge of architecture,' Rory said. 'When we took Razzle for a walk along the coast path, Molly pointed out some interesting features on Saint Martin's . . .'

'You got Rory outside?' Miriam had picked up her sundae spoon but held it suspended in mid-air as she digested this piece of information. Rory rolled his eyes.

'I thought a bit of fresh air would do him good. He spends too much time cooped up in this big old house, as beautiful as it is. I'm trying to persuade him to do his running outside on the basis that you, erm, *we* live in such a beautiful part of the country and the spectacular view and sea air have to be better than jiggling about on that silly machine and staring at a wall.'

Rory's parents exchanged a look and Miriam dipped her spoon into the creamy mascarpone. 'Simply wonderful,' she said, as she swallowed her first mouthful. 'The tiramisu, I mean.'

'Perhaps you could also convince him to shave that ginger monstrosity off his face, while you're at it,' said his dad. 'You wouldn't know it to look at him, but underneath all that fluff he's quite a handsome fellow. Takes after his old man.'

'I'm working on it,' I said with a massive grin. Rory caught my eye as I stepped back from the table and picked up the tray. I thought the corner of his lips twitched slightly, as if he was suppressing a smile.

'If you'll excuse me? I need to get on or I won't be home until midnight.'

A little while later, I brought through a platter of cheese and biscuits. Although this course was not Italian in origin, I'd selected a couple of Puglian cheeses and served them with olives and some rosemary crackers. The meal was intended to be Italian in flavour, not necessarily an authentic Italian experience. I wasn't prepared to start with antipasto, primo, secondo, corntorno . . . it would have taken all night. Maybe one day I would produce a proper Italian meal to make Nonna proud. But right now, it was baby steps.

'Join us?' his mum offered again. 'There's more than enough to go around.'

'That's kind of you, but I want to get on. There's a lot of clearing up to do.'

'We can help with that. Can't we, dear?' She looked across at Rory.

'Not on your birthday, Mum. Besides, it's what I'm paying Molly for.'

I returned to the kitchen just as the weather started to deteriorate quite rapidly. The summer storm was about to descend in dramatic fashion. As I scraped the plates and waited for the first dishwasher cycle to finish (the trouble with having a culinary disaster was extra washing-up), a distant rumble of thunder made me jump. The ceiling spotlights flickered but recovered and there was a repeated thunking sound as the first heavy raindrops pelted the glass. I pulled the open window closed as the suffocating temperatures had eased and I didn't want rain flooding the worktop.

'We're leaving now, Molly, but I didn't want to go without saying goodbye and thank you for such a beautiful meal.' Rory's mum swung the kitchen door open a little while later. 'As good as any restaurant, and a break from the cooking for me.'

I grabbed the tea towel and wiped my hands. 'It was my pleasure, and it was lovely to meet you. I'll just say goodbye to Mr Brooker.' I smoothed down the front of my cotton dress and walked towards the hall, but she pulled the door ever so slightly closed as I approached.

'We really appreciate all you are doing for Rory,' she said in a low voice.

'It's only a bit of housekeeping and I'm being paid for it.'

'I know, but I don't think you realise what an enormous achievement it was to get him outside, and I'm sure that wasn't part of the deal. I just wanted to say, out of earshot, that it made my day. I don't know how much he's told you, but he was ill a couple of years ago. He recovered so well to start with, but then he stagnated, and it was the lack of friends that worried me most. You being around and your friendship, which is plain to see, has pushed him to take another forward step. And for that I'm thankful.'

'It's not a problem. I like him.'

301

She smiled and patted my bare arm. 'If only you were a few years older, you'd have been exactly the sort of young lady he would have gone for.' There was a pause. 'And exactly the sort of young lady that he needs right now. Shame.' She squeezed me before letting her hand drop and opened the kitchen door, ushering me through to the hall.

As everyone said their polite goodbyes and Rory opened the front door, a sudden crash of thunder made the lights flicker again.

'Are you sure you're going to be okay?' Miriam asked Rory and then turned to me. 'He never did like thunder as a child. Or the dark. Bit of a troubled sleeper, weren't you, love?'

'I'll be fine. Stop embarrassing me. I'm not seven,' Rory said, sounding seven.

So she embarrassed him further by pinching his cheeks and planting a huge mother-kiss on his forehead.

'You're sure we can't drop you home, Molly?' Clive asked. 'This storm's building up to be a humdinger.'

'Thanks, but a bit of rain doesn't bother me. I'm not a scaredy-cat, like Rory.' He huffed. 'I'll be at least another hour and I live *really* near. The storm will have passed by then.'

'Do you need a hand?' Rory asked after they'd left.

'No, I've got it. You go and lift some weights, tinker about selling Indonesian oil reserves, or whatever. I'll only talk too much and annoy you.'

'Let me help?' He sounded pleady.

'But you're paying me to do it, so if you help it will be done faster and then I'll only get half the money.'

'I'll round up your fee to a hundred for tonight?'

I did a double-take, hands on hips. He was being ridiculous.

'I feel like doing something normal. Something sociable,' he said.

'Okay then. But you don't have to pay me extra.' Especially as I'd cheated.

'Great, I'll get the rubbish . . .' and he moved towards the bin.

'No!' I said too quickly. The tiramisu container and sauce tubs were at the top. I stepped between him and the evidence, finding myself facing his chest and a cascade of beard. 'I'll get that. You can unload the dishwasher. The first cycle must be nearly finished.'

He looked down at me as I looked up. The ends of his beard tickled my nose. He smelled of sea kelp shower gel and a rather intoxicating spicy aftershave. For the tiniest fraction of a second, I didn't feel like the young girl he thought I was. I felt very much like the fully grown woman I actually was. My body came alive for a brief moment and neither of us moved. What the heck were my nerve endings playing at? And what was up with Rory? He was looking at me in a peculiar way. Everything about this high-octane situation was confusing and unexpected.

The dishwasher clicked to signal the end of the programme and broke the spell.

'I'll get that,' he said, spinning away from me. 'Watching you bustle about the kitchen tonight has made me realise that I want to start cooking again.' He was looking everywhere but back at me. 'I used to enjoy it.'

'The only thing stopping you is you,' I replied, trying to be all sage and wise and move on from what had just happened. 'Proper cooking needn't take long. My granddad swears by *Jamie's 15-Minute Meals*. He's always YouTubing clips.'

'Funky granddad.'

'You have *no* idea,' I said, thinking of his latest Facebook status – 'Walter Butterfield *is feeling motivated*. How spicy is too spicy?' I did warn him the post could be misinterpreted but this just made his eyes twinkle – the way they used to twinkle when Grandma threatened to whack him with the fish slice for stealing her cheese straws.

Lightning flashed through the dark window and lit up the garden like a massive explosion of fireworks and I saw Rory's body tense out the corner of my eye.

'One Mississippi, two Mississippi, three . . .' I started to count, to work out how close the storm was. Then there was the most almighty clap of thunder and all the lights went out.

We both stood still for a moment, expecting the electricity to come back on, but nothing happened.

'Molly?' Rory whispered. 'Where are you?'

He sounded surprisingly anxious.

Chapter 48
Percy Gladwell
1895

Despite frantic attempts to contact Violet, it was not until the following morning I finally received word. My night had been restless. I knew something was wrong, but it seemed overly dramatic to assume some disaster had befallen her just because she'd failed to keep our appointment. The matter was finally resolved when Freddie burst through my office doors, making my ruler slip, and I drew a deep jagged line through my work.

'We have just had word from Mr Marston's secretary. Mrs Marston was taken seriously ill yesterday.'

I let my pencil fall from my fingers and it rolled to the edge of the drafting table. I leaned forward and felt my fists clench.

'Confound it, man. Details?' I snapped. 'What was said exactly?'

'Sorry, sir. That was about the sum of it. She was taken ill and he apologised that she'd been unable to keep your appointment.'

Ill – the word was damnably vague. Had she a headache or had she contracted a life-threatening disease such as smallpox?

I needed to know.

*

An hour later I was on the doorstep of their Kensington residence. Freddie had cleared my schedule for the morning and I hammered on the heavy panelled door.

It was Mary who answered.

'Is Mrs Marston in?'

'Oh, Mr Gladwell. Did no one get word to you? She was rushed into hospital. She collapsed yesterday morning and Mr Marston had a physician here within minutes. I'm sorry. Mr Marston's secretary said he would notify you.'

'Yes, yes, I was notified, but was given no details and I am greatly concerned about her welfare. How is she?'

'You'd best step inside, sir. I don't want to be one of those that talks in the street.'

She held the door and I entered the narrow Italianate hallway of their townhouse. She lowered her voice and stepped closer to me, all the time wringing the edge of her white apron between her hands.

'We were in London, because she'd been peaky of late and Mr Marston had arranged for her to see some doctor on Harley Street. And then this happened – she was in so much pain, sir. And I didn't know what to do. She was nearly bent double with it. And there was so much blood . . .'

The poor woman burst into tears, so obviously distressed that I placed a hand upon her shoulder and tried to calm her, but I did not need details of the events; I needed the outcome.

'There, there. You did all you could. I know how fond you are of Mrs Marston, but has there been any news since?'

She looked up at me, clearly not sure what she was and wasn't allowed to say. 'P'raps it's best you see the master,' she eventually said, avoiding the question and shaking her head.

'I'll let him know you are here.' And she scurried down the hall.

Her inability to tell me Mrs Marston's present condition could only mean one thing – whatever had befallen Violet, she had not survived it.

I had lost her for ever.

Chapter 49

Present Day

'I'm a few steps to your right,' I replied, the dark now *so* dark I couldn't make out any outlines or shapes. I heard Rory's breaths getting faster. He wasn't going to flip out on me, was he? I wouldn't know what to do. The revelation that he'd tried to take his own life was still fresh in my mind.

I moved towards the sound of his shallow breathing and waved an arm about like a blind person. I brushed against his shoulder and gripped it. His other hand came up swiftly to find mine.

'Sorry. Totally ridiculous of me. Don't like the dark.'

'I'm here. You're not alone.'

'No. No. I'm not alone,' he repeated. 'Heights, small spaces, flying, spiders, snakes – in fact, any vicious, petrifying creature – I can do. Just not the dark.'

'That's all very impressive as long as they don't attack you at night, then,' I said.

'Ha, I'm ready for them,' he joked. 'Point me in the right direction.'

I was about to ask if he had any candles but then had a better idea.

'Just getting my phone. Don't move,' I said. I slid my hands along the worktop where I'd left my mobile, but caught it with my searching fingers and sent it crashing to the floor.

'Damn.'

'I'll help,' he said. There was much shuffling and wafting of hands as we both crawled about on our knees trying to locate the dropped iPhone. Trying to work out where he was, so we didn't end up smashing heads, my fingers bumped into his and neither of us moved for a second. Feeling something warm after scrabbling about on cold slate tiles sent a small voltage through me.

There is something about the dark that magnifies your remaining senses. Take away sight, and your body focuses on the others in an attempt to compensate. I could feel the icy cold of the hard floor on my bare legs, strangely cooling in this sticky heat, and the tiny pieces of grit embedded in my knees. The hairs on the back of my arms were bolt upright like the feather-duster-tail of a petrified cat. I could hear Rory's slow, deep breathing, the shuffling of his legs, and of course the unrelenting rain beating against the glass of the windows. There was a noticeable absence of the sounds you don't register when sight is your primary sense: no hum of a fridge, or tick of the cooker clock. The power cut had suspended the heartbeat of the house. I could smell faint traces of garlic from the meal, but the musky scent of Rory was closer and somehow more overpowering. Another dramatic flash of lightning lit us both up like a wartime searchlight beam and I could see his wide eyes and worried expression.

As he sat back on his legs, I spotted my phone, illuminated by the lightning. I grabbed it.

'Are you okay?'

'Not really. Sorry. I'm supposed to be the adult here.'

'Not at all.' I moved closer, inching across the floor on my knees, and put an arm on his back, rubbing him gently like a mother might comfort a child.

What had Google taught me? Distraction.

'So what's trending in the heady world of trading? Is the pound strong against the dollar? Should I be putting all my money into Japanese yen?'

'These are silly questions, Molly. I know what you're trying to do.'

'Do you?'

'Yes.'

'Is it working?'

'Yes.'

I let my arm drop as his breathing returned to normal, fumbled for my mobile and activated the assistive light, inadvertently shining it in his face. He put up a hand to shield his eyes.

'Guess I need to man up,' he announced.

'Don't say that. I hate the way men feel they have to be strong and silent. You're allowed to express your emotions, deal with your anxieties and communicate both to the people around you.' I wondered if that had been the problem, and that an inability to talk about his worries had led to his breakdown.

'After my experiences, I couldn't agree more. But this is a bit deep for kitchen-floor talk,' he joked, noticeably calmer. 'You've gone all sociologiser on me and we've got the aftermath of a dinner-party to clear up.'

For the next half an hour, we worked by candlelight, Rory having found a bag of tealights in the pantry. It was atmospheric, working in the flickering tiny dots of yellow, and would have been quite a romantic setting if it wasn't for the fact I didn't feel that way about him. Although, perhaps if he'd been a bit younger, not so beardy or my boss . . .

Sneaking slugs of dessert wine from the opened bottle when he wasn't looking, I hand-washed several saucepans as Rory dried. Thoughts of the people who had lived at Acacia House in the past drifted into my head. Had Violet and her husband stood together in this room? Had they kissed in the candlelight and then walked up the fairy-tale staircase, hand in hand, to continue their love story? I felt the happiest I had been in a very long time.

I looked out the window and noticed the rain was softer. 'Would you mind if I stood outside for a bit in the cooler air?' I asked.

'I'll come with you,' he volunteered and I wondered if he didn't want to be left alone. 'We could finish up the Barolo, as long as you don't get me into trouble for giving alcohol to a minor. One small glass won't hurt you. I think we've earned it.'

'Good idea.' I didn't mention the Prosecco or the sweet dessert white I'd been swigging. 'Anyway, there isn't a legal age limit for drinking at home. I often have wine with meals,' the Holly-me said.

'Hopefully not when you are looking after all your siblings.' He cocked his head to give me a parenty-type look.

'Well, no, not then. Obviously.'

'Without wanting to lead you astray . . .' He picked up the half-empty bottle of Italian red and two clean glasses, '. . . and only if I'm not holding you up.'

'It's fine. Grandd—erm, my mum isn't waiting up or anything. She knows it's going to be a late one.'

The rain was now barely a patter. I put some of the tealights in a large glass bowl and carried them out to the garden room. The air was clean and fresh, and the storm had left behind a glorious damp earth smell. It was as lightless as the triangular cupboard, and I must have resembled a gigantic glow worm as I made my way through the kitchen door.

'This was my grandma's favourite part of the house,' I said, placing the tealights on the wicker table.

'Oh yes, I keep forgetting your granddad lives in a similar house.'

'Actually, it's absolutely identical, down to the very last brick. It even has the same hinges on the fitted cupboards, crenellated newel posts and the stained-glass geese. I should have said. I couldn't get over how *all* the details, from the crawling window to the chequerboard herb garden, were the same when I first came here. Particularly considering the houses are two hundred miles apart. It's partly why I began the research – I was convinced there was a connection.'

Rory looked interested and rubbed at his ginger fuzz. 'You said they were built by the same architect . . .'

'Yes, but it *has* to be more than that. I know he lived in Granddad's house until his death, but I'm starting to wonder if he had a bit of a thing for the lady who lived here: Violet Marston. It's the only explanation that makes sense.'

Rory looked interested and leaned closer, his bright eyes shining like lamps through the dark red tangle of hair and beard. 'In what way?'

'Because, not only was there a box of possessions personal to Violet hidden in Granddad's house, presumably hoarded by an infatuated Percy, but also the house should have been built of materials local to Dorset, not local to here. It was one of Percy's guiding principles and he went against it. Granddad lives on the Jurassic coast, not far from Weymouth, and the local building material is quarried stone from Portland. So I have to ask myself why such a renowned architect would use flint and brick when there was a wealth of outstanding building material on his doorstep?'

Rory shrugged. 'Unless Violet's house had special significance.'

'Exactly.'

'And she was happily married to Mr Marston all her life?'

'Yes, until he died, according to my research.'

'Perhaps if he couldn't have the woman he loved, and his

love was unrequited, he decided to build an exact replica of the house he'd designed for the Marstons. Because to walk in the rooms she walked in, to look out of the windows she looked out of, perhaps even to sleep in the bedroom she slept in, would be the closest he would ever get to her.'

It was the same conclusion I'd drawn, although after reading her coded letters I suspected Violet returned Percy's love. It wasn't unrequited – just impossible. She was married and divorce wasn't an option in those days. I had no proof for our wild speculation over Percy's reasons for building Hawthorn Place, but somehow it felt right. After all, he loved the house so much, he remained there until he died.

I took several sips of the delicious red, even though a beer would have hit the spot. The wine fuzzed through me and made my legs wobble. I leaned against the high-backed wicker seat and felt content. Rory and I chatted companionably about everything and nothing, and I even opened up about Grandma, admitting we'd quarrelled last summer but without going into detail. Good company was the best, and it made me realise how much I'd missed Izzy. Phone calls and social media weren't the same as face-to-face interaction.

As my second *large* glass of red, which I'd topped up and gulped down surreptitiously in the dark, kicked in, there was a sudden torrential downpour – an encore from the passing storm. Heavy streams of rain falling in vertical sheets. Fuelled by the alcohol and remembering Harrison's philosophy of embracing the here and now and to hell with the consequences, I stood up and ran to the lawn.

And for five minutes, not caring what Rory thought of the mad girl spinning about in a sodden linen dress and singing wildly out of tune, I danced in the rain.

*

'The wine seems to have gone to your head. You're all wet,' Rory said as I returned to the relative shelter of the garden room, breathless but happy.

'And you're all dry. Budge up, old man,' and I shoved him along the wicker sofa, instead of returning to the single chair. There were two outdoor cushions, made of some stripy water-resistant fabric, and I wriggled about to get comfortable.

'You're a funny one,' he said into the darkness. There was a pause. 'If only there were some stars, we could have stargazed. Mind you, I only know one constellation.'

'That's one more than me. I can just about identify the moon. Let's rain-gaze instead.'

'Sounds perfect.'

I picked up my glass and clicked his. 'Cheers. To better times to come.'

'I'll drink to that.' And he knocked back what was left in his glass, as we settled down to gaze at a black and hypnotic sky, as raindrops glistened like diamonds in the reflected glow from our candles.

I woke with a jump. My dreams were suddenly floodlit as power was restored to the house, and all the appliances that had been on when the electric went out burst back to life. I'd fallen asleep with my head on Rory's lap, with one of his arms draped across my body. His head was resting on the back of the sofa, flopped to one side, a low snore coming from his mouth. He took longer than me to stir.

'Wha ... What time is it?' His head rolled forward and he focused on his rogue arm. I'd never seen him move so fast, withdrawing it as if I was on fire. His back went ramrod straight and he adjusted his shirt, running a hand down the front as if to check no buttons had been tampered with. As if.

'Half five,' I said, glancing at my watch as I sat up and ruffled my tufty hair.

God, I must look dreadful – not that it mattered what Rory thought of me. It was hardly like waking up with a boyfriend, when it was vital to look immaculate and alluring at all times. However, I ran a finger under each eye, in case there were traces of stray make-up, and licked my dry lips.

'Good grief, we've been asleep for nearly six hours. That's a record for you, isn't it?' I said.

He furrowed his brow and rubbed the wild beard with his hand. 'Yes, it is.' He rotated his head, stretching his neck and rolling back his shoulders.

'Not surprised you've got a stiff neck – sleeping in a chair,' I said, as I got to my feet. My dress was claggy and clinging to every curve. Or more accurately, every jutty hip and sticky-out bone on my body. I pulled it down, self-conscious of my dishevelled form as we both actively avoided eye contact.

Where had the ease of last night gone? There was an awkwardness pervading the atmosphere. It was like waking up next to a complete stranger after a drunken and ill-advised one-night stand, knowing you had crossed intimacy barriers and seen each other at your most vulnerable. But the sexual element surely wasn't a factor here, so it didn't make sense.

'I'd better go. Thanks for everything,' I said.

'I need to pay you . . .'

I was already backing away, towards the door. 'No, honestly. I'll grab my bag. Pay me next time. It's fine.'

'Okay, if you're sure.'

And as I went through the door into the kitchen, I looked back and saw him drop his head into his hands in despair, clutching at it as if he wanted to rip out his troubled brain, for all the world looking like a man who'd just been tried for murder and handed a life sentence.

'Where were you last night?' Harrison asked, flicking geranium petals at me. 'I was so bored. Everyone was busy.'

He'd called at the house just before Sunday lunch, but I'd been asleep. Granddad explained I'd not got back until the early hours, but Harrison insisted I was woken up, so I'd chucked on some jeans and stumbled downstairs. At least my short hair was always Good-to-Go.

'Working. I did tell you.'

We sat in Granddad's garden room, which was back to the welcoming space it had always been under Grandma's loving care. Recently purchased summer bedding plants were bobbing their colourful heads in newly washed terracotta pots and Granddad had swept it out and re-varnished the garden chairs. I'd made some simple bunting with pinking shears and ribbon from scraps of fabric in Grandma's sewing box, following instructions from the housekeeping guide, and it was once again an enchanting area to watch the sun go down of an evening – especially with a glass of pea pod in your hand, and with your most beloved grandparent by your side.

'For this fancy banker bloke you're always going on about?'

Did I talk about Rory more than I realised? Perhaps I did. But it was only because the connection between the two houses meant he was often on my mind.

'Technically he's a trader, not a banker, but yes. He paid me to cook and serve a birthday meal for his mum.'

'Bloody long meal if it went on until Sunday morning. Anyway, you told me you couldn't cook.'

'I'm learning . . . besides, I might have cheated a bit.' I turned to him and gave a conspiratorial smile. 'Posh supermarket pasta sauce and a pre-made tiramisu. I hid the containers.'

He relaxed a bit. 'Sweet. Talking of food, how about I take you out for lunch? The Barley Mow is always popular on a Sunday.'

'If you like.' Wow, he was treating me to lunch. That was a first. Perhaps he wasn't such a bad boyfriend after all.

I told Granddad we were heading out and looped my arm through Harrison's, feeling alcohol-fragile but happy. It was still unbearably close and cloying. There hadn't been any storms sufficient to break the weather in Summerton yet – they were coming across from the east – but we'd had a light show of rain overnight. Drooping flowers that had flopped in the summer heat were quenched and perkier. The soil was a rich brown, and that delicious smell of the damp earth filled my nostrils. But we needed a more substantial downpour to properly clear the air. The vegetable patch would certainly benefit from a good soak. We fell into step as we followed the brick path off the property and hiked up the hill into the village.

'So where does he live then?'

It took me a moment to realise he was still quizzing me about Rory.

'Oh, he has a house on the Norfolk coast. It's set in a really beautiful garden and reminds me of here – the smells and sounds of being near the sea.' I didn't add that it was unnervingly identical to Granddad's. Every time I'd tried to talk about the houses he'd lost interest. History wasn't his thing. I was beginning to wonder if I was.

Harrison yanked his arm away from mine and stopped walking.

'You've been to his Norfolk home? When was this?'

Oops.

'I . . . erm . . . he told me about it.'

'What are you hiding, Moll? You're so damn mysterious about him every time I ask. Where does he live? I'm not talking about his fancy Norfolk holiday retreat, his local house. The one you spend all your time at, trying to convince me it's work. I don't know any Rorys and I've lived here all my life.'

'I'm not hiding anything. He's old enough to be my dad – give me some credit. He's got this godawful ginger beard and is all reclusive and moody. He looks like Chewbacca, for goodness' sake.'

'If you've got nothing to hide, let's walk there now, before we head over to The Barley Mow. You said it was only five minutes away.'

So I lied through my freshly brushed teeth.

'He's got guests. I don't want him to spot me hanging around the house on a Sunday morning. It will look odd.'

'Do you fancy this bloke, or what?'

A shiver ran the entire length of my body as I analysed my feelings for Rory – a complicated man with mesmerising eyes, who was never far from my thoughts. And then I told another lie, to myself and to Harrison.

'Absolutely not,' I said.

Chapter 50

'Can you get this, babe?' Harrison handed me the bill without making eye contact, and continued to stare at his phone.

We'd eaten at The Barley Mow, but I wasn't particularly hungry, completely distracted by my adamant assertion that I had no romantic interest in Rory. The longer I sat there, the more I realised that I did find my boss attractive. I'd failed to be honest with myself and the truth was I wanted him to feel the same way about me.

Harrison had the mixed grill and ate like a man who'd been fasting since Christmas, but I'd only ordered a bowl of chips and picked at them. All that was left on his stadium-sized oval plate was a tiny pile of peas – unlike me, he didn't do green.

'But *you* invited me. I assumed it was your treat. I haven't got any money.'

'You've just pulled an all-nighter at Mr Geriatric Banker's.'

'I haven't been paid yet. I didn't even bring my bag.'

'Bloody hell, Molly.' He scrabbled about for his wallet and flung his card on the circular tray. Now I understood why he'd ordered such a large meal.

I stared at his handsome face, all scrunched up in irritation, and realised it wasn't me he'd invited to lunch; it was my purse.

I calmly placed my hands on the spray-polished table in front of me and looked into the eye that wasn't hidden behind a curtain of hair, trying to sort out my muddled thoughts.

'When did you say you were planning to leave for your big trip again?'

'Any time now really. I've been getting my rucksack together and planning the first few weeks.'

Being with me hadn't made him change his plans then. And his half-hearted suggestion that I join him had never been followed up with any practical suggestions. He hadn't even asked me if I held a current passport. So where was this going? Was he using me? And why had it taken me so long to realise? I was a convenient sexual partner, a babysitter for his not-daughter in an emergency, a time-filler until his big trip, and a bankroll for his social life. And when I didn't stump up the funds, he lost interest. He was like a cat, circling my legs and purring for food, but as soon as I wanted him on my metaphorical lap, he was out the cat flap faster than a bolting rabbit.

'What are we doing?' I asked, leaning over the table as he typed his PIN into the handheld card machine.

'Whatever you want. We could nip back to mine and you could show me how grateful you are I've bought you lunch?' His sexy grin reappeared, now he thought he might get something for his unexpected financial outlay.

'No, I mean where is our relationship going? You're off around the world soon so it's going to come to a natural end. Why are we dragging it out?'

'You can come along for the ride? There's nothing holding you here. No big career. We could be travel buddies?' he offered, but both of us knew it wasn't any more genuine than the last time.

'And Freya?'

'At the end of the day, she isn't mine. Abby is going to meet someone and I'll be the spare part. I'll miss her cheeky little smile and cute chatter though. It's been the only thing holding me back.'

'That and the lack of money?' I suggested, it now blatantly obvious I was never reason enough for him to stay.

'Yes. That too. But I'm not heading off for ever. I've decided, after all those things you said, to give it a year. I may be shallow and a bit hedonistic, but I'm serious about the kid. I'll send her postcards and stuff.'

'Because postcards are practically the same thing as having a person in your life,' I said. But, give him his due, he recognised his own shortcomings, and he was brilliant with Freya and Abby. He'd offered them both stability and friendship in trying times.

I swept my hand through my hair. It was getting longer now as trips to the hairdresser weren't a financial priority. I'd decided to grow it anyway. Brian would be pleased.

'I have to do this, Molly Coddle. Get out of this small-time place and see the world before I end up like my dad, working in the village I was born in and married to the girl across the road. And I have to do it for Ben and all the things he'll never get to experience. You have to live a bit of life in case the chunk you think you've got left gets snatched away, y'know?'

My heart flipped as I thought of a young life extinguished without warning and the impact this had on poor Harrison.

'But you need money,' I said.

'The compensation money is through.' He'd kept that quiet.

'The compensation for an injury you don't actually have,' I pointed out.

'Drayton's is a big firm. They won't miss a few thousand. Let those who have it share it with those of us who don't.'

'But it's not your . . .' My words trailed off. There's nothing like being confronted with a version of yourself, however distorted, to make you realise how you are perceived by others. In a funny way, I wasn't angry with Harrison. He wasn't a bad person, just a freeloading one. There was an element of the big kid about him – restless and bored by his small-town life. It was a mirror to my selfish behaviour with Brian and even my time with Rupert, and when I looked at the reflection, I didn't like what I saw looking back at me. Harrison was and would always be a seriously sexy package. Just not one I felt attracted to any more.

'I'm not sure I do know,' I said, my face furrowed in thought. 'I think there's a point in your life when you have to grow up. Don't get me wrong – I was late getting there, too. But I think it's time to put on my big girl pants and do some serious adulting. So I'm calling time.'

'You're dumping me?' He half-laughed. 'Not cool, babe. I'm the best thing about this poky little village.'

'I know. My loss.' I pushed my chair back and stood up, bending back over the table to squeeze his hand. 'Thanks for the memories, Harrison. It's been one hell of a ride, but I'm getting off now.' I grabbed my phone from the edge of the table.

'You can't walk out on me. I've just bought you dinner. You owe me.'

'I don't. But there are some people in my life I do need to pay back. Big time. Thanks for helping me focus.'

'Bri?' I was lying, tummy down, basking like a very skinny tattooed pencil, in the hot sun. My mobile signal was adequate, I was young, free and relieved to be single. Life was good.

'Hello, Molly. I'll fetch your mother . . .'

'No, it's you I wanted.'

'Really? Oh, okay. How's it going in Dorset? It's been kind of

you to stay on and look after Dad, but your room is here waiting for you when you return.'

'I know,' I said, picking at the lawn and snapping off daisy
heads. I was at the end of the garden, looking back at the house,
watching Granddad mow the lawn and occasionally stop to
take a selfie. I'd created a monster, but a totally adorable one.
He'd gone from one screen obsession to another, but at least he
was interacting with people now. And knew how to cook things
other than toast. The smell of the freshly cut grass and the unusual proliferation of butterflies flitting about added to my general
state of simple contentment. Grandma had been right: the views
and the fresh air were free, and they made me happier than so
many of the material things in life.

'So, what can I do for you, sweetheart?' He sighed.

'I'm not after anything. You've done more than enough for
me over the years.'

'Oh . . .' His voice was cautious and hesitant. He was waiting
for the catch.

'I simply rang to tell you about Wally's progress. He's back in
his bed, rather than falling asleep in the armchair downstairs.
Our diet has improved considerably, now that both of us are
learning to cook. And you should see the garden – I really believe
the old Granddad is back.'

'That's wonderful to hear, Molly. Thank you. We've been so
worried about him, I won't lie. Perhaps we could pop down
tomorrow? I know it's a weekday and very short notice, but
we've been trying not to step on your toes.'

'It would be lovely to see you. I'll cook.'

'Really? Okay. That would be . . . great.'

'And I'm sorry I kicked off when you wouldn't bail me out.
I'm planning to see the summer through here because this time
with Granddad is precious. I realise now exactly how precious.

If I'd known Grandma was going to be snatched away from us all like that, I would go back and do things differently that last summer.'

'We all would, Molly, but sadly you can't flick through life like a book and see what's coming.'

'I know, and then at the end of the summer I'll come home and sort my life out. I thought I might make use of my abysmal degree and maybe look at teaching or a research role somewhere. I have been so consumed with investigating the history of the house that I've spent half the time on unrelated tangents because the subject matter has been so fascinating. I'll have to start at the bottom but I'm keen to learn.'

'Right.' Brian seemed totally lost for words. 'Wonderful news. And great to hear you've been investigating the house – Dad mentioned as much. I'm so proud of you.' His words meant more than I expected. 'I've missed you . . .' he added tentatively.

'I missed *both* of you – very much. Love you, Brian.'

'Love you too, Molly,' and I heard his voice break as he put the phone down.

Chapter 51

'Let's crack open a bottle of the dandelion,' I suggested. 'It's surprisingly good. And, as the meal is home-cooked, it would be nice to continue the theme. Plus, I think Grandma would be pleased we're still enjoying her efforts.' I turned to Brian. 'Could you get one while I stir the sauce?'

Mum and Brian had arrived the following day as promised and were both milling aimlessly about, not used to feeling so redundant, because Granddad and I had everything in hand.

'Are they still kept in that silly little cupboard under the stairs?' he asked.

I nodded and Brian pulled an unreadable face.

'Erm, Dad, could you choose one? I'll only get it wrong.' Brian's hand went up to the back of his neck and he rubbed it as he took in a long suck of breath.

'Don't tell me you're *still* scared of that little cupboard?' Granddad teased. I looked over to them both for explanation. 'Always nervous of it since he got shut in as a nipper. Briggie said it was the start of your claustrophobia.' I tried to hide my surprise, but one eyebrow bopped up as I lifted the wooden spoon to my lips to taste my masterpiece. I said nothing.

'So much you cared. You never did sort that latch.'

'Big girl's blouse,' Granddad said, playfully tapping his son on the backside as he walked past to fetch a bottle of Grandma's potent wine.

Even though we were deeply entrenched in summer, Granddad had a fancy for a roast, but this was no ordinary roast. M&S had nothing on me: slow-cooked herb and cumin lamb shanks, with lemon and harissa chantenay carrots, garlic-laced savoy cabbage and crispy duck-fat roasties. It occurred to me now that I might have gone overboard with the taste sensations, but after a glass of the dandelion wine, no one would care.

'You did all this yourself, honey?' Mum asked, watching the plump, shiny, bright orange carrots tumble into an old-fashioned vegetable tureen as I prepared to serve the meal.

'Don't look so shocked.'

'To be fair, the most extravagant dish I've ever seen you produce is a Cup a Soup,' Brian chipped in, and instead of pulling a scowly face, the new me grinned across the table at him.

'I know. I certainly needed to up my game. We've been using Grandma's cookbooks for most of our meals. I'm not going to find a recipe for a fragrant Thai curry in there but it's great for the classics.'

'We?' Brian questioned.

'Yeah, Granddad cooks a mean Yorkshire pud.' I looked across at my dear grandfather, who gave me a cheeky wink and tilt of the head.

'Secret's in the hot fat,' he said and tapped his nose.

'Whilst we're on the subject of my dad, what have you done to him?' Brian put a hand on his father's arm and gave a gentle squeeze. 'A few short weeks ago he could barely operate the TV and now, before I'd even stepped through the door, he was waving an iPad at me, trying to show me a selfie of him in the garden.'

'Got myself a dapper phone as well, son. You can't slip the

pad thing in your pocket and I like to stay up to date with my Facebook friends.' Granddad tapped his shirt pocket – the rectangular bulge of his smartphone visible through the checked fabric.

Brian spat out his mouthful of wine. 'Facebook? Now you're winding me up.'

'No. Seriously, he's joined several Facebook gardening groups and even made his own selfie stick from bamboo canes and garden twine,' I said. 'He's got nearly a hundred friends already.'

'It's mostly local people or family, like my cousin in Surrey and her kids. You wouldn't believe how her grandchildren have grown. That little Mikey was a babe in arms and now I see he's drumming in some band called Gravity Falling.'

'My seventy-seven-year-old father is on Facebook?' Brian clarified.

'Yes, and a local da—' Granddad began.

'Who's for apple pie? Homemade shortcrust.' I interrupted Granddad. Now wasn't the time to announce he'd subscribed to a local seniors dating site. ('Not for romance, you understand, love. For companionship.')

And as the dinnertime conversation progressed, I couldn't help notice Mum sit back from the chatter, letting the banter and gossip go on around her, while she merely looked from face to face and smiled to herself.

The trouble with ninjas is they are covert agents. They sneak in, do what they have to do, and you never even know they've been there at all. What was she up to?

Or had she already done it?

I slipped from the cupboard and out through Rory's front door, but my stomach had more knots in it than a scout leader's entire repertoire. It would be the first time I'd seen Rory since his mum's birthday meal and our accidental garden room slumber party.

It was a colder morning in West Creeching than I'd left behind in Summerton. I shivered as I stood under the shelter of the porch and rang the brass doorbell. There was no obvious movement from inside and I was about to press the bell again when I saw his blurry figure approach through the stained glass by the door. The lock clicked and he swung the heavy door inwards.

Neither of us said anything as I slipped in through the gap and put my bag down by the stairs. I couldn't even bring myself to make eye contact at first. Why was there this atmosphere? Nothing had happened the other night, even if I was beginning to wish that it had. Certainly nothing worth updating a social media status for. I spent some time with my employer, helped him through a power cut and we fell asleep in his garden room after sharing half a bottle of wine.

No sex. No drunken things said that we needed to unsay. No inappropriate gestures or advances. Only a stray arm.

'I didn't see you come down the path. Which is odd, because I was in the gym.' He was the first to speak.

'I can assure you I wasn't dropped off by the TARDIS. You must have missed me.' I felt uncomfortable and unnecessarily scrutinised.

He frowned. 'Erm, your money is in the usual place. I've given you a bit extra for Saturday night.'

'There's no need . . .' I tilted my head up and took a deep breath. This was silly. Our eyes met briefly – long enough for me to know I wasn't imagining the atmosphere. Goose pimples broke out in a frenzy.

'Please take it. And I can't be disturbed today – under any circumstances. I have to work.'

'Would you like a cup of tea in a bit? I can be as silent as . . . erm, an empty shoe.' Nothing like sheer desperation and the sight of neatly paired trainers to make you say the stupidest of things.

'No. No tea. And can you let yourself out when you've finished? I'll be on the phone non-stop and busy with . . . things.' He walked towards his office but stopped after a couple of steps. I waited for him to turn back or say something. There was a heartbeat and then he continued, pulling the door firmly shut behind him.

I set about my work. I had a routine now, and because I was on top of things, I whizzed through each room like a domestic queen, albeit without a crown.

The kitchen bin was full again, but I was pleased to see vegetable peelings and plastic meat trays that implied he'd done some proper cooking and not been surviving on fling 'em and ping 'ems. I changed the bag and took the full one out the back of the house.

If he was 'super busy' then I was the Pope – white skullcap included. Rory worked from home and was in control of his hours. Nosy, disbelieving me decided to walk around the back of the house and have a peek through his office window.

He had his back to me, facing his multiple trading screens – none of which were switched on. The phone was untouched in its cradle. His desk was empty and he was hunched forward with his head resting on one hand; the other was playing with a stray computer cable.

He sat up and kicked the wastepaper basket with some force. It toppled forward and balls of paper and chocolate bar wrappers rolled out. Rory just watched them scatter and slumped into his hands again.

Perhaps it was to do with his illness. Perhaps he was having some sort of relapse. I understood mental health issues didn't just disappear – there would be good days and bad days – but I'd not witnessed any bad days since I'd been working for him. Not like this – sitting and staring at nothing.

The three hours flew by and it was nearly time for me to finish. I was focused and hardworking, and despite the uncomfortableness of the situation, I was humming to myself, earbuds in, and flitting about.

I didn't notice him at first – a great big Honey Monster leaning on the door jamb and watching me. I wondered how long he'd been there and my arms fell to my sides, as if I'd been caught stealing cookies from the biscuit tin. I wiggled an earbud out.

'Sorry. Didn't mean to startle you,' he said. 'I wanted to catch you before you left.'

'No problem. Did you get all your work done?' I looked him straight in the eye and he shuffled his feet and looked away.

'Um, yeah. All done. Look, this isn't easy, and I don't want you to take it the wrong way, but I don't think I need you any more.'

'Oh.' My stomach collapsed. 'Do I make too much noise? I know I hum without realising, but I can't help the vacuum. I do try to be quiet. And everyone breaks things occasionally. I can replace the plate, but accidents happen.'

'It's not you. You do a perfectly competent job.' Not a brilliant job, I noticed. 'I . . . I think I can probably manage now. You've got the house back on track so I should be fine.'

'Right.'

'Sorry.'

'And it's not because I finished off the Prosecco Saturday night, then had all that wine and danced in the rain?'

'No. It's not you.'

I laughed then – unable to stop it slipping out. 'Please don't say, "It's me" – like someone trying to break up with an unwanted girlfriend.'

What little flesh was visible on his forest of a face went pink. He cleared his throat. 'I can give you a reference. Jot your address down or leave me your email.'

'I don't want a reference. *I want a job.*' It wasn't about money any more; it was about being able to hold down steady employment for my own sense of pride. And possibly, being near him.

'I know. I know. You need the money for school, so I'll give you some extra to tide you over. I feel shitty about it and everything but this is the way it *has* to be.'

He sighed and walked away, and I was left wondering what the hell that was supposed to mean.

Chapter 52
Percy Gladwell

1895

'Mr Gladwell? My secretary was told to inform you that my wife wasn't able to make the appointment. You shouldn't have come. The Norfolk house is of no consequence at this moment.' Edward stood with his back to me, not turning immediately.

'I am truly sorry to intrude upon your grief. I . . . I—'

'A little premature, Gladwell, although at this stage, we have no assurances my wife will survive. And of course, in cases such as these, it is probable that she will not.' He eventually turned, drawing on his pipe.

Unable to hide my relief that Violet was still alive, but not my horror at the bluntness of his statement that she was not expected to recover, I reached out for the back of a chair to steady myself.

'Of course. I'm not here with regard to the house. I came here as a friend, to enquire about her condition and offer my services in any way I can.'

Edward gave a dismissive shake of the head, as if he couldn't understand my concern. 'It appears the child was growing outside the womb. She has lost a considerable amount of blood and required immediate surgery. Luckily, the surgeon has worked under that Lawson Tait fellow in Birmingham. He's had success with this type of surgery for several years – life is all about contacts, eh? Had she been born fifty years ago, she would be dead by now. Although at present her fate remains uncertain, we have, at least, got her through the first twenty-four hours.'

Violet was pregnant? I'd been frustratingly slow. Of course, I saw it now. She was expecting when I saw her last. Not touching her cake, looking pale, and her desire to finish the house. It was all she ever wanted – a child. And now that wish had nearly killed her. And perhaps would still.

'Is there *anything* I can do?'

'Kind of you, Gladwell, but I fear all we can do now is pray.'

In that moment, I knew I would give anything for her to survive – even if I was never to see her again. Naturally, I would pray for her, but I could not help but feel God was playing a cruel game. Punishing us both for feelings we could no more prevent than a child could stop the tide eroding a castle in the sand. Especially as those feelings had never once been acted upon or openly discussed.

'I understand. Please pass on my best wishes when you see her.'

I wasn't a particularly Godly man, but it is strange how we turn to Him when all other options seem closed to us. I spent the entirety of that night upon my knees, having had no further word from Kensington, praying to be absolved for sins that had been in thought alone, and begging that He had the grace to spare her.

Chapter 53

Present Day

A few days later, lying on my tummy and looking out of the crawling window at Granddad's burgeoning garden, not even July's finest display of flora and fauna could lift my heavy heart. Birds hopped about on the lawn, periodically pecking at the grass; flower borders had been tamed and were rewarding us with a psychedelic display; and the vegetable patch, although slightly behind with the crops, was thriving. Even the beans were going up in the world – with creeping tendrils twirling around the canes and seeking out the sun. My life seemed stagnant and colourless by comparison.

Losing the cleaning job was a real blow. I wanted everyone – Mum, Brian, Izzy, Rory ... even Rupert – to know that I'd changed, that I'd matured.

So, what should the mature Molly Butterfield do? Fight for her job. Go back and confront Rory in a grown-up and reasonable way, and persuade him to reinstate her?

I shuffled to my knees and stomped downstairs with all the determination of a woman who was exceedingly determined and flung open the little under-stair cupboard door. I clambered in and it closed behind me with a click. The wine crates disappeared, like always, and I shuffled forward to check the coast was clear.

Voices drifted through the cupboard door, so I paused.

'I liked her.' I recognised Miriam's voice. 'You were silly to let her go.'

'I didn't ask you round to give me grief, I asked you for help with the housework. I just couldn't face it this morning and I didn't want it spiralling out of control again. Cooking is one thing – I'm glad I've rediscovered my passion for good food – but clearing up is quite another.' I heard feet patter across the hallway and the front door open.

'Like I said, I don't mind helping out short-term but you either need to get someone else in or get that lovely young girl back.' There was a shuffle and a pause. 'Do you know what I liked most about her?'

'I expect you're going to tell me, regardless of my answer.'

'She made you *you* again.'

'What's that supposed to mean?'

'Two years of therapy and all these steps you've taken to reduce stress – quitting your job, taking up sport, employing Mrs Gammell and stepping away from a destructive social life. You became a recluse, Rory, and I didn't say anything because I recognised it was your way of coping. But a few weeks of this girl bouncing into your life and you're outside these four walls, cooking proper food, and interested in living again.'

'Right. Have you finished? Or is this the start of a lengthy lecture on whom I can and can't employ?'

'Give me a moment, I'm putting my shoes on. And another thing . . .'

I heard Rory sigh.

'She made your eyes light up and you've started to laugh again. I mean really laugh. That's something you haven't done in a long time.'

Yeah, *at me*, not with me, I thought.

'Mother, she's seventeen.'

'For goodness' sake, Rory, I'm not suggesting you marry the child. Friendships don't have to have sexual undertones, or overtones, or whatever. I'm saying she was good to have around. Like that mate of yours from school . . . what was his name?'

'He moved up north and started a family.'

'Yes, but you were always relaxed with him, not poncing about in expensive shoes and pretending to be someone you weren't – unlike when you hung around your jumped-up city types. Molly was a positive influence and, while there was absolutely nothing wrong with Mrs Gammell—'

'Who at least knew how to work a washing machine,' Rory interrupted.

'. . . she never went on walks with you or made you address your scruffy wardrobe. Don't pull that face. I've said my piece now, so I'll leave you to think about my motherly words of wisdom. I'll post these for you. Same time next week?'

I heard the front door open and there were kisses and goodbyes.

I didn't want to risk Miriam being in the front garden as I crept outside. Just my luck, she'd still be dawdling along the path deadheading something flowery and dead. Turning up now might be too much for poor Rory, so I clicked the door open a fraction, then closed it again – letting the cupboard do its magic. And went back to teach Granddad how to video call.

'Molly? Erm, what can I do for you?' Rory opened the front door to me a couple of hours later and looked both surprised and panicked. His hand went to his collar and he fiddled with it as he talked.

'I've come to ask for my job back. Beg for it, if necessary.'

'Did you bump into my mother this morning?' His eyes narrowed.

'No,' I said honestly. He scrunched up his face, not totally convinced.

'You make it sound as if you were sacked. I simply didn't need you any more.'

Even if I hadn't overheard his earlier conversation, I knew I was being fobbed off.

'You *do* need me . . .' He raised an eyebrow. 'You need me to clean and help you keep on top of your life. The whole idea was I freed you up to work. Plus, if you're honest, I think you secretly loved my singing.' I paused for breath. I was going for a combination of hard facts and gentle humour.

'Molly . . .' He started to shake his head. I could see where this was heading, and despite the new, mature me resolving not to resort to emotional blackmail, it appeared some habits were hard to break.

'Please?' The biggest, drippiest tears formed in my lower lids and politely waited to take it in turn, as they plopped from each eye and ran down my face. I was surprised how easily they came, and even more surprised when I realised this time they were genuine. The strength of my desire not to be cut out of his life overwhelmed me.

'Oh, God. Don't do this, Molly. I can't cope with someone else's tears.'

'But I *need* this job. I have to save for the bus fare next term and my family is so huge and so poor and I went to church and prayed about it and everything . . .' The tears were flowing faster now and my voice was getting squeakier. And the lies were getting bigger.

He stepped closer and I saw him flex his fingers, as if he was contemplating a conciliatory pat on the back or a friendly ruffle of my hair.

'You can reduce my hours, if money is a problem?' We both

knew it wasn't. 'You needn't even see me. I can be like a sleeping partner – except I won't be sleeping and I'm not a partner. But you know what I mean? Unseen and highly efficient, like a silent housework shadow.' His face changed. Maybe that one was closer to the mark. Maybe he did have a problem with me – my humming or my ineptitude. He tugged at his bottom lip with his teeth.

'Okay.'

I sniffed and the tears stopped. 'Okay, as in I can have my job back?'

He battled with some inner thoughts, and nodded.

'But I won't be around. Perhaps I'll get you a key cut or something. I trust you.'

'Thank you,' I gushed, flinging my arms around him, not mentioning I already had a key.

The look of utter horror that flashed across his face as I administered my grateful embrace reminded me that not every-one appreciates physical contact. I pulled a contrite face and bowed my head slightly.

'And I promise not to give you any more random and totally inappropriate boss hugs,' I added.

For a couple of weeks, things returned to normal. I did my hours at Rory's, and continued the dog walking for Mr Pickersgill and babysitting for Catherine. I'd totally got to grips with small kids now, although it turned out Amber responded better to being treated like an equal. Fine by me – I made her read to Oliver whilst I picked up the toys and ran their bath. I even managed to get Razzle to walk to heel – sort of.

Jean, who I still saw from time to time because it turned out I enjoyed the cycling, even when I could afford the bus fare, asked me if Granddad would be entering anything in the Summerton

Fayre, but I pointed out everything we'd put in was late and nothing would make show-worthy size.

'I didn't even know there was a fayre in Summerton,' Granddad said when I told him about my conversation. 'I'll have to be more organised for next year.'

'Jean said there's a gardening club held in the village hall once a fortnight. Newcomers are always welcome.'

'Did she now. Well, maybe I'll drop by and see if she's got a contact number.'

'You could always Google it,' I suggested, playing devil's advocate.

'Hmm, yes, but I think it would be better to speak to her in person,' he said, and I smiled. No one could ever fill the shoes of the indomitable Bridget, but Jean could at least bring her own pair round and slip them under Granddad's table occasionally.

'Dave and I are looking for a flat together,' Izzy announced, as we had our weekly video call.

'But you hardly know the man,' I whined. How can things have moved on so fast? I'd only been away for three months.

'Sometimes when you know, you know,' she said. My heart gave a walloping thump, rolling over at her words as if to tell my head it had missed something, but my brain skittered on regardless and we talked of more mundane things. I questioned her about the realities and practicalities of full-time employment (only twenty-eight days' annual leave?) and shared my top low-budget nineteen-fifties cleaning tips. It was a far cry from our conversations only a few short weeks ago.

Armed with a head full of architectural knowledge and a million questions, I cycled back to Bickerton Manor, making full use of my free entry. Michael was pleased to see me and I rather monopolised him while I was there, chatting about Percy Glad-well, the decorative arts and the evolution of architecture.

'If you've got time on your hands, young lady, you could always volunteer,' he said, after we'd covered all the topics extensively. 'We could do with people like you – enthusiastic, knowledgeable and personable.'

'I'm not sure how long I'll be in the area. I really need to start looking for a full-time job after I've seen the summer out with Granddad. Although I don't have a clue what to do with my life or where to start looking.'

Michael rubbed his chin and narrowed his eyes. 'What sort of thing are you looking for? And, as a graduate, do you have a starting salary in mind?'

'I honestly don't care. As for salary . . .' I laughed. 'I think I'll be lucky to get something that pays minimum wage. I'll probably end up stacking supermarket shelves, but at least it's a start.'

'Don't read too much into this, but would staying around here be a possibility?' Michael asked.

The question threw me for a moment. I'd assumed I'd be heading back to my bedroom in Brian's house, but if I really wanted to grow up, perhaps I should be thinking not only outside the box, but also outside Brian's Georgian three-storey house. After all, Izzy was deserting me, and Mum and Brian would always be enough for each other. Maybe there was an old man with an unused self-contained attic in his oversized and quirky house that might take on a paying lodger. An old man who could do with the company and a general cheerleader in his life.

'Possibly,' I said. 'If something comes up to keep me here.'

As I witnessed a glorious sunrise two days later down at the bay, my phone pinged with an email asking me to consider a job at

Bickerton Manor. There was still a formal interview to attend and references to supply, but this was simply red tape as Michael indicated the final decision was his. The wages weren't great, but the work would be varied: caring for the collections, updating inventories, interacting with the public, helping to set up exhibitions and so on. I'd been thinking about relocating permanently to Dorset since our conversation, although I'd yet to approach Granddad. With a potential job in the offing, perhaps now was a good time to sound him out.

Lumpy pebbles dug into my bottom as I wriggled about to make myself more comfortable. I placed a rolled-up jumper behind my head and leaned back on the shingle bank to watch the sun finally clear the horizon and let her warm light bathe the bay.

'Molly Coddle?' a voice called from behind. I turned and as the figure got closer I realised it was Harrison. 'Your granddad said I'd find you down here. Not sure he likes me much though.'

'He likes you more now we aren't going out,' I offered helpfully.

He frowned. 'Anyway, came to say goodbye. I know you brutally dumped me in a public place and everything, but you kinda got under my skin, and I wanted to check we were cool.'

'As a summer breeze,' I replied.

He squatted down and joined me on the bank. 'I got a good deal on a last-minute flight, so I'm heading out tomorrow,' he said. 'I've been planning stuff for months so I'm good to go.'

'I hope you have a brilliant time. Make good memories,' I said, touched that he'd taken the time to seek me out.

'Yeah, Ben never got to travel – he never got to do much, really. I like to think he's high-fiving me from some place in the ether.' I gave his arm a comforting rub and neither of us spoke for a moment. 'So –' he cleared his throat – 'I'm starting in Oz, working my way up through India, and finishing in Europe. I'm still thinking just a year, after our conversation, y'know? Freya will miss me, and they can change a lot at that age.'

I grinned at him and he looked confused.

'What?'

'My little boy is growing up,' I said. 'And he's going to be just fine.' I threw my arm around his back and rested my head on his shoulder. He let his head fall to meet mine and we stayed like that for a long time, watching the breeze dance across the surface of the sea, and listening to the gush and hiss of the tide toying with the pebbles by the shore.

Chapter 54

I knew Rory was deliberately keeping out of my way. When I turned the key in the front door, his office door was hastily closed, shutting him in his silent world. Or shutting me out.

I finished the housework in record time, and there were no other instructions, so I texted him to ask if I could tidy up the flower borders – ridiculous as he was less than six metres away from me. He replied I could help myself to anything I needed.

It was an absolute scorcher of an early August day. I popped on a floppy-brimmed sun hat from my rucksack and went to investigate the shed.

There was an assortment of hand tools in a basket, which I took outside, and then selected a pair of snippers to cut back the invaders, quickly establishing I should have worn gloves as the brambles pricked and the nettles stung. It was partly guesswork and partly newly acquired knowledge, but I worked out what plants to keep and what to pull out.

The sun was approaching nuclear explosion temperatures and was now directly overhead. I glanced at my watch and realised I'd been longer outside than I'd intended. There was some laundry to put away, so I decided to call time. I was thirsty from the heat and achy from bending over.

Before I turned back to the house, I sensed him. I didn't need to look at his office window to know he was standing there. Quite how long he'd been watching me, I didn't know, but as I made my way to the shed, I was aware of him stepping back into the shadows of his office.

He didn't want me around but still felt the need to keep an eye on me. Did he think I was about to make off with his rake or something? And how had we gone from our budding friendship and the easy chatter of the birthday meal to this? Was it to do with his depression? Or was it personal to me?

It made absolutely no sense at all.

'I thought you were downstairs.' Rory looked most put out that I'd appeared on the upstairs landing in front of him.

'No. I was bringing up the clean sheets.'

'So I see.'

The awkward silence crept like an invisible mist and filled the space between us. Was I really that bad he had to avoid me completely?

'I'm taking Razzle down to the cliffs when I finish here. Would you like to come?' If he was feeling low, the fresh air would help. Maybe we could even talk this thing out.

'No thanks. Besides, I went for a run this morning along the coast path and back through the dunes.'

'You did? That's fantastic.'

'Nice and early, half five, before people were about. It was good. You were right, Molly. Fresh air and open spaces. I've been cooped up here for far too long. It's still baby steps for me. I'll get there in my own time, but I'm making progress.'

'I'm pleased.' And I meant it. He was such a lovely man and deserved to find his way again.

I smiled and held his eyes. He broke away quickly and turned his head sharply, as if I'd slapped him across the face. He'd shut down again and I watched him retreat downstairs, and my own body underwent a wave of sensations I couldn't quite define.

Five minutes later there was a knock at the front door. Apart from the postman, who'd already been, very few people called at Acacia House. Not knowing if Rory had heard it, I went downstairs, but he was already standing in front of the open door.

It was Holly. What the hell was she doing here?

'Hello. Gemma, isn't it?' She noticed me hovering at the bottom of the stairs.

'Erm ...' I could feel both sets of eyes bore into me, Holly waiting for confirmation, Rory waiting for an explanation.

I uttered an indeterminate sound, but however hard I tried, nothing coherent came from my mouth.

'This is Molly and I'm Rory Brooker,' he said. 'What can I do for you?'

'Hi, I'm Holly.' She stuck out her hand towards Rory, who reluctantly took it. 'We never actually got to meet.' My heart started to thump violently. She was going to ruin everything.

'My middle name is Gemma.' It was a pathetic and desperate lie. 'Some of my school friends use it, so I get called both.'

'Holly and Molly. They could get confused.' Rory tipped his head between the two of us and gave a half smile.

I nearly choked on my words. 'Funny coincidence. Anyway, I must get on ...'

'I'm here to deliver this from Mrs Gammell.' Holly thrust a carrier bag at Rory. 'She's sorry she hasn't been up to see you since her surgery, but it's been a slow recovery, so I offered to drop off some of these jars of marmalade. We made a batch together last week. And, not that I'm trying to steal Gemma's job ...' She shot me an evil glare – enough to remind me that's exactly what I'd done to her. 'But if things change, or she moves on, I'm still interested in any hours you have available in the future. Every little helps when you're a student.' Rory looked confused. 'After all, we spoke for so long on the phone and you offered me an interview when—'

'Thanks then. I'll put these in the kitchen,' I said, stepping forward and grabbing the bag of clinking jars from her. And I shut the front door in the startled face of my nemesis.

Rory would have to be stupid not to realise something wasn't adding up.

And Rory wasn't stupid.

Chapter 55

Percy Gladwell

1895

Several weeks passed. I made daily enquiries as to Violet's condition, and the hours spent on my knees were rewarded. Each night she survived she grew stronger, until she was eventually out of danger. I was informed Violet would return to West Creeching to convalesce and contrived to visit her as soon as I was able.

I took the train up one October morning, and was seen into a small drawing room, where Violet lay on a daybed, with a large tapestry across her knees. Her faithful servant Mary sat quietly in the corner. My heart stopped as I noticed the words of a medieval love poem across the panel, interlaced with poppies and cornflowers. It was the poem from the book I had given her back in June.

'Violet?'

'Oh, Percy. You came?'

She was pale and thin, her glorious hair wild about her face, but my arrival brought colour to her cheeks.

'Of course. I tried to see you in London but your condition was too precarious. I asked Mr Marston to pass on my best wishes for your speedy recovery.'

'You find me engaged in needlework.' She looked down at her lap. 'A bed curtain inspired by a beautiful verse that always brings me to tears. *For weal or woe I will not flee To love the heart that loveth me . . .*' She tried to arrange herself into a more comfortable position and gave me a piercing stare. '*That heart my heart hath in such grace That of two hearts one heart make we . . .*'

'Please,' I said gently, as my heart pounded violently, 'do not exert yourself. I will not stay long. I do not wish to tire you when rest is undoubtedly the best medicine.'

'On the contrary, I am bored out of my mind. You know how I hate to be confined? Even reading is becoming tiresome.' And she indicated a small pile of books on a tripod table beside her.

'*Marcella* – Mary Augusta Ward,' I read from the top volume. 'I understand it to be an engaging book and have considered reading it myself. A strong woman, engaged to a wealthy Conservative, who is taken with socialism – perhaps it is as well Edward did not investigate these books too closely,' I teased.

She smiled then. Her rare and precious smile, and I at once felt as if I had been bestowed with the greatest treasure in the world.

'Edward merely tutted when he saw the titles. I'm not convinced he paid much attention to their content. I'd forgotten that we share a love of unsuitable fiction. Perhaps that is why I like you so much . . .'

My eyes darted across the room to Mary, but she was staring out of the bay window, her hands neatly folded in her lap. The epitome of a discreet and invisible servant.

'It is merely snobbery that prevents people from reading a good book,' I continued. 'One that will have them turning the pages and living a thrilling adventure through the words. The loss, my dear, is theirs.' I smiled at her gaunt face and she slid her hand across the folded down blanket and over her tapestry, towards mine – resting it near the edge of the bed. The tips of our fingers touched for the briefest moment and then she withdrew her hand again.

'I thought I'd lost you.' My voice was low, but Mary was humming a hymn to herself and appeared engrossed in the view from the window. 'I prayed every night that God would spare you, and you know I am not a man given to prayer.'

'I, too, believed it was my time, but something kept pulling me back. Perhaps it was your prayers?' Our eyes met and held.

'I think it was something far more powerful; I believe it was love . . .' My voice faltered but I found it again. 'You are loved by so many people, Violet, that God couldn't bear to take you from them.'

Mary's gentle singing came to an end and Violet gave a small cough.

'Did you stop at the house first? I do so wish to see it.' She tried to smile again, but her heart wasn't in it.

'I did and it's progressing nicely. We are still on schedule.'

'How wonderful. Then I shall be living there as the garden comes to life. I ordered so many bulbs, perhaps too many, but there should be colour in every bed. And I desperately need colour in my life at this time . . .'

I didn't know how to respond. The details of her recovery weren't known to me, nor much beyond the circumstances that had led to her collapse. It was not proper to ask. Violet, however, did not seem to share my sensitivity around the subject.

After a small pause, she continued. 'You see, it is possible, Percy, I can no longer have children.' Her eyes clouded.

'Now, madam,' Mary walked across the room and stood between us, adjusting the blankets of her mistress. 'That is not what the physician said at all.'

Violet turned her head to the window and a solitary tear rolled down her pale cheek.

Chapter 56

Present Day

'What's going on, Molly? You were the only person I interviewed for the job. Or at least, I thought you were.' Rory looked directly at me, his eyes narrowing.

I looked down at my shoes and kicked at the doormat with my toe. 'Nothing's going on. I don't know what you're talking about.'

'Okay. I'll catch up with that Holly girl and ask her.' He moved to open the front door and I put out my hand and grabbed his sleeve.

'Okay. I might have *slightly* misled you when we first met.'

I don't think there was ever a moment in my life when I felt so totally rubbish. A heavy feeling rolled my stomach over and made me feel sick. My arms started to tremble as I stared intently at the stupid doormat, covered in a rainbow of light from the stained glass.

'It was Holly who was recommended by Mrs Gammell,' I began. 'And it was Holly you spoke to on the phone and invited round for an interview. But it was me who found myself in your house at six o'clock that evening.'

His brow wrinkled and his eyebrows met for a quick chat in the middle of his head.

'But *you* assumed I was Holly.' My voice was stronger now, as I tried to shift the blame. 'I did correct you. I told you I was

Molly but you carried on, drawing me in with all your talk about this job and the money when I was at a point in my life desperately needing both . . .'

I wanted him to say something. Perhaps acknowledge he had played a small part in this whole mix-up by his rash assumption. But he said nothing and continued to stare at me with his horrified emoji face.

'And then you offered me the position, so when I saw Holly coming up the path, I told her the job had gone.'

Still nothing from him, just green eyes that were losing their sparkle the more I spoke.

'I thought it would be easy – cleaning. I mean people do it all the time in their everyday lives. But it wasn't, because I've been spoilt and I had to learn fast. And none of it was helped because Holly is some kind of wunderkind with the domestic abilities of Mary Poppins, so you had all these high expectations after the phone call, and I . . . I really struggled.' I could feel tears pricking at my eyes but these weren't manufactured, unlike the ones I'd engineered so many times in the past to get my own way with Brian. My despair was real.

He finally spoke. 'Stop with the fake tears, Molly. I just want the truth.' We locked eyes and I swallowed hard. I had such confusing feelings for him, but I had to be totally honest, because I knew I couldn't live with myself if I was anything less.

'I lied at the interview. I wasn't qualified and pretended to be someone I wasn't. And Holly needed the job just as much as me. If not more. You should give it to her. You're right, I'm clumsy, I hum too much, and I'm pretty abysmal at housework – although I've learned masses and tried really hard not to let you down. I don't blame you for asking me to leave before.'

'You think I got rid of you before because I didn't like you, or thought you weren't up to the job?'

'Yes, and because I got tipsy that night in the garden room – all that dancing and then falling asleep across your lap.'

It was his turn to look uncomfortable. He fiddled with the damn beard, pulling at a piece with his fingers. 'Who are you then, Molly? Was this all an act?'

'No, I really *am* that abysmal at housework. I can't be quiet when I'm asked to be. And I don't always have proper control of my spindly limbs. I'm gawky, awkward, spoilt and selfish. But I'm not a seventeen-year-old, church attending schoolgirl who's never had sex and has five billion siblings. I'm a twenty-four-year-old university graduate who has had a comfortable middle-class upbringing, and a failed long-term relationship behind me – something else in my life that I managed to mess up.'

'You're not seventeen?' His hand dropped sharply. '*You're not at school?*'

I shook my head.

'But you look so young,' he said, almost to himself. I was fully aware my boyish figure gave me an adolescent appearance. But then my behaviour hadn't helped. 'Jesus, Molly. What have you done?' His shoulders slumped and he stood shaking his head, like the bobbing Churchill dog from that stupid advert.

I looked blank. I thought I'd just listed enough misdemeanours; surely that covered the present crimes. What more did he want?

'Do you not realise what's been going through my head?' His glorious soft, throaty voice was building to a crescendo. 'From my initial delight at the friendship I'd formed with my young employee, to doubting whether my feelings might be something more. The connection we had, your surprising flashes of maturity, the infectious way you embraced life – all jumbling around and not allowing me to think straight. I've been so worried about people's misconceptions, even though nothing inappropriate has taken place. Have you any idea how all of this might make me feel? *Have you?*' He was almost shouting now, his angry face getting redder and closer. It was scary, because Rory didn't do angry; he did quiet, withdrawn and introspective.

'You have feelings for me?' I frowned. Was *that* what this was all about? He actually *liked* me? In a maybe-I-could-kiss-her way? My heart flipped.

'I thought perhaps I did. Not any more.' His head moved slowly from side to side and the flash of anger subsided almost as soon as it had appeared. He was trying to dislodge these feelings, flinging them away with each shake of his head. I let the bag of marmalade slip to the floor and put out my hand.

'But that's good.' He didn't move, but stared at my hand as if I'd thrust one of Razzle's poo bags at him. 'Then I didn't imagine it. We connected. There is something, isn't there? We can start again. I finished with Harrison – you were right about him. And I don't care if you're old enough to be my father, age doesn't matter once you're an adult. What's twenty years? Look at Michael Douglas and Catherine Zeta-Jones.'

A frown crossed his face. 'For God's sake, Molly. How old do you think I am?'

I paused. Horrible question – worse if it comes from a woman – but I still didn't want to offend him.

'Erm, well, there's the little bits of grey hair, and your past career, those slippers, and of course it's difficult to see your face under all that fuzz ... I thought, well, assumed really ...'

'I'm barely thirty. All the men in my family go prematurely grey – look at my father. These stunning silver highlights started peeking through when I was in my early twenties.'

I realised my jaw had dropped open and I tried to arrange my features in a slightly less OMG expression – because that would have been rude. He'd spent the last couple of months thinking I was seventeen, and I assumed he was hurtling towards fifty, when in reality there was only six or seven years between us. How blind we'd both been.

He moved out of my reach and his head dropped. 'This is irrelevant now, Molly. You lied and pretended to be someone you weren't. All these weeks of deceit can't be undone by a simple sorry.'

'It wasn't a lie exactly ... well, yes it was a lie, but sort of with good intentions ... well, not good intentions exactly, but you started it ...' Sometimes I still sounded immature, even to myself. No wonder people consistently mistook me for a teenager and Rory had believed I was still at school. Accepting this and being forced to take a proper look at myself over the past few weeks hadn't been the most pleasant experience.

'Stop behaving like a child, Molly, especially as we have now firmly established you are far from that. Collect your money from the kitchen and then I really don't want to see you again. This time you *are* fired. I don't tolerate lying from an employee. Under *any* circumstances.'

He walked towards the office. 'And don't start with the tears again. Especially when you don't have starving siblings, a widowed mother and the help of God to back you up this time. You are a destructive force and you've nearly destroyed me. Stay out of my life, please, because I don't want you in it.'

Chapter 57
Percy Gladwell
1895

'I'm sorry, Charlotte, but I can't do this any more. It's not fair to me and it certainly isn't fair to you. You deserve better.'

Nearly losing Violet, even though she wasn't mine to lose, had made me realise there was no way I could marry Charlotte. I'd returned to Dorset and arranged to visit the Hamiltons – her mother gushing over me as I arrived, and then tucking us away in the front parlour with a knowing and conspiratorial smile.

'I don't understand . . .' Charlotte's round cheeks drained of colour and she began to pick at her fingers. Moments before, she too had gushed at me, apprising me of her recently acquired domestic skills, the long list of items secured for her bottom drawer, and bombarding me with questions about what area of the county I should like to live in. 'Are you saying you no longer wish to marry me?' Her bottom lip started to quiver.

'Yes, that's exactly what I'm saying. And I think it's kinder to tell you now rather than let this drag on.'

'But you *promised*.' Her voice cracked and she clasped both hands to her chest.

'When, Charlotte? When did I promise?' My voice was gentle but resolute. 'I spoke to you last Christmas and asked you to give me a year before I made any commitments, and now I find you consider us engaged, when I have never formally proposed.'

Her nostrils flared as she considered my words. 'But you *implied* we were to marry. You let me talk of our future, and knew, whether a formal proposal had been made or not, that I *believed* we would be together . . .' Tears started to roll down her plump cheeks, and my heart ached for her.

There was undoubtedly blame on my part. I'd gone along with her plans, not correcting her assumptions, hoping perhaps marriage would help me forget Violet and move on from the unhealthy infatuation over a woman I could never have.

'Yes, and it was wrong of me,' I acknowledged.

'Is there someone else? Was I the poor saphead that you took pity on, knowing I would not get another offer, whilst you considered other options? Are you in love with another?'

'I have no expectations elsewhere, Charlotte,' I replied, choosing my words with care. 'I am fully expecting to see out my days as a bachelor. But it would not be right to marry you, knowing that I do not love you, when you are a good woman, who deserves to be loved, and will make a most excellent wife.'

If I had never met Violet, I could perhaps have been happy with Charlotte. But I knew I would rather live alone than be with someone who could never compare to her. I would come to resent Charlotte and she did not deserve that. If I could keep Violet in my life, even if only as a friend, it would be enough.

'Do you not understand, Percy? *You were my last chance*,' she yelled.

Her body collapsed across the chair and she threw her head over her folded arm. The sobs grew louder as she entered a total state of despair. My heart bled for her, as it was not in my nature to be unkind. I had to hope she would see, in time, that I had made the correct decision.

I put my hand on her shoulder but she shrugged it away.

'I was never foolish enough to believe you loved me, but was content with our match – even if you had merely agreed to it out of pity,' she cried into the chair.

'Pity is not reason enough to marry. And you should place greater worth on yourself than that. You are a kind, God-fearing woman, Charlotte. You deserve better.' As she thought about my words, her resolve strengthened.

'Of course I deserve better,' she spat, sitting back upright. 'But who will have me now? I have wasted a year with you, Percy – a year I did not have to spare. How do you think that makes me feel?'

'Wretched?' I answered honestly, because that same feeling was eating me up inside. 'There will be someone out there who loves you and appreciates—'

'You have destroyed me, Percy Gladwell, and I will never, *ever* get over this. You are an evil man to play with my emotions in such a manner.' The sobbing stopped and she stared at me with unblinking eyes. 'You have condemned me to the life of a spinster, never to bear children or to have the opportunity to raise my station in life. I hate you for giving me false hope and I heartily wish you dead. You do not deserve to live a happy life, for you have surely destroyed mine.'

Chapter 58

Present Day

'What's up, love?' Granddad finally said that evening, as I pushed my perfect homemade steak and ale pie around my plate. Not one forkful had made it to my mouth.

'I've lost my job.'

'Which one? You've got about fifty,' he joked.

'The one that mattered,' I said, trying not to get emotional. 'The cleaning.' Although I'd had to ring Mr Pickersgill and explain that I couldn't walk Razzle any more. I'd suggested a local girl, Holly, and he'd been understanding.

'Oh, you'll get another one. People are always crying out for cleaners. Not like in my day when only the rich could afford to employ others to do their housework. And now we have women going out to work to earn money to pay for a job they could do themselves.'

I looked at my darling Granddad then, across the table from me, pulling a silly face and tucking into the pie as if he hadn't eaten for a fortnight. And I mean *really* looked at him. About ten years had fallen from his furrowed brow and stooping shoulders since I'd come to stay back in May. His pale skin had been tanned by the summer sun, and the unbearable weight of grief was no longer bearing down on him. He was standing tall and his love for life had returned.

There was a prolonged silence as I played with the pastry, finally stabbing a piece with my knife. He looked up at me, noticing my silence, and scraped the last of the buttery mashed potato on to his fork.

'What was so special about this job, then?'

'The employer.'

'You haven't gone and fallen for the boss, have you? School-girl error.'

Wincing at his choice of words, I let my cutlery drop from my fingers. It clattered on the plate. 'If that wasn't so close to the truth, I'd laugh.'

'And he's not interested?'

'He was, and then I went and cocked it up so badly that even a powerful fairy godmother with the biggest magic wand on the planet couldn't sort this mess. But it's okay, Granddad. I don't want you worrying about me.'

'I understand. You don't want to be talking to an old man about your personal problems. I wish Briggie was here. She'd have you sorted and back to your old self in no time.'

'Yes,' I sighed, acknowledging the truth of his words. 'She'd whip up a Victoria sponge with butter icing and homemade jam, and everything would be all right.' I smiled as a memory of her standing in the kitchen, hands on hips, floral apron around her generous middle, telling me to pull myself together came to mind. She would have said something profound, like, 'You may have detoured but if you're meant to be, you'll find each other again,' and then gone back to peeling a mountain of potatoes.

'Do you remember when I fell over the wheelbarrow as a teenager, knocking a shuttlecock around the garden?' I said. 'I really bashed my elbow and had a huge bruise on my leg. By teatime, there was a Dorset Apple Cake on the table, next to a pot of clotted cream? I instantly forgot about the pain and practically ate the whole thing. Good memories.'

Granddad chuckled and then put a weathered hand up to his chin. 'Because, as she always used to remind us, cake makes everything better?'

'Yes, sometimes it really does . . . Oh, Granddad, I miss her so much.'

'Well, you still have two Butterfields who love you; you have me and you have Brian,' he said. 'Not that our baking could ever measure up.' There was a pause and then Granddad heaved out a long, slow sigh. 'Brian really loves you, you know?'

'But he didn't choose me, did he? I was part of the deal, whether he liked it or not.'

'Briggie and I didn't choose the house, it was gifted to us – a bloody great house we couldn't afford to run, away from our family, and at the time, my job. But we fell in love with it and I can't imagine having spent my life anywhere else.'

'I *do* love him,' I said.

'Then what's the problem?'

I focused intently on my plate, but I wasn't really looking at it. I bit at my thumbnail. Did I even know why I'd been so distant with him over the years? To be fair, we'd jogged along okay at the beginning, despite my initial resentment at sharing Mum with him. It was the teenage years when things got trickier, but then all adolescents kick out and rebel. He was an easy target because I could always fall back on the 'You're not my real father' line. I'd been unfair to him. I could see that now.

'You know he can't have children?' Granddad continued.

I narrowed my eyes and stopped biting my nail.

'I think it was a big factor in the failure of his short-lived first marriage. He was totally upfront about it when he met Annetta because it had been a deal-breaker in the past.' There was a pause while I digested this new information. 'So don't be sure, young lady, that he didn't want you as much as he wanted your mother.' He scooped up a forkful of carrots and studied my face. 'If not more.'

What a summer this was turning out to be. I had so many lessons I needed to learn and they'd seemingly been crammed into a few short weeks. Poor Brian. Poor Grandma. Poor Rory. The one person I wouldn't allow myself to feel sorry for was me. I didn't deserve my own sympathy.

'Why don't you take a little walk down to the bay and see if that doesn't clear your head, love? Blow all your troubles away,' Granddad suggested.

I scraped my chair back and walked over to this dear old man who could somehow make things better without the need for baking, and planted a small kiss on the top of his soft, pink, bald head. He was right, of course; a bit of sea air and a bracing walk would help me focus.

When I returned two hours later, there was a lopsided, slightly burnt Dorset Apple Cake sitting in the middle of the kitchen table.

And an awful lot of mess to clear up.

Chapter 59

Now that I was no longer funding Harrison's social life, and my own had come to an abrupt halt, I had an overwhelming desire to visit Mum and let her hug everything away. I did two nights of babysitting for Catherine, which gave me enough to get home. It would have been cheaper if I'd booked an advance ticket but speedy access to the healing hugs was worth every extra hard-earned pound.

Izzy was pleased to hear I was popping back and made plans for the gang to meet up Saturday. I reluctantly agreed but insisted on Friday at home with Mum. And Brian.

He met me from the station and I quietly slid into the front of the car and yanked the seatbelt over my tummy. Brian looked at my face and kept quiet for the first few minutes.

'Are you okay, love?'

I think he was expecting me to snap. Or grunt. Or both. I looked across at his concerned face, half concentrating on the busy road, but throwing me repeated anxious glances.

'No. I've messed up big time. And there's nowhere quite like home when you need a bolt hole. Plus, I've missed you both so much.'

'You have?' He threw another quick glance in my direction before his attention was diverted by the roundabout.

'Yes, I *really* have,' and I reached out for his knee.

*

Ninja Mum took one look at me and poured two sizeable gins.

'Leave your bag there. We can deal with it later. Come and sit out on the decking. The evening sun is glorious.'

We sat together on our expensive rattan cube patio furniture, on the microscopic square of decking in our tiny piece of west London. I sipped my pink raspberry gin and let the heat of the evening sun warm my bare shoulders. Brian discreetly left us alone and insisted on preparing the meal, but not before I'd hugged him and thanked him for picking me up from the station. If he was surprised by my sudden displays of affection, he hid it well.

'Work? Man? Or friends?' Mum finally asked in a deliberately disinterested fashion, staring ahead and swirling the contents of her glass. She rubbed a thumb over her glossy, manicured nails as if they were the focus and the question was merely throwaway.

'Work,' I said. 'No. That's a lie. Man.'

'Yes, they're the worst. Jobs don't destroy your heart in quite the same way.'

The hum of the traffic and the slightly fumy air seemed to stagnate around us. Shouts from some argument in a nearby garden drifted over the tall fence and I realised there was a distinct lack of sky. I had to look straight up to find it, past the rooftops and the proprietorial six-foot-high boundaries. It was so different from Dorset. Or Norfolk. There was no salty sea air or sense of space. It was all somehow more cloying, less fresh, less wholesome. It made me realise that whilst it was wonderful to see Mum and Brian, I didn't belong here.

'It would be funny if I wasn't so desperately heartbroken,' I said.

'Walter mentioned there was a boy. Said he's off travelling soon. It's always the realisation you aren't enough. That they don't want you as much as they want something else.'

'It's not Harrison.' I scrunched up my face. 'He was a waste of my time, as it turned out. Fun but selfish.'

Mum remained silent, letting me continue in my own time, and took another sip of her fragrant flamingo-coloured gin.

'Anyway, Rory is far from a boy,' I continued. 'Part of the confusion really. He's got this speckled grey around his temples and a godawful ginger beard that hides most of his face. I thought he was about fifty – much older than he really is. But the really funny thing is he thought I was much younger. Like, seventeen. I mean, can you believe that?'

There was a pause.

'Yes,' said Mum.

Okay, I'd walked into that one. Mum took another sip of her gin. It was the liquid equivalent of flicking uninterestedly through a magazine. Ninja mother was listening, willing me to open up to her, but doing it from a distance. I decided to spill everything. There was no point in delaying my shame; we both knew I'd tell her eventually. And she had enough gin to wait all night if necessary.

I coughed to clear my throat and prepared to lay my troubles on the line.

'At first I thought he was old and boring, and I'm pretty certain he thought I was inept and annoying, but we got to know each other and somewhere along the way I sort of fell for him. Turns out he sort of fell for me as well.'

'So what's the problem?'

'I told these massive lies to get the job – pretended I was someone else, someone who was still at school, and good at all the things I'm no good at.' I couldn't look at her and tilted my face away, towards the sun. I let it blind me and half-closed my eyes, shielding myself from any judgemental looks she might throw my way. 'Meanwhile, he struggled with this massive guilt about his confusing feelings towards someone he thought was technically a child.'

Saying it out loud was the first time I'd appreciated how serious it was from his point of view, and I felt awful that I'd needlessly put him through all this.

'I really messed up. And now he doesn't want anything to do with me.' I picked at my fingernails as uncomfortable emotions flooded my body.

'Brian gave up on me,' Mum said. 'After weeks of being asked out and rebuffing him, I told him I wasn't interested and threatened to resign if he kept harassing me. He stopped immediately and stepped away. You know what a sweetheart he is?'

'Yes,' I said, a lump forming in my throat.

'And then I realised all the reasons that had stopped me from dating him – worrying about the impact he would have on you, people gossiping about the single mother who'd wooed the boss to solve her financial problems, how my parents would be devastated if I dated a non-Catholic, non-Italian – they all paled into insignificance, because I loved him. He was kind, loyal, trustworthy. He was generous and calm – never pressuring me and promising to put you first. And he had this sexy little shy smile that made my insides flip when I looked at him.'

On cue, Brian poked his head around the back door. 'Dinner will be served in twenty minutes, ladies. Anyone for a top-up?' He waved the gin bottle, the tonic in his other hand, and Mum held out her empty glass. All smiles, he almost skipped out to us, topping Mum up but noticing my glass had barely been touched, and retreating inside once more. The fleeting look that passed between them as he left was one of two people very much in love. Had they always been like this? So devoted and in tune with each other?

'I had to swallow my pride before I lost him,' Mum continued, when Brian was out of earshot. 'I stood behind his huge, imposing desk on a wet Friday afternoon, when everyone else had left for home, and told him I was wrong. Admitted I'd lied and that there was nothing I wanted more than to be with him.'

'It's not the same. My lies were calculated. That's not so easy to forgive, is it?'

'No.' She put her glass on the table and picked at a stray thread of rattan. 'But perhaps if you can forgive me for what I've done, I think this Rory should be able to forgive you . . .'

'You've lost me.'

'You aren't the only one who's done something they feel ashamed of. Something they don't think can be forgiven. Something with ripples that reached further than anyone thought possible.' She turned to look at me for the first time in the whole conversation. 'And you are those ripples, my darling child.'

I'd hardly touched the gin, but now took several big gulps to prepare myself. I knew she was about to deliver on her promise. She was about to tell me the truth about my father. My body went rigid in anticipation.

'Silly lies and evasions of the truth that went on for so long that it was hard to face. Feelings of guilt and embarrassment that haunted me when I least expected them to. And then it all boils down to when is the right time and how do you find the right words to tell your precious daughter that you have absolutely no idea who her father is?'

Chapter 60
Percy Gladwell
1896

Acacia House was finished in the late spring of 1896. I was busy with clients in the north of England for much of June, preparing plans for a row of workers' cottages, and was only able to visit West Creeching two weeks after Violet had taken up residence. It had been an unpleasant time for me, Charlotte's heartbreak always at the forefront of my mind. I constantly wrestled with my guilt for not correcting her assumption earlier, and worried for her future. My fondness for her, my admiration of her drive, and even my respect for her uncompromising faith, were genuine, but I did not and would never love her like she deserved. Instead, I turned my face to brighter things.

The journey from London was almost unbearable. It was a sticky day and the heat of the carriage made me feel quite unwell. As soon as I stepped on to the platform, the sea breeze greeted me like a long-lost friend, making the walk from the station far more pleasant.

The façade of Acacia House looked magnificent on my approach, reminding me what a complicated game Violet's marriage was. Although my social circles were not those of Edward, his philanderings were common knowledge, if one took the time to enquire. He wasn't a bad man, nor were his activities unusual, but my darling Violet was merely a pawn to him – a means to an end – and her quiet acceptance of this was heartbreaking.

The door was opened by a young girl I didn't recognise, but I knew the household staff had increased now she had moved from the cottage, whereas before the staff had merely been Mary, a cook, and a maid-of-all-work. The girl checked her mistress was happy to receive me and then saw me through to the drawing room.

Sitting beneath the subtle Morris Willow Boughs wall-paper, with soft green furnishings and dark mahogany furniture that only enhanced the deep reds of the brick fireplace, Violet looked serene. '*Ego semper tecum sum quamquam procul absumus*' across the fireplace made my heart leap – words we had chosen together and that had special meaning for us, whatever Edward had been foolish enough to believe. The house was all I had imagined and more – perhaps because I had given so much of myself to it. I knew that the love we had both invested in its design was a conduit for the love we could never openly give each other.

She stood as I entered, still pale all these months after her loss. Mary was in the corner, by the door to the garden room, her head bent over a book.

'What do you think, Percy? Isn't the house perfect? Everywhere I look, my heart lifts. Your thoughtful touches, your clever design ... I shall never live anywhere else. Being here makes me so happy when life sometimes causes me to feel so sad.' Her face revealed flashes of the old Violet, before she paused and allowed herself to consider her present circumstances. 'I can only hope that the crawling window is one day put to use, and that the beautiful mural is appreciated by others than myself.'

'Now, now. Don't distress yourself, Violet. There is no reason to think you cannot have another child. Give it time.'

'I needed that baby, Percy. I needed someone to love, and someone to love me . . .'

Her words hung in the air between us for what seemed an eternity. We both knew the truth of her marriage and we both knew the truth of the feelings between us. And yet it was strange: I had never spoken of Charlotte to Violet, as though to admit there was even the possibility of someone else would be a betrayal. I was hers. I would always be hers.

'You have that, Violet. You have me,' I whispered.

For a moment neither of us spoke nor moved. To openly acknowledge everything that had passed between us this past year was dangerous. So far we had merely alluded to feelings neither of us dared voice. But we both knew. We had known for a long time.

Mary moved silently to the garden room door, I had almost forgotten she was there, muttering something about seeing a heron near the pond. And we were alone.

'If I say it aloud once, will you never ask me to say it again?' She lifted her head and her wide Aegean eyes looked up at mine. My hands rose from my sides, almost without any conscious effort on my part, and cupped her cheeks.

'I have never asked anything of you,' I said.

'I know. You are a good man, Percy. I hope you find someone who deserves you.' There was a pause. 'And who loves you like I do.' The hairs on my arms rippled like the grasses in the sea breeze. 'See? I have said it now. I love you. But we both know that it can never be.'

She gave a little shrug of her shoulders and they dropped. Conversely, my heart soared to stars as yet uncharted by man. To have a woman such as Violet admit such feelings, to choose me over the tall, self-assured, wealthy Edward, was somehow almost enough. Almost.

'It is sufficient to be your friend and to have spent these past few months getting to know you. Don't grieve for things that can never be.' My hands remained about her face, my gaze fixed on hers.

'Promise you will always be in my life, Percy. Always?' It was a desperate plea, as if I was somehow necessary for her very survival.

'I promise,' and, without thought, I moved my head towards hers and our faces hovered only inches apart for a few brief moments. Had she pulled away or given me any indication my intentions were unwelcome, I would have withdrawn immediately and apologised, but our breathing was steady and slow. It was Violet who finally moved her lips closer to mine, but before they touched, there was a noise from behind and we pulled apart to see Edward behind us in the doorway.

'What the HELL is going on?' His voice was thunderous and his face red. The young girl who had let me in appeared behind him in the hall and began to speak.

'Madam, your husband has—'

'Leave us please, Lily.' He dismissed the girl and walked into the room, slamming the door behind him.

'Have you both lost your voices? I asked a question and I expect an answer.'

I moved away from Violet, who reached out for the back of the nearest chair.

'There is nothing going on. Your wife was upset and I was consoling her,' I said.

'I bet you damn well were. I know what I saw, Gladwell. Don't treat me like an imbecile.' He reached out a rough hand and grabbed at my shirt. 'I trusted you. I thought she would be safe with you. I thought you were . . . Oh, it doesn't matter what I thought. Seems I was wrong.'

Violet rallied and walked towards her husband, and in her immeasurably calm and dignified way she spoke directly to him.

'Edward, you are being foolish. I have never been unfaithful to you. Since the day of our wedding my lips have not touched another's, nor have I shared my bed with anyone but you. I have kept my marriage vows and I can promise you that before God. Can you say the same?'

He loosened his grip on my collar but chose not to answer Violet's direct question. He didn't have to. His actions answered for him, and instead he directed his vitriol at me.

'Your overwhelming concern for my wife during her recent illness is clear to me now. An architect does not go to such great pains to enquire about the welfare of a client. Your final bill will be met, Mr Gladwell, but your association with our family is over. I wish you to leave this house immediately.' He turned to Violet. 'This man is never to step over the threshold of this house again unless I am present. Do you understand? Not one foot is to pass through this front door.'

'I understand, Edward, and I promise.'

Chapter 61

Present Day

'I don't understand.' The big reveal I'd waited so long for. The missing piece of my genetic jigsaw. Was my mother telling me it would never be answered?

'It was a drunken night at a house party,' she began, finally placing her gin on the table. 'I lied to my parents – good Catholic girls don't go to those sort of parties. And if they do, they don't get so drunk they can't remember much past the second bottle of cider. Molly – I couldn't even stand up without holding the wall. And there was this guy, he'd chatted to me on the stairs, I vaguely remember thinking he was attractive, and he was funny. I practically dragged the poor lad up the stairs by his hair. We sort of ended up in one of the bedrooms, over a pile of coats. I'm sure you don't need a diagram for the rest.'

'His name?'

She shook her head from side to side, her eyes flickering. 'I can't even remember if he was dark or fair, tall or short, and I certainly never caught his name. Less than an hour of my life spent with this total stranger and, like I said, ripples that went on for years. I made a concerted effort to find him when I realised I was pregnant, but I didn't even know who'd hosted the party – it was a casual invitation from a group we were talking to in the pub. For weeks I looked at every face on the Tube, every stranger in a queue, hoping to recognise him, but I didn't know what I was looking for. It was hopeless.'

The remainder of my gin was knocked back in one go and I let the empty glass rest on my knee as she continued.

'It took my father three weeks to talk to me. Mum kept weeping and praying to the effigy of the Virgin Mary that stood so accusingly on the sideboard. But however disappointed they were, they never abandoned me or suggested I got rid of the baby. And for nine years, they supported me and helped raise you. You were the light of their lives, even though my final insult was to call you Molly. Nonna was bitterly disappointed I didn't give you an Italian name – but I didn't want that for you. I'd spent my entire childhood trying to fit in, trying not to be the odd one out, with parents who spoke poor English.' She looked at me for a moment. 'It was like when you cut your hair. I understood. You were rebelling against Brian, even though he loves you as much as my parents loved me. But you kick out when you are young. It's all part of growing up. And it's okay.'

I don't know whose tears fell first, but she looked across at mine and misread them.

'Don't ever think, sweetheart, you weren't wanted. That's not what I meant.'

'I know.' I put out a hand to reassure her.

'So?' Mum asked.

She wanted to know my reaction to this piece of news, but the truth was, I didn't know how I felt. Of all the wild scenarios I'd imagined over the years, this hadn't been one of them. I thought perhaps he was married, or he hadn't wanted anything to do with me. Not once did I imagine Mum had absolutely no idea.

I knew then that she'd been right to delay telling me. If she'd delivered this news back in May, I would have flipped out and turned on her. But I'd changed. My priorities had changed and I knew now which people in my life were the most important to me. And then I thought about Grandma and how I would give anything to go back in time.

'How could you think, even for one moment, that I wouldn't forgive you? I love you.' I reached out for her hand and squeezed it. 'And when you love someone, you can always find it in your heart to forgive.'

'Exactly.' And Ninja Mum gave me her sweetest smile and squeezed my hand back.

I met Izzy at The Dog and Duck the following evening. Most of the gang were there, and she introduced me to Dave, who looked totally besotted with my friend and barely acknowledged anyone else. Ah, young love.

'Loving the hair. Are you growing it out?' one of the lads said, sliding his arm around me and bending down for a cheeky kiss. 'You're looking hot.'

'You're looking drunk,' I replied.

'That's our little Molls.' And he ruffled my hair. The action rankled. I didn't want to be treated like a child any more. I couldn't do much about my height, but I could do something about my behaviour.

Sitting outside on the waterfront, the sun about to depart, I took a sip of my ice-cold Guinness and looked about me. The pub was next to the Thames – its beer-garden running down to the water's edge. As lovely as the river was, it wasn't the sea. There were no crashing waves or sweeping vistas. I could only see as far as the imposing town houses the other side of the river. There were no distant horizons where the pale blue of the sky met with the dark blue-black of the water. And there were people everywhere – all crowded on to a thin strip of grass that edged the concrete and met the water – as if that counted as countryside.

Later, we moved pubs, closer to town. Another round of drinks and then we hopped on the Tube at Richmond and headed to Shepherd's Bush for a club. It was hot and airless underground. Men writhed up to me, as we all clung to our poles in the crowded carriage, their sweaty bodies embarrassingly close. And then we filed out like ants, along the artificially lit tunnels and into the city that would never truly be dark, even in the dead of night.

The club was no better. Fluorescent lights flashed and the thump of the drums from the colossal speakers pounded in my head. It was okay, I loved dancing, but not as much as I remembered. I tumbled into the open air with relief as the club was eventually abandoned at one o'clock in the morning.

'Where next?' asked Dave, a proprietorial arm around Izzy.

'Home for me,' I said.

The evening had been fun but I'd had enough. And as I sat on the Central Line later, a few isolated souls dotted along the blue fuzzy seats, all avoiding eye contact with the rambling drunk further up the carriage, I looked at my reflection in the window opposite: a slight girl, with short hair and sunken eyes. The city was great, but somehow draining. The coast was home, and I missed Summerton and West Creeching equally, and for very different reasons. Salty air, bracing winds, and that delightful sense of space that you can only get from staring across the rolling sea. I didn't belong in the city.

Not any more.

Chapter 62

'Shove up,' I said to Brian. 'You are sofa hogging. There's definitely room on there for two.'

He moved along and I flung myself down, swinging my feet over his knees and leaning back on the arm. He looked slightly alarmed at the addition of my legs to his lap but said nothing.

'I'm going to stay in Dorset and sort my life out,' I announced. Mum looked up from her magazine and smiled.

Lying awake the previous night, turning over possibilities in my slightly tipsy head, I'd asked myself some serious questions. Where was I happiest? Who mattered to me? What should I do with my life? And for the first time ever, I made an important decision with no grown-up help. Even my choice of university had piggybacked on Izzy's research.

Seeded by Michael's offer, an idea had germinated, taken root and started to poke through the earth.

'I'm going to ask Granddad if he wants a paying lodger. I'm thinking of moving down to Dorset.'

'Permanently?' Mum asked.

'Certainly for the foreseeable future. A potential job offer has come my way but even if it doesn't come off, London doesn't rock my world as much as it once did,' I said, traces of Harrison lingering in my choice of words. 'If Granddad agrees, the house lends itself to a workable split. Don't forget, Grandma had all those lodgers in the eighties.'

'So you're not put off by the ghosts then?' Brian teased.

'There aren't any ghosts,' I said. 'At least, I've never seen any.'

Brian shrugged. 'Don't get me wrong, I love that house, but there was some weird stuff going on when I was little. I got caught in the cupboard once and had the strangest experience . . .'

'I expect you'd been at Briggie's homemade wine,' Mum said. 'We all know how potent that stuff is.'

Brian looked indignant. 'I was a child, Anna. I hadn't touched a drop. Anyway, that silly cupboard is so low, it's only children who can get inside properly.'

'Just a bad dream then, sweetheart,' Mum said.

'I didn't fall asleep in there, if that's what you mean. And I wasn't sleepwalking. Never saw the boy with the teddy though.' Brian shuffled up straighter in the sofa. 'So with me *and* Mum, that's two of us who had weird experiences. And my mother would never imagine things – she simply wasn't the sort.'

'No,' Mum agreed. 'She most certainly wasn't.' And they smiled, remembering the no-nonsense woman that was Grandma.

My mind, meanwhile, was connecting some very wobbly dots. The ghostly boy with the one-eyed teddy . . . who only appeared in the nineties . . . And then I thought of my sleep-walking boss and the shabby teddy bear in his closet – and my mouth dropped open as everything fell into place.

It made sense that if I could travel through the cupboard, then others could as well. Yes, it was a way of me getting to West Creeching and back, but it was also a way others could visit Summerton. And the cupboard was small. Most adults wouldn't need to climb all the way in, and even if they did, they wouldn't let the door close behind them.

I smiled to myself. How could I explain to Brian there was no ghost? That it was just a sleepwalking little boy who'd crawled into a tiny cupboard and come out two hundred miles away? Much as Brian had so clearly done as a child. But I didn't want to share this revelation. For now, the cupboard was mine – part of an unusual house built by an architect in love with a woman he could never have. Perhaps that love had been so powerful it had translated into something magical. And perhaps it still had some magic left to work. After all, love would always find a way . . .

'Ghosts aside, I love Hawthorn Place so much I can't even begin to put it into words,' I mused.

'Well, at least I know what to do with it when Dad passes on.' Brian bent towards me and kissed my head.

My eyes flashed wide. 'Oh no. I didn't mean—'

'I know you didn't, but it would be nice to know it was being lived in by someone who appreciated it and all its oddities.'

'And how does Rory fit into these big plans?' Mum asked. Brian looked between the two of us, the name meaning nothing to him, but he didn't comment.

'I'd like him to be part of my life. But even if it all goes pear-shaped, I'm staying with Granddad. Besides, the crops are coming thick and fast now from the veggie patch. I put a lot of hard work into that garden. I want to enjoy the fruits, or more precisely vegetables, of my labours.'

Later that day, Brian offered to run me to the station, but I told them I would make my own way. I knew which bus to catch, and besides, gone were the days I expected people to run around after me.

'Thanks for having me. I'll see you soon.' We gathered in the hallway to say our goodbyes.

'Good luck getting your man,' Mum said, as I hugged her.

'Even if you do relocate to Dorset,' Brian said, 'you might

consider coming to New York with us at Christmas – my treat. The hotel was so lovely, we've decided to go back. After all, you've given up your summer to care for Dad. You deserve a break.'

'Maybe.' I stood on tiptoe to kiss his soft cheek but caught Mum's eyes flickering in panic, and I replayed Brian's words in my head. Hotel? I thought they'd done a house swap . . . And as I stood there, several things fell into place.

'Could you just check I haven't left my phone on the work-top?' I asked Brian, knowing full well it was in my pocket.

'Of course, darling,' he said, nipping back up the hall.

As soon as he was out of earshot I turned back to Ninja Mum and gave her a stare even Paddington would struggle to muster.

'The last few months – *it was all you*.' I looked her in the eye and she didn't break contact. 'You didn't want me back here, lounging about and feeling sorry for myself, so you pretended the house wasn't available. Did Granddad really think of asking me down, or was that you too?'

She shrugged. 'I merely mentioned that you were homeless and needed somewhere to stay . . .'

'No wonder you got in quick with the house swap announce-ment when Brian arrived home that night. Poor love didn't know a thing about your plan, and I bet you knobbled him so he wouldn't lend me any money. That man has always put his hand in his pocket to help me out.' Still she remained silent. 'You knew if I stayed with Granddad I'd be forced to become independent because, unlike everyone else I've ever lived with, he wasn't in a fit state to run around looking after me.'

'I don't know what you mean. It was all *you*, Molly.' She smiled a slow and measured smile.

'Well, it worked. Thank you, Ninja Mum,' I said, reaching

out and squeezing her hand as Brian bumbled back into the hall looking apologetic.

He was a good man, a kind man, a man who had always been there to plaster the grazed knees and hug away the disappointments, and who had often fought my corner as Mum wrestled with the tough job of parenting her wayward daughter. He *never* came down hard on me, and was consistently my biggest fan. All he wanted was a daughter, and all I'd done was shut him out.

'Silly me – it was in my pocket all along.' I shrugged. 'But thanks so much for looking.'

Whatever the truth of Mum's manipulation, it was important not to undermine this gentle man. I had accepted the revelation about my real father with a calm resignation. It no longer mattered to me who he was, because I'd had a loving father from the age of ten – a man who didn't care about genetics when it came to dishing out his boundless love, and had stepped up to give a fatherless little girl all the love in his heart, even though there were times when she most definitely didn't deserve it.

Despite my earlier kiss goodbye, I threw my arms around him one last time. When I finally pulled away, I looked up at his darling face.

'Bye, *Dad*,' I said, emphasising the tiny word that had such enormous implications. 'Thanks for everything.'

And all three of us tried really hard not to cry.

Chapter 63

Percy Gladwell

1896

Never having been a drinker, it was surprising how quickly I embraced the habit. A glass of wine or port had always been sufficient to relax me after a long day bent over the drafting board, or difficult meetings with disagreeable clients. However, it transpired that a whole bottle could dull the pain of a man racked with guilt and riddled with despair. Weeks, not months had passed since Edward had forbidden me to make any contact with his wife and, with each flip of the calendar, my pain increased. The liquor helped me to forget that I was not permitted to visit her again, that I could never be near her, to laugh over frivolous works of fiction or nieces with over-active imaginations. It enabled me to put aside the guilt I felt over a heartbroken Charlotte and face each dawning day.

But I would invariably sober up and all these things would come crashing into my life again.

'Do you think you will find an answer in the bottom of this?' Mother tutted, as she collected the empty port bottle from the floor. Mrs Cooper had let her in despite my insistence that I was unavailable.

'It's not a regular thing. Can't a man enjoy a drink after a hard day's work without having to justify his actions?' I was slumped in the easy chair in the corner and had to raise my arm to shield my eyes as she drew back the window-curtains.

'Look at yourself, Percy,' she said. 'It's three o'clock in the afternoon and you've not been at the office for several days.' I looked across at her, wondering how she knew my movements. 'Freddie is a loyal lad, but not quite sharp-witted enough to fool me,' she explained. 'I stopped by Great Marlborough Street first, under the misguided belief that you would be at your place of work.'

'I've not been well.' I waved a vague hand in the air. 'Heart trouble,' I quipped, referring to the broken nature of that particular organ. I thought I was being clever, but mothers have an unnerving ability to see through the bluff. Perhaps it is all those years observing their offspring as children. They learn the body language and little tics that invariably give them away.

'I'm sorry about Charlotte,' she said, sinking on to the edge of the unmade bed. 'I should not have pushed. I didn't know there was someone else.'

'What makes you say that?' I sat up straighter now.

'A handkerchief I found once underneath your pillows. And I do not ask who she is, or the story attached to your heart-break, but you must pull yourself out of this melancholy, Percy.'

'Why?' It was a simple question and I was curious as to the answer. What did I have now in my life? My buildings were no longer enough. I had tasted real love and had it snatched away. Why does a man devote his life to a career and the accumulation of wealth, if not to provide for a wife and family? I would have neither. I wanted neither, if they were not with Violet.

'Because you are loved and it's breaking your mother's heart.'

'And Charlotte?' I enquired, thinking of another heart I had broken.

She avoided my eyes and took a deep breath. 'She will rally.'

'Charlie said the Hamiltons have been ignoring you at church and refusing to acknowledge you in the street.' My brother had told me this in confidence but I was tired of playing games. 'There is no need to pretend. I've caused a great deal of hurt and upset.'

I suspected she had withheld this from me, racked with guilt about the whole situation, even though I placed no blame at her feet. The errors had been mine: allowing Charlotte to believe there was hope, and failing to keep my true feelings hidden from Violet. Had I managed to hide them, I believe she would not have risked doing or saying anything that went against her marriage vows, and Edward would not have parted us.

'You have, but not through design. Time will heal the pain, for both you and Charlotte.'

I was unable to stop the tears from falling down my cheeks, even though my face remained rigid. It was suddenly all too much.

'I don't know what to do, Mother,' I said.

'Then you shall come home with me and time will do the rest.'

So, reluctantly and because I had simply run out of options, I returned to Weymouth with her for the summer. But I was delaying the inevitable. I still sought solace in the bottom of a bottle and allowed myself to spiral downwards into a place so dark, I couldn't see beyond my own misery.

Finally, with each day darker than the last, I penned a letter to Violet, feeling that I at least owed her an explanation for my imminent actions.

I took the train to West Bay and stood atop the majestic cliffs that I had often visited in my youth, another bottle about my person, and let the afternoon sun of that bright day bring me a last moment of light.

I questioned God then, as I stood looking across the endless sea. Why show me such a wondrous thing and then deny me? If it was a test, I had failed. If it was a punishment, I could think of no crime I had committed in my thirty-one years that truly merited such cruel retribution.

Asking for forgiveness only from Violet, and not from my unjust God, I consumed the entirety of the Cockburn's and stepped off the cliffs, letting the last few weeks of crippling hurt and absolute despair rush past my ears as I hurtled towards the sand.

Chapter 64

Present Day

I missed Rory desperately, even more so when I returned to Summerton. Silly connections to him plagued my every waking moment: a ginger cat strolling across the street, a clip of Chewbacca on the television, even opening a jar of marmalade brought a lump to my throat. I couldn't sleep. And when I did, his stupid, furry face kept popping up in my restless dreams.

I rang him a couple of times but he didn't answer. I began to worry about his state of mind. All the problems I'd caused him were bound to affect his moods, and I didn't want to be responsible for another downward spiral.

I tried texting, but still got no response. The longer this went on, without so much as a *Leave me alone, Molly* from him, the more I worried. It occurred to me that he might have done something stupid, or been shipped off to hospital with stress, and this uneasy feeling snowballed until I decided to find some answers.

'Sorry to bother you, but I can't get hold of Rory and I wanted to check he was okay.' Miriam's number had been easy enough to come by – I simply called Mr Pickersgill, and he didn't question my motives.

'Molly, how lovely to hear from you. What a lot of silly nonsense about nothing. He'll get over it, my dear. He's huffing and puffing at the moment but a bit of time will give him some perspective, I'm sure.'

I was embarrassed that Miriam knew about my lies but pleasantly surprised that she didn't seem unduly angry. If she could be reasonable about it, I didn't see why Rory had to bear a grudge – I'd apologised, after all. The most important thing, however, was I'd established Rory was okay.

'Would you tell him I called? And maybe, reiterate how sorry I am about everything?' Perhaps she would fight my corner. I could but hope.

'Of course, although I'm guessing, if he hasn't been in touch, you haven't heard our other news?'

'No ...'

'Clive did some more digging into my family tree, including talking to my elderly uncle. He's been all fired up about the house again since our conversation. You won't believe this, but it turns out Rory and I do descend from the couple who built the house, although from the younger son. The oldest son didn't have children and there was a complicated lineage to follow, through various daughters, which is why we lost the Marston surname. I knew the house had been in the family a long time, but I never once suspected the family had kept it since it was built.'

'Rory is descended from Edward and Violet?' I said, a shiver running through me.

'Yes, and he was very excited to have a personal link to the house – especially as it will be his one day. But then I've always felt the house told a story and it makes me happy that the monument to Edward and Violet's love has remained in the care of those who are a result of it.'

I knew then that if Violet was their great, great, times several, grandmother, then the letters deserved to go to the Brookers – however hard it would be for me to part with them. But before

I shared this with Miriam, I wanted to check Granddad didn't mind, go through them again and maybe get them photocopied. I even wondered if I could use them as leverage to see Rory one more time.

With promises to keep in touch (Miriam clearly liked me, even if her son thought I was the devil incarnate), I put the phone down and thought about what course of action to take.

I loved Rory. It was as simple and as complicated as that.

If Miriam said he needed time, I'd have to be patient – not one of my virtues. But then I thought about everything and realised there was a way I could see him, just be near him for a while, and for purely selfish reasons.

Deep into the night, I crept downstairs, slipped into Granddad's cupboard and emerged in a dark, silent hall two hundred miles away. As I closed the triangular door, I remembered Rory's sleepwalking. Hopefully I wouldn't bump into him on the landing, restlessly striding about the house in his sleep – possibly clutching a teddy. But there were no sounds to indicate anyone was awake. Only a hum from the kitchen and a green glow from the Wi-Fi router on the hall table.

I put a tentative foot on the first stair. I couldn't recall them being squeaky but then I'd usually been bumping a heavy vacuum up behind me, so I took each step slowly and listened for any movement.

The door to his bedroom was open. There was a glow by the bed where his mobile phone was charging, and a plug-in night light – probably to counteract his fear of the dark. The large lump in the bed was emitting something close to a snore.

His eyes were firmly closed and he was deep in sleep. I looked at him for a while, his face cast in white light, slivers of moonlight from the gap in the curtains highlighting his handsome face.

'Sorry,' I whispered. Somehow it was important to say the word out loud, even though I knew he couldn't hear it. 'Sorry I lied. Sorry I thought you were about fifty. Sorry I crashed into your life and mucked everything up. And sorry I scuppered any chance of us.' It was my saddest sorry. I'd been so ridiculously slow to realise that I had feelings for this gentle, reclusive man and now I'd blown it. Who could blame him for wanting nothing to do with me? Lies were no foundation for a relationship.

He shuffled and flung an arm out of the covers. I froze, hoping I hadn't woken him, and waited for him to settle and for the heavy breathing to resume.

'I promise to learn from my mistakes,' I continued. 'I won't tell any more lies, I won't rely on others to look after me and I will sort my life out. The humming? Well, that's never going to change.'

I put out my hand to stroke his thick, dark, ginger – possibly auburn – hair. Still he slept the sleep of a hundred years, so I risked perching on the edge of his gargantuan king-sized bed, determined to say all the things I needed to, even if Rory was unaware I was there. Hopefully I could then move on from this sorry mess.

'You were doing so well and you didn't need me, crashing into your life and putting your recovery back, but I had to check you were okay.'

I bent over to kiss his head, letting my lips linger for as long as I thought I'd get away with, and inhaling the familiar and comforting scent of him. And then I went downstairs to return to my Rory-less world.

Chapter 65

Percy Gladwell

1898

Two years had passed since my foolish act. The doctor suggested that the excessive alcohol in my system may have saved my life. A drunkard does not brace himself for the moment of impact and consequently his injuries may not be so severe, but they were severe enough. In my inebriated state, I had also failed to walk to the highest point and my fall was of a shorter distance than intended. My physical injuries took several weeks to heal but the mental damage was to take much longer.

And yet, every morning since my moment of foolishness, I awoke with the same thoughts – thoughts I had wrestled with since Edward had discovered us. What was Violet doing at that precise moment? I knew she would be in her beloved Acacia House, but where was she sitting? Did she appreciate the views from the garden room? Would the stained-glass geese make her smile as she walked down the corridor? Did she look upon the inscription above the fire-place and think of me? I couldn't have Violet and I had always known that. But, after several months of enduring self-pity (and enforced abstention from the demon drink) I realised I could have the next best thing. There was a way I could connect with her, that I could share in her life, even if only in my imagination.

After several weeks of hunting, a patch of land was secured in Summerton, not far from my beloved Weymouth. Violet had always hoped I would be happy in Dorset and, having so nearly lost me, Mother was delighted I would have a residence nearby to enable her to keep an eye on me.

'But it's down a funny dip.' She looked sceptical as we surveyed the land. 'Not a practical site, Percival, I am surprised at you.'

'It's not my intention it should be a showy house,' I said.

'Yet you tell me it's to have six bedrooms. For one man living alone, I consider that showy. And you're shipping down materials from Norfolk? Such folly.' She tutted her disapproval and edged closer to the dip, totally bemused by my choice of plot.

Still a graceful woman in her sixtieth year, she was one of the most important people in my life. She had nursed me back to health and not rushed me nor judged my actions. The back was a little more bent and the hair a little more grey, but she remained a formidable and impressive woman.

'I think I could be content here,' I said. 'The building of this house will help me to heal.'

'Then I approve,' she announced. 'Give it twenty bedrooms and build it of marzipan if that will make you happy. It was all I ever wanted for you.'

'I know,' I said.

She reached out for my hand, and we stood at the top of the track, looking down a tree-covered dip at a most unpromising parcel of land.

But it would take a further two years, the building of Hawthorn Place and a small miracle for me to pick up the pieces of my broken life and finally be at peace with the world and my God.

Chapter 66

Present Day

My interview at Bickerton Manor was a breeze. I studied hard for a couple of days beforehand, and was armed with an encyclopaedic knowledge of the house and its history. The black nail varnish was removed and I even found some colourful, smarter clothes. I was offered the job on the spot and was asked to start the following Monday at nine o'clock. Prompt. The bike and my buttocks were mightily relieved that I had sufficient bus fare funds.

Granddad was beside himself when I asked if he would consider a permanent lodger, and we set about sorting the attic into a habitable flat. With all the activity and excitement, Rory wasn't quite as prominent in my thoughts. I only worried about him every ten minutes now, instead of every waking moment.

'Where do you want this, love?' Granddad asked, holding out the box of Violet's letters.

'Thanks. I'll take them up to my flat.' I hadn't told Granddad yet that I was intending to pass them on to the Brookers. Multitasking, with an armful of spare bedding I'd dug out of the airing cupboard, I missed the first curly step and slipped. The contents of the box spilled across the floor, so I bent down and carefully bundled everything back together.

And then I saw it.

Tucked under a cardboard flap at the bottom of the box was an envelope. I pulled it out and saw it had Violet's name on the front – no address, just her name, as though it had been hand-delivered. I opened two sheets of faded paper inside and saw it was a letter from Percy and dated 1937 – the year of his death. I sank on to the bottom step and began to read his words.

My darling Violet,

This is the second goodbye letter that I have written to you – the first over forty years ago when my exit from this world was planned by my own hand. Thank God, in his infinite wisdom, for saving me from my folly. This time, however, a bottle of port will not prevent the inevitable.

I know now the time I have left is measured in hours not days. It's not sudden news, nor overly distressing. I'm moderately comfortable as I lie here on the bed, the nurse fussing and flapping around me, until she heaps so many pillows behind me I am virtually in my own lap.

We have both suspected for some time things weren't right: the coughing up of blood and general fatigue that have plagued me these last few weeks. But it is my inability to descend the stairs that I find the hardest to bear. A prisoner in this room, however beautiful the prison may be. This oak four-poster bed has become my cell, yet the embroidered hangings from the canopy remain a comfort, more so in my final hours. I don't need to see the words of the poem to know they surround me, interwoven with delicate cornflowers and striking poppies, all the verses etched across my heart, and embroidered by your fair hand.

I'm not complaining. I have had my three score and ten, and find, looking back, I've spent them well. My buildings will stand proud in the landscape of this fine country long after I am dust and bone. My name will be in architectural volumes of the future, and people will stumble upon forgotten articles in Country Life *where my finest works were showcased and my principles espoused. The impact I had, although small, has been significant. Perhaps it would have been greater still had I undertaken commissions abroad, but I was never prepared to leave you, my dearest, for it is you I must thank for your guidance with my career and enduring faith that I could return to the profession I had abandoned so recklessly . . .*

This letter implied he'd written her a suicide note at that tortured time in his life. I knew Violet had remained married to Edward, but it made me happy that she'd nevertheless had some sort of relationship with Percy, and that they'd stayed in touch until his death. He'd clearly turned his life around after that dreadful time and become a great success. It was sad that they'd never been able to embrace or express their love, but it would have been unbearable had he died before he was able to make peace with it all.

And then I read the final page of the letter and my heart stopped.

I stood up, sat back down again, and reread the last few paragraphs. I couldn't give Rory any more time to get over my deceit – I had to show him this *immediately*.

Because, before me, in the elegant handwriting of an important and nationally renowned Arts and Crafts architect, was the truth of his life and his love.

I had the end of Percy and Violet's story.

Chapter 67

Percy Gladwell

1905

Nearly nine years had passed since I'd been forbidden to put a foot over the threshold of Acacia House. And nine years since I had foolishly and selfishly sought to deal with my misery by stepping into oblivion.

It had been a period of great change for both myself and the country as a whole. A new century dawned, filling everyone with hope and optimism, marred only by the death of our sagacious Queen. Worries about the accession of her scandal-tainted son proved groundless and there was even a degree of wary optimism about the King. My own life had undergone a shaky rebirth: I had gradually found my feet and was at last back in a place where I could be truly happy once more.

The turning point for me had been the arrival of a note from Violet during my recovery, when I was convalescing and utterly wretched. How she had tracked me down, I did not know, but I am eternally grateful that she did.

. . . however desolate you feel, I can promise it is nothing to the state of utmost despair I was in when I received your letter. Do you not understand, Percy? It is only the thought that you are

somewhere in the world, going about your business and making it a more beautiful place, that keeps me going. I cannot believe you gave up on us so easily, when I can promise that love will always find a way, even if we both must be patient and allow it to do so. Do not give up, my darling, for my sake as well as your own . . .

And somehow love had indeed found a magical and unfathomable way to keep us together.

Technically, in those years, my foot had never crossed the threshold of Violet's house in West Creeching. That part of Edward's demands I had at least kept to. But today was different. The invitation had come from Edward himself – his hand forced by a mutual friend, and one whom Edward was desperately keen to impress.

It was ironic that Edward's breaking of me had been the making of me. Like a phoenix from the ashes, I had risen again and was to fly higher than ever before. And Violet had been there to help me soar.

The train journey was arduous and I was glad to finally arrive at my destination. It had been so many years since I had disembarked at West Creeching station and walked up the gentle hill to her house. It was spring – the season for new beginnings and fresh growth. I passed the row of cottages on the approach, and noticed that the low box hedge in front of the vicarage had matured and filled out. Daffodils nodded a welcome and crocuses led the way. But more than anything, the air was indescribably good after the stench of the city.

I had only officially visited Acacia House once subsequent to its completion – the day Edward had arrived home unexpectedly. As I looked across at the façade of the property for the first time since that day, I noted, yet again, how the light fell differently in this part of the world. The sky was a wider canvas. Perhaps it was the absence of hills and undulating landscape. East Anglia was a flat country but no less beautiful for its lack of dramatic topography.

It felt alien to approach the house along the herringbone path, and I was delighted to see a bed of petunias – something I had laughed about with Violet many years ago. Mary answered the door and saw me through to the drawing room. Violet's face briefly lit up as she abandoned her sketching to the window seat, brushing an anxious hand across her skirts as she faced me.

'Mr Gladwell. How perfectly charming to see you after all these years. I trust you had a pleasant journey?'

'The train from London was tiresome but my spirits were lifted by the walk up the lane. I had forgotten how pretty Creeching was. I have not been to the north Norfolk coast for many years, although I recently completed a small commission to the east of here, in Great Yarmouth.'

'You will notice many changes since your last visit. The garden is now nicely established. You wouldn't believe how high the poplar is now, and I often think of our discussion when I look out at it.'

'Yes, I remember.'

Our eyes met and held as long as we dared. Mary was still hovering in the doorway, not yet having been dismissed and doubtless awaiting instructions.

'And, of course, my house is now filled with children,' she said. 'Although perhaps two is a slight exaggeration of the definition. I would have dearly loved more but must consider myself exceptionally lucky to have even had two when I believed all hope had gone.'

Of course I knew that she had fallen again, a year after the tubal pregnancy that had nearly ended her life. Mary had been right. The damage had only affected one side, and although not without risk, she'd gone on to have two carefully monitored pregnancies, but the doctor had advised against a third.

'Ah, yes. May I offer my congratulations, Mrs Marston. I understand you now have two healthy sons. They must keep you fully occupied.'

We avoided further eye contact of any significant length, both conscious of Mary. The maid coughed and Violet walked towards the sofas.

'Mary, please could you arrange a tray of tea? And then be so kind as to notify Mr Marston that our first guest has arrived.'

Within a few moments Edward appeared. He looked older than I remembered, greyer around the temples, and his face was worn and heavily lined. The result of hard living. I wondered if it stuck in his craw to be in contact with me again.

'Mr Gladwell.' I prepared for the crushing handshake, but his grip had lost the strength it once had. 'I hope this afternoon will be profitable for us both. You were specified by Lord Hollingbroke after the success of the municipal buildings in Manchester. I would have preferred to meet in London, but he was keen to see Acacia House, and our private affairs need not interfere with this project. We will both benefit immeasurably should this come off. I trust we can both be civilised for the duration of the meeting?'

Business was going well for Edward, but only because he'd had the foresight to invest heavily in electric trams. That, along with the continued growth of the railways, ensured he continued to be a wealthy man – so wealthy, in fact, he no longer felt the need to conceal his dalliances. No wonder Violet never dared visit the city.

'You are aware I have two sons now?'

I nodded.

'Edward is my eldest. A fine lad of seven with a strong will and a lively mind. Then we have Samuel – very different in temperament and looks to his older brother. I think perhaps he takes after his mother, although I am not sure that is necessarily a good thing.'

Violet cast her eyes to the floor and I wondered if Edward's statement was an attempt at humour. If it was, it fell flat.

'I am sure they are both fine boys . . .'

Before I had finished my sentence, there was thundering of feet as two small lads burst through the drawing room door and halted abruptly in front of me.

'Hello, sir. Pleased to meet you. I'm Edward Marston.' The confident Edward junior stuck out a grubby hand, which I took and shook heartily. His clothes were soiled and scruffy – clearly a lover of the outdoors and adventure. I resisted the urge to say, 'Yes, I know'.

The younger Samuel was wide-eyed and silent as he also stuck out a tentative hand. He resembled a baby bird. Eyes too big for his delicate head and a paler complexion. By this point my heart was beating so hard I had trouble focusing on what I should and shouldn't say. I bent to my haunches, level with the smaller child.

'Percy Gladwell.' I took his hand. 'Pleased to meet you.'

'Mama said you built this house and I thought it must have taken such a long time to put all the bricks on top of each other.'

Violet was now behind her sons, a hand resting protectively on Samuel's shoulder. He was the quiet one. This I knew. He was the thinker. And the artist.

'Well, now, I didn't actually build the house. Much stronger and more able men than me did that. I merely designed it. With your mother's keen overseeing eye, of course.' I risked a quick glance and was graced with one of her sweet smiles, but a guarded one. This was a different Violet to the one I knew. To me she would always be Violet the untamed – a passionate woman, my equal and my raison d'être. With Edward she became Violet the wife, the no one, but I knew that her time with me enabled her to cope with being the other Violet.

'I love the castle stairs,' Samuel continued. 'But Father doesn't like us playing on them. He says we make too much noise when he's in his study underneath. But he isn't here terribly often so we do it when he's away.' Edward junior struck out a leg to kick his brother in the shin and remind him their father was standing nearby.

'And do you play games of fearless knights? Do you defend the tower and protect your mother?' I asked.

'Sometimes. But I like the library best. And the seats in the window.'

'Ah, a reader? You will go far, young man, for a person who reads lives not only his own life, but the lives of every hero he reads about.'

Yet a man who truly loves, needs to live but one life, I thought to myself.

The meeting was a great success. Lord Hollingbroke was open to my ideas and I secured a sizeable commission. Edward was equally content by virtue of finding Hollingbroke an architect who shared his vision and therefore earned his gratitude.

Afterwards, I adjourned to the garden room for a most splendid afternoon tea. Edward remained in the dining room with Hollingbroke, sharing coffee and cigars, but for the sake of my lungs, I made my excuses.

Violet sat with me, watching the children toss quoits across the lawn and enjoying the late afternoon sun. She owned to having made the cake herself, but I knew she was a competent baker. I had tasted her baking on occasion in recent years – usually in the middle of the night, candlelit and in companionable silence.

And never once did my foot cross the threshold to the house. That promise we kept, even if we had other sins to atone for.

The boys proved companionable fellows. Edward was confident and took after his father in both looks and manner, but I liked him enormously. In my efforts not to favour Samuel, I gave his older brother more of my attention as he talked about the train set he hoped to get for his birthday and how much he adored his governess. Samuel, only four years old, began to look weary and clambered up on the bench by my side. He remained more cautious of me than Edward junior, but the tiredness eventually won out and he soon curled up beside me, sound asleep. Again, I struggled to keep my emotions in check as his tiny head rested near my knee. I risked placing my hand upon his blond head and ruffled his hair. Edward was at my right side, having retrieved a volume on wild animals from his father's modest library.

After a while, I pulled out my pocket watch, its heartless counting down of this precious time taunting me, but as the sun at last dipped her head below the horizon, I sighed.

'I fear I must take my leave,' I reluctantly said. 'My train leaves at half past.'

'Such a shame, Mr Gladwell. I had hoped to take you around our extensive gardens.'

'Another time, perhaps, for I would very much like to see how the planting has progressed these past few years.' I gazed at the sleepy child half across my lap and my heart was once again heavy. We both knew how hard it was for me to go.

Edward junior and a sleepy Samuel got to their feet and stuck out their hands.

'It's been smashing to meet you, Mr Gladwell,' Edward said.

'The pleasure was all mine.' I shook them both by the hand. 'Take good care of your mother.'

'We will,' said Samuel, his face earnest. 'I don't want to lose her like I lost my teddy bear. She is the only one I've got.'

'A precious woman indeed,' I said. 'Absolutely one of a kind.'

As I turned to follow Violet to the house, a tear pricked in the corner of my eye. Determined not to let it fall, I took a deep breath and smoothed the front of my frock coat. It was unlikely I would be formally invited to Acacia House again, and in many respects, it was better that way. I knew being in contact with things that you could not own was hard – a lesson learned in those early days with Violet. Every time we'd parted and she'd returned to her husband had chipped away at my very soul. As a man always taught to embrace my emotions, and not to shy away from them, the next few steps were the hardest I'd ever had to take.

Without looking back, I walked along the brick path, and left two pieces of my heart behind.

Chapter 68

Present Day

Acacia House was silent, but then it usually was. Rory was a great lover of peace and quiet – at least he was until I came along.

Clutching the precious letter, I crept out of the cupboard, headed to the front door, as I'd done a hundred times before, and turned the latch. It was locked. I jiggled the handle, but it wasn't going anywhere. Okay, that meant he'd locked it from the outside. Unusual, because he never went anywhere, but not impossible. Perhaps he was visiting his parents, was out for a run, or was even shopping. I could but hope.

Then I noticed a small pile of post on the floor by the letterbox which suggested he'd gone away. Goodness, he really had got brave. Why had I been so worried about him? He was obviously making great progress. Maybe he'd taken a little holiday.

I had a quick scout around to see if there were any clues to his whereabouts but there was nothing obvious. The kitchen was unusually tidy and bare. His new cleaner must be super-efficient. Probably the flawless Holly. She'd doubtless got her scrappy little butt in here as soon as I'd gone. And she'd be everything I wasn't – except old enough.

I took my mobile from my back pocket and dialled Miriam again, to ask if she knew where Rory was and when he'd be back.

'He's gone away, dear. Don't ask me where. Mothers are always the last to know. Clive and I were worried at first, but he's been texting us and seems upbeat. He said he's sorted himself out and knows where his future lies. Off to see a friend, he said. I'm fairly certain he was London-bound, so one of his city friends probably. I suppose I should be pleased he seems to be getting back to some kind of normal.'

'Did he give you any indication of how long he'd be gone?' His sudden unexplained absence was frustrating in the extreme.

'I asked the same question but he either doesn't know or doesn't want me to know. But then I was so pleased he felt up to travelling, I didn't push it. Don't think that car of his has been used more than half a dozen times this year.'

'But I must get in touch with him. I have some important news.'

'I'll certainly pass the message on, but when I mentioned you recently, he waved me away and said it was irrelevant now. I'm sorry, Molly, I tried.'

It was then I knew it was over. He couldn't forgive me, not even to pick up a phone and ask my news. Instead, he'd gone off to find himself and get away from deceitful girls who couldn't operate washing machines and hummed out of tune. I had to accept I'd totally blown it, but I secretly hoped he would always wonder, like me, how things might have turned out if I hadn't told so many lies.

I sat in Granddad's kitchen with my head slumped in my hands. Yet again, I wished Grandma was still alive. She would know just the thing for a broken heart. Probably in the form of a cake. I could do with her no-nonsense approach right now.

And a chance to apologise.

It always made those vicious knots pull tighter when I thought about how we'd left things – how she'd gone to her grave so cross with me, thinking I was ungrateful and rude. I wanted her to see that I'd changed and grown up.

'All right?' Granddad asked, wandering into the kitchen, clutching a brown paper parcel.

'Sort of. I was thinking about Grandma.'

He pulled up a chair and sat beside me, placing the parcel on the table.

'I've been thinking of her a lot recently, too,' he admitted. 'Do you think she'll be mad at me if I ask another lady round for a spot of supper? Just as a friend,' he clarified.

'Jean?' I asked, and his wrinkly cheeks flushed pink as he nodded. 'I think she'd be delighted. And it would be great to have a *friend* –' I stressed the word – 'who shares your passion for the garden. You can pass on your expertise.'

'Oh, I think she'll be the one passing her knowledge on to me. I found out recently she's descended from Charlotte Hamilton – *the* Charlotte Hamilton of Hamilton Nurseries.' I looked blank. 'The huge nurseries outside Bridport. Everyone's heard of Hamilton Seeds . . . Set up her own nursery over a hundred years ago, became quite a wealthy woman by the time she was forty and eventually married some penniless vicar. Jean's father was one of two boys she had late in life. She told me that she positively adored her grandmother. Grandmas hold a special place in your heart, don't they?'

I nodded and tried not to cry. 'And granddads,' I said, reaching for his hand. 'Never heard of Hamiltons though,' I admitted, 'but I think Jean is lovely. Let me know when you're having her over and I'll pop along and say hi.'

He smiled. 'Anyway, I'm going off at a tangent,' he said, and he patted the package. 'I was sorting through the study earlier and came across this huge parcel for you, long forgotten under a bundle of papers. It's a cookbook Briggie bought for you at the end of last summer. I'd forgotten about it, to be honest. She was going to post it but then . . .' His voice trailed off, unable to finish the sentence.

'A parcel she was going to post to me *after* I left?' I clarified, the timeline vitally important.

He nodded. 'Open it then,' Granddad urged, sliding the package in front of me.

My name and our London address had been written in her distinctive handwriting across the front but no stamps had been added. It was clearly a parcel wrapped and ready to go. Granddad sensed me hesitate.

'We quarrelled . . .' I began, my words getting lodged somewhere between my throat and my mouth. 'Last summer – the reason I left early. I was really—'

'Over as soon as it had begun, I'm sure,' Granddad interrupted.

'But I was so—'

'Briggie never mentioned anything to me and I'm sure you don't want to be dragging up petty disagreements, or things said in the heat of the moment. And she was quite outspoken, our Briggie, so you should take anything she said with a pinch of salt. I loved her dearly but she was an opinionated madam.'

'But in this case, I think she was right with the things she said.' I was determined to get this off my chest, even though I couldn't physically get it off my hip. 'Brian will be so disappointed when he finds out what I've done.'

I stood up from the table and lifted my T-shirt. Give Granddad his due, he didn't so much as blink.

'Oh, how pretty. Very Gothic,' he said. 'All the youngsters have them nowadays. It's a kind of art form in its own right. I know it must be frustrating that Brian sometimes still thinks of you as a little girl, but I know Annetta will recognise that it's your choice. And I bet Briggie was only jealous because her body was such an undulating canvas. Mind you, I loved every inch of it.' There was a pause. Granddad was clearly having none of my self-pity. 'Come on, love, open this up and let's see what's inside.'

My hands trembled as I slid a book out from the brown paper and ran my fingers down the shiny cover of a brand-new hardback entitled *Stunning Cakes for Beginners*. I opened it up and there was a handwritten inscription inside, dated a few days after our quarrel.

To my darling granddaughter Molly

I didn't get to bake you a sorry, so I'm sending you the next best thing.

Everyone makes mistakes, even me, but cake can always be relied upon to make everything better.

Grandma Bridget x

'I'll say this for her,' said Granddad, leaning over my shoulder and peering at his wife's words. 'She never was one to bear a grudge.'

'But I was so mean,' I sniffed. 'In fact, I've been mean to a lot of people in recent years.'

'Come now,' he said, patting my shoulder. 'Don't you think we went through all this with Bri? He was a nightmare teenager. Told us we were small town and out of touch. Berated us for not having a telly – not having electricity, come to that. Didn't we realise how embarrassed he was to ask mates round? Got worse when he grew taller than me – strutting around the house like some sort of puffed-up cockerel.'

Kind, gentle Brian? I was surprised.

'And then he pushed me so far one day that I pinned him up against this very wall. I might have been shorter than him, but forty years tilling the soil and working in the council gardens made me pretty damn wiry.' He chuckled at the memory. I tried not to let my mouth fall open.

'That stopped him in his tracks. The fact his old man wasn't the pushover he'd assumed. Interestingly, we jogged along much better after that.' He smiled at the memory. 'You were just being a typical teenager – getting your curly, swirly flower thing done was all part of the perfectly normal rebellious stage.'

I didn't want to point out I was actually twenty-three last summer and should have been beyond that behaviour. But perhaps he was right. And maybe I'd grow to love it. It would be a reminder of who I was and who I'd become – and that was cause for celebration.

Granddad retired to the living room to leave me alone with my thoughts. As I flicked through the beautiful cookbook, my tears started slowly but built to a crescendo. All this time I'd felt so churned up because I hadn't had the opportunity to make things right with Grandma, but she'd already forgiven me – probably the very moment I'd stormed out the room. All that was left was for me to forgive myself and to do this, I had to go to the bay and have a chat with her.

Summerton beach was busier now that schools were finished for the summer. Small groups littered the shoreline as evening descended and people tried to eke out the last of the day. Tiny plumes of smoke drifted up from disposable barbecues and I could hear the familiar 'pffft' of beer cans in the distance. I trudged along, heading for a quiet patch of pebbles under the cliffs and away from everyone.

And as I walked, I said all the things to Grandma in my head

I'd wanted to say since the day Brian had walked into the kitchen, phone hanging limply by his side, and turned to Mum, sobbing, 'She's gone, Anna, she's gone … '. I apologised for the unkind things I'd said last summer, for all the times I could have stood with her in the kitchen and learned from her, and for the swims she had in those last few years without me. I was full of regret and self-pity. For how I had treated her son, for my laziness and my misplaced sense of entitlement.

When people love you relentlessly, their love washes over you like the incoming tide, and it's so easy to take their love for granted – to assume that the tide will always come in and wash the misunderstandings away. But Grandma had died unexpectedly and the tide hadn't cleansed the littered beach of my selfish behaviour.

I took a deep breath, wriggled out of my shorts and slipped my vest top over my head.

'Wait up, Grandma,' I shouted to the omniscient sea, not caring who heard me. Tears filled my eyes and finally surged over my lids and down my wind-whipped cheeks. 'I'm coming in …'

Chapter 69

Funny how you look for the familiar, even when you know it's long gone. There was no canvas bag of towels as I scrabbled my way back up the pebbles and the realisation hit me hard. Perhaps I had fooled myself that she was in the sea with me, maybe doing her elegant, old-lady breaststroke to keep her shampoo-and-set hair above the water. And as long as I didn't turn around, she would continue to swim behind me.

I'd stayed in the water longer than was prudent because I knew returning to the shore would break the spell. A young couple had come up this end of the beach since I'd entered the water. They lay together on a rug, sharing a bottle of wine, too wrapped up in each other to notice me stagger up the pebbles back to my abandoned clothing. Only a few weeks ago that had been me with Harrison. Now I was here alone.

I threw the towel about my shoulders and was about to sit down when I noticed a figure in the distance leaping over the little stream that fed into the sea. There was something about the man that drew my attention. It was as though he was heading for me, but that was ridiculous. I didn't recognise him, not even as one of Harrison's extensive entourage.

Suddenly the figure broke into a run, even though running was tricky on the shingle. He scampered down the banks and raced along the shoreline towards me with complete abandon.

Despite the warmth of the early August evening, I was starting to shiver as the water evaporated from my body and a cool wind from the sea bit at my skin. The figure was getting closer – a handsome man with auburn hair and magnetic green eyes. A man who was starting to look vaguely familiar. A man who seemed to have misplaced his beard . . .

'Rory?' My heart flipped in my chest and I squinted to get a better look.

He halted directly in front of me, slightly breathless after his exertions.

'Everyone should embrace their inner Razzle,' he said, letting out a long breath and momentarily closing his eyes in what I can only describe as a moment of pure contentment. 'This amazing girl . . . woman I know taught me that.'

My insides did a triple Arabian flip. He was talking about me, right? I opened my mouth to ask a hundred questions. How had he found me? Why was he here? Was he still angry with me? – but nothing came out.

'Your grandfather said you'd come down to the bay,' he explained.

'But . . . but what are you doing in Summerton? You barely leave the house, never mind the county.'

'Yeah. It's been rather a hellish week. I've done it in stages. Plus, I didn't really know where I was going. I spent a few days trying to track you down in Creeching but no one had heard of you apart from Holly, and she didn't know much.'

Hold on – was *I* the friend Miriam mentioned he'd gone off to see? This was a massive road trip for him to undertake merely to find out what my important news was.

'The only thing I thought was real was your grandfather's

house in Summerton, so I thought I'd start there. I had to do a bit of detective work, and I've been several nights in various hotel bedrooms. A big deal for me, as you know.'

'You could have just rung my mobile and asked,' I said, trying to remain calm and not get my hopes up.

'I wanted to surprise you.'

'You certainly managed that.'

There was a pause and the sea breeze rippled across my damp body, which shuddered involuntarily.

'You're shivering.' He looked concerned.

'I've been swimming with my grandma,' I said. 'The dead one.'

'Ah. She would have liked that.'

See, that was why I loved him. He totally got it. Shame I'd probably buggered up any chance of an us with my lies.

'So . . .' I pulled the towel tighter around me and started to rub down my shoulders. 'Long way to come to hand me my P45.' The shivering intensified and it wasn't just from the cold.

'I wanted to show you the ginger monstrosity had gone,' he shrugged, pointing to his chin. Yeah, right. He'd come two hundred miles to show me a few square centimetres of pink flesh. I wasn't born seventeen years ago . . .

'It suits you. You look almost auburn in this light.' Suited him was an understatement. He'd gone from middle-aged sugar daddy to, quite frankly, a bit of a heart-stopper with a few quick flicks of the razor.

'I *am* auburn.'

Another awkward pause.

'I had this really weird dream about you,' he said, looking at his feet, kicking at a couple of pebbles. They tumbled down the bank into the receding froth of the ebbing tide.

'Oh?'

'Standing by my bed. Saying stuff. It seemed very real and it got me thinking. Guess I was missing you if I was conjuring up such convincing visions.'

The shivering stopped and a warm feeling flooded my body.

'I'm actually very missable. I'm the sort of person it's good to have around with all my tuneful humming and whizzy domestic skills. And because I'm so good at keeping quiet. Obviously.'

Our eyes met briefly and then his fell back to the pebbles.

'I told Mum about your lies – about making me think you were seventeen and pretending to be someone you weren't.' My heart sank. Surely he hadn't come all this way to give me another telling off? 'I was so angry and wanted her to be angry too – especially as she was so fond of you.'

'And?'

'She broke out the biggest smile, told me it was the best thing she'd heard all year, and asked what was I waiting for.' Ah, Miriam had my back all along. Bless her.

His eyes lifted from the ground and crept slowly upwards. I could almost feel an invisible touch as his gaze slithered up my body like the hands of a particularly proficient lover. I looked into those mesmerising eyes of his and then studied the mouth that had been so obscured all these weeks. God it was kissable. Why did I ever think he was Brian's age? This was one youngish, attractive man standing before me.

'But you must understand what a big deal this was for me, Molly. I thought you were still at school. It nearly broke me . . .'

I was losing patience with all this side-stepping. 'Look, I mucked up big-time. I got tangled in a knot of lies and my behaviour was ill thought out. But I've done some serious growing up in the last few weeks and sorted myself and my jumbled emotions out.' I swallowed. 'I love you, Rory, and have done for a lot longer than my obtuse brain realised. I can't be doing with guessing games any longer. If you've driven all this way to tell me you feel the same, then *just say so.*' I was almost pleading.

Nothing happened for a few seconds. A crowd of shrieking gulls called out overhead and a rogue wave rushed up the pebbles and covered my toes. Had I got it all wrong? Perhaps he was only here to clear the air between us. Perhaps he wanted to be friends. This could be awkward.

'So,' he said.

I frowned. 'So?'

And then the penny dropped into the sea with a resounding splash.

'Just say "so",' he clarified. It was a definite statement this time, and his arm swept up behind me and I was pulled towards him. That delicious scent that had hooked me from the beginning drew me in. His lips hovered millimetres from mine and I savoured one last second of anticipation before Rory showed me just what an extra few years of life experience did for a man, with a kiss that really did rock my world.

We reluctantly pulled apart and I got lost in his eyes and the smile that was slowly creeping across his face. And then I remembered that he didn't know. He hadn't seen the letter.

'I've been desperately trying to contact you,' I said. 'I found a letter from Percy to Violet – it was tucked under a flap in an old box of Percy's things Grandma found in the house years ago.' In my head I'd written Percy's last few hours. I wanted to believe Violet had been with him at the end, and that she had gathered up the letter and all those precious mementoes of their love and tucked them away in a place she could perhaps return to them from time to time but that would not be discovered in her own house.

'And?'

414

'And you won't believe how it finished. You're seriously going to have to brush up on your architectural knowledge because, it turns out, you have it in your blood. But it wouldn't be right for me to give you spoilers and tell you the end of their story. I have to show you.' Although there was a little bit of cupboard shenanigans I had to explain first. I gathered my clothes and slipped my shoes back on.

'So you were only trying to get in touch to tell me about some old letter?' he teased. 'And there was me making this grand gesture – travelling halfway across the country . . .'

'Well, that and to tell how much I loved you – natch. Plus, I wanted you to know I've got a job at Bickerton Manor – a proper full-time one. The salary isn't enormous but the work is amazing. I get to pass on my historical knowledge to unsuspecting members of the public. Michael was impressed with my enthusiasm.'

'I'm pleased for you.' But his smile had disappeared. It was odd being able to see so much of his face. I'd kind of got used to the fuzz and missed it now it was gone. At least I could read his expressions better now without an acre of tangerine fur obscuring his features. Perhaps there was an in-between? A subtle stubble that wasn't quite a beard but was still the fuzzy face I'd fallen in love with?

'But?' I prompted. I knew there was a but.

'But, I'll hardly ever get to see you, Molly. My home is West Creeching. It would be difficult for either of us to uproot, especially as you have a job down here. Now that I've found you, I need you in my life full-time. Guess I'm an all-or-nothing kind of guy. I don't think I can bear occasional weekends or an online relationship.' His hand came up to my face and his thumb stroked my cheek.

'About that . . .' I said, reaching my arm up to his broad

shoulder. 'There's something else I haven't been totally honest about. Something you have to promise you'll keep secret. Something that will make our relationship a whole lot easier and is going to blow your tiny, middle-aged, ginger mind . . .'

I grabbed his hand and led him back to Granddad's, towards the small triangular under-stair cupboard that had somehow been forged from a powerful love between two people who had no other way to be together over a century ago. And to show him a letter that would irrevocably connect him to not only Acacia House, but Hawthorn Place as well.

'Auburn,' he grunted, as he trailed behind me.

Chapter 70

Final letter from Percy Gladwell to Violet Marston, continued . . .

1937

. . . Ego semper tecum sum quamquam procul absumus – *we feared we would soon be parted when we chose this inscription and yet, through some miracle that I will never truly understand, there were periods of our lives when we saw each other every night. I truly do not know who was the more surprised the morning you stumbled from the under-stair cupboard and back into my life once again. Could the power of our love have forged such a thing? Let us not question it, but gratefully accept the miracle bestowed upon us by a universe that defies explanation.*

I was never expected to make old bones and the doctor once remarked I was a modern miracle – he was not to know that you were the drug that kept me going all these years. But I have lived a life I would choose again a thousand times, for all its restrictions and secrecy. I have been loved and have loved with all my heart in return. Not a conventional relationship, yet a relationship still.

I recall a conversation we had many years ago about my niece and her fanciful houses. We were like the architect's compromise between Millicent's unorthodox and whimsical drawings and the laws of engineering and science that determine how a house can be built. We found a path between what we wanted and what we could have. But compromises can be beautiful things in their own right . . .

In the dead of night you will come through our little cupboard, and creep up my stairs, as you have done so many times over the years – pray God I last that long. You will sit by my bed and take my hand in yours and we will talk again of silly geese and jumping into petunia beds. I will laugh, I will cry, and you will kiss my brow and put a glass of water to my lips. And all will once again be right with the world, even if I depart from it before the dawn.

For while I am proud of my churches, my manors and my almshouses, my real legacy is made of flesh and bone. And whilst he may never know me as his father, I am proudest of all of Samuel – our son.

> Farewell, of hearts that heart most fine,
> Farewell, dear heart, heartly to thee,
> And keep this heart of mine for thine
> As heart for heart, for loving me.

Percy Samuel Gladwell
13th November 1937

Acknowledgements

A huge thank you to my wonderful editor Kate Byrne for taking a chance on *The Secrets of Hawthorn Place*, and to the whole team at Headline Accent, particularly Versha Jones for designing such a stunning cover. Thank you also to the smiley and enthusiastic Hannah Schofield, who became my agent just as this book was taken on. Ours will be a fabulous partnership – I can feel it in my bones.

For research help I would like to thank Darren Lawrence for his insight into city trading, and to Eleanor Parker for her beautiful translation of the medieval poem and being generous enough to let me use it. Also, Amanda Rendell for organising the enlightening trip to Kelmscott Manor (where William Morris lived for the last 25 years of his life), and for her hen party gift many years ago of the glorious 1960s Good Housekeeping's *Running a Home is Fun* – which proved jolly useful to both me and Molly.

I had very limited architectural knowledge when I had the initial idea for this book, or even what time period I wanted to set the historical thread in, and it was only as I began my research that the Arts and Crafts Movement leapt out at me. I have found the research fascinating, so much so, that this late Victorian/early twentieth century period has now become my firm favourite as an author. I can't wait for our topsy-turvy world to return to normal and to once again visit the stunning country houses and museums around me. There really is nothing like stepping into these old buildings to send shivers up my spine and neurons racing around my author brain.

Sometimes, as weird as it sounds, authors have very little control over certain aspects of their stories, and Rory's hair colour was always a given. So a virtual high five to all the wonderful auburn-haired beauties out there, particularly Caitlin McKie, Oliver Lawrence, Louise Bartram, Amanda Rendell, Emma Strain, Stephen Taylor, Lucy Bashford and Kenny Sayers. Ginger, strawberry blonde, red or auburn – it's sensational and you all wear it well.

Thanks to my beta readers, Linda and Clare, and, as always, to the RNA for giving all writers of romance a home. My friends within the organisation are many, but big love to Heidi Swain, Rosie Hendry, Ian Wilfred, Kate Hardy, Claire Wade and Clare Marchant, who saw me through lockdown and kept my spirits up when the book struggled to find a home, even though I could happily list another fifty authors who mean the world to me.

Everyone knows that it takes more than just an author to create a book; from keen-eyed copy editors and creative cover designers, to understanding family and patient friends. To any I have accidentally omitted, please know I am eternally grateful to each and every one of you.

Finally, to all the beautiful readers out there. I hope, like me, you found solace in some fabulous books during the pandemic, and that you have enjoyed Percy and Molly's stories now that we are (hopefully) out the other side.

Jenni x